LAST OF THE GREAT BOONDOGGLES

ALEX FLEMING

Published in 2009 by New Generation Publishing

First Edition

Published by New Generation Publishing

FOR AUNT CLARICE

Missing

"Yes?" said the Sergeant, raising an eyelid. Peruvian pipe music played.

"I'm looking for my husband," said the woman, stepping forward to the counter.

"You're what?" said the Sergeant.

"My husband," said the woman. "I think he's gone missing."

"You think." The Sergeant barely looked up at all. He had far more pressing things on his mind.

"Yes. I'm almost certain."

The Sergeant sighed aloud, adjusted his position and opened a big red book. "Name," he groaned.

"Jollygoode," said she.

"What is," asked he.

"My name," answered she. "Susan Jollygoode."

"Is that a name?"

"Well, yes. I believe it is."

The Sergeant paused to scratch his chin.

"Husband's full name," he said, taking out a pencil and wetting the lead.

"Oh. Duncan Jollygoode."

"And you last saw him when?"

"Monday night."

"Monday night. Address."

"One Pudding Lane, Upper Hooey."

"…Upper Hooey." The Sergeant wrote each detail in his book with utmost diligence but very little passion.

"Do you want the postcode?" the woman asked obligingly.

"No," he replied, lifting the hatch. "One minute."

And he disappeared through the side door into my office. The Peruvians got out their guitars.

It was one of the driest summers since records began.

Well, that was when I heard you were missing. Missing upstairs, more like! What on earth could have possessed you? Anyway, we know where you are now, and that's the main thing. Now I hope you'll reflect on what's happened and understand that you have done a very stupid thing indeed. It won't be easy, I know. But I'll stand by you, because I know you're not a bad person at heart. I'll always be here if you want anything. Can I send a parcel? Do you still like Eccles cakes?

A Very Large Hole

I'd been loath to abandon my game of solitaire that day. Why should I be bothered, after all? Anywhere else, the report of a missing person would be met with little but apathy, sanctioned by the rubber stamp of officialdom. But this, of course, was *not* anywhere else. This was Nether Hooey. And I simply had nothing better to do, save my game of solitaire.

It had fallen to me, then, to interview Susan Jollygoode on that warm-ish Thursday morning. Susan Jollygoode – a woman who appeared to be *not quite all there*. As if something was… well, yes. *Missing.*

"He went to have a bath and never came back?" I asked, looking her squarely in the eye.

"That's what I said, *Inspector*" she said, oddly placing stress on the final word.

"He failed to reappear?" I asked again.

"That's right. He failed to reappear," she repeated as if to mock me. Her accent sounded curiously familiar. Highlands and islands, perhaps. "He never came out of the bathroom."

"Could he have slipped out somehow?"

"No. The door was locked. On the inside." Highlands and islands. Definitely.

"On the inside?" Come to think of it, her face was curiously familiar too. "So how did you get in?"

"I unlocked it. With a screwdriver."

"Your bathroom door can be unlocked from the outside? With a screwdriver?"

"Yes. It's quite normal. Isn't it?"

"And it can also be *locked* from the outside, presumably?"

"…I suppose so." Susan Jollygoode seemed taken aback by the thrust of my inquiry. My police training hadn't been altogether wasted, then.

"Could he have gone out through the window?" I continued, on the front foot now.

"No. The window was closed."

"And it can't be closed from the outside?"

"No."

"Have you tried?"

"Well… no."

This was going well. The keenly inquiring mind of the professional detective had already exposed gaping holes in the informant's account. *Amateur!*

"Does your bath have a particularly large plug hole?" A sudden change of tack. Always good for unsettling the opponent.

"Not particularly. Anyway, the bath was still full of water. So he couldn't have gone down there." Barmy! Was she playing with me? Or was I playing with her? It was hard to tell. She seemed to be suppressing a smile – stifling a laugh – sharing a joke…

"Can anyone hear us in here?" she suddenly asked, looking around towards the door.

A loud rasping cough from the Sergeant issued over the Intercom. I looked across at the monitor to see him pruning a large philodendron.

"No, but we can hear them," I replied.

"What's with the music?" she asked again, as if we were suddenly in on something together.

"What music?"

"That crazy music out there. What's it for?"

"Ah, *that* music. Well, it's all part of the 'softly softly' approach, madam. Designed to put you at your ease."

She stared at me with a look of befuddlement.

For all her apparent ambiguity, Susan Jollygoode was not unattractive, albeit in a peculiarly Scottish way. She had an alluring way of tilting her head as she spoke, almost coquettishly, casting a questioning look into the eye of the beholder. Her eyes were the colour of hazelnuts, her lips more than suggestive. Her pale skin had the look of a delicate marble, or possibly a rare kind of cheese. A full mane of flaxen hair was held in check, tied by a black ribbon that danced teasingly around the line of her neck.

She spoke as if her husband's disappearance wasn't really that big a deal. As if he was some object she'd lost down the back of a sofa, something she'd misplaced in the laundrette. Of course, it was easy to conclude that her husband had *simply upped and left her* while she wasn't looking. And she was nutty enough not to have noticed.

Duncan Jollygoode ran his own business, she said – Jollygoode and Jollygoode. "What about the partner?" I asked. "You know, Jollygoode *and* Jollygoode?" She replied straightfaced that *she* was the partner – well, secretary. "Accountants and solicitors should always have two names. Don't you think?" And he was which? Accountant or solicitor? Neither – he was an estate agent. Where did he work? He worked at home. An estate agent who works from home! Did he have any enemies? Anyone who would want to *harm* him in any way? After all... an estate agent... But there were none. None at all. Not even a client with a grudge. Because he didn't have any clients. "He's only just started," she explained. It was a new business. Progress so far: zero.

"What about debts?" I continued undeterred.

"Only the usual."

"Nothing that would make him want to vanish?"

"Nothing that I know of." She seemed to be losing interest. As she crossed her legs, the hem of her skirt lifted above her elegantly crafted knee.

"And how would you describe your relationship?"

"Well, we're married."

"An affair, perhaps?"

She held my gaze for a fraction of a second too long.

"...Affair?"

"I mean, is there anyone else in your husband's life?"

"Oh, no. He would never do anything like that... Would he?"

Gently Does It

An estate agent with no enemies, no debts, no affairs. Nothing to go on at all. Duncan Jollygoode was as good as fictitious, I concluded. What would make a fictitious person disappear?

"Quite a case," I commented to the Sergeant at the counter. "Most baffling."

"It doesn't help that it's your first case, does it sir," the Sergeant said as he took my notes for filing. He'd already changed the record: *Moon River* by the Mantovani Orchestra. "And on your first day, too. Now that's what I call a turnip from the blue."

"Hmm."

"A turn-up for the books," corrected PC Mabey from the staff area behind the counter.

"Yes," agreed the Sergeant. "It is a bit of a surprise."

"Not one of yours then, Sarge?" said the goatee-bearded Mabey, feet on desk, pencil in ear.

"No. I thought it was one of yours." The Sergeant put the notes in a buff-coloured folder and started to water the pot plants.

"Must be one of Cake's."

"Hold on, hold on," I interjected, beginning to feel irrelevant. "What do you mean, 'not one of yours'? What's going on here?"

"It's just a turn of phraseology," the Sergeant said in mid-irrigation. "Nothing to concern yourself about."

Mabey snorted with amusement. "We did say we'd tell him, Sarge."

"Tell me what?" Now I sounded like a small boy who'd lost his mummy.

The Sergeant straightened his back and looked at me squarely. "Well, sir. If you'll pardon me for appearing disrespectful. We have ways of doing things here that might not be quite what you expected. But being as it's your first day, it's probably best to take things little by little. Best wait till Cake's here. Then we can thrash it out man for man over a pot of tea."

"And that's another thing. Where's Cake?"

"Ah." The Sergeant sighed in a manner suggesting a can of worms being opened. "Surely you know about that, sir. The part-time aspect of it all."

"I know nothing about any 'part-time aspect'. All I know is that I'm here to fulfil a public duty."

"Yes. You'll certainly be wanting to do that."

As he spoke, the Sergeant shifted a large pot plant across the counter, crouching slightly to gauge its visual effect on the visitor. The counter was high and L-shaped, more reminiscent of a betting shop or court-room than a police station. A small boy could have remained hidden behind it for days.

I had been briefed. Of course I had. I was to make my way to the Dribbleside village of Nether Hooey, there to take up the post of Detective Inspector. I was to be assisted in my duties by a Sergeant Burley-Hogg and the two PCs, Cake and Mabey. Together, we would be responsible for policing the village and its outlying area, including the smaller village of Upper Hooey and the easily ignored hamlet of Neither Hooey. Though not the estuary town of Dribblemouth. That was all.

"Never mind, sir. Cake'll sort it out," Mabey commented with a sarcastic snigger. "He always sorts things out."

I'd had my reservations about taking the job in the first place, but this was getting ridiculous. Perhaps they were right. Perhaps Cake would sort it out.

"What time's he due?" I asked.

"Cake? Midday is his normal time, sir," answered the Sergeant.

"Very well. Staff meeting, twelve thirty sharp."

"That's our lunch hour," said Mabey, opening up a newspaper. "It's against union regulations."

"One o'clock?"

"One thirty."

"One thirty then. In my office."

"Right you are, sir. We'll be there at one thirty. Won't we Sarge." The Sergeant chuckled.

"And one more thing, Sergeant."

"Yes sir."

"Why did you send the Jollygoode woman in to see me? A routine case like that? Surely Mabey could have dealt with it."

"Well. I just thought you'd like something to do, sir."

"Do? I'm here to deal with murders, embezzlement, kidnappings. Serious crime. Not a piffling disappearance."

"I'm afraid we don't get that kind of incident here, sir. In fact we don't get much crime at all. If I gave everything to Cake and Mabey, you'd be sitting around twiddling your heels all day. "

"Don't get much crime?!"

"Anyway, how do you know it's not a murder, sir? If you don't mind my asking."

"It isn't a murder. Yet. Because we have no body. Until then, it's a routine incident to be dealt with by uniform. Is that understood?"

"Loud and clear as mud, sir," the Sergeant said with a two-fingered salute to the temple.

"Right. We'll speak further when Cake arrives." My illusion of authority temporarily restored, I returned to my office and closed the door.

Mabey's laughter rang out over the Intercom.

It didn't make any sense at all. I'd been sent to Dribbleside to spark a revolution in law enforcement. Soft-touch policing, they called it, justice

10

with kid gloves. My alternative training in the Netherlands had produced a number of fruits, all of which my superior, Commissioner Painter, was keen to hurl at this small rural community. Exciting, radical new techniques of crime management that I was simply itching to apply in the field.

In that case, why had I been sent to a village where they 'don't get much crime'? For that matter, why had I been sent to a village? A community of law-abiding inbreds in the middle of nowhere was no place to test novel techniques of policing, I'd already protested with commendable sensitivity.

"Relax," the Commissioner had said to reassure me. "There's as much crime in Dribbleside as there is anywhere else, man. No more, no less. These new techniques will take time to settle. For that, you need good country air. You don't want a murder every five minutes, now do you? What do you think this is, a television programme?! In any case, policing isn't only about solving crime. Good God, no. Policing is just as much about serving the community, preventing crime from happening in the first place. Dribbleside is the place for you. Believe me."

Now I was beginning to doubt that. As a police officer, it was always good to know there would be cases to solve, offenders to apprehend, victims to comfort, bridges to mend. But if there weren't even any cases to solve, what was the point?

PC Cake marched in on the stroke of noon. No sooner, no later. It soon became perfectly clear that exactness and punctuality were his forte, just as inexactness and ambiguity belonged to Sergeant Burley-Hogg and slovenly insolence to PC Mabey. Cake was tall and upright, as rigid as the minute hand on the vestibule clock – so tall, in fact, that he had to stoop when entering my office. In that respect he provided a fine contrast to his colleagues: Burley-Hogg, thick and stocky as a draught ox, Mabey small and slight as a mere footnote to humanity.

"Sorry, sir, did nobody tell you?" Cake said when questioned in my office after lunch. "I start at twelve on the dot and finish at six on the dot. Mabey starts at eight on the dot and finishes at two on the dot. That's the theory, anyway. Sarge doesn't believe in dots, but he does two jobs. He mans the desk and looks after the vegetable garden as well. And he has other business to see to besides."

"What other business?"

11

"His farm and horticultural business, sir. Did nobody tell you?" he repeated, somewhat irritatingly.

"No, nobody told me."

"He's all right as long as you let him talk about soil and fertilizers. And of course, that means he's only here when he isn't busy lambing, calving, ploughing, planting, harvesting, mucking out or threshing."

"And what is your other business then? Or do you just get up late?"

"I'm a baker by trade," he said proudly. "Forty loaves in, forty loaves out. Forty loaves in, forty loaves out. And so on. And so on. Crack of dawn till eleven on the dot. You'll find us at the back of the High Street, sir. Behind the Committee Hall."

So this was what the Sergeant had meant by 'the part-time aspect of it all'. I couldn't help wondering why Commissioner Painter hadn't bothered to tell me about it. Did he even care?!

"What about Mabey? What's his business?"

"He runs a pub. Did nobody tell you? The Copper Inn. He doesn't let us in there, though. Claims the locals would object to a police presence. It would sour their ale, he says. Now, I suspect—" and he suddenly leant to me with a knowing look—"that he either dilutes the ale or has an illicit still. And he lives with a woman who isn't his wife. Most scandalous, an affront to common decency. But what can we prove if he doesn't let us in?"

"Right. Mabey runs a pub. He works – no, sits here in the morning, then goes to pull pints. You do your honest baking, then come and sit here all afternoon. Is that it?"

"No sir. Most certainly not, sir. I do not merely sit here. I have important police work to do." Cake rubbed his elongated nose in self-satisfaction.

"And what would that be, in your case?"

"Why, directing traffic in the High Street, of course. Checking the lamps and other equipment on bicycles. Everything must be to the correct standard. Occasionally restraining sheep. And of course, an endless mountain of paperwork to deal with."

"Paperwork? There isn't any crime, what paperwork could there be?"

"Well, you know… Paperwork." For the first time since he'd walked in, Cake appeared less than forthright. Something was bothering him.

I would test the water. "Of course, we did have a case today. So there'll be some paperwork there."

"A case, sir?"

"Yes. The disappearance of Duncan Jollygoode. Wasn't that one of yours?"

"One of mine, sir? I'm not sure I know what you mean."

"I think you do."

There was an awkward silence as Cake thrust out his chin and adjusted his tie. A silence broken only by the clumping of the Sergeant's great boots and the clinking of cups and saucers on the other side of the door.

"Tea sir," his muffled voice announced. Mabey roused himself sufficiently to open the door, revealing the Sergeant bearing a tray replete with pot, cups and dainty little plates with floral edges. "Can we make some room, boys?"

With commendable alacrity and a visible air of relief, Cake cleared the top of my desk while Mabey lazily gathered chairs around. In no time at all we had the basic setting for a tea party. An odd time of day for it, I thought, but then I was beginning to think everything was odd in Nether Hooey. The Sergeant placed the tray on my desk with a look of satisfaction, then turned to Cake. "And finally, the tour de resistance?"

"Ah yes," answered Cake. "Strictly speaking, it's not yet one thirty, so strictly speaking we shouldn't be starting yet. Nevertheless," and he went to fetch something from the reception area with bony index finger raised aloft. The theatricality of his gesture took a knock when he had to stoop through the doorframe, but was restored to its full digital glory on the other side.

"We thought we'd give you a little welcoming party," explained the Sergeant. "Just a little something to make you feel at home from home."

Cake walked back in, stooping where appropriate, with what looked like a bomb on a plate. The bomb was dark brown and round like a cannonball, and had a burning fuse protruding from the top. I flinched momentarily, my sheer animal instinct divided between diving under a chair and jumping out of the window. Mabey and Burley-Hogg seemed hugely amused at that.

"Welcome to Dribbleside, Inspector Gaskett!" Cake declared cheerily while carefully positioning the cake in the middle of my desk. "I made it myself, sir. Half a pound of chocolate, two hundred mills of cointreau and a carrot, gas mark five for forty minutes," he explained as the sparkler fizzed out.

Burley-Hogg was Mother while Cake cut the cake. And Mabey…?

"Know what rhymes with moondoggle, sir?" he asked uselessly. I could but assume it was some kind of party game. The Sergeant eyed him warily as he poured the tea.

My bemused look was all Mabey needed for an answer. "Moondoggle rhymes with boondoggle, sir. Boon, doggle. Know what a boondoggle is, sir? It's a public service that no longer serves any purpose but to waste taxpayers' money. And that's what we are. A boondoggle. No crimes to solve, no arrests to make. A complete waste of time and space. Isn't that wonderful."

"Milk and sugar, sir?" the Sergeant said a little too forcefully. It was as if he wanted to shut Mabey up. Or at least shorten his lead.

"Just milk, thanks." I turned back to Mabey. "But you're happy to keep drawing your salary?"

"Half-salary, you mean. Huh! That's going to pay the bills, isn't it! But if the Ministry knew we had nothing to do, they'd close us down. And we wouldn't want that, would we. Oh no. We wouldn't want that." Mabey looked across at Cake and rolled his eyes mockingly.

I watched as Cake carefully measured a quarter spoonful of sugar to put in his tea. His thoughts were clearly elsewhere.

"Try the cake, sir," urged Burley-Hogg, at last taking his seat between the two constables. "We all had a hand in it, so to speak. I grew the carrot, Mabey supplied the liquor. A·kind of welcoming gesture from all of us to all of you. Go on sir, it won't eat you."

"All right. Cheers then." I cautiously took a bite from the huge wedge of chocolate-carrot-and-cointreau cake passed to me by Cake. It was utterly, unthinkably, inconceivably divine.

"Shall we start this meeting early, sir?" said Mabey. "Seeing as we're all here."

I nodded, not being in a position to speak.

"You see," Burley-Hogg attempted through his own first mouthful, "it's as I said before, sir. Nothing much has ever happened here. It's too far from the maddening crowd, if you like."

"Trouble is," Cake took over, "if we weren't here, who knows what might happen. It's entirely possible that our disproportionately large police force is what stops crime from occurring in the first place. Our very presence acts as a deterrent. That's how I like to see it."

"With us so far, sir?" asked Mabey. I wasn't sure. "Good."

"So now," Cake continued. "What would you do if you were the Commissioner, or the Ministry, or the government, knowing we have no crime? You'd close us down of course, and spend the money elsewhere. But if you closed us down, the crime would surely return. It's a Catch 22 situation. So what must we do to make sure they don't close us down? We have to make it look as if there's actually plenty of crime going on here after all. In other words…"

"In other words…" echoed Burley-Hogg as he put his teacup down.

"In… other… words…" said Mabey, rolling his hand in that *'you know what comes next'* gesture.

Sweet baby Jesus. They were committing the crimes themselves. Or at least inventing them.

"Nothing too gory, mind," Cake hastened to add. "No one ever gets hurt. Order is maintained, and everyone's happy."

I turned my mouth up, took a deep breath and surveyed the three of them. On the left, Mabey stared back at me while loudly sipping his tea. On the right, Cake self-consciously wiped a darkish crumb from the side of his mouth. In the centre, Burley-Hogg's chair squeaked rhythmically as he rocked on his heels.

"You realize I'm obliged to tell Commissioner Painter about this," I said at length. "It can't be allowed to go on."

Sergeant Burley-Hogg tilted his head to suggest disagreement. "I would advise against such action, sir, if you don't mind my saying. If the Commissioner knew, we would all be out of a job. Then our village would have to be policed by telephone from Dribblemouth. What about the villagers? They can't go all the way to Dribblemouth just to get a village bobby. Have you no compunction?"

Compunction or compassion, there was little doubt the Sergeant was protecting his own interests rather than those of the villagers. But in a way, he and Cake had a point. Enlightening Commissioner Painter and thereby getting the station closed down would have left the villagers utterly at the mercy of malice. And in any case, we now had a real case on our hands…

I sighed in resignation. "Let us say no more of this matter. We have the Jollygoode case, after all. I assume it isn't any of yours? I mean, your public-spiritedness wouldn't stretch to making a person disappear?"

"Indeed not," said the Sergeant.

"Though I've often wished it," Mabey added with a dark glance at Cake.

"By the way," I said. "What happened to the last Inspector? The Commissioner didn't really say."

Mabey and the Sergeant quickly brought cups to lips, leaving Cake to explain.

"He disappeared, sir. Did nobody tell you?"

Some Kind of Plot

"Vegetables have to be rotated every year, sir," the Sergeant explained in his rough country burr as we sauntered around his well-tended vegetable plot. Certainly thrilled, he was, to have a new listener. I nodded. "Otherwise disease takes hold. And then where would we be? I'd have nothing to take home to Ethel, and I'd be in her dog books again. But put potatoes where the cabbages were last year and, well, you're in business so to speak." I nodded again. "Now, beans, for instance, they produce nitrogen, you follow, so growing beans puts more nitrogen in the soil."

"Nitrogen."

"You put in what you take out, you see."

"Yes, I see."

Agriculture was the only culture as far as Burley-Hogg was concerned. A man of fearsome stature, he certainly looked capable of lifting an iron ploughshare or pulling a stubborn pair of oxen with the minimum of effort. His hands were massive – *farm hands*, indeed. His fingers were as thick as carrots, his head as broad as a prize pumpkin and the width of his chest little short of a sheep hurdle. His legs were like ten-year-old spruce trunks and his backside was difficult to describe in any genteel way.

Yet the physical appearance of the man was so much at odds with the delicacy he displayed when tending to the station's potted plants, window boxes and hanging baskets, not to mention the jealously guarded flower borders around the vegetable plot. He appeared to be communing with his flora at those times, as if they understood him better than any human could, and for this he repaid them with unerring affection. Not that he lacked affection for his two-legged cousins; he simply could not abide time-wasters. There were far more important topics on his agenda.

"Irrigation is the key, of course. Nothing'll grow without water."

"So…"

"That's right, sir, the drought. If we don't get some rain soon, this year's crop will be the worst in living memory, including the war years. By God, we had it easy then!"

We walked past a row of onions.

"By the way, Sergeant," I said, sensing the time was right to broach more relevant issues. "Any results on the Jollygoode search yet?"

"Ah, yes! I'm glad you reminded me. Well, we traced him through the Inland Revenue, in fact." Burley-Hogg came to his senses, a hint of professional pride relieving the ruddiness of his rustic features. "He set up his own business earlier this month."

"Here in Hooey?"

"Upper Hooey, that's right."

We sat on a bench at the bottom of the vegetable plot, pausing for a moment to survey the scene before us. Our position commanded a breathtaking view of the Dribble Valley and beyond, a landscape of which any Brueghel would have been proud. Down below a brambly thicket in front of us was the old railway line. Behind that, the river meandered past an old windmill into the distance. Fields and meadows on either side of the Dribble were parched brown with drought, their thirsty colour relieved only by winding green hedgerows of hawthorn, hazel, dog rose and crab apple.

A blue summer sky, interrupted by the occasional whale-shaped cloud, provided a most pleasant backdrop. It was certainly quiet here in Dribbleside; there was little sign of human habitation, save the occasional farmhouse and fisherman's tent. But over there to the left was the village of Upper Hooey. It seemed to hover in mid-air on a dramatic rise in the topography, as flocks of crows circled the sky above its ancient oaks and beeches. Below it, hilly slopes of scorched grass stood on either side of a sweeping depression. Shadows formed by parallel lines of mediaeval field ridges resembled a human rib cage as the afternoon sunlight glanced across them.

"His name is also on the rental agreement," added the Sergeant.

"One Pudding Lane?"

"Yes, and the gas and electricity contracts, not to mention the council tax. And the marriage certificate. And he's a paid-up member of the Dribble & District Dangerous Pastimes Society."

I sensed a moment of triumph. "Dangerous Pastimes…?"

"Associate member. Never turned up."

"Oh."

"He's registered on the electoral roll, too."

"So that's all in order, then?" I asked.

"Well, yes and no, sir. The curious thing is, all this happened in the last two weeks. And there's no record of him anywhere before that."

"Nowhere?"

"That's right, sir."

"So we have a missing husband who might not even exist...?"

"Well, sir. I think you may have hit the hammer on the nail there."

There was a lengthy silence.

A sparrowhawk hovered high over a field in the valley.

A jet scrawled noiselessly across the sky.

"They're watching us, you know," my companion said at length.

I gave a start. "Who are?"

"Them. The vegetables. They're watching."

"How do you know?"

"Ah. I know. They're cleverer than we think. You may think they're just vegetating, but they're not." The Sergeant leaned towards me, one chubby finger prodding the side of a turnip-like nose in that clichéd mannerism. I could only think he was making merry at my expense.

I looked at my wristwatch and rose quickly to break his spell. "Good God, is that the time? We have work to do, Sergeant."

"As you say." He bent to deadhead a marigold.

I hurried back up through the vegetable plot as the Sergeant went to fill his watering can.

I typed my report on the case. Made a copy for Commissioner Painter. Made some calls. And left for home.

Home

'Home' was, for the time being, a signalman's hut from the days when the Dribble Valley Railway still came through these parts. The old station mistress had kindly let me use it until I could find more fitting accommodation.

The hut was conveniently located at the end of Signal Box Turn, a narrow lane leading down to the disused railway from the High Street. The crumbling edifice of the old station was still visible from my back window. Beside the ghosts of weary travellers let down by the service yet again, my only neighbour was the station mistress, a white-haired woman of ninety who seemed to think the trains were still running.

Every morning, with blue cap on head and whistle dangling from breast pocket, she would put out a sign saying "DOWN TRAIN DELAYED", and every night she would take it back in again. She rarely ventured into the village, but instead seemed to spend all her days examining her pocketwatch and tutting like Alice's white rabbit. "Oh, good! An inspector at last!" the old dear had declared on handing over the ticket clipping implements. If anyone had ever informed her of the railway's sad demise, she certainly didn't show it; she merely remained under the illusion that the trains were running a little late, as ever.

The home she provided me was rudimentary, in a very real sense: coal stove on one side, bed on the other, and a pair of time-honoured chairs in between. Television, telephone, telegraph receiver. Enamel wash basin, prehistoric bathtub. At the back, a collection of strange levers and handles I preferred to leave well alone. A stack of old advertising boards – Bovril, Skegness, Andrew's Liver Salts – and a miniature hob on which to prepare my rustic breakfasts. For anything beyond that, I would probably fall back on Cake's pastries, Mabey's bar snacks and Burley-Hogg's seasonal produce.

Once inside, I quickly produced a copy of *"What To Do In Tricky Cases of Missing Persons"*, a supplement to the standard issue Ministry of Hedges Policing Manual (1949). The supplement had never been used and was sadly neglected. As I opened the Contents page, a small moth flew out from between the covers.

And I read. Chapter 1, The Case, Section 1, Ascertaining the Facts. Well, I'd done that. Section 2, Corroborating the Facts. This I would now attempt to do.

Corroborating the Facts. Witnesses in cases of missing persons are notoriously unreliable. They fall into three categories. One. The spouse or close relative of the missing person. Two. Neighbours, work colleagues, and other peripheral persons. Three, the murderer.

Witnesses in category one, the spouse or close relative of the missing person, are unreliable in that they tend to distort facts in a wanton or otherwise highly obstructive fashion. Cf. Crown vs. Littlejohn, 1924, when the victim's daughter saw him drinking in a pub, while the son swore he had been repairing the gutters on his house.

Category two, neighbours, work colleagues, and other peripheral persons, are unreliable for a number of reasons. One of these is sheer disinterest. Another is the exact opposite: so keen are they to be involved in the case that they will provide a complete fabrication of lies in order to maintain that involvement. A third reason is intense dislike for the missing person. Cf. Crown vs. Pauper, 1911, when the victim's ballet rival claimed she saw her disappearing into a brothel.

Category three, the murderer, only applies when the missing person has been murdered. This witness will not usually give reliable evidence.

So which am I, Inspector? I'm so reliable. You so want to believe me. Of course you do. How could I be unreliable? Look at my knees. Aren't they shapely. Don't you think? Look at the way I glance at you. How would you describe our relationship? An affair, perhaps? Come on, then… Come on… Woof! Come on… Woof woof! Come on… Woof woof woof!

"Come on!"

"Woof!"

"Open up!"

"Woof! Woof!"

As the banging on the door continued, the supplement fell from my lap with a thud.

"You said to come over?" said Four-Eyed Bob through the pouring rain as I stood in the doorway.

"Yes. Yes, of course. Come in."

Miss Marple stood aside to let Bob in, as she always did. She then shook off a spray of her own raindrops and wiped her feet vigorously before entering.

"You can take the shades off, Bob," I offered.

"Whoa! It's far too bright in here," he countered, collapsing into a chair.

We did laugh.

Miss Marple settled into her favourite position at Bob's feet. Laughter always put her at ease.

"Sorry, I must have dropped off," I explained.

"Working too hard?"

"No. No, quite the contrary, in fact."

"Not enough excitement, then."

"Could be."

"Country air."

"It's this new case, Bob. The mysterious Duncan Jollygoode. There's something not quite right about it."

"Yes, I think we should."

"…Should what?"

"Use it as a test case."

"That's right. Just what I was going to say."

Miss Marple mumbled something as she slept.

I'd known Four-Eyed Bob since way back. When? It's hard to recall. I cannot remember, nor even imagine, a time when I didn't know Bob, so great was the impact he'd had on my life. His philosophy was simple: trust your inner voice, yes, but above all else, trust *your nose*. The way something smelt could tell you all you needed to know about it.

Of course, his blindness helped in this respect. "Eyesight does so complicate things," he would claim.

Bob liked to name his dogs after fictional sleuths. At one time, his companions had been a pair called Poirot and Columbo. Poirot, a sleek border collie, displayed somewhat more intelligence than her canine sidekick, a shaggy mongrel. Bob once demonstrated this to me in a telling experiment. He sat both dogs at the end of a corridor, then walked to the other end. "Poirot!" he called, and both dogs came padding down the corridor with tails a-wag. He then sent them back to the far end. "Columbo!" he called, and only Columbo made the journey. "That takes the biscuit," I commented, as Bob rewarded each of them.

Bob was what you might call 'nasally presentient'. They say the blind have enhanced powers of hearing, but for Bob, it was all in the nose. He would be the one to give not an eyewitness account, nor an ear-witness account, but yes, a nose-witness account.

It was he who'd encouraged me to answer the police ad that had brought me to Dribbleside in the first place. The post was conditional upon a six-month training period in the Netherlands, where the new techniques, known as 'De Bloemensterk Beweging', had long been established. And during this Netherlandish training, I realized that Bob's *nasal dexterity* could surely be put to use in serving the community. I would ask him to assist me in any way he could; it was the very least I could do to thank him. "Bob…," I'd started. "Yes, I'd be delighted," he'd replied, without batting an eyelid. Almost as if the whole thing was *part of his big plan.*

Miss Marple was a shiny black labrador whose nose was mostly moist. Through some strange quirk of fate, her own eyesight had started to fail her from the earliest time; now the poor dog was almost as blind as a bat. In a way, she and Bob were the most complete companions. Bob refused to give her up, so they just carried on. The blind leading the blind, you may say. But somehow they managed to stumble through life without major mishap.

By complete coincidence, Four-Eyed Bob lived in Neither Hooey, the forgotten village in the Dribbleside triangle. The sure knowledge of his invaluable assistance – not to mention my indebtedness to him – had put me in no doubt at all that I should accept the Dribbleside post.

"What's the usual rule in missing persons cases?" Bob continued over a glass of Droichead single malt whiskey. "Play the waiting game," he replied to his own question as he nosed the peaty flavours of his wee dram. "And what does that mean?"

"Do nothing."

"More or less. Place the person on the missing persons register, *then* do nothing. For a week or so. Often the person has just gone to the shops and couldn't decide whether to buy a twelve pack or a six. Or they've gone to the hills to get away from their families. A lot of time is wasted on missing persons who aren't missing at all."

"OK. So what you're saying is that we in fact do nothing?"

"No. Not in this case. You have a very strong feeling that all is not well with this missing Mr Jollygoode; I agree, it doesn't sound or smell like your usual missing persons case. So I suggest you do the opposite."

"The opposite?"

"Don't play the waiting game. Don't do nothing. Go over to the woman's house. Make a real nuisance of yourself. Put her under pressure. Why did she bring you this cock and bull story? There must be something else behind it. Get on her back. Badger her. Treat it as a priority case. Something is bound to emerge."

"Well, it *is* a priority case. It's the *only* case."

"So much the better. Concentrate all your resources. Proactive policing, that's what it's all about. Humour the victim, nip it in the bud, get it all in the open before this woman can make complete and utter fools of the entire police force."

I poured him another whiskey.

"You know, it reminds me of the famous Human Pyramid Case a few years back," Bob continued.

I knew what was coming next. It was one of Bob's little quirks. After only a couple of drams, he would launch into some long anecdote that I was supposed to find edifying, enlightening or otherwise useful. His tales were like little vignettes, little stories within stories that he'd saved up for years and now felt were relevant to our conversation. He never told me how he felt them relevant. At the end, he'd always say "That's for me to know and you to work out." Not that I minded. He knew more about the world than I did, and every little helped.

"Human pyramid?"

"On the Paris Metro. A troupe of circus acrobats led the gendarmes around by their noses for months."

"How?"

"I'm just going to tell you. The acrobats, being generally penniless, would habitually travel on the Metro without paying, or without the proper ticket. They would all be dressed in everyday shabby clothes just like everyone else, totally anonymous. Suddenly, as they reached their destination, they would form a human pyramid at the ticket gate, and would use this to vault over the station staff. Those at the base of the pyramid would perform double backward somersaults over the gates. Then they would all merge back into the crowd and disappear.

"Of course, they were professionals. They could build their pyramid in nanoseconds, before the station staff could even react. At first, people were just stunned. They would look on in awe, then burst into spontaneous applause when the feat was complete. The ticket collectors were quite powerless."

Miss Marple lifted an ear as she slept.

"The Human Pyramid started to appear all over Paris, always in the Metro. As it did, it of course gained a certain notoriety, and the public started to support it. People would close ranks to shield the fleeing acrobats, or deliberately create a diversion when a ticket collector appeared about to nab them. The trouble was, no one knew when or where it was going to happen. Sometimes there would be three or four sightings in a day, sometimes none for weeks. The stations appeared to be chosen completely at random. So the gendarmes had no way of predicting the troupe's movements and thereby apprehending them.

"To make matters worse, members of the public started to act as 'decoy pyramids', whether simply in support of the troupe, or to cock their noses at the pathetically incompetent authorities. The police sent plain clothes officers on every train, at monumental expense of public money, and attempted several arrests. But each time, their purported 'offender' was simply an innocent member of the public.

"Soon, the whole affair became a real *cause célèbre*. Sightings were reported on daily news bulletins, TV documentaries filmed, articles written in magazines by prominent psychologists. Members of the public started wearing '*On a vu la pyramide!*' badges. Stations that had been visited by the pyramid started putting up colourful signs boasting of the fact. It came to be a matter of pride that a station was chosen for this brilliant show of acrobatic prowess.

"Media commentators started noting subtle variations in the pyramid formation, depending on the day of the week or the meteorological conditions, and there was much speculation as to whether some kind of code was being used. Meanwhile, financial experts calculated the massive losses in Metro revenue due to the free use of its transport service. To make matters worse, ordinary members of the public had also started to travel without paying, as it was now the fashionable thing to do.

"Other, more shrewd commentators noted that the Metro was conversely making huge profits thanks to the publicity. The number of paying passengers had in fact doubled due to public curiosity. Everyone wanted to say they'd seen the pyramid, if not once then twice, if not twice then three times. Bookies offered odds on where the next sighting would be. Some individuals scooped massive winnings, while the betting companies themselves had a field day.

"The phenomenon disappeared as quickly as it had started. As every week went by without another sighting, the public and media gradually lost interest and turned to other pressing issues such as the nocturnal habits of the Prime Minister's girlfriend. There were rumours that the leader of the troupe had died in a terrorist attack, and this was neither confirmed nor disproved. There were also rumours that the Metro had planned and executed the whole thing as a profit-making venture. As if to prove the point, a spanking new line was built and opened to the public only six months after the final sighting."

There was a short silence.

Miss Marple awoke with a start and looked up at Bob.

"So… What has that to do with the case, Bob?" I asked.

"That, my boy," he replied with a final gulp of whiskey, "is for me to know and you to work out. Come on, girl. We'd better be off."

The rain had eased by now. Bob felt his way out into the twilight. Miss Marple almost collided with the umbrella stand as she followed him out.

I never quite understood how they got home on that bicycle.

Dear Aunt Clarice,

I'm thinking of writing a novel. What do you think about that?! It all started when a woman came in and said she'd lost her husband, and then it just took off from there. Well, there's nothing much to do here, and it'll help me make sense of it all. The whole story was going to be imagined by someone who was actually in a coma, but then I saw a series on TV about a man in a coma who imagined he was a detective, so I changed it to brain surgery! Then they changed the TV series to make people think the man was having brain surgery. So I changed my story to madness! And then – you guessed it – they changed the TV series to madness too!! I always had the idea first. But that can't be possible – can it? They have to plan these programmes months or years in advance. Then I thought, perhaps I really am writing the TV series and this is just a dream! What do you think? Hope you're well.

love

John

PS Thanks for the Eccles cakes!

Identity Crisis

"Yes?" The Sergeant happened to be pruning a very large rubber plant when Susan Jollygoode walked in for the second time. Satie's *Gymnopédies* filled the air.

"The Inspector called me," she said.

"Did he."

"Yes."

"Inspector Gaskett, you mean?" Burley-Hogg didn't really mean to be obstructive. It was just that he had far more important things on his mind than merely doing his job.

"Yes. I think."

"You think?"

"If that's his name."

"It is."

"So… What's it all about?"

"I can't be sure. I can't be sure."

"Well, could you find out then?" The woman's patience was growing thin.

"Find out?"

"Yes, would you? Please?"

"Of course. One minute."

The Sergeant ceased his pruning and disappeared through the side door. Susan drummed her fingers on the counter to the rhythm of the next *Gymnopédie*.

"Thanks for coming," I announced with deliberate insouciance as Susan Jollygoode stepped into my office that day. I did well to conceal my irritation; she was more than half an hour late.

"What's it about, then?" She looked and sounded decidedly unimpressed.

"I want you to take a good look at these local citizens."

I had invited seven Dribblesiders to take part in an identity parade. "That's what we usually do," Burley-Hogg had assured me, "whenever we need some figures for the books. Positive ID, if you like." He was talking about the fabricated offences, of course. Certain procedures had to be *seen to be done*, rather than actually *being* done, and the identity parade was occasionally one of them. The idea was to find a suitable 'witness' to a fictitious incident, gather upstanding citizens of as many shapes and sizes as possible, and record the witness's reaction to them. Not to mention their reaction to the witness. Then engage in some genial banter, share some light refreshment at MoH expense, and all go away happy in the knowledge of another month's funding safely secured.

The 'unusual suspects' rounded up for such convivial occasions were usually the same magnificent seven. Well, that was the only way to do it here. There were no 'usual suspects'. Because there was no crime.

In the case of Susan Jollygoode's missing husband, however, the village parade took on a new, hitherto unimagined significance. For it would tell us whether any of the 'suspects' recognized the woman, or could ever recall seeing her husband – or whether we were merely being led a merry dance. And that was why, on this occasion alone, I agreed to go along with the atrocious deception by my well-meaning colleagues.

The Seven Dribblesiders were naturally only too pleased to take part. A cheerful lot they were, with a generally positive outlook on life.

Besides, there was a certain amount of interest in my appointment, and they were all keen to see me in the flesh. "*A New Inspector for Dribbleside! But Why?*" the local rag had mused.

Anyway, there they were, standing in a line along one side of my office. Sylvia Grainger, a retired and unknown actress. Medium height, medium width, medium depth. Ralph Morpurgo, an intellectual. Small and bent. Angela Hall, keeper of the Big House. Tall and gaunt with a permanent crick in her neck. The brothers Jeffrey and Jeremy Green, builders. One shorter than the other; standing side by side, they resembled a simple stepladder. Peter Mowforth, plumber. Small, compact, like a removed section of pipe, always stuttering. And Karen Gutteridge, clerk to the Nether Hooey Council, thick as a plank. All perfectly ordinary people. But all splendid characters in their own right.

"Why?" asked Susan Jollygoode.

"Clues, Mrs. J., clues," I replied. "One of these blemishless citizens could hold the key to your husband's disappearance."

"...The key?"

"Yes. They may shed light on his whereabouts, in their own special idiom."

"...How?"

"Leave that to me, Mrs. J. We have ways and means, and this is one of them. See it as another avenue of enquiry, if you like. Now. Please have a good look at these seven good people. Which of them do you recognize?"

"Which of them do I recognize?"

"Which of them do you recognize."

"Well... That man there." She pointed to Peter Mowforth. "He drives a blue van."

"Do you?" I asked him.

"Y-y-yes, I d-d-do!" stammered Peter Mowforth, beaming with misplaced pride.

"Well done, Mrs. J. That's one down."

"Excuse me, *Inspector*, is this some kind of game?" Susan Jollygoode asked with a look of disdain. And there was that stress again.

"Who else do you recognize?" I continued regardless.

"Oh... Well... That woman there. She lives in the thatched cottage by the post office."

"Yes! Yes! You are quite right, my dear," said Karen Gutteridge.

A terrible cry suddenly issued from the staff room.

Cake stormed in.

"Who's been at my sandwiches?!" He held out an open sandwich box – empty, bereft of lunch, save for a family of crumbs huddled in a corner. Wholemeal bread, perhaps a hint of Branston's.

"Oh!" the Seven Dribblesiders gasped as one.

"Oh dear," explained Sylvia Grainger. "I'm afraid *we* did."

"You ate the Constable's sandwiches?" I interjected. "Why?"

"Oh, but look at the box, darling."

The lid of the box bore the inscription: *Cake – Help Yourselves!*.

"We were waiting in there such a long time. I'm afraid one or two of us started to feel rather peckish."

"Yes, we particularly enjoyed the nectarine," added Jeffrey Green, trying to help.

"Yes, the nectarine," echoed Jeremy Green. They even spoke in different tones, about half an octave removed.

"We thought you'd prepared the refreshments early this time," said Angela Hall. "We were most grateful, we really were. Cheese and tomato sandwiches, a nectarine, an apple and a small Eccles cake. Most delicious."

Cake – Help Yourselves. The logo used by Cake's bakery. The seven should have recognized it, but they'd been blinded by a false conviction. How easily can delusion conquer reality! The poor man was beside himself.

"We are most awfully sorry," said Karen Gutteridge. "May we buy you a baguette, as a replacement? They sell them in the Deli."

"I ought to arrest the lot of you," replied Cake, none too happy. "A night in the cells would do you good."

Ralph Morpurgo now saw his chance to wax philosophical. "You might agree, however, that your sandwich box is more than a little misleading in its representation?" he posited. "And that you compounded the effect by leaving the box for all to see, and, moreover, by not being there yourself to give it an identity *sine qua non*? For when, we may ask, is a lunchbox *not* a lunchbox? And I think we have the answer. Your very absence rendered it a mere *box of lunch*. Logically speaking, we should have confined ourselves to the cake alone, since only the cake is offered by the ill-advised logo of your establishment. But who acts logically these days? Alas. It would seem to have been a case of *quid non consumandum est*, or perhaps *noli me edere*. Perhaps we could put this down to a simple misunderstanding and forget the whole matter forthwith."

A short silence ensued while all digested the weighty worth of Morpurgo's postulate.

"There is the small issue of my lunch, sir." Cake remained grumpy. His rigorous attention to uprightness and propriety meant that he was, by nature, predisposed to bearing lengthy grudges for any perceived injustice. This one would surely take a while to be resolved.

Susan Jollygoode stepped forward. "I'll take you out. Have your lunch on me."

A hush descended on the room. We stood there open-mouthed at the brazenness of it all. A witness at an identity parade, asking a police constable out to lunch, *in the middle of it.*

Nobody spoke. Cake looked up at Susan, down at his sandwich box, across to me, around at the Seven Dribblesiders, and finally back at Susan Jollygoode.

He paused. Everything hung on his next pronouncement.
"All right then," he said. And out they walked.

Anything to Get Out of There

"Well?"

Sounds of the Amazon rain forest. We could certainly have done with some of that here – *rain*, that is; the mercury was hovering in the mid-nineties as Cake returned to the station, much the better for his free lunch. I accosted him in the vestibule and handed him my report on the identity parade for filing.

"Sir?" he said obtusely.

"Did you learn anything?"

"Oh, yes sir. I certainly did," Cake replied as he unstrapped his helmet and placed it on the counter next to the report.

"What, then?"

"Well, I didn't know they did ploughman's at the Plough, sir."

"I meant *about Susan Jollygoode*," I persisted.

"Oh. Oh! Yes… No. Nothing at all." He seemed more interested in the report than in giving me any useful information.

"What did you talk about, then?"

"Oh, this and that. You know. She kept asking questions. Obviously, I couldn't stop too long. I had to get back on duty."

"But you *were* on duty, Cake! It was your duty to get as much information you could in connection with this damned case!"

"Was it? Oh. Sorry, sir. I didn't realize that." Cake was nothing if not ordinary. For despite his ridiculous physique – absurd height, fine wedge-shaped face that narrowed towards the front, long bony fingers that would have performed admirably well in an accountant's office – he was otherwise nondescript in appearance, undistinguished in thought, of medium density and average intelligence. He would be the last to boldly go where others feared to tread.

"What sort of questions?" I continued.

"Pardon?"

"What sort of questions was she asking you?"

"Oh, you know. This and that. Did I like my job. All about the village. Had I noticed anything strange. Was there anything else I knew. And about you, sir."

"Me?"

"She asked a lot of questions about you. How long you'd been in the village. Where you'd been before that. Where you lived. What you did in the evenings. That kind of thing."

My God. The woman fancied me. How did I feel about that? Ambinanimous. Is there such a word? I felt a certain heat rising behind my collar.

"So, in conclusion, you, a police officer, allowed yourself to be interrogated by a member of the public, whom it was your duty to question in connection with our only case. Congratulations."

"Thank you sir."

"Carry on, Cake."

A curious picture was emerging. Not only had no one ever met Duncan Jollygoode, but it seemed his wife was completely unknown as well. The Seven Dribblesiders proved as much; none of them could recall ever seeing her, anywhere. So why did I have the distinct sensation that I'd met her before? Perhaps I was the victim of an elaborate hoax. Perhaps we all were.

I turned to enter my office.

"Sir?" The Constable stopped me at the door. "Just a thought…" He brushed a rogue crumb from his chin.

"Yes?"

"Well, you know at the Identity Parade…"

"Yes?"

"It says here that Susan Jollygoode recognized at least two of the participants."

"Correct."

"But further down, it says '*They had no recollection of seeing her*'."

"Yes?"

"Well, it doesn't make sense, sir."

"What doesn't make sense."

"How could she recognize them, but they never remember seeing her? It just doesn't make sense. Unless she's been spying on them, that is." Cake obviously had a propensity for spotting errors. One of the basics of good detective work, for sure.

"Good God! Well spotted, Cake."

"Thank you, sir." He seemed truly flushed with pride.

"Well spotted," I said again for effect.

"Thank you."

"That must mean—" interjected Burley-Hogg from behind the counter.

"Yes! They're all lying!!" I exclaimed. It seemed quite beyond doubt.

The two looked at me with mouths open and eyes agog. Yes, I felt a momentary twinge of remorse at destroying their irrational faith in the honesty of their fellow villagers – villagers selected specifically for their presumed honesty. But that was just the kind of imbedded traditionalist attitude I'd been sent here to challenge. For the basic assumption of the 'softly softly' approach was, ironically, that all citizens were inherently dishonest; the 'law-breaking majority', indeed. "*Shake 'em up and sort 'em out*," Commissioner Painter had roared then guffawed.

"That's the only explanation!" I continued in total confidence.

Cake could hardly believe his ears. Ever wishing to trust the positive qualities of human nature, it was just too much for him to bear. "What, everyone who took part, *lying?*"

"But why?" the Sergeant asked in equally shocked sympathy.

"Why what?"

"Why would they do that? Why would they lie?"

"Why would *anyone* lie?! Because they're… hiding something, yes, that's it, they're all involved in some kind of collusion! They're all in it together!"

"What, even the Clerk to the Town Council?" The concept of corruption in high places was clearly anathema to Cake.

"Possibly. Possibly." Now I was not so sure myself.

31

"What is it they're hiding, d'you think?" asked Burley-Hogg.

"I don't know. I don't know. That, as they say, is for us to find out."

"Righto sir."

"Good. Well done, Sergeant. Well done, Cake."

I returned to my office with a sense of breakthrough. Elation, even.

Where Time Stood Still

"I'm quite interested in poetry," Mabey said with a stroke of his goatee beard.

We were on our way to Susan Jollygoode's. Being my first venture into Upper Hooey, I had asked the Constable to come along – and instantly regretted it. I should add that I'm no great friend of poetry.

"You are?" I said to humour him.

"It's a hobby of mine."

"Excellent."

"I do some writing, too, when I've time."

"Yes?" Admire the landscape. Swat at a midge on the windscreen. Anything but listen to poetry.

"When things are quiet at the pub. Or the station."

"Good."

"'Trees stride out across the land, Set in flow by nature's hand. Then there comes the race of men, And they all fall down again.' That's one of mine."

"*YOU STUPID BLOODY FOOL!!!*" I shouted. A bespectacled girl on a bicycle flew out in front of us as we passed some waste land. She was across the road before I could hit her.

"Being a poet, you see the world in a different light," the slightly bearded one continued. "You position yourself on a higher plane."

"What?"

"When you're a poet, I mean. You're on a higher level."

Looking in the wing mirror, I watched the girl disappear round the bend behind us. Where had she come from? Where had she gone?

"I think it's helped me," Mabey carried on regardless. "I think it has."

"Has it."

"I'm a poet, and I don't half know it!"

I did my best to disregard the piece of lofty culture emanating from the passenger seat. Some police force, the Dribbleside constabulary; it didn't even have a serviceable patrol car. The tax disk had run out. Besides, none of the officers were roadworthy. I'd understood that you needed a driving licence to join the police force, but not here, apparently. Cake was still taking lessons; nothing if not a plodder, he'd spent two years without even approaching his test.

Burley-Hogg had no time for such things anyway. His *modus movandi* was the bicycle. Mabey, for his part, had been banned from driving due to repeated traffic offences in a previous life. "Poetic licence," he would claim. "Ordinary rules don't apply".

And so, my car became the official vehicle. Send petrol receipts to the Ministry of Hedges, I was told.

I looked at my watch. Twenty to one. That meant we would arrive early. If the Sergeant's information was correct, Susan Jollygoode wouldn't be back from her nursery job until one. We could wait outside her house and appear impatient, thus taking her off guard. That always appeared to be the best tactic.

"Next turn on the right," came Mabey's instruction.

We had passed *The Point of No Return*, an aptly named pub at the very edge of Nether Hooey. From the main road running up the Dribble Valley, a small white marker indicated the turn to Upper Hooey, as instructed by the irritating little man. After the turn, the road dipped under an old railway bridge.

And beyond the bridge, everything changed. The scenery became instantly more rustic in an olde-worlde picture postcard way, its colour almost sepia. Well, the drought was largely to blame for that. Haywains stood in fields. The weather was somehow foreboding, with dark clouds hanging low on the horizon. The mood was distinctly gloomy.

"T.S. Eliot," Mabey announced, pulling out a pocketbook without warning. "He's one of my favourites. Did you know his name's an anagram of Toilets?"

Even as I drove on, he lifted the book to my face, describing a clockwise circle with his index finger over the letters on the cover. It did indeed read 'Toilets', as the T.S. has been placed above the Eliot.

"Strange that a person whose name was an anagram for toilets could write such stimulating verse, don't you think?" He opened the book and started to read. Something about an old man being read to by a boy. What, you expect me to memorize poetry while I'm driving?! "Very fitting," Mabey commented. "Except I'm not old and you're not a boy. And you're not reading to me." More poetry. It all sounded like madness to me. "This is the beauty of the poet's art. Not bog standard. Not bog standard!" And on he read.

The narrow country road continued to wind and meander among the hedgerows and grass verges of a different world. Pheasants flew up in astonishment. Cows turned and stared as we passed. As we started to climb towards the village, the rib-cage hills fell away on both sides. Dark clouds blotted out the sun. A wind of unknown origin blew wisps of straw haphazardly past our craft while sundry rodents scattered for cover. It felt like an ascent into hell.

"Turn right here."

As we came over the brow of the hill we left the relative comfort of the asphalt to turn onto a simple farm track. Deep tyre ruts straddled a Mohican strip of wild grass, only offering passage for a single vehicle. The grass caressed the underside of the car as we passed over it, the occasional bump provided by the occasional exposed boulder.

After a few minutes of this ordeal, the road smoothed to a chalky surface as we pulled into the village of Upper Hooey.

There were the thatched houses, there the rose gardens. Just as I'd read in the *Village Almanac – A Tale of Two Hooeys*. The road was virtually empty, but for the odd agricultural vehicle and schoolboys playing French cricket. Double yellow lines had been painted near the verges, possibly explaining the absence of parked vehicles. But who would have parked there anyway? The lines had clearly been painted freehand, their thickness and the gap between them varying wildly and quite unpredictably. At one point, they departed from their kerbside role and drunkenly depicted the shape of a chair. Had it been too much trouble for the painters to remove the chair that stood in their path? This was indeed the impression.

"Left here."

It was quite absurd: Mabey in the passenger seat, issuing instructions and regaling me with poetry, while I, a newcomer to these parts, and, what's more, theoretically his superior, was at the wheel, like some kind of visiting taxi driver.

"That's the house," he announced, thrusting an outstretched digit across my face towards the opposite side of the road. One Pudding Lane was a yellow-plastered rustic property with doors and window frames painted green. It seemed somehow familiar to me, like a distant memory; I was sure I'd seen it before.

A rough gravel path led through a sadly untended garden full of parched wild grasses and overgrown shrubs to a generous porchway fashioned from rustic logs. Somewhat more conspicuous was a huge oak tree standing on the boundary between the house and its neighbour. Large enough to live in, I thought. Perhaps that was where the husband had gone.

Susan Jollygoode was burying something in her front garden. "Shouldn't you be at the nursery?" I complained as we approached her from behind, footsteps crunching on the gravel.

"Yes… No… It's my day off. Not that it's any of your business." Our initial strategy had failed, but we'd taken her by surprise nonetheless. In truth, it didn't seem hard to achieve; the woman was distinctly edgy.

"So… What can I do for you?" she asked as she rose. Her tone suggested that she would prefer not to do anything for us at all.

"Just making some routine enquiries, Mrs. J. Can we go inside?"

With an uncertain glance at her earthwork, she downed gardening tools and wiped soiled hands on overalls in some irritation. "Yes, I suppose so," she said, and led us in.

The house itself was neat enough, but somehow unloved. It hadn't been dusted in a while. Without thinking, I corrected the tilt of the Van Gogh in the hallway as I entered. Long Grass with Butterflies. Most apt. Probably some kind of clue. Susan Jollygoode ducked under a low wooden lintel to enter her kitchen. I followed suit and my colleague had to remove his helmet. Good job it wasn't Cake. He would never have crossed the threshold with that height.

"You've met PC Mabey?" I said with a peremptory wave of the hand in the Constable's direction.

"Ma'am." He saluted her with an insolent lift of the chinstrap.

"I'd like to ascertain the groundwork," I continued. "Lay a few facts." Now that was a Burley-Hoggism. The Sergeant's idiom was catching.

"About…?"

"Your husband, Mrs. J., your husband."

"Ah, my husband, yes." Susan Jollygoode seemed entirely unfocused on the matter at hand, little concerned over the disappearance of her spouse. I wouldn't have minded, but it was *she* who'd brought the problem to *us* in the first place.

"For example, where exactly did you last see him?"

"I've told you all about that." She cast me a look of utter perplexity. That old *you cannot be serious* look. But I was serious – deadly serious.

"I need to see it. For myself."

"Very well. It's upstairs."

The phone rang. Susan Jollygoode turned to give it a worried look, then glanced up at me. Mabey had time to compose a poem. *Aren't you going to answer that?* I thought. She snatched up the receiver nervously.

"Hello? No, he's not here at the moment. I don't know. What?" She turned away to continue in a furtive whisper.

On the farmhouse kitchen table, pine, made to look antique, lay a large parcel. It was addressed to Duncan Jollygoode. Unopened. Next to that, some bills. A letter. A document headed simply with the initials 'D.E.F.F.' Behind these, on the wall, a photograph of Susan Jollygoode sitting on a bench with a man and two children. They were all smiling happily, dressed as Disney characters. She as Snow White, he Mickey Mouse. The children were those two chipmunks. In the background, the unmistakable fairy castle of Disneyland. Which one could it be? Florida, Paris? Tokyo? One I hadn't yet heard of?

I was suddenly overcome by an unbearable feeling of sadness.

"Er – Inspector?" Susan called from the kitchen doorway, where she and Mabey stood awaiting me.

"Yes? Of course. Upstairs."

We followed her up a creaking flight of stairs, negotiated a mid-flight landing and soon stood before the bathroom. The door was indeed unlockable from the outside, given a screwdriver.

"Is this just how he left it?" I asked. "You haven't touched anything?"

"Of course I have," she snapped. "I live here, don't I?"

I glanced down at the bath. It was still half full.

"It's different water," she explained.

"Different water…" echoed Mabey.

I tested the window. "Yes. Just as you say. Can't be closed from the outside. Good."

I sat on a wicker chair, and like some crazy game of unmusical chairs, Mabey nabbed the toilet seat while Susan Jollygoode perched reluctantly on the edge of the bath.

"I'd like to ask a few questions, if I may," I said, whipping out my notebook.

"Fine. If you must."

"How long have you known your husband, Mrs. J.?"

"Oh… Quite a long time. A few years."

"A few?"

"Four. I think."

"Shall we say four then."

"Yes. Why not."

"You moved here two weeks ago?"

"Yes."

"Where did you live before that?"

"Where did I live? Oh… Wales. It was in Wales."

"But I thought you were Scottish."

"Scots can live in Wales, can't they?"

"Can they?" *Always answer a question with a question.*

"Anyway, I'm not Scottish. I'm a Shetlander."

"Ah. And you lived in Wales with your husband?"

"Yes. He's Welsh."

"Welsh?"

"That's right. Swansea."

"That's where you lived?"

"No, he was from Swansea. Is, I mean."

"And where did you live?"

"I told you. In Wales."

"Where in Wales?"

"Oh… F–f–Ffestiniog. I think it was."

"You think?"

"Where the railway is."

"Do you have a memory problem, Mrs. J.?"

"No. No. I have a problem holding conversations in my bathroom." She rose abruptly. "Come on, this is getting ridiculous. Can we go downstairs now? Have you finished up here?" Well, there were one or two things left unresolved. Ideally, I would have liked to attempt a reconstruction. But then again, as I'd already surmised, the whole story may have been fabricated anyway. What would have been the point?

We moved to the relative comfort of the kitchen. But the result was the same: Susan Jollygoode seemed singularly unable to give a clear answer on anything. Though she *was* able, when pressed, to provide a small photograph of her husband: a man who appeared not to have a single distinctive feature. "We'll have this blown up," I said helpfully as I slipped it into my wallet, knowing all the while that no manner of photographic machination could help the man's plight.

"Last seen wearing? Something daring?" asked Mabey, pulling out his own notebook.

"I beg your pardon?" gasped Susan Jollygoode.

Mabey sighed wearily. "What was your husband wearing when you last saw him, madam?"

"Well... *clothes*, I suppose."

"*Clothes*, you suppose?"

"I don't remember too well..."

"Nothing more specific than that? *Clothes*? It's not much to go on. Were they fashionable? Dowdy? Lightish or darkish? Come on."

"Perhaps he was in fact naked?" I offered, genuinely trying to help. "If you say he was in the bathroom."

"We can't very well put that, can we sir," Mabey countered. "*Last seen wearing nothing.* It would attract entirely the wrong sort of attention, don't you feel."

"Shall we invent a suit of clothing for him, then, just for the sake of decorum?"

"I'm not inventing anything," Susan Jollygoode inserted with a look of hurt pride.

"Anyway," I continued, "if he *had* been naked, he would obviously have thrown a towel around his loins before dashing out, wouldn't he? At the very least."

"All right then, *Last seen wearing a bathtowel around his loins, toga-style?* Would that help, sir?" Mabey sucked on the end of his pencil with leaden irony. Susan Jollygoode looked from one to the other of us, then back to the first one, shaking her head in disbelief. I grunted and turned my attention outside.

The kitchen window looked out on a self-enclosed back garden of generous proportions, with a sunny south-facing aspect and ample scope for improvement. A stepping-stone path down the middle and grass on either side. Sunflowers rampant in the heat. Long grass with butterflies, dried out and brown, could do with a good mowing. A shambolic mix of hardy perennials and low shrubs at the edges, tall and unkempt, mixed with all kinds of weeds and backed by deciduous and coniferous trees. All overgrown.

"You've let the garden go," I commented absentmindedly. "That's a shame."

"Yes well... It's hard without a man around the place," said Susan. That did seem the very obvious and convenient answer.

"If it were me, I'd have cut the grass before digging holes at the front," I fished.

"Look, have you come here to discuss gardening? I thought there were more important things on your mind."

A squirrel flung itself from the top of a beech tree to the hanging fronds of a nearby mountain ash, scrambling frantically as the branch gave way under its weight.

"Where did your husband work?" I continued as I contemplated the shed at the bottom of the abandoned garden.

"At home. I told you." Susan Jollygoode remained as obstructive as ever.

"Yes, but where? Which room? I'd like to see it."

"Oh… Yes. Well. It wasn't exactly a room, you see… because… he worked in the *shed*." It was as if she'd hit upon the idea at that very moment. I turned to find her giving me an oddly meaningful look.

"In the shed?"

"Yes. He worked in the *shed*," she said more decisively but with an equally meaningful look, and perhaps the hint of a wink.

"All right, can we see it then?" I ploughed on regardless.

"Yes, you can see it. There it is," she said, pointing a finger through the window into the ether.

"No, I mean can we see *inside* it?"

"I'm afraid not. It's locked and I haven't got the key. Do you see, Inspector? I haven't got *the key*."

"He took the key with him?"

"He must have done. I never saw it anyway…"

Why would a man disappear and take the shed key with him? Because he didn't want anyone messing with his trowels and hoes? Or perhaps he didn't fancy a tax inspector going through his settled accounts while he was away? That would suggest an intention to return…

"Let's go and have a look," suggested Mabey.

Susan Jollygoode now looked decidedly uneasy. "What would be the point of that?"

"No, it's a good idea," I agreed. "We might spot something of note. Even if we can't get in."

We stood at the door of the garden shed. Seen from closer quarters it was a rather inappropriately grand structure, with a round cast-iron knob and windows on either side of the door. More like a summerhouse, in fact.

"He might be inside," said Mabey. I wanted to believe he wasn't trying to provoke me. "Shall we break the door down?"

"Have you got a search warrant?" Susan Jollygoode blurted out in evident panic.

"No, that won't be necessary," I said in the hope of calming her. "Let's just look through the window for now."

Through the grime of the shed window I could just make out what looked like a desk, a filing cabinet and a waste paper basket. Yes, the missing man had worked there. But of course, they could equally have been a workbench, a ladder and a garden bucket. And there, at the back, was what appeared to be some kind of time machine. More likely a lawnmower, of course. In that case, the unkempt lawns could unwittingly provide Susan Jollygoode with her silent witness; they looked like the business end of a witch's broom, and hadn't seen a mower, or a weekend-gardening husband, for some weeks. Make that months, as the drought would have slowed the growth anyway. But of course, that would only prove the absence of gardening, not the recent disappearance of the gardener. Do estate agents mow lawns? They might, if they had to sell the house. They might not, if they wanted to describe the garden as 'a delightful mix of wild grasses in a country setting'. The evidence was inconclusive.

"We may want to access this property at some stage, Mrs. J.," I said.

"Fine," she replied. "Bring a search warrant. And find *the key*."

"And I think that'll do for now. Good day."

We returned to my car, she to her digging. Until Mabey remembered his helmet. "Sorry, ma'am," he explained, "left it on the kitchen table. Can't do without me helmet, ma'am." And out he came with his helmet under his arm.

"She's making it all up," was Mabey's verdict as we prepared to leave. "A pack of lies, is my surmise."

I gritted my teeth and buckled down for a long journey back.

Dear John,

That's a nice idea about the book, I hope it makes you happy and keeps you busy. Be sure to give it a good story, that's what I say. I can't abide books without a good story. Otherwise you'd be like that man who writes off the top of his head, what's his name. I was listening to him on the radio the other day. He didn't seem very sure of himself at all. You have to be sure of yourself, that's what I always say. Decide on what you're going to do, then just go ahead and do it. Of course, that's difficult in your situation, I know. But you've always got to look on the bright side. Always find something to keep yourself busy. The devil finds works for idle hands, as it says in the Bible. I've always kept myself busy, and it hasn't done me any harm. I'm afraid to say this isn't a dream, John. I wish it was, for your sake, but no, what's happened has happened and the sooner you accept that the better. You were responsible for what you did, I won't mince my words. It's no good trying to bury the truth. Well, I'd better be off to the post office before they close. Make sure you wrap up warm now, what with the evenings drawing in.

love
Aunt Clarice

Memory Jogging

"How many Disneylands are there?" I asked, once back in the safety of the station vestibule. Fittingly, it was the soundtrack to *Jungle Book* this time.

"None if I can help it," said the Sergeant none too helpfully.

"I think three," I said to start the bidding. "Florida, Paris, Tokyo."

"California, Hong Kong," corrected Cake in his customary fashion. "Makes five."

"Hong Kong? That hasn't happened yet, has it?"

"Wales," Mabey said casually. It was the time of day I was coming to dread: the change of shifts between Cake and Mabey. What always ensued was always something like a squabble between two schoolboys – Cake, tall and gaunt, proper and righteous, stubbornly cautious, bridling indignantly at the constant mocking of his colleague; Mabey, shorter and sarcastically lightweight, cynically unconventional, smugly stroking his artist's goatee as he revelled in another moment of knowing things that no one else knew.

"Pardon?"

"Wales, sir. They built one there a few years back."

"I've never heard of that." Cake was on the trail of righteousness again.

"Carmarthen. Car something. Cardiff. One of those."

"So how come we've never heard of it?" I asked.

"It was a financial disaster. They hushed it all up, of course. Went to the pre-opening trial with my boy. Rained the whole time. Couldn't understand the announcements. Not your classic Disney experience."

Wales? Susan Jollygoode said she'd lived there. Could there be a connection?

"But what was Susan Jollygoode doing there?" I continued, trying to maintain some semblance of cohesion. "She hasn't got any children, as far as we know. And yet there were two kids dressed as chipmunks in that photograph."

"Maybe they were chipmunks," jested Mabey.

"Maybe they were from a previous marriage," Cake offered more constructively.

I wasn't sure about either proposition. "She doesn't look old enough to have had a previous marriage."

"Ah." Mabey sensed another of his special moments. "You're never too young to have a previous marriage. When man and wife are wed, it's in and out of bed. Isn't it."

"Of course, you'd know all about that," said Cake, thinking to repay some of the cumulative hurt.

"I haven't had a previous marriage, mate. Have you, Inspector?" asked Mabey.

"Never mind that. So the man in the photo wasn't Jollygoode? If not, who was he? Could he be involved in the case? Is he a secret lover? Or just her brother? These are the kind of things you should be asking. Not whether I've had a previous marriage. What sort of coppers are you?"

"Yes, but sir, if I may intervene," said Mabey, intervening, "the man in the picture was dressed as Mickey Mouse. Now, as you know, everyone when dressed as Mickey Mouse looks like Mickey Mouse. Consequently, I feel the photograph lacks the necessary qualities whereby we can start to build a case, in this case. Would you not agree?"

It was true. It would have been utterly impossible to gauge whether the man in the photograph on the kitchen wall was the same as the man in the photograph in my wallet. For while the latter had a conspicuous lack of distinctive features, the former had an abundance of them. Large black ears, for starters.

Two fine pictures of health and fitness jogged past the open door of the station in their running gear. He, fair of hair and tanned of face, wore a salmon pink T-shirt, white shorts and mustard-coloured socks, while she, petite, brunette and tanned of face, wore the opposite. A mustard-coloured T-shirt with little sleevettes cut away to the shoulder, little white shorties and cute salmon pink popsocks. Both were panting most gaily, in an entirely heterosexual way.

A large black cat dashed up the road behind them. It was trying to catch little cords tied to the back of their shoes, which the cat must have mistaken for mouse tails.

"Nick and Nicolette from the post office," explained the Sergeant from behind the desk. "Taking their cat for a run. Same time every day. They do say cats have their own alarm clocks, don't they sir."

I'd never heard that one, but it set me thinking nonetheless. If ever you needed information in a country village, where would you go? To the village post office, of course. That's where locals would stand gossiping idly while they waited for the person in front to complete a road tax special exemption application form. Perhaps our two panting joggers, or possibly their cat, could point us in the right direction.

"Post office?" I asked.

"On the High Street like everything else, sir," said Burley-Hogg. "Turn right and it's on your left. You'd have to be blind not to miss it."

And I didn't. *N. & N. Down, Proprietors* said a hand-painted sign nailed to the oak lintel of the doorway. Like most of the properties in the High Street, it was a modest Georgian structure built in an age when people were shorter. A huddle of villagers lined up outside, waiting for the Downs to open up after lunch. What was quite so urgent for them I couldn't fathom, but I supposed their flow must be hard to stop. Rather like a dripping tap.

"Good afternoon, Inspector," proclaimed Nick Down with a jaunty leap in his voice as he opened the door to let the huddle in. "I trust it's not about the counterfeit pension books?"

"No, no, I'll leave those to you," I joked back, little wondering how he knew my identity already. "Can I have a word?"

Nick left his wife to the mercy of the baying throng and led me into the back room. I explained the case of the missing husband and asked him to monitor all mail addressed to the Jollygoode residence. All terribly hush hush, of course. Needless to say, he could only reinforce what I'd already heard from the Sergeant – that nothing at all was known about the Jollygoodes.

"Do you play tennis, Inspector?" Nick asked as we rose to resume our daily lives. "My wife and I are always on the lookout for new partners."

"Ah," I sighed apologetically. "I'm afraid I have no partner."

"No partner? How very unfortunate," the postmaster sympathized. "We could always set you up with one. We have to be very diverse these days, after all. We must offer diverse services," he suggested with a wink. The *double entendre* was unbearable – whether intentional or not.

"Well, you know," I responded with a vague waggle of the hand, "in my profession it's best to remain unattached, if you follow. You know the kind of thing: candlelit dinner in exclusive restaurant organized for wedding anniversary meal, wife sits and smoulders alone because detective husband has been called out to investigate a murder. 'Sorry darling, you know how it is' he says on his return, as she throws her serviette down in disgust. No, I don't think I could stand that. Thanks, all the same."

"….I meant, a tennis partner?" Nick Down ventured, seemingly undeterred.

"Ah."

"A threesome, perhaps? We've done it before. We take turns to play with each other, while the third one watches from the side, occasionally retrieving balls from bushes and the like. We laughingly call it 'Singles a-go-go'. The other one is 'Swap'n'mix doubles'. We play a set, swap partners, play another set, and so on until everyone has played with everyone else and we're all completely exhausted. It's great fun and it certainly keeps you fit, Inspector." He glanced at my questionable middle for the briefest of seconds. "We have to be versatile these days, after all."

"Right. Well, maybe we could do one of those," I replied as I turned for the door, knowing in myself that it was never going to happen.

The post office cat leapt down from the windowsill and came curling around my legs. "Don't mind Aubergine," called Nick with a laugh. "She's just marking territory."

Two postcard-sized notices on the wall caught my eye as I squeezed past the queue of villagers towards the door. "*Invitation to a Party: Introducing The Matrimony Course – How to Build a Healthy Marriage that Lasts a Lifetime, Sat. 24th June 8:00pm, Community Hall, Drinks and Desserts, Music & DVD, £5 per married couple RSVP: Nick & Nicolette Down*" read one. And below it: "*Penelope – Psychic, Medium, Spiritual Counsellor – Gentle, reassuring, helpful. Tuesdays only*".

That set me thinking of another line of enquiry. In the Netherlands, it was common practice to enlist the help of psychics, spiritualists and mediums in solving crimes. Bodies had been found, hidden jewellery uncovered, second wills revealed and guilt proven, all thanks to those sundry voices from beyond. Faced with a missing husband who may never have existed, a supernatural aid suddenly seemed a perfectly viable option.

Dear Aunt Clarice,

Thanks for writing back. The man who writes plays off the top of his head was probably Harold Pinter. I certainly don't think I'm Harold Pinter. I'm almost sure of it, but I sometimes have my doubts! I've heard he starts writing without planning anything and just lets the story develop naturally. I'm not sure which path I should take; at the moment I'm just bumbling on through the undergrowth, clutching at branches to keep myself afloat, if you see what I mean. I'm sorry I haven't planned it as you suggested. I know I should always take your advice, but I keep forgetting. If I'd listened to you I'd never be here in the first place! But I had no option, you see. It wasn't my fault. She made me do it.

love
John

Unhappy Medium

Penelope Slack opened the door of her maisonette on Laughingstock Street. She wore a pink taffeta dressing gown and fluffy pink slippers, had her hair in curlers and a fag hanging from her mouth. She couldn't have been more than forty, but seemed bent on imitating the style of my grandmother. I wouldn't have been surprised to learn she had false teeth.

"Yeah?" she drawled in mid-expiration of cigarette smoke.

"Inspector Gaskett. We spoke yesterday?"

"Oh, right!" she breathed in mock surprise. "I wasn't expecting you so early, like."

"Ten o'clock, wasn't it?"

"Was it? Well, fuck me. Sorry love. Memory like a sieve."

Laughingstock Street had an interesting history that seemed suddenly pertinent. In the late 17th century, as the *Village Almanac* informed me,

45

stocks had been erected here for the chastisement of witches, adulterers, wifebeaters, charlatans, quack doctors, confidence tricksters, sellers of bogus remedies, incompetent builders, ale-diluting innkeepers, Catholics, Papists, Jacobites and all other fashion of unspeakable miscreants. But instead of the grisly punishments meted out to these unfortunates in other parts of the country, here in Dribbleside they were simply locked in the stocks and laughed at, for days on end if necessary. Consequently, the aptly named Laughingstock Street came to be the default residence of villagers with, shall we way, more imaginative professions – and Penelope Slack certainly fell under that description. As if to prove the point, the stocks still stood right outside her maisonette, encircled by chain fencing and oft snapped by tourists.

"You better come in then," she said, turning to blow smoke through the corner of her mouth as she backed against the door to let me in. The front of her dressing gown slipped open to reveal a healthy eyeful of cleavage.

Penelope Slack's front room was full of rubbish. Not the kind that is gladly thrown away, but the kind that is all too regrettably kept. There were prints of tropical sunsets and herds of stampeding elephants on the walls, pink tasselled lampshades on the lights, faerie queen figurines bedecked with hanging beads and glittering sequins, huge square candles bearing single Chinese letters on their sides. Disney character cushions on sofas, placed incongruously over drapes spirited away from an Afghan bazaar. And in the middle of the room, a plastic mat bearing the signs of the zodiac and a motley collection of mystic symbols. How anyone who claimed to be psychic could display such an egregious lack of prescience when it came to taste was quite beyond me.

The impression of chaos was augmented by the random positioning of ashtrays crammed with dog-ends, some piled so high that any new addition would have sent the whole lot tumbling to the floor.

"You here for a quickie or the full works love?" Penelope asked in the doorway to the room, arms half-folded in that languid manner known only to smokers. Two large ripe apples nestled on the folded forearm of her non-fag-holding hand.

"Police business," I replied. "I thought I'd made it clear."

The woman hurriedly drew together the front of her dressing gown. "Sorry love. Thought it was a joke. 'Inspector Gaskett'. You know, 'Excuse me, mate, I've come to inspect a gasket'?" Her face was momentarily wreathed in smile wrinkles, like an old tangerine. Sadly, the lines gave her an appearance of pain more than anything else.

I stood and eyed her with a stony expression. It was the kind of taunt I'd suffered since childhood, 'Gaskett' being unhealthily close to 'spastic' in the febrile schoolboy's mind. Even Mr Idle, the school careers adviser, had suggested I enter the motor repair trade, on the pretext that people often find professions that are uncannily reflected in their names. 'Besides, it would be good for advertising,' he'd enthused, little knowing the hurt I was feeling inside. But now, to be taunted once more by the village's eminent seer...

A burning smell emanated from another room. "Bugger me, left the toaster on," she shrieked as she rushed out to the kitchen with smouldering fag held aloft.

I amused myself by rummaging through a loose pile of Tarot cards while Penelope Slack doused the fire in her kitchen and went to make herself decent. It was a complete waste of police time, but I was *choosing* to waste it and had no one but myself to caution for it. The Tarot cards were scattered on a low coffee table placed in front of the Afghan-draped sofa. Some had spilled onto the zodiac chart on the floor; some were showing their faces and some their backs. All the familiar images were there: the Wheel of Fortune, the Hanged Man, the Magician, the Tower, the Hermit, the Lovers, the Fool, the Madman... Mr Pint the Milkman, Mrs Sole the Fishmonger's Wife, and the Knave of Spades from Alice in Wonderland.

"I'm one card short of a pack love," said Penelope on her return, mistaking my curiosity for genuine interest. "I ain't got *Deff.*"

She meant 'death'. I resisted the temptation to relate everybody's favourite anecdote, that *Death* doesn't actually mean *death.* "You interested in that kind of thing, are ya?" she continued. "You got *Deff?*"

"No, I haven't got *Death*, and I doubt that cards such as these could be of any use to my enquiries. Whether Master Bun the Baker's Son killed Colonel Custard in the pantry with a 14th century Persian ruby-encrusted dagger is very much by the by, I'd say."

Penelope Slack burst into laughter. "Fuck me that's funny," she chortled in an entirely exaggerated way. Though her language remained indecent, she had at least had the decency to cover herself up. She now wore a loose-fitting, short-sleeved, pale green cotton top and matching floppy pants. The pink slippers were there by default, and the curlers would have taken far more time to unravel than I was prepared to allow.

"Do you use these for your divinations, then?" I asked, indicating the cards with a sweeping gesture of the hand.

"Fuck me no," she answered in her now familiar style. As if to emphasize the point, she stubbed her cigarette on the nearest ashtray while turning to blow the last vestiges of smoke through a corner of her mouth. "Tarot's just a con. Didn't you know? They belong to my kids. Well, I say kids, they're my partner's kids. Well, they're not his either, strictly speaking. They're his old bird's. When her bloke left her for another woman, she looked after the kids. Then she shacked up with my Harry, and they both looked after them. Then she went and topped herself, and Harry kept the kids. And that's when I met him."

"So you're looking after children that don't belong to either of you?"

"That's it. You're bloody quick, entcha Inspector."

Penelope Slack's life was evidently even more chaotic than her maisonette.

"So how do you do your divinations, then?" I persisted in some hope of getting my day back on track.

"Brains, Inspector," said Penelope Slack with a little too much relish. She moved over to a chest of drawers covered with arcane memorabilia. "My little helper," she added, removing an object from a drawer. "Say hello to my little Brains."

Clasped firmly in a sandwich of her bony hands, a large chameleon was already eyeing a fly that buzzed ingenuously from pillar lamp to post box. The creature's huge eyes rotated and twisted until they settled on me, whereupon its colour turned a deeper shade of purple. It seemed somewhat redundant to enquire whether she had a proper licence for it.

"He tells me things by changing colour," the woman announced, plonking her psychic sidekick down on the zodiac chart. "He went mauve to say how surprised he was to see you." Well, anyone could have worked that out. "People kept asking me 'Where's your crystal ball? Where's your crystal bleedin' ball?' So I thought 'balls to that' and called him Brains, seeing as he's cleverer than a crystal ball. His real name, if you want to know," I didn't, "is Aztec Chimera the Third. I got him off a highly respectable Mexican dealer, and before you ask, he was legit, all right? And yeah, before you say chameleons don't grow in Mexico, he said he got it off a highly respectable dealer in Africa. Not all chameleons change colour, he said, and I said, well, mine bloody better do, or you're in trouble mate. I don't want me clients coming here and calling me a fraud 'cos I got a chameleon that don't change colour. Did you know they don't have ears? They communicate by extrasensual perception. All I have to do is listen to their inner bleedin' voice." Yes, I was getting altogether too much information here. I would need to hurry the conversation on.

"Let us cut to the chase, Miss Slack," I said, keeping an eye on the eye of the beast.

"*Ms*, if you don't mind."

"Sorry – *Ms* Slack. Why am I here? Yes. Well, a woman in the upper ward – I'll protect her identity for now if I may – has reported her husband missing. I thought perhaps you might apply your abundant gifts to help us find him."

"I'd have to see the woman, wouldn't I. More to the point, she would have to see my Brains."

"Ah. I have an inkling she would only reluctantly agree to that. Is there nothing you can do in her absence?"

"You having a laugh? What, find the whereabouts of a missing person just on your say-so? Not likely. Can you do that, Brains? …No, he says he can't. Tough cheddar mate."

"I've got a photograph."

"A photograph…?" Brains had gradually settled into the grey-black hues of the zodiac chart. "Give us it here then."

I handed her the miniature passport photo of Duncan Jollygoode, which she placed on the zodiac chart in front of her squamate companion. The animal jumped back a quarter inch and suspiciously trained its rotating bug eyes on the faded print. I could hardly describe its reaction as recognition of any sort; something more on the lines of "*Jesus* what's that shiny piece of paper?!"

"Now I need to prepare meself," said Penelope Slack as she started placing objects at various positions on the chart. A Chinese candle went on Gemini, a Tibetan prayer bell on Taurus and a glittering oyster shell on Aquarius. "What sign are you?" she asked.

"Sign?"

"Star sign?"

"Oh. Aries."

"Bugger me. Aries. The ones who don't believe in star signs. We got a right one here, Brains," she muttered as she placed him on the sun, the photo on the moon. "Now. Absolute effing silence please." She lit an incense candle fashioned in the shape of a Hindu deity and sat in the lotus position facing the whole assemblage.

With chin lifted high and eyes firmly closed, my psychic host started to quietly emit a low, reverberating hum that was surely not the product of any mortal being. I could see no hidden speakers, no telltale trail of electronic cordery. She was somehow producing this unearthly sound herself. Brains remained motionless, gazing now at the photograph, now at his transcendental mistress, evidently considering her insane.

The sound continued for a good two minutes with barely perceptible breaks. Meanwhile, the smell of incense began to mask the all-pervading reek of stale cigarette smoke.

At length, Penelope opened her eyes and exhaled. Brains turned his eyes towards me as if to say, "*That any good mate?*"

"There's nothing, Inspector. No being emanates from the picture, he says. I'd say this man is long dead."

I was stunned. "But you can't be sure?"

"But I can't be sure." Brains continued to survey me. "Wait a minute... What's that you say? Well fuck me rigid. He's saying something about *you*... You're a landscape gardener at a wildlife park, Inspector? Is that right? You're pretending to be something else, though you don't know it yourself... You fancy this woman... She's good enough, quite good... Jolly good?... You've reached the point of no return, he says... Brains, you dirty beggar! I can't repeat that!... You wear odd socks... And... And... AAAAAHHHHHhhhhhhh!!!" She issued an exaggerated cry of anguish and keeled over sideways onto the floor. Brains diverted his gaze towards her. I checked her pulse. There were signs of breathing, chest movement... She could not be dead.

"*Leave money on table. Forty quid. See yourself out,*" said the chameleon.

Faced with a host who was senseless and a deputy who couldn't hear, I sensibly followed his bidding, while still marvelling at Penelope's performance and wondering how she'd managed to make the animal talk. It seemed futile to claim that I was executing a public service and should be exempt from payment. I stepped out into the rising heat of Laughingstock Street, having learnt nothing about the missing husband – save for a growing conviction that there was nothing to be learned at all.

Dear John,

I hope you're settling in now. Are they treating you well, as far as can be expected? As long as it doesn't feel too much like a prison. Although heaven knows, it should be. I would come up to see you, only my legs are getting worse and the hours are so limited. You being so far away doesn't help, of course. How are you filling your time? Did you make any progress with that book you were talking about? I could send you some ideas if you like. You wouldn't believe the stories you hear these days. On the news the other day they said some people had been arrested for eating a policeman's sandwiches while waiting for an identity parade. I ask you! The cheek of it. There are plenty of funny little stories like that. But please don't say it wasn't your fault. You must have known what you were doing, and the sooner you face that fact the better. No one made you do it. Well, I'd better get those bulbs planted. I wouldn't mind betting it's going to rain.

    love
    Aunt Clarice

A Growing Conviction

Cake was having none of it.

"No, I can't be having that," he said, happy to employ his preferred idiom.

It was lunchtime, and of course, the Constables could find little to do other than lounge about in the staff area behind Burley-Hogg's counter, taking verbal swipes at each other or exchanging gripes about their pay as they trawled through the Positions Vacant column in the Daily Dribble. For the Sergeant, it was the ideal moment to spray the pot plants to the sound of *Your Glockenspiel Favourites.*

"But it's obvious, innit." Mabey, well irritated from his morning's paperwork, was engaged in his second favourite pastime: winding Cake up.

"What is?" asked Cake.

"She does him in, then makes out he's disappeared, doesn't she."

"What, so you're saying Mrs Jollygoode actually killed her husband?" Cake had to check.

"That's what I'm saying."

"What would she do that for?"

"Insurance, of course. Stands to reason." Mabey plucked a grape from the staff fruit bowl.

"No, no, no. She would never do that kind of thing." Cake was equally firm in his conviction.

"Either that, or there is no husband," his tormentor continued, mouth full of grape. "He just doesn't exist."

"What do you mean?"

"No one knows him. No one's ever seen him. So maybe he just doesn't exist."

"What did she report him missing for, then?"

"Seeking attention. Or maybe she's got a soft spot for our Van der Valk in there." How glad I was to have installed a two-way intercom system with recordable CCTV.

"No, I can't be having that," Cake repeated. "She's the victim here. The husband has deserted the marital home and left her to pick up the pieces."

"She's really got you in her pocket, hasn't she. And all it took was one ploughman's lunch! Ha!" In his enjoyment of the moment, Mabey leant back in his chair and laughed loudly at the ceiling.

"Tell you what," Burley-Hogg broke in, even as droplets from his spray gun landed softly on the leaves of the maidenhair fern. "Why don't you have a bet on it?"

Mabey leapt out of his chair with unprovoked excitement. "GOOD IDEA!" he yelled in a rare show of anything positive. But there would have to be money involved: "A fiver says the man doesn't exist."

"All right," said Cake, rising to the bait. "My money's on desertion of marital duty."

Cake and Mabey produced the readies as the Sergeant took a note of the bets.

"So that's one desertion and one complete fabrication," echoed Burley-Hogg, jotting the predictions down with his stubby fat pencil. "And I'll go for murder. Homocide. Come on lads, it's got to happen sooner or later."

"And no tampering with the evidence," said Cake with an accusing glare at his senior. "Like last time."

Mabey had to laugh. "What, you think Sarge would wave a magic wand to conjure up a non-existent husband out of thin air, then do him in, just to win a bet?! You wouldn't do that, would you Sarge?"

Burley-Hogg said nothing but chuckled with amusement as he recorded the official time, place and meteorological conditions of the bet.

"Well, it wouldn't be the first time, would it," said a deflated Cake.

"Sarge ain't a murderer. Are you, Sarge."

The Sergeant chuckled again. "Oh, I don't know. I've done some slugs in my time."

"You know what I mean," said Cake. "That time when you bet I'd lose my truncheon and I found it stuffed down your trousers."

"Oh yeah! The fastest fiver I ever earned!" Mabey laughed again.

"aaaaaaaaaaaahhhhhhhhhhhHHHHHHHHHHH!" A banshee's wail could be heard hurtling along the High Street and up the steps into the station. And a picosecond later: "My Brains is missing! MY BRAINS IS MISSING!"

Followed a microsecond later by the calm riposte of the desk sergeant: "My brains *are* missing, madam. My brains *are* missing."

"No! You don't understand! My Brains, my Brains!"

I slid out of my office in time to save the day, mentally cuffing the snorting Constables on my way through.

"I'll deal with this one, Sergeant," I said with a pretence of proper authority, then turned to face the psychic visitor, Penelope Slack. "You have lost your companion?"

"He's gone, Inspector, he's only fuckin' gone and gone!" The woman was distraught.

"Language," warned Burley-Hogg with chubby finger erect.

"When did you last see him?" I asked.

"Well…" she said, even now beginning to draw her own conclusions. "When *you* were there, Inspector! When I awoke from my tantric trance, you had both disappeared!" Penelope Slack clawed at her hair like some demonic health inspector searching for headlice. That hair was straw-like, long and straggly; the curlers had evidently been wanting of effect.

"I assure you I didn't take him!" I pleaded.

"Then who did!" she bawled.

"I don't know!"

"But you're a detective! You're supposed to know!"

"And you're a psychic! You've got special powers!"

"Now you're just taking the piss!"

It could have gone on. Fortunately, at that moment a referee stepped in to part us.

"Sir. Madam. With respect," started the Sergeant, and again, "with respect, what exactly is or are your brains? Let us deal with this in an adult fashion. It's not good for the plants."

I volunteered an explanation as Penelope wheezed for breath. "It's a chameleon."

53

"A comedian?"

"A chameleon. It appears to have disappeared from the lady's mais-onette."

"I hope you've got a licence for it," said Cake, eager as ever to enforce the letter of the law. The woman muttered some new profanity as she fumbled another cigarette to her mouth.

"Ah. But can the lady be sure?" continued Burley-Hogg, ignoring Cake. "The chameleon, if I'm not mistaken, has the uncanny knack of merging with its surroundings. Could you not simply be overlooking it, madam?"

"*HIM*," retorted Penelope testily, glad of a chance to give the Sergeant some of his own medicine. "Could I not be overlooking *him*."

"Well... Could you not?"

"No. I could not. I see him with my paranormal senses, not with mere eyes. He ain't there, I tell ya."

"But of course, for members of the public that caveat will not apply," I said. "Who will be able to see your Brains when he merges with his background?"

"...Only me," the woman replied forlornly.

"Then surely," interjected Mabey, sensing a poetic moment, "he will exist and not exist at the same time. *Essence* without *existence*, as Sartre would not have had it."

"Oh?" said the Sergeant, turning to him.

"See, if your variable-coloured pet were in the next room, in *essence*, does that prove his *existence*? When we walk out of a room, does the room continue to exist?"

"Course it does, you prat," intervened Cake, not without good reason this time. "Stop being so bloody *poetic*."

"Ah, you may call me a *prat* and mock my *poésie*, but you cannot prove at this point in time that the fine lady's chameleon exists, nor that it ever existed, nor that any chameleon has ever existed, nor that you yourself existed before this very moment!"

"Eh?"

"Or this moment!"

"Look—"

"Or this!"

"SHUT UP!" cried Cake, utterly exasperated. "I know I existed before this moment, because I remember it. I remember everything."

"Aha!" yelled Mabey with an air of victory. *"Cogito ergo sum*! I think, therefore I am – *I think*! As the old saying goes. The problem is that our chameleon friend does not think. So then, does he exist?"

"OY! Do you mind?" For psychic Penny, who until now had followed their exchange in bemusement, as if watching a game of sub-intellectual ping-pong, this crossed the threshold of good taste. "How the fuck do you know he don't think? He thinks more than you do, fuckwit!"

"Language," reprimanded the Sergeant, raising a digit once more.

"I could have you arrested for that," said Mabey. "Linguistic violence. The penalty is severe."

"I don't think that will be necessary," I said, attempting to defuse a tinderbox situation. "We'll put up a notice. You know the kind of thing."

"Yeah," said Mabey, self-esteem sorely bruised. "Missing. One chameleon. Colour: Variable. Size: Smallish. Unmistakable."

An awkward hush fell on proceedings, none present feeling sufficiently qualified to provide further useful comment. Until –

"This could be a philosophical matter, could it not," said Sergeant Burley-Hogg, turning to me. "Perhaps you should see the Doctor."

"What doctor? I'm not ill."

"Doctor Morpurgo. Professor of Philosophy at Halfheart University."

"The one who attended the identity parade?"

"That's right, sir. He lives in Probability Mews."

"But Sergeant – *philosophy*?? How can that possibly be of help? Every-one knows philosophy has nothing at all to do with the real world."

"I wouldn't be so sure. His imagination has come in handy on many an occasion, sir. He might know if there's an osteopath on the loose. He might provide logical recourse to the animal's whereabouts, and at the same time give useful pointers in the missing or hopefully, no, *possibly* murdered husband case, sir. He's always up for that kind of challenge."

"Always up his own arse, more like," said Penelope Slack as she knocked ash onto the vestibule floor. It sufficed for the Sergeant merely to raise a finger this time.

"Philosophy appears to some people as a homogenous milieu," Mabey threw in, reading from a book. "There thoughts are born and die, there systems are built, and there, in turn, they collapse. Others take Philosophy for a specific attitude which we can freely adopt at will. Still others see it as a determined segment of culture. In our view Philosophy does not exist."

And by the time he'd finished reading, everyone else in the room had simply disappeared.

Absinthe Mind

A visit to Probability Mews was to prove unnecessary, for I happened upon the Professor himself, sitting alone at a round table in the corner, on my next visit to the Point of No Return. An ale man he, I arrived at the very moment when his next instalment was due.

"Another?" I offered with my usual generosity.

"Gladly," Morpurgo replied, "I've been waiting for you."

He must be talking figuratively, I deduced, and went to order his poison – Highly Extraordinary. The ale at last replenished, I then set about picking his labyrinthine brain. "We have a conundrum of some proportions that you may be able to resolve," I started, taking care to avoid normal language as far as possible.

"Oh yes? And what shape might that conundrum take?" asked the Professor.

"A shape that cannot be defined. A shape that hath no shape."

"Come again?"

"It's a mystery. We have a missing husband of whom there is but little or no record, and now a missing psychic chameleon belonging to a psychic woman, possibly our only chance of finding said husband. All other avenues having been exhausted, I wondered if you'd care to apply your philosophical wit to the issue."

"Ah yes, the case of the missing husband. The most alluring Ms. Jollygoode and the incident of the mistakenly scoffed lunchbox. Most amusing, most amusing indeed. And now there is a further twist in your curious little detective story – a missing beast of the order *Squamata*. Yes, you have set yourself quite a difficult task, placing yourself in a topos where, by definition, nothing much ever happens. So far so good, but difficult to maintain in the long run. Something was sure to happen sooner or later, was it not? And now you have realized that your life is sustained by a stream of incident, not constrained by the structure of police procedural. Most profoundly intriguing." Morpurgo paused to sup his ale. "Most intriguing indeed," he repeated, licking his lips.

"Well… Could you perhaps throw any light on the affair?"

"Affair? Has there been an affair? Quite possibly, quite possibly, though I very much doubt it involves your missing man and the equally missing beast."

"The affair as in the *matter*."

"What's the matter?"

"The matter of which I speak."

"Ah. You see it as matter? Definable matter? Yes, that is also equally feasible. Now. In what way could the disappearance of a mysterious individual and the evaporation of a lizardine creature be connected in reference to definable matter? Our first hypothesis would be to suggest that the two are *co-existential*. That is to say, they are *one and the same*. Now, of course, in the real, physical world, no one would claim a human being and a leathery-skinned animal could share *identity*. And indeed, I would deduce that the times of their respective disappearance are at variance, as you omitted to mention the *latter* on my appearance at your station to investigate the *former*. Nevertheless, they may be seen to share an identity in that they have both vanished. Beast-*qua*-husband, as it were. I would go further to posit that, as a result of said shared identity, they have both become *imaginary constructs* of your mind. They in themselves have essence, but in your mind they are one and the same. You have, as it were, projected the character of your missing husband onto that of your chameleon, and vice versa, and for that reason the missing husband may seem able to alter his colour or appearance to suit his surroundings while the chameleon may be found loitering around the home of the aforementioned, highly delectable *Madame Jollygoode*."

I looked at him goggle-eyed. "And the second...?" I eventually managed to enquire.

"The second? Steady on, I haven't finished the first yet," counter-posited the academic, raising his glass.

"The second *hypothesis*?"

"Ah. The second hypothesis. You mentioned that the chameleon is psychic. Now, being a Doctor of Philosophy, I effortlessly retain all information to which I am randomly or purposefully made privy, as I am sure you will know already. I have in my head whole libraries full of information, painstakingly catalogued with shelf numbers, row numbers, aisle numbers and annex numbers, information that I have the power to retrieve in the fluttering of an eyelid. I am walking down an aisle at this very moment, and now carefully pull out, oh but from the topmost shelf, the information that you are a policeman. Why are you investigating a disappearance if you are a policeman? And the answer is computed instantaneously: because a crime has been committed, or at least you suspect as much. And then I ask myself: why would a psychic chameleon be the next to disappear? Answer, once again: because it knew too much about said crime. Some person – we know not who – was concerned that the oracular reptile would reveal the solution to the crime, a crime that said person has perpetrated, and has therefore taken steps to purloin it. And so, once again, your chameleon and your missing husband are found to share the same identity: for not only are they both disappeared entities, but they both share a connexion with the same crime." Yes, he said *connexion*.

"…And are there any more?"

"More what?"

"Hypotheses?"

"But yes. Shall I tell you the third one? Is your non-philosophical mind not saturated with a surfeit of wisdom already?"

"Tell me the third," I replied with growing annoyance.

"The third hypothesis is that the whole affair, yes, the whole matter is being played out in your imagination. I mentioned some hours ago the concept of *imaginary constructs*. I was merely jesting then, as I had not yet downed a sufficient quantity of ale to be truly serious. What you must remember is that all matter is nothing but *illusion*. Not *delusion* – I am a philosopher, not a psychoanalyst. I would lay no claim to examining your mind as an individual being, but the mind of all humanity, the *human condition*. I am not interested in your *delusions of grandeur* but in your *illusion of greatness*. The heavenly Susan Jollygoode entered your office and told you her husband was missing… *and you believed her*! Your belief transformed the notion of his disappearance into reality. But in *reality*, the man is nothing but a fiction. He has no body, and therefore he is *nobody*. And on to your chameleon. You have heard that he is missing; and so you believe it to be true. You believed the psychic woman could communicate with the brute, but she could do nothing of the sort. For it, too, is nothing but an illusion."

I started to wonder if the famous Doctor Morpurgo might himself be an illusion – his ideas were certainly bereft of any substance – and, more worryingly, that I might be too. But no. I could not be an illusion to myself. I had thoughts, I had desires, I had a pain in the back of my neck…

"This is the beauty of fictional constructs," he droned on. "The human mind sees what it wants to see, to the exclusion of all else. For example, you so keenly desired to see me here, and in your mind you created the fiction that I would be sitting here alone. So enslaved are you to your illusion that you have failed to notice my good friends who share this table with me, and have done for some half a day now."

Good grief! There, seated around the small round table with us, were two others enjoying measures of what appeared to be absinthe in special edition etched glasses. "My absinthe friends present themselves," said the Professor with a smirk and a chuckle, before introducing them as Slowcoach and Selbydate, the missing members of his 'unholy trinity'.

"All right?" said Slowcoach with a wink as Selbydate absentmindedly twiddled an ornate spoon. I managed to force a smile.

"So now you are thinking, which is illusion and which reality?" the Professor continued. "Am I myself, perhaps, illusory? Perchance this whole scene is naught but a *solipsism*, Latin: *solus*, alone, *ipse*, self, the philosophical idea that *My mind is the only thing that exists*, an epistemological position that knowledge of anything outside the mind is unjustified? That the external world and other minds cannot be known and might not exist? Or perhaps you yourself are merely the product of someone else's imagination, the *solipsism* of another? But please understand. I have not created these illusions: I am no magician, no *illusionist*. No. I have merely suggested them to you, and your poor human mind has itself created the illusion." We were alone again. "I hope this makes it perfectly clear. Your missing husband, and your so-called chameleon, may exist in *essence* but you will find them nowhere in *substance*."

Curiouser and curiouser.

I was fairly sure I was not the solipsism of another. How else would I have those thoughts, those desires, that pain in the back of my neck? True, the Professor had introduced a useful element of *perspective* into the case, and for that I was somewhat thankful. Police training and common sense had already taught me to trust no one and take nothing for granted; yet they had never suggested that a crime, a suspect or a witness could be *illusory*. Just as his own use of Latin phrases, archaic con-structions and impossibly contorted logic gave the impression that he was intellectually predisposed and therefore of use to society, so Susan Jollygoode's testimony had conjured up the illusion that some incident had occurred – when in fact, nothing may have happened at all.

I drank up and took my leave. I needed something more concrete to go on. Something altogether more *corporeal...*

Some Body

They found the body on Sunday afternoon.

A game of croquet in the vicarage garden was getting overheated. As Sarah blocked his ball with her foot, Peter hurled her mallet into the bushes. "Dad, Peter hurled my mallet into the bushes!" "No, but Sarah blocked my—" "Peter, this is the very last time, do you hear?" "Yes, dad. Sorry, dad." "Where is it?" "Over there." "Here?" "No. There!" "Here?" "Yes." "Hold on... Oh my goodness. Oh my gosh. Peter, go inside. Sarah, call your mother. Oh my golly." "What is it?" "Just go inside." "Mum!" "Phoebe! Oh my God." You know the kind of thing.

It was my dubious pleasure to attend the crime scene with Cake on that lazy summer afternoon. The body of a man lay face down behind a large rhododendron bush, in a narrow strip of woodland between the perfectly manicured lawns and low outer wall of the vicarage garden. Contrary to earlier speculation, the body was neither naked nor wrapped in a bathtowel, toga style, but wore a darkish suit and lightish tie entirely consistent with estate agency. Despite a conspicuous lack of nudity, it was therefore easy to conclude that the body was Duncan Jollygoode's, though no identification was found to prove it. The man certainly resembled the photograph in my wallet. But then again, so did so many other men.

Cause of death: Blow to back of head by blunt instrument. Possibly some kind of mallet.

Time of death: Hard to ascertain. Wound still fresh, slight aroma of fish – herring, perhaps. Murdered *after lunch*, I concluded, before ordering a collapsible crime scene unit and pathologist set from Constabulary Headquarters.

The Reverend Oscar Melon and his family were huddled together in the drawing room in a state of shock. It was evidently quite upsetting for them to find a corpse lying in the spacious grounds of their sumptuous Victorian property; perhaps it was a skeleton in their closet come home to roost. And yet Oscar Melon, breaking off occasionally from attempts to comfort his sobbing household, claimed not to recognize the deceased, nor ever to have heard of the Jollygoodes. That Susan was not a churchgoer was easy to infer from her general demeanour. All the same, Upper Hooey fell within the parish of Saint Sebastian's, and it was surely the vicar's bounden duty to know all his parishioners, in a strictly non-biblical sense.

Some kind of subterfuge was afoot, I decided, but couldn't decide what or why. Why commit a murder then barely conceal the body in your own back yard? Because the appearance of a chance discovery would deflect suspicion away from you, of course. It would have looked somewhat bleaker for the vicar if the body had been found buried under his aucuba.

Well, that was one way of looking at it. There could of course have been an alternative explanation. It could, for example, have had something to do with the missing chameleon.

"It could have been suicide," proffered Cake, keen to bolster his lingering hopes of winning the bet. "That's right. He couldn't take it any more. Not only was he in a profession he considered dishonest, but he wasn't even getting any business. And he'd deserted his wife because she'd rejected him." The phantom of Cake's £10 winnings danced in the air before his eyes. "He didn't fancy leading people down any more garden paths, so he came to make his final confession to the vicar. But... something happened... so he couldn't go through with it, and topped himself in the bushes instead."

"But he's not Catholic."

"How do we know? It's hard to tell the spiritual leanings of a dead man," Cake said with uncharacteristic lyricism. "And he may have had a deathbed conversion, anyway."

"The *vicar* is not Catholic. He wouldn't take confessions."

"Ah," Cake pronounced victoriously with finger raised, "but the dead man wasn't to know that, was he? Not being a churchgoer, as the vicar said, he wouldn't have known the difference. And it may have been the realization of his error that finally tipped him over the edge."

"You're just being silly now. Who on earth would commit suicide by whacking themselves over the back of the head? And how?"

"Er... Well, of course, the blow to the head could have been incidental... The real cause of death could have been... er... something else..."

It all reminded me of an anecdote Four-Eyed Bob had once shared with me. On seeing a newspaper article with the headline "*Woman found strangled – by our crime reporter"*, an enthusiastic young constable had promptly taken himself to the newspaper company to arrest the journalist for murder. He had only desisted from his task on convincing himself that the woman had not been *strangled* by the crime reporter, but merely *found* strangled, whereupon he arrested the poor hack for not reporting a crime through due process. Then it was pointed out that the woman had not been *found strangled* by the reporter, but that he was merely reporting what he'd been told by the police in the first place. Whereupon the hapless constable reported the newspaper's editor to the Fair Trade Commission for misleading use of punctuation, entered the headline in a competition for famous gaffes in print, and started looking for a new job.

"Flowerbed conversion," I muttered as I eased down the handbrake.

"Beg pardon sir?"

"He didn't die on his deathbed. More likely a *flowerbed.* Flowerbed conversion."

"Oh!" Cake laughed disingenuously. "That's jolly good, sir."

Informing Susan Jollygoode of her husband's death was going to be the hardest thing I'd had to do since – well, *ever.* At the very next opportunity, which happened to be the following morning, I consulted *"How to Break Bad News to Relatives"*, a supplement to the standard issue MoH Policing Manual (1949).

The supplement had never been used and was sadly neglected. As I opened the Introduction page, a small moth flew out from between the covers.

Breaking Bad News to Relatives. This is one of the hardest things you will ever have to do. Bad news to be broken to relatives can take a number of forms, including: (1) Death of a relative, (2) Arrest of a relative, (3) Proof that a relative is not a relative, (4) Discovery of a relative not previously known to be a relative, and (5) Discovery of a relative previously thought to be deceased. In some cases, (6) Release of a relative from custody. The latter applies particularly to psychopaths and other dangerous individuals.

The procedure in such cases is uniform. First, the situation requires perfect calm. It is recommended that you drink tea, not coffee, prior to your visit. Second, make sure your facts are correct beyond any possible doubt. All too often, regrettably, case (1) above is followed almost immediately by case (5). Moreover, be sure to visit the right house. Cf.

Gittings vs. Worcestershire Constabulary (1917), when the claimant was mistakenly informed of her brother's arrest on terrorism charges, resulting in her hurling Molotov cocktails at the local police station. NB. Claimant won a substantial award plus cost of materials.

(1) Death of a relative

Method: Direct visit to the relative in question. Wait to be asked in. Do not look around to see if others are listening. Do not give bad news on the doorstep. This might be misapprehended as a trick.

Avoid using the telephone, unless the sheer distance involved would delay identification of the body. Never, ever give bad news by telegram. The reasons for this are self-explanatory, but include (1) the wrong person may receive the information, and (2) the telegraph operator may make a typing error.

Direct approach – Correct information – Calm mind. These are the four key phrases.

"I think you'd best just tell her," said Four-Eyed Bob, standing at the door of my office.

"Yes," I agreed.

"Tell her it might be him."

"Yes."

"But don't say it might not."

"Right."

"See how she reacts."

"Woof." Miss Marple was back from her walk around the vegetable plot. Good for the soil, Bob had explained.

"Right, old girl. We'd better be off."

"All right, then. See you later, Bob." Gregorian chants. Bob and his dog stepped out into the searing heat of the street.

I asked Mabey to make me a good, strong cup of tea.

He said, not when he was off duty.

I said, but you *are* on duty.

He said, not 'tea-making duty'. That was what he did in the pub, when he wasn't illicitly distilling liquor or diluting beer.

Burley-Hogg made me a good, strong cup of tea. He was in an exceedingly generous mood anyway, now that the odds on him winning the bet had shortened significantly. "Looks like I'll be pocketing those fivers, Constable. Just a matter of crossing the i's and dotting the t's," he said as he handed me a mug in the staff room.

"Drat, should have stuck with me hunch," replied Mabey in mock disappointment. "What'll you do with your winnings, Sarge? Live it up large?"

"I might book myself a nice holiday. Yes. That would be grand. Still, it's early doors yet. We still have to prove she did it, don't we."

"Shouldn't be too difficult," said Mabey. "These things can be helped along. No point in leaving them hanging mid-air, eh?"

"That's right. No one would thank us for procrastivating, for sure," agreed Burley-Hogg. I had my doubts over the ethics of police officers betting on the outcome of a case; it surely wasn't right. I wouldn't go as far as to suspect the Sergeant of committing homicide for the sake of £10, but it did seem quite in his interests to falsify the occasional piece of evidence in this case.

"We have to keep an open mind, of course," I warned.

"Of course we do sir, indeed we do," agreed the Sergeant. "An open mind at all times."

"That's if we've got a mind," added Mabey with a snigger. He even mocked Cake *in absentia*.

"In any case, a murder's been committed," I said soberly. "And a pet has been stolen. Don't you think a little less frivolity would be appropriate?"

"That certainly is also true, sir," Mabey conceded frivolously. "We wouldn't want to be frivolous about murder, would we. Still, look on the bright side, eh? At least we don't have to make the crimes up any more."

I downed my tea and prepared myself for the ordeal ahead.

"It'll be all right, sir," said Burley-Hogg, as if to console me. "We all have to come to terms with things. We all have to move forward."

"Yes. Thank you, Sergeant. That does make me feel a lot better. By the way, Sergeant."

"Yes, sir."

"Let me know as soon as you get the autopsy report, won't you."

"Righto, sir. Yes. I'll do that, sir."

So it was that I set off on my second visit to Upper Hooey, on that hot midsummer morning. And this time, I chose to go alone.

The Longest Day

"And you'd like to see more central involvement in regional issues?"

"Yes, that's right. Devolution can only go so far, I feel. Of course, there are things local people can and should decide for themselves, and that's only natural."

"Such as?"

"Such as when and how often to clip roadside hedges. The gender mix of local councils. Which roads to surface with asphalt. And so on."

"I understand. Carry on."

"But there are some things, I feel, that central government should always be deeply involved in. School education, for example. Building hospitals. Litter."

"Litter."

"Yes, of course. Litter isn't a regional problem, it's a national one. It's a problem of national mentality. We once made goods and products of which we were rightly proud. But this nation has no pride in its products any more. Once, it would have been considered taboo to simply cast aside an empty box of Swan Vestas or a used bottle of Marmite. These were prized and valued items in their own right, even when empty. They would be discarded, with reverence, in the proper way and through the proper channels. There was, as it were, a sense of harmony between people and their waste."

"I see."

"And now? Products, wrappings, packages... Well, they have no inherent value at all, do they. Consequently, it seems perfectly acceptable to toss them aside at the earliest possible juncture. Now in Sweden, they've found a way of addressing this problem, which was never that great there in the first place, to be fair. In Sweden, they burn garbage to fuel local power supplies. But instead of the local authorities picking up their rubbish, they buy it from the people, at modest rates it has to be said. The result is that the streets are constantly being scoured for litter by people of lower incomes, thus eradicating the problem. Litter has become, in other words, a valuable commodity. The people who used to drop it are now picking it up. And it has certainly helped the unemployment problem, which was never that great in Sweden in the first place, it has to be said."

"I'm talking to Andrea Payne, Spokesperson of the Campaign for Administrative Reform. In a moment, we'll be talking about state pensions. First, some travel news."

"If I had my way, they'd all be strung up on——"

I turned the radio off. I was having some trouble finding the turning to Upper Hooey; I'd already passed The Point of No Return, near the spot where we'd turned the previous time, but could see nothing. Nothing but an endless stream of litter blossoming up through hedges and scorched grass verges.

I knew I'd gone too far when I reached Neither Hooey, the forgotten village, two miles down the road. I made a U-turn and turned back along the road. Sure enough, there, a little way before Nether Hooey, with the Point of No Return visible up ahead, the white marker post stood as clearly as it possibly could. 'Upper Hooey – No Through Road'. How could I have missed it? My mind must have been elsewhere.

I ducked down under the old railway tunnel after the turn, and everything changed in an instant. There was no roadside litter, for a start. There were also, it seemed, suddenly no other cars. The surface of the road was wet, evidence of a recent downpour; but the weather had been fine on the journey so far.

More than that, though, there was something different in the air. The hedgerows were murky, sinister. Crows circled aimlessly in the air above lonely windswept fields. I looked up at the sky, now filled with clouds of gloom. It had that same sense of foreboding as before.

A tractor suddenly and quite irrationally pulled out of a field onto the road ahead of me. I swerved desperately to avoid it, but it was too late. The tractor had already ploughed into the passenger side of my car. I got out in a hurry, ready to give my first caution.

The driver, an unhealthily tanned middle-aged fellow with an insolent blondish coif, climbed down from his cab. His massive frame towered over me as I attempted to prepare a strategy. "You're in a hurry, aren't you," he said with a distinct undertone of violence.

"Police," was the best I could offer as I frantically fumbled in my coat pocket for some ID.

"That'll be fine," he replied, relieving me of the obligation with a dismissive hand gesture. "In a bit of a mess there, aren't you," he continued. Steam rose lazily from the bonnet of my car. The wing on the passenger side was buckled beyond recognition.

I tried to gather my composure. "Name."

He gave no reply but merely eyed me with a look of menace.

"Name, please."

"I don't think that'll be necessary. They'll never take your word against mine, for a start. I have not had a single accident in thirty-seven years, and everyone in these parts knows it."

"Perhaps your time was due, then."

"You are to blame. You were going too fast."

"I am not apportioning blame. I need to make my report."

"Oh, your report, is it? All right, then, for your report, you can say my name is Farmer Hector the Hedgehog, I live on the Old Grassy Knoll under the Old Oak Tree in Old Upper Hooey, and my solicitor is Peregrine Falcon-Browne in the City of London."

"…Falcon-Browne?"

"Peregrine Falcon-Browne."

"No further questions. You may go."

No one, anywhere, messed with a client of Peregrine Falcon-Browne. There would only be tears in the end if they did. Providing he was paid enough, his devilishly legalistic brain could find a loophole in any law. His clients were the trustees of bogus charities, celebrities on drink-driving charges, company directors who'd frittered away their employees' pension funds. He had ruined the careers of several high court judges and caused the resignation of at least one Attorney General. If someone said they were a client of Peregrine Falcon-Browne, it meant not only that they were rich enough to buy your silence, in one way or another, but also that you could never win a legal argument with them. Even if they were a farmer. Especially if they were a farmer.

Hector the Hedgehog climbed back into his cab and revved up the engine. Without so much as a hearty farewell, his tractor backed away and trundled off along the hedgerows until it was out of sight.

It did of course strike me, after the event, that he could have been lying about Peregrine Falcon-Browne. It was so easy to say, after all. Like the dictator of a third world republic claiming to have the atom bomb. You don't just march in there, do you. He might *not* be lying. You'd only march in if you were fairly sure he *didn't* and *wasn't*. Well, in that light, Farmer Hector's misdemeanour didn't seem so awfully severe anyway.

But there I was, stuck with an undriveable car, having completely and utterly alienated my only chance of rescue. I turned the key in the ignition anyway, just to be sure. The engine offered nothing but a jarring, whirring cacophony of mechanical discord.

The car had yet to be fitted with two-way radio; given the distinct lack of criminal activity in the village, that was low on the list of low-priority tasks anyway. Communication was therefore out of the question. What I needed was some kind of portable telephone that you could carry everywhere with you, but that appeared to be technically impossible. Where would you put the cables, for a start?

There was no escaping it. I would have to walk the remaining two or so miles to Upper Hooey, then deal with the problem from there. So off I set, having secured the car as best I could. It would have to stay there until I could get help from the village.

Despite the summery season, there was a sudden chill in the air. Murky grey clouds continued to jostle with each other in the sky. Sporadically ferocious gusts of wind started to bend grown trees double. I turned my lapels up and tucked in my chin. Things did not bode well.

As I walked, teams of rabbits came to mock me through gaps in the hedgerow. When I turned to confront them, they would dart into unseen hideaways, whence to mock me some more. Sheep would simply stop, look up and gaze with expressions of bemusement. Wood pigeons were posted at forty-yard intervals along the telegraph wires. Their job was to monitor my progress along this interminable road. Occasionally, one of them would hurtle past on its way to make a report. Some were unavoidably indisposed, to be replaced by collared doves. They did pretty much the same job, but were not so alert. I felt I could trick them. But not the wood pigeons. They even aimed their droppings at me as I passed below.

The road was endless. Could it really be only two miles to Upper Hooey? Long stretches of asphalt, lined on both sides by hedgerow, would continue as far as the eye could see. As I reached the end of a stretch, the road would suddenly twist and turn in meaningless, mad contortions for a few hundred yards, before straightening out again. And then the same sequence would be repeated.

I heard footsteps on the road behind me. Oddly, they seemed to be keeping pace with my own, neither coming closer nor tailing away. When I stopped and turned, I saw… no one. The footsteps also stopped. The road had dipped into a shallow cutting, grass verges forming embankments on either side. I must have been hearing the echoes of my own footsteps.

I heard the whinnying of horses on the road behind me. The sound seemed to be following me along the road. I turned; there were no horses. I heard the clamour of agricultural machinery on the road behind me. I turned; there was no agricultural machinery. The sounds were being picked up by the wind, I decided, and carried far across the fields on the wings of tiny flying insects. That was the only possible explanation.

I heard the squeaking, creaking, clanking of an old bicycle on the road behind me. This time, it seemed to be approaching rather than keeping pace. Soon, I heard a gentle wheezing of breath. A slight panting. And a screeching of brakes. I turned to see my old friend Bob. Was I relieved to see him.

"It is you, isn't it?" said Four-Eyed Bob.

"Bob!" I cried. "What... Why... When...?"

"I had a feeling you were in trouble," he said. Miss Marple looked up from his basket with an expression of utmost sympathy.

"Yes, I—"

"You had a disagreement with a tractor, yes. Came straight out of a field without looking, didn't he. Yes. Insurance write-off, of course." How could he know such things? I'd long since given up asking. "Let's walk together for a while, shall we? Don't stop for us. You have to reach Susan before sundown, after all. Out you get, girl."

Miss Marple plopped out of the basket and down onto the road. As we continued on our way, she walked alongside us, tail hanging low.

"Farmer Hector the Hedgehog, it was," I said.

"What was?"

"The driver of the tractor. A right prickly character."

"Hedgehog?"

"Yes."

"Strange name."

"You don't know him?"

"Can't say I do. Did you get his number?"

"No, I... Well..."

"In that case, anyone could say they were Farmer Hector the Hedgehog, couldn't they."

Miss Marple agreed.

"Never mind. We'll find him," Bob said confidently.

"Best be careful, though."

"Client of Peregrine Falcon-Browne?"

"That's right..."

"Oh dear, oh dear." Bob laughed. "That's what everyone says around here. It's a local tradition. Whenever there's trouble brewing – whether it's an argument over a land boundary, a false accusation of infidelity, or what have you – just say 'I'm a client of Peregrine Falcon-Browne.' It defuses the situation and everyone goes home happily."

"Ah."

"Yes, I'd say your Hedgehog is in for a roasting when we get our hands on him."

We walked along silently as I reflected on my own idiocy.

The wind had softened to a gentle breeze. A summer school of swallows screeched in excitement as they soared and swooped over our heads. The sunshine returned, and for once, Bob didn't look out of place in his shades.

"Do you believe in dreams, Bob?" I asked, finally.

"Why yes. I believe they exist."

"No, I mean—"

"But as to whether I have faith in them. That's a different matter. The only thing I have faith in is my own intuition. My nose. And my dogs." Miss Marple gave a muffled sneeze by way of affirmation. "What have you been dreaming about, then?"

"All sorts of things, since moving here. Weird things."

"That's trauma, my boy. You've had a big upheaval."

"Possibly. Last night I dreamt I was in a hospital. You were a doctor and Miss Marple was a nurse."

"What, a dog dressed as a nurse?"

"No, an actual nurse."

"How did you know it was Miss Marple then?"

"…Because you called her that."

"Could we see? With our eyes?"

"Yes, you could see. I was the one who couldn't see."

"I see. I see."

We did laugh. Miss Marple looked up, perfectly content. Her tail was wagging now.

"It must be because we take such good care of you," concluded Bob.

So why, in this dream, was Susan Jollygoode my mother? *She* was taking care of me. Now that was rich. Susan Jollygoode seemed hardly capable of taking care of herself, let alone anyone else.

Susan Jollygoode. Perhaps she really was the murderer. She'd killed her husband and dumped his body in the vicarage garden. Perhaps he'd been having an affair with the vicar's wife, or a gay tryst with the vicar. I hadn't thought of that. I might have to say, "I regret to inform you that your husband is dead, and by the way you're under arrest." Why was she always so evasive? Why did she seem unable, or unwilling, to answer any question with a straight answer? And what had she been burying in her front garden that day? But no. Surely not. She might well be scatty, one saucer short of a full tea set, but I couldn't believe she would hurt even the tiniest of flies. The Sergeant may well have won the bet, but Susan had played no part in the crime. I was sure of it.

Then again, why did her face, her voice, her manner seem so very familiar? Could I have met her somewhere before?

It was really rather pleasant now. Dull grey clouds had been replaced by fluffy white ones. The road ahead had an agreeable curve to it. Dunnocks and wrens flitted among the hedgerows; butterflies and bumblebees stopped to admire wild flowers along the way.

I turned to share this warm sensation with Four-Eyed Bob.

And he was nowhere to be seen.

I stopped and looked back. There was no sign of man, dog or bicycle. Had they moved on while I was lost in thought? Or had they never been there in the first place?

I could but carry on. The village would appear soon, I felt sure.

What did appear was a single, monumental rain cloud. It hurried in briskly towards centre stage, then simply hung there, filling the whole sky with its ominous presence. It was so low that I could almost touch it. It felt moist, cold. The darkness of night fell over the surrounding countryside, leaving just a bright edge glowering along a distant horizon.

And then the wind picked up again, without notice. The trees were bending once more, their foliage rustling with a suddenly returning urgency. Tree bark and other arboreal debris started to fly past me, leaves and twigs swirling through the air as they continued their windborne journey to nowhere. I was sure I could see small rodents, and the odd sheep, being hurled across the fields along with them.

As cracks of thunder issued in the distance, the first raindrops started to fall. They were about the size of golf balls. What size is a golf ball? Not being a golfer, I could but guess. A golf ball was about the size of those raindrops. Each great globule fell like a precision-guided missile onto the helpless ground below. I could see a pattern of watery trails emerging on the road ahead. Was it a map? An electronic circuit? No, it was just a lot of rain. And now it was pouring down in relentless torrents. It actually hurt.

The road started to climb Copse Hill, flanked on each side by the rib cage of field strips I'd seen from the vegetable plot. It was a steep climb, made worse by the rain lashing down on my head and the wind whistling past my ears. I didn't remember putting on my raincoat, but there it was. I lifted the back and shoulders over my head to fashion a makeshift tent. It collected water like bilge in a ship's hull. Every now and then, the contents would slop onto the ground with a terrific crash. My raincoat was a great sou'wester.

Through the gloom, I could see a figure standing by the road ahead. He seemed to be beckoning. Was there something he wanted to share with me? His hat, perhaps? As I drew closer, the figure turned to face me, shaking spasmodically in the wind. Rain continued to pelt down in diagonal lines, like something from a Hokusai print.

The figure was now just a few yards ahead. It suddenly looked less like a man and more like a young woman, standing just inside the field to the right. The gleam from the horizon illuminated her golden hair. It was jagged and somehow lifeless. She shook in convulsions. She was certainly in need of help.

A sudden sheet of lightning revealed her. Yes, she had no legs, but a wooden broom handle thrust into the ground. She was dressed in a rustic coat and hat, straw protruding loosely from her outstretched arms. Her hair was made of hay; fragments of which blew away in the wind. Her head was an old football, her mouth the little hole where the pump would go.

"Thank you, Ma'am," I said with courtesy and a bow, swiping the hat from her head. "That will do nicely." And it did do nicely, for a while, as the rain swept down with persistent ferocity. Water flowed along the edges of the road in little rivulets. Veins coursing to the heart of the land.

But soon, as the slope of Copse Hill levelled out, the sky started to brighten once more behind me. There was another peal of distant thunder, then an unearthly silence fell. Only the relentless squelching of my own footsteps reassured me that I hadn't lost my ears in the rain.

I looked up to see the guilty cloud scuttling off into the distance, grumbling morosely about some grievance or other. In its place came a clear, pure blue sky, spreading sunlight to every corner of the Dribble Valley. My elongated, late afternoon shadow marched off along the road ahead of me. And there in the distance beyond, I could see the thatched roofs and whitewashed walls of Upper Hooey.

Late afternoon shadow? I looked at my watch. It was eight o'clock in the evening.

But I'd left Nether Hooey in the morning. How could I possibly have taken nine hours to walk two or three miles? Without eating or drinking? Or needing to?

As I mused, birds reappeared in the hedgerow. Horses started to frolic, no longer required to look miserable on three legs. My surroundings were, once again, quite genial.

I turned a gentle corner and the road disappeared. It simply ran off into a field and ended there. And yet – there was the village, on the far side of the field.

One thing was for sure: we had not driven through any field on my first visit here.

I started across the field. The ground still heaved with rainwater, yielding generously to my every step. Each time my shoe sank in, a newly vacated hollow gurgled as it refilled with muddy water. Soon, the whole field was playing a symphony of babbling squelches. Worms surfaced to check out the commotion. Blackbirds and thrushes gratefully yanked them out.

At length, and all the muddier for it, I reached the far end of the field. A broad farm gate was the only thing between me and a chalky lane leading down a gentle slope into the village. On the far side of the lane was an open orchard where sheep grazed under fruit trees; beyond that, a huge farmhouse.

The gate was tied shut with a length of frayed plastic rope. So keen was I to finish this journey that I could have vaulted the gate in one. But, mindful of my social standing as a guardian of the peace, I decided to climb over with dignity.

That was a big mistake. The gate was quite rotten, and the wooden crossbeam gave way without a hint of resistance as soon as my whole weight was on it. It didn't so much snap, as simply collapse in a pathetic heap. My precarious position, and the momentum it afforded, sent me flying over the gate onto the other side.

A group of children rushed over from the orchard to enjoy my misfortune.

"Look! The man has fallen over," said a girl of about three, looking down at me as I nursed a sore ankle.

"What a silly man," said an older girl, possibly her sister. They all had the same face anyway. There were five or six boys and a similar number of girls, none of whom looked old enough to have started school.

"Shall we tickle him then?" said the first girl.

"No! Let's steal his hat!"

"Steal his hat! Steal his hat!" they all started chanting.

One of the older boys, obviously the bravest, came over to where I lay sprawling, and whipped the hat off my head as I struggled to my feet.

"Come on, kids. I'm from the police," I protested with a false chuckle. Pulling rank with pre-school children was not my proudest moment.

"It's a policeman! It's a policeman!" they squealed with renewed delight. "We've got a policeman's hat!"

The introduction of that concept merely enhanced their excitement. They passed the hat amongst them as they ran across the road into the orchard. I chased them around apple trees, pear trees, plum trees and more apple trees, scattering sheep in all directions as I went. Just when I thought I could grab the hat, another child would whisk it away from under my nose.

"Policeman's hat! Policeman's hat!" shrieked the younger ones, giggling with mirth. With their nimble darting movements and their tiny elastic legs, they could easily outmanoeuvre me. I would give chase, then slip and land on my backside again, pounding the wet turf with my fists in frustration.

This just wouldn't do. I was here to police a community of thousands, yet I couldn't even control a handful of children. As the child with the hat danced rings around me, others grabbed my arms and legs, pulling me down again.

Then the brat with the hat, the youngest boy of three or four, made a fatal error. He put the hat on his head and ran across in front of me, waving his arms about wildly like a safari park baboon. He took his eye off the ball for a fraction of a second. I stuck out a leg and brought him crashing down. The children all stopped dead and stood open-mouthed with fear. I pinned the boy's neck to the ground with one hand and retrieved the hat with the other. Yesss. This was a most satisfying moment, a moment of supreme triumph.

"You there. May I ask what on earth you're doing?"

I froze. It was a schoolmarmly voice, harsh and unforgiving.

"Oh. G-Good evening. I-I—" No sound of any greater substance would issue from my throat.

The boy on the ground was crying. The others started to sob in unison.

"And you enjoy tormenting children, I suppose?"

"No, I— Not at all, I—"

"I've a good mind to report you to the police."

"No, but I—"

It was Mrs. Hardcups, my old schoolteacher. I was six years old. I'd been caught stealing apples from an old lady's garden. Well, I ask you. The tree was leaning over the road. They were asking to be picked.

"Pay attention! And look at me when I'm talking to you."

"*Yes, Mrs. Hardcups. Sorry, Mrs. Hardcups.*"

"That's better. Now, I'm willing to let you go this time. But I warn you. If I ever catch you molesting or abusing these children again, you will wish you had never been born. Do you hear?"

"*Yes, Mrs. Hardcups. I'm sorry, Mrs. Hardcups. Please don't tell my father. Please don't.*"

"All right. Now go!"

I took my hat and scuttled away without further encouragement.

"But he's a policeman. He said so!" the youngest girl claimed on my behalf.

"Nonsense. He was just saying that to frighten you."

"Why was he so dirty, Nan?" asked another. "What's he doing here? Is he Jesus?"

"Don't be silly. Now come on home."

"Yes, Nan." Their voices faded into the distance behind me.

"Why did he call you Mrs. Hardcups, Nan? And in that silly voice?"

As I dusted myself off and made the swiftest possible withdrawal from the scene, a thought suddenly struck me. I hadn't the faintest idea how to reach Susan Jollygoode's house from the orchard; I hadn't the faintest idea where I was at all. All I could do was to continue walking down the chalky lane into the village. Perhaps something would jog my memory. It was not a large village, after all. Or perhaps I would come across a friendly villager. Did they exist? In the meantime, I could dry out a little and present myself with a little more dignity at my destination.

I walked past the Old Post Office. The Old School. Next to it, the New School, a yellow house. Neither of them looked remotely like a

75

school. The Old Bakery. The Olde Pubbe. Well, that was a pub. The Old Stables. The Old Barn. The Old Lockup. The Old Forge. The Old Policeman's House. Had there once been a police presence here? Or was it where an old policeman now lived?

It seemed that everything was 'Old' in this village. 'Old' in this context usually meant a building that no longer fulfilled its original purpose. What had happened? The lifeblood of the community had been sucked dry, to be replaced by city commuters in their sports cars and landrovers... or so I assumed. But there were no sports cars or land-rovers. No sign of undue wealth. Quite the opposite, in fact; Upper Hooey had every appearance of a community that had forgotten itself. Deadly nightshade, old man's wort and wolf's bane grew in clusters on the verges, poison ivy crept low along the ground and clambered over roadside walls. Hedges were overgrown with blackberry brambles and Russian vine, trees strangled by ivy and Virginia creeper.

The chalk track led me to a pond surrounded by a small village green. There was no sign of life in the pond, save for some unruly clumps of aquatic vegetation protruding from its dank, murky depths. The top of the pond was amire with concentric rings of grime. As I approached, a frog hopped out of this uninviting morass onto the safety of a lily pad.

To the left of the green was an old stone cross, its inscription rendered illegible by centuries of weathering. Beneath it, a small white sign: 'No Ball Games, No Picnicking, No Scattering of Ashes'. Next to the cross stood a signboard displaying an old map of the village. The green could be found in the centre of the map, its colour faded to sepia. I traced my route thus far: there was the Old School, there the Old Forge. And there, opposite the cross, was Pudding Lane. I turned to find it behind me.

Good Night

Susan Jollygoode was planting something in her front garden. A small tree, a type I didn't recognize. Burley-Hogg would know; I could take a furtive clipping later. Was it relevant to the case? Anything was relevant to the case. Keep your eyes and ears open at all times. "Or ears and noses, in our case," as Four-Eyed Bob would say.

"What kept you? —Oh. Sorry." Susan shielded her eyes from the sun as it set behind me. She had clearly mistaken me for someone else; perhaps she thought I was some kind of second coming. "You look as though you could do with a drink."

"I think I might need one. May I come in?" *Wait to be asked in.* First rule broken.

"Not with those muddy boots on. Wait a minute. I'll get you some house shoes."

She was unusually friendly today. And surprisingly lucid. Perhaps planting the tree had switched her on.

"What's the matter, anyway?" she asked as she reappeared with the substitute shoes.

I looked around to see if anyone was listening. Second rule broken. "Well, Mrs. Jollygoode," I started.

"Oh, go on. Call me Susan."

That seemed a good idea. "Well… Susan…"

"Yes?"

"We've – we've – we've found a body…" Third rule broken.

"A body? Of what?"

"Of… somebody. We're not sure. We think it might be…"

"Yes?"

"…Your husband."

"…My husband?"

"Yes. I'm afraid so."

"Oh, my *husband*! I'm with you now." She laughed as if it were some kind of joke known only to us, then immediately changed her expression to an exaggerated frown. "Really? That's terrible. Come on, get those shoes off. You need that drink."

"It might not be, though."

"Might not be what?" Susan moved back into the house with an utter lack of concern.

"It might not be your husband."

"I bet it isn't," she called from the kitchen with another laugh. "Where's your friend, by the way? The policeman?"

Was I not a policeman?

"Erm… otherwise engaged. Talking of which, might I possibly use your telephone?"

As I struggled to prise my muddy shoes off, I stumbled into the hallway and collapsed onto the floor. Susan came to help me up.

"What a chump you are!" she said, giggling sexily as she patted me on the chest.

But I'd just told her we'd found her husband's body. Something wasn't right here.

"The phone's out of order. You'll have to go to the post office. Why do you need the telephone, anyway?"

"My car broke down. I need to call a taxi."

"To go where?"

"To go and identify the… er…"

"Oh yes. That."

'*That*'. Some way to refer to your deceased spouse.

"We can go in my car," Susan offered nonchalantly.

"Can we?"

"Do you want this drink first?"

She led me into the kitchen. The table had been cleared of papers, and a vase full of freshly cut white carnations was planted in their place. The photograph on the wall, the one taken in Disneyland, was no longer on the wall.

"Here," said Susan. I'd omitted to ask what the drink might be. I held out my hand, expecting much, and received a glass as small as a thimble. "*Lao jiu*," she said. Something incredibly rude in Welsh? "Taiwanese. That'll bring the colour back to your cheeks."

"Oh. Well. Cheers." She downed hers in one. I took a sip. It tasted like some kind of medicine. A thick, syrupy, burnt taste. Perhaps it *was* medicine.

"Where did you get that hat?" she asked with a look of considerable amusement.

"A scarecrow lent it to me."

"Well, take it off. And the coat."

I took them off. She hung them in the hall. We entered the living room, where she bade me sit on the sofa while she knelt before me on the floor.

"Another?"

"Thanks." She poured another thimbleful.

"What's your first name supposed to be?" Susan asked. "I can't keep calling you Gaskett."

"Everyone calls me Gaskett. Inspector Gaskett. Or just sir."

"Oh, come on."

"Well, all right. Let me think. Would you like a riddle? Well, here it is. My *first* is... a bird."

"Robin?"

"Er – no. My *second* and *third* an expression of surprise..."

"Jesus."

"No. And my fourth is... just... N."

There was a pause.

"Justin?"

"No."

"A man's name ending in n. Simon?

"No."

"Another drink?"

"No. Yes. Thanks."

"Stephen?"

"No, not Stephen."

"Adrian?"

"No."

"Not Julian?"

"Not that."

"Ivan?"

"Certainly not Ivan."

"Maximilian."

"By no means."

"Ron?"

"That ends in d. As does Donald."

"Kieron?"

"No."

"Colin, then?"

"Never Colin."

"Aaron?"

"Not Aaron."

"Glen?"

"Not."

"Martin?"

"God no."

"Ben, perhaps?"

"Nope."

"How about Tristan?"

"How about it?"

"Or Jonathan?"

"In your dreams."

"Kevin? Kelvin? Calvin?"

"No! No!! No!!!"

"Brian?"

"Not on your nelly."

"Harrison?"

"No way."

"Adrian?"

"Said that."

"Aidan?"

"I'm afraid not."

"Nathan?"

"As if."

"Marlon?"

"Get outa here."

"Alan?"

"NO!!! NOT ALAN!" I was beginning to wish I'd never started it. Perhaps I should just have told her straight.

"What is it then?" she asked, looking pretty fed up herself.

"It's John, OK? It's John."

"Oh. You poor sausage. You poor, poor sausage." Susan stared at me with an expression of pity more than anything else. Which was puzzling. I'd never considered the name John to be much cause for sympathy. And I couldn't remember when I'd last been called a sausage.

"Yes I see," she said, her look changing to one of growing enlightenment. "Jay is a bird. Oh! an expression of surprise. And 'N' is 'n'. J-OH-N. Very clever."

Time passed in no time. Of what we spoke, I could not say, nor much remember. My initial resolve, my original purpose in coming to the house had evaporated at the moment I'd set eyes on her in the garden. She had bewitched me. I made no further mention of the body at the vicarage. Nor did I go any way towards eliminating her as a suspect, as I'd hoped to do. On the contrary, I was now beginning to suspect her more than ever. For her behaviour appeared to be a deliberate ploy to deflect me from my true path, and in that quest she had succeeded admirably.

We'd quaffed copious amounts of *lao jiu* by now. I emptied the last few drops into Susan's thimble.

"Could we leave it till tomorrow?" she said demurely, like an eight-year-old asking her daddy for a sweet.

"What?"

"The identification… thingy."

"Oh. I suppose so."

"You look exhausted. I don't think you're in a fit state."

"No, I suppose not."

"And I've been planting fig trees all day. We'll both be better in the morning."

"But—"

"You can stay here. If you like."

And so it was that I slept in Susan Jollygoode's house. The house I seemed to know so well. I had no ulterior motive, as such; I wasn't letching or leering or groping, not at all. She simply asked me to stay, and I fell straight into it. But I confess that, at the moment of her invitation, I was overcome by a sensation of long-endured lust about to be consummated.

"Where? Exactly?"

"Exactly where you are, of course. Cheeky. I'll get you some sheets."

So I would sleep on the sofa. The anticipation of bodily union was put on hold. All the same, it was pitch black outside and I was completely shattered, not to mention a little drunk. My resistance to this new idea was zero.

"There," she declared with a flourish on completing the rudimentary bedmaking. "You know where I am. If you need me."

"Yes. Thanks." I didn't, and I did.

"Night, then." She closed the door very quietly behind her. I sank down onto the makeshift bed and fell asleep instantly.

"Come over here… You whose name ends in N."

She was lying next to me on the sofa. Looking up at me with teasing eyes and a coquettish half smile. Her flaxen hair untied, the black ribbon spread out over the pillow.

"Come to me, John. It's now or never."

I awoke to see her standing at the window. Silhouetted in the moonlight, the curve of her slim waist X-rayed through her satin nightdress. The curtain swayed and lifted under the influence of a cool night breeze. Susan revealed the mallet in her hand as she approached me with menace.

Ah. 'Twas but a dream. Of course it was.

Dear Aunt Clarice,

Thanks for the tips! Well, since my story is all about crimes of various sorts, ideas like that would be very welcome. You may think it odd, me writing a police story when I'm surrounded by them all the time. But police stories are funny! Why do you think that is? So yes please, the more the merrier. We have a library here, but it's very limited. It's not much bigger than those vans that used to come round. Do you know what the Internet is? It's basically a system of getting all sorts of information through a computer. Everyone thinks it's a virtual world, floating in space, but it still has to have cables everywhere. One day there won't be any cables at all! Anyway, I'm getting a lot of ideas from there too. The trouble is, I tend to get sidetracked and bogged down on a subject that's not strictly relevant. Still, it keeps me busy, and that's the main thing, as I'm sure you'd say! Hope you're well.

love

John

World's Smallest Post Office

"The post office is on the far side of the green," Susan said as she collected my cup. "You can't miss it. It's the smallest post office in the world."

I'd slept like a baby. Fitfully, waking every half hour at first, then so deeply that nothing would wake me. In the end, my hostess had to physically push me off the sofa.

"But you'll have to be patient. The postmistress is a bit of an ogre."

"Is it really that small?"

"Tiny. You'll see." She opened the door. "What about your hat?"

"Will you keep it? I don't think I'll be needing it now."

"All right. See you later."

I stepped out into fresh summer sunshine.

A girl with plaited hair and thick-lensed spectacles was standing in the neighbouring driveway. She absentmindedly tossed a huge orange basketball in the air, let it hit the ground, then caught it as it bounced back up. This she continued to do, watching me all the while.

Ignoring her stare, I walked down Pudding Lane towards the old stone cross by the village green. Water boatmen and skaters skimmed across the still, rancid waters of the pond, the only semblance of life on a lifeless morning.

It was an odd kind of green. Not surrounded in any comforting, reassuring way by quaint flower-bedecked cottages, cute doggies wagging tails at garden gates, and perhaps a winding lane at one side passing under a lych gate on its way to the calming idyll of a village church, this 'village green' was nothing but a rough patch of sun-scorched grass, beside which the odd residence grudgingly presented itself. There was no heartwarming dialogue, no life-affirming air, but merely the lonesome silence of rural alienation. *Skull Cottage*, announced a crooked sign on a nearby gate. It didn't feel like home. Not at all.

There was no sign of any post office. A red post box stood on the far side of the green, with an old Morris van, fifties-style, post office red, parked diagonally on the grass next to it. Beyond that, a donkey chomped dandelions in a field. And further off stood another large sprawling farmhouse.

The post office van had seen better times; its wheels had been removed. As I moved towards it, I could see cables and wires of all types and sizes issuing from every orifice, trailing across the grass into the distance. Perhaps the telephone was inside the van. POST OFFICE: ENTER THROUGH REAR DOOR, said a sign pasted on the side of the vehicle. Not only was the telephone inside the van, but the van itself was a post office! I looked through the round window on the back door to confirm my surmise, then tried to open the door. The speckled chrome handle creaked and squeaked to voice its opposition. It must have been some time since anyone had used this service.

Inside the van was the unmistakable smell of vintage cars: leather, old engine oil, worn-out carburettors. Wooden boxes lined the sides of the vehicle; all had keyholes, all presumably locked. An archaic cash register was chained to the floor. And there was the telephone – the old-fashioned candlestick type with separate mouthpiece and receiver – attached horizontally to a board behind the driver's seat, so that the candlestick pointed back towards the door. A kind of 'mobile telephone' that wasn't going anywhere. The mouthpiece and dial were so positioned that the caller was obliged to crouch on the floor of the van to use them; that was the only possible way. I tried lying on my stomach, propping myself on my elbows and lifting my head up to the mouthpiece. This immediately proved far too painful. So I turned over and lay on my back. That would have to do for now.

Next to the telephone was a sign: "Dial S for Service". This I duly did. Whereupon a bright arc light illuminated the inside of the vehicle, accompanied by a noise that sounded like a power generator.

As I held the receiver to my ear and waited for an answer, I could hear the faint sound of a telephone ringing in a house nearby. No one answered. "*Be patient,*" Susan had said.

"Yes?" said a woman's voice on the nineteenth ring.

"Oh... I—"

"Come on, I haven't got all day! Stamps, is it? Postal order, what?" I assumed my interrogator to be the postmistress. *A bit of an ogre* seemed to be putting it mildly; the woman had obviously never contemplated the notion of civil courtesy. She spoke with an aggressive country burr that gave every impression of impending risk to personal welfare.

"Sorry. I'd like to use the telephone."

"You are using it."

"No, I mean, to make an outside call."

"Go on, then."

"What, just dial?"

"Yes, dial, man! What are you, stupid?"

"What about the charges?"

"Put them on your account. You are who?"

"I'm... Well, I don't live here."

"Don't live here? What do you mean?" The ogre seemed taken aback.

"I'm staying at Susan Jollygoode's".

There was a long silence. A crackle. A hiss.

"Hello?" I said plaintively. In a way, I was rather hoping that would be the end of it. But it wasn't. Not quite.

"Put money in petrol tank. Ten pence per minute. Now would you mind? I've some cows to milk."

"Yes. Thank you—"

The line went dead. Ten pence per minute? Daylight robbery!

Though rapidly tiring of my position, not to mention the glare of the arc light, I now endeavoured to call the station.

"Police."

I didn't think I could ever be so relieved to hear Burley-Hogg's gruff tone.

"Yes, it's me, Gaskett."

"Inspector Gaskett, yes sir. We were wondering what had happened to you."

84

"I'm in Upper Hooey. I'll be taking Mrs. Jollygoode to HQ this morning to identify the body. Or rather, she'll be taking me."

"Yes, the car. We know all about it, sir. It's all in hand."

"In hand?"

"It's been towed away, sir. A complete turn-off. They've arranged a courtesy car to tide you over."

"A courtesy car? That is most kind." Life was not so bad after all. But who were 'they'? "By the way, do you know a farmer called Hector Hedgehog?"

In the receiver, I heard the noise of something being dropped. The sound of hysterical laughter. A crackle. A hiss.

"Can he hear us?" A woman's voice.

"I hope not!" A man's. More laughter.

A hiss. A crackle.

"Did you say something, Sergeant?"

"I said, *Hedgehog?* That would be an unusual name," said Burley-Hogg.

"He's the one who caused the accident," I explained.

"There is a Hector *Hodgkinson*."

"Hodgkinson?"

"Perhaps you didn't hear correctly, sir."

"Possibly."

"He's my brother-in-law. Quick-tempered so-and-so. But harmless in the end. His bite's worse than his bark. What about him?"

"Oh... Nothing," I said, quickly relenting. My agricultural adversary had not only claimed representation by the best lawyer in the land, but also had the police in his pocket. "I'm sure it was nothing."

A hiss. A crackle.

"Poor old Derek. But at least it worked."

"Yes. What ... next then?"

" ... the treatment. We've ... go-ahead from the Ministry."

A crackle. A hiss.

"Is there someone with you, Sergeant?"

"Oh, there you are, sir. I thought the line was dead."

"I thought I heard voices."

"No, I'm quite on my own here. Just been weeding the broccoli."

"Right. Well, till later then."

"Right you are, sir."

"By the way, Sergeant. Is that autopsy report in yet?"

"No, sir. Not yet, sir."

"Right. Carry on."

I replaced the receiver and gratefully crawled out of the van. The door was as reluctant to close as it had been to open. I found the petrol cap by the rear wheel, on the side of the vehicle facing away from the green. The cap had been modified to accept cash. Taking a coin from my pocket, I pushed it into the crudely fashioned slot, sending the coin tumbling noisily into the petrol tank. How on earth would it be retrieved? Perhaps it wouldn't. It seemed for all the world that no one had used this particular service for a good many years.

"Thank you kindly, sir."

I looked up to see an old man, an immensely old man, sitting in a wheelchair in the shadow of the van. He must have been a hundred, if not more.

"Can I help you?" I asked.

"Security," was his reply. The old man was dressed impeccably: white trousers, white blazer, white shirt, white shoes, white hat. Green bow tie.

"Are you all right?" I asked again.

"Security. Security is my business."

"Security?"

"Work for the Post Office. Security. Breathe in, hold your breath, breathe out. It's my job." He was a living security camera.

"I'm very glad to make your acquaintance, Mister...?"

"Security. Breathe normally. It's my job." His voice was hearty but strained with age, like the sound of a gale-force wind squeezing through gaps in a larch-lap wooden fence.

In a corner of my eye I could see a large ruddy-faced woman, bucket in hand, scarf on head, wellington boots on feet, watching us from the open door of a cow shed some way off. The postmistress, no doubt. What a good thing not to have wanted stamps.

"Excellent. A splendid job. Well, goodbye for now," I said, moving off.

"Security. Work for the Post Office." He raised his voice in increments to match my growing distance from him.

My head was thumping as I staggered back to Susan's house.

The girl with the plaits was still playing with her basketball in the neighbouring driveway. Throw down, one bounce, catch. Throw down, one bounce, catch. Look up. Throw down, one bounce, catch. Watch as front door opens. Hold. Throw down, one bounce, catch.

"You could have warned me," I moaned as I stood on Susan's threshold.

"What about?"

"God, my neck aches."

"The post office?" Susan laughed mischievously.

"Yes, you could have warned me."

"I did say it was tiny."

"Yes, but you failed to say it was an exercise in contortion."

"What was?"

"The upside-down telephone, of course."

Susan eyed me with a look of disbelief, combined with pity, compounded with the barely restrained impulse to make jolly at my expense. The result was a battle royale for dominion over her facial muscles. "Oh no, you didn't... No, tell me you didn't..." She laughed again in a wholly carefree manner.

"What? Didn't what?"

"You're supposed to flip the board on its side to make calls! There's a little wooden support underneath. Didn't you realize that?" I was speechless. "Come on, chump. Let's be off," she continued cheerily.

"All right then. What about the security guard?" I asked as I climbed into her car.

"The old man?"

"Yes."

"Alzheimer's. Lovely old chap. It used to be his van, forty years ago."

"And he's sat there ever since?!"

"He gets wheeled in for meals. He's just happier out there."

"Wheeled in where?"

"The postmistress's house. She's his daughter."

Susan Jollygoode certainly knew a lot about the village, I thought, as she drove up Pudding Lane and joined the chalky road at the top. She knew a lot more than would have been normal for a newcomer. But perhaps she was just nosy.

Soon we were bumping and rumbling along the rutted cart track out towards the real world. The track described a generous circle around the village and eventually joined the asphalt road at a T-junction. This was the turn Mabey had taken on our first visit; I'd walked right past it without noticing in the previous day's rain. Everything now made perfect sense.

"It's that wretched farmer," Susan said after I'd explained my mistake. "He thinks he owns the place! Well, he does, practically. He's filthy rich, rolling in land. He had the asphalt road end up in his field just to spite the other villagers."

"Which farmer is that?"

"Hodgkinson."

"Hector Hodgkinson?"

"That's it. Do you know him?"

"Let's just say I bumped into him."

As we started down Copse Hill, we came to the bend where the hatless scarecrow should have been. It wasn't there. Maybe it was another bend. It had been dark, after all.

We came to the spot where I thought the accident had happened. There was no sign that anything had happened at all. Well, Burley-Hogg did say they'd removed the vehicle. I looked forward to receiving my 'courtesy car'.

In stark contrast to the previous day's ordeal, today's journey out of Upper Hooey was smooth, trouble-free, and actually rather agreeable. The road sauntered happily along, curving playfully around silently acquiescing hedgerows as if inviting us to a game of hide and seek. Clumps of poppies stood and swayed at the edges of occasionally exposed cornfields, awoken from their ancient slumber by the farmer's plough. Farmer Hector's plough, no doubt.

"His wife runs the post office," said Susan, bringing me sharply back to heel.

"Pardon?"

"The farmer's wife. She's the ogre who runs the post office."

"Ah." Was there anyone in the village who wasn't related to the postmistress? Apart from Susan Jollygoode? The girl in the plaits, perhaps?

"They've got a son called Santiago. Thinks he's God's gift."

"You wouldn't have him on your sofa then?"

"Certainly not! You naughty thing."

I really wanted her at that moment.

Constabulary Headquarters were in Dribblemouth. Susan turned left at the white marker post and hurried on through Nether Hooey. Past the Point of No Return, past the Community Hall, past the police station.

Mabey was standing outside with his shirt unbuttoned and his hands in his pockets. I didn't care.

Predictably, Dribblemouth was where the Dribble dribbled out to the sea. Though, of course, even that was not quite as simple as it sounded, as the *Village Almanac* had explained in some detail. For the River Dribble met the briny mass at exactly the same point as another, much larger and much more significant flow – the Nilby, a major waterway along which barges and tankers carried cargoes of oil, chemicals and perhaps paperclips deep into the industrial heartland beyond. That was why the estuary town was listed as a Grade 2 port, boasting a sizeable harbour for fishing boats to boot. As such, it was known by all and sundry, the whole world and the BBC, as Nilbymouth. And that's how it appeared on maps, anglers' guides and lorry drivers' hand-scribbled route instructions.

Trouble was, the Dribblesiders weren't very happy with that. Ever since the Middle Ages, when a settlement had first been established around a hospice run by Benedictine monks, there'd been controversy over which river should give the town its name. People in the Dribble Valley pointed out that the first settlement had been on the right bank of their river, firmly in Dribbleside territory. That, in fact, was where the old town with its fishing port still stood. The Nilby camp, conversely, used complicated measuring equipment and set-squares to argue that the left bank of the Dribble met the right bank of the Nilby at a distance deeper into the estuary than the entire width of the Dribble, thereby inferring theirs to be the principal water. And anyway the Nilby was wider. It mattered little that, even today, almost the entire geographical area of the town including the Follicle shopping centre lay on the Dribble side, with only the docks, a caravan site and a greyhound stadium in the Nilbyside domain. To the watching world, it was Nilbymouth and that was that.

Attempts had of course been made to find a compromise that would suit everyone. The most notable effort came in the lean years of the early 1920's, when an economist of national renown noted that local workers on either side of the divide were spending more time destroying each other's capital equipment than doing anything productive for the region. It was suggested that the town be called Nilby-cum-Dribblemouth, or else Dribble-cum-Nilbymouth, to satisfy all parties. This merely served to exacerbate the problem, however; as each faction broke into two sub-factions, one claiming that the first-named river was unfairly awarded greater prominence, the other that the second-named remained tied to the 'mouth' and was therefore unfairly deemed to be superior. A satirical rag then proffered a solution in the composite name of Dribblymouth, whereupon the entire campaign collapsed on both sides.

Further back in the Victorian days of munificence and charitable causes, a local philanthropist had tried to solve the age-old rivalry by establishing a new community of timber houses on the spit of land between the two rivers, calling it 'Mesopotamia'. "*We shall herewith enter a new age of social tolerance and liberal virtues*," the Mayor of Nilbymouth had proclaimed as he cut the ribbon to declare the community open. The timber structures were promptly destroyed by fireboats from the Dribble side and ballast dredger cranes from the Nilbys.

As for the present, my colleagues called it Dribblemouth, and that was good enough for me.

Tracks of His Tyres

Farmer Hector Hodgkinson stormed into the police station. He was not a happy man.

"I've come to report a theft," he said gruffly and with a hint of barely controlled violence.

Flight of the Bumblebee.

"Morning, Hector." Burley-Hogg barely looked up from his Pest Control Monthly.

"Some bugger's stolen my wife's hat!" yelled the farmer.

"Your wife's what?"

"Her hat, man! My wife's hat!"

"Where did this happen?"

"Does it matter? East Field, man. It was on a scarecrow in East Field!"

"When?"

"I don't know! It was in the field yesterday morning."

"What did it look like?"

"The field?"

"The hat."

"What do you think it looked like? It looked like a hat!"

"Colour?"

"No. Just a hat."

"Do you have a photograph?"

"Of course I don't. What do you take me for?!"

"Well, we'll keep an eye out for it, Hector." Burley-Hogg moistened the end of a finger and turned another page of his magazine.

"Aren't you going to write it down, then?" demanded the agriculturalist.

"Oh, yes. I am going to write it down."

"Good. Because when I find the bugger that stole it, I'm going to wring his rotten bloody neck!" Hector shook a clenched fist at the blameless Sergeant.

Burley-Hogg was not unduly perturbed. He knew how to handle his brother-in-law, and any other threat for that matter. He'd had this overhasty tiller of the land in his pocket ever since he'd started courting Hector's older sister Amelia some forty years earlier. The technique was simple: wait. Remain calm. Let the other person empty his bag. Make him feel just a little bit silly.

"How do you know it was a man?" the Sergeant asked at length.

"How do I know what was a man?" returned the farmer.

"How do you know it was a man who stole the hat?"

"It's a man's hat, that's how."

"Your wife wears a man's hat?"

"Why shouldn't she?"

"So if your wife wears a man's hat, couldn't the thief also be a woman who wears man's hats?"

Hector paused. "Oh. I hadn't thought of that."

"As I say, we'll keep an eye out. We will be vigilante, have no fear."

"Right then." Deflated, diverted, re-directed, Hector could barely recall the cause of his wrath, let alone put it in words.

"How's the potato crop then?" asked Burley-Hogg to ram his victory home.

"Terrible. Blight," bemoaned the farmer.

"Oh dear. Did you try that chicken manure I mentioned?"

"No. I used pigs' muck as usual."

"There you are, then."

"Anyway, I can't stand here nattering all day," said Hector, his customary impatience starting to course through his veins again. "I've got pigs to feed."

"Right-o. Be seeing you, Hector."

"And let me know if you find it," Hector added as he turned to go.

"Find what?"

"The hat, you old bugger, the hat!"

"Oh, the hat. I will let you know, of course." The Sergeant put a finger to his forehead by way of a valedictory salute.

Farmer Hector Hodgkinson stormed out of the police station, not because his anger had returned but simply because he knew no other way of leaving a building. Outside, PC Cake was contemplating the location of Hector's tractor, his head tilted to the same angle as that of the offending vehicle on the pavement. Perhaps he was trying to remember some bylaw governing the angle of a vehicle's tilt or the gap left for pedestrians to squeeze by, as if mounting the pavement with eighteen-inch tractor wheels weren't crime enough. Cake eventually concluded that it was a breach of Municipal Regulation 257-1 Subsection 3 (C), and reached into his top pocket for his booking book. The farmer brushed the Constable aside, clambered into his tilting cabin and roared back down the High Street in his tractor, leaving behind a trail of stippled mud patterns from the tracks of his tyres.

Whose Body is it Anyway

We pulled up at Dribbleside Constabulary Headquarters. This was a real institution, manned by real, qualified people who really knew what they were doing. Telephones rang ceaselessly, now here, now there, while junior staff and senior detectives earnestly examined minute details on their paperwork as they hurried and scurried along corridors. That there was never a collision between them was, I decided, entirely the result of their consummate skill and training in handling the demands of the modern office environment. Yes, these were the grown-up men and women of the real world.

Susan Jollygoode was visibly shaken on entering the Mortuary. There, the cadaver lay on a pullout ledge, covered in a white sheet, no longer smelling of fish. The flesh had turned rather purplish in hue; perhaps the sight of that alone was enough for Susan. Or perhaps she now realized, at last, that her husband was in fact dead.

The non-speaking assistant pathologist gently pulled the top of the sheet away from the corpse's face. Susan drew in a sharp breath and put both hands to her mouth as if to brace herself. She gazed at the face for a few seconds, then breathed out again.

"No," she said at length.

"No??"

"That isn't my husband."

"Are you sure?"

"Of course I'm sure."

So what was I to make of this. Now we had a missing person *and* an unidentified corpse; two unsolved cases, and a local constabulary that was entirely unequipped to deal with either of them. Not to mention a disappearing chameleon.

"Can I go now?" Susan asked coldly. It was astonishing – both she and her voice were utterly transformed. She was a stranger again.

"Yes, of course. Sorry to have bothered you."

"Right."

She walked out briskly and without further ceremony. I signalled to the non-speaking assistant pathologist, and the body returned to its icy cubbyhole.

My means of transport now gone, I wondered how I could possibly return to the station eight miles away in Nether Hooey. But as the front door of the building swung shut behind Susan's trailing leg, I caught a glimpse of something familiar in the street outside: *Cake – Help Yourselves.* Cake's red logo on a gleaming white van parked by the kerb. Cake couldn't drive. How did it get there? I strode over to the clerk at the front desk.

"Excu—"

"Ah," said the clerk, with an unmistakable tone of condescension. "Inspector Gaskett. A lady here to see you."

There she was, standing by the desk, all jeans and effervescence. "Victoria Cake," she said, proffering a hand. "Call me Vicky."

"You're Cake's wife?!"

"Sister. He'll never marry. Much too fussy."

"So... What are you doing here?"

"Oh! Silly me. Well, I've come to take you back to the station. Only we heard about the accident, see. The Sergeant said you'd be here. Vinnie can't drive, of course, so we decided I'd come and collect you. You don't mind, do you? Only I was passing through to deliver a wedding cake. I made it myself, you know. My cousin's marrying one of the Fisher boys next week, and I had to bring the cake up here today. I know it's a bit too soon and all that, but I'll be too busy to do it next week and the Fishers have got a climate-controlled freezer, see. So we'll have to deliver the cake first, then I'll take you back to the station. I hope you don't mind. I would have gone already, only I didn't know when you'd arrive. Well, I just popped in on the off chance, to be honest. Then I saw that woman come out and I thought it might be her. So I came in and asked if you were here, and you were, so here I am."

"...Vinnie? Who's Vinnie?"

"Vinnie Cake, my brother. Short for Vincent. Sorry. Thought you knew."

No, I was not yet on first name terms with my staff; I was too busy enjoying their surnames for the moment.

"Well... Yes, that will be splendid. Thank you very much. I was just wondering how—"

"Good! Come on, the van's outside."

The inside of the van gave off a sweet aroma of fresh pastries and vanilla essence, just as you'd expect. Victoria Cake's cake was sitting on the passenger seat, resting on a large silver base and delicately cloaked in cling film. It was quite unlike any other cake I'd ever seen before. Not the standard multi-tier iced job for the Fisher boy. Oh no. His cake was fashioned in the shape of a fishing boat, with himself standing astern in tuxedo and bow tie, gripping a large fishing rod. At the end of the line was his bride, a white mermaid holding a posy of flowers. She was beaming with joy, apparently happy to have been 'pulled'. He too, for all his exertions, grinned buoyantly.

"Quite a work of art!" I commented generously.

"I call it my *fish cake*! Get it? The sea is made of passionfruit coulis. The bride is covered in Swiss white chocolate. Her tail is made of angelica. That's because her name is Angelica. The outside of the boat is hazelnut icing. Vinnie said I should just make a three-tier cake like everyone else, but I prefer this. Don't you?"

"Yes. Well, it's certainly... What shall I... How should I... "

"Oh. Sorry! Here's me going on like this. Can you rest it on your lap? It's not heavy." She lifted the cake out and held it while I squeezed into the passenger seat. "I can't put it in the back, it'll move about too much. I like to have it in front where I can see it. If you know what I mean."

And so it was that I was driven through the streets of Dribblemouth with the Fisher boy's boat-shaped wedding cake perched precariously on my knees. I was rigid with fear. One false move, and the fish cake would have been the cat's dinner. Luckily, Victoria Cake was one very careful driver. So careful, in fact, that we barely seemed to be moving at all.

"Angelica's my cousin, actually. Did I say?" Victoria continued, barely pausing to breathe or even check the rear view mirror.

"The mermaid?"

"Yes. The mermaid." She laughed loudly. "She's my cousin."

"Angelica Cake?"

"No, Green. Angelica Green. We share a grandmother."

"Oh."

"She's pregnant."

"Ah."

"—Angelica, not the grandmother! No one knows who the father is. But it's one of the Fisher boys. She's been with all of them."

"All of them?"

"All of them. Hopefully it won't be a fish."

"How many Fisher boys are there, then?"

"Just three. Three Fisher boys, all good and strong."

We were navigating a road made of brick cobbles that led onto a kind of wharf. The passionfruit coulis rippled worryingly.

"Desmond, Denholm and Declan. All good lads. I went out with them at school. All good lads."

As we drove over the wharfside cobbles, I couldn't help but notice an overpowering stench of rotting fish. Angelica's angelica started to wobble. I clung on to the cake for dear life; the last thing I wanted was Desmond, Denholm and/or Declan on my back.

"Presumably she knows which one she's marrying?"

"Oh yes, she knows all right. Declan. The best of the lot!" Victoria almost seemed to levitate with excitement.

"Doesn't he mind, then? You know, about the other two?"

"Of course not. It's just sex, sex, sex round here! And what's wrong with that, I say."

"Quite. Quite." I decided a change of subject was in order. "Are we nearly there?"

"Yes, it's the next boat but five."

"Boat?"

"They live on a boat. All three of them."

"Three brothers living together?"

"Yes, on a boat. Isn't that fab?" Victoria brought the vehicle smoothly, almost expertly to a halt. "This is the one."

It was not so much a houseboat as a converted fishing boat, complete with poop deck and gallows. Its bow bore the name *'Three Herrings'*. I could well picture its 'climate-controlled freezer' – huge, industrial and full of frozen fish. It would certainly add a special aroma to the wedding cake; but there again, considering the story being acted out on top of the cake, perhaps that was entirely part of the plan.

Victoria stepped out and came to relieve me of the cake. "Won't be a mo," she announced cheerily, then waltzed over to the Three Herrings moored there by the wharf's edge. She was met at the side of the boat by a youngish, thickset man wearing a knitted woollen hat. Desmond? Denholm? Declan? He asked her something, pointing vaguely in my direction with his chin. The answer appeared to be satisfactory, as he immediately looked over at me with a broad smile and a cheery wave.

A second young man, equally thickset but wearing a rugged turtleneck pullover, emerged from the cabin of the boat. Denholm? Declan? He winked at Victoria, then asked her something, pointing vaguely in my direction with his chin. The answer appeared to be satisfactory, as he immediately looked over at me with a broad smile and a cheery wave. The first young man said something to him and they both laughed heartily.

A third young man, equally thickset but wearing great wading boots, emerged from the cabin. Declan? He grinned at Victoria, then asked her something, pointing vaguely in my direction with his chin. The answer appeared to be satisfactory, as he immediately looked over at me with a broad smile and a cheery wave. The second young man said something to him and they all laughed heartily.

A much older man emerged from the cabin. He had the ruddy, rugged complexion of a seafarer, with waves of luxuriant grey hair swept back from his temples. He said something to the three and they all laughed heartily. Victoria passed the fish cake to him. As he turned to take it back below deck, he caught sight of me in the van and stopped. The expression of joviality drained from his face. He stared at me for a moment, then said something to Victoria. He seemed quite unsettled. She waved a hand as if to make light of it. Then, with a peremptory gesture, he disappeared below deck with the cake.

Victoria kissed each of the boys in turn before returning to the van.

The boys waved and smiled affably as we drove off. I somehow doubted their sincerity.

"What was all that about?" I felt compelled to ask.

"Oh... Nothing," Victoria replied with unusual terseness.

"Who was the old chap, then?"

"Derrick Fisher. The father."

"Right."

We drove back over the brick cobbles into the commercial district of Dribblemouth.

"We were just having a little joke, that's all," she added by way of an excuse.

"About Peregrine Falcon-Browne?"

"Pardon? No, something else." She was clearly preoccupied.

We had left the town behind us and were travelling through open country before she spoke again. "Have you been invited to the wedding, by the way?"

"No. Should I have?"

"Well, I just thought... seeing as you're Vinnie's superior, you know."

"No... We have a different kind of relationship."

"Yes, he's not very forthcoming, is he."

"Loyal, though."

"Yes. Very loyal."

"Is your family close, then?" I asked, merely seeking to continue the conversation.

"Oh yes, close. Yes, we're close. You know, our family's been baking bread for three hundred years? Maybe that's why we're called Cake. But perhaps we should have been called Bread?" She laughed, and so did I.

I felt relieved to be returning to the village. These last twenty-four hours had felt more like twenty-four years. In my state of barely justified exhilaration, I invited Victoria to lunch at the Plough. I had Cumbrian Ghoulash, she Fenugreek Moussaka.

Dear John,

It was nice to hear from you again. I must say you seem in relatively high spirits, considering all that's happened. Perhaps writing about that kind of thing gets it out of your system. But you mustn't forget what you're there for in the first place. Always remember your debt to society, but keep yourself busy too. I've never heard of this 'Internet' thing. And where is the computer you mentioned? I didn't realize people in your position had access to that kind of thing. Anyway, if you want any more ideas, I can send you some clippings from the Echo, they always have funny stories in there. It's amazing what goes on in the world, isn't it. You'll never guess what's happened here, for instance – the vicar has run off with the postman's wife! I always knew he was a bad lot, that one. Most unchristian. Apparently they've been carrying on for years, but it all came out one morning when the postman rang to deliver a parcel and saw his wife's shoes in the hallway. Would you believe it? The things that go on. We'll, I must get on with my winter repotting, so I'll close here. Take care, and remember to keep yourself occupied.

love
Aunt Clarice
PS. Enclose some cuttings to keep you going

LONDON (BBC): A farmer has painted stripes on his sheep to camouflage them after rumours of a panther on the loose. 21-year-old Charles Hardcup from Ribbleside spray-painted green, yellow and red stripes on six of his sheep through cardboard stencils after reading about the sightings. He said: "Panthers prey on sheep, and there was no way I was going to allow any of mine to fall victim. So I decided to make them merge with their surroundings, like chameleons." Mr Hardcup, who studies graphic design at Clitheroe School of Art, said it only took 15 minutes to paint each sheep. He told the Daily Record: "It doesn't matter that the colours are bright. It is the patterns that are important because cats only see in black and white. The colours are a tribute to Mark Rothko."

Curiosity Cornered

I strode in to the police station with a zip in my bounce and a spring in my step. *Fly Me To The Moon*, Sinatra crooned.

Burley-Hogg was repotting some seedlings. "Ah, there you are sir," he said quietly without looking up. His thoughts were clearly elsewhere.

"Geraniums?" I inquired to gain his attention.

"Delphiniums, sir. Can't be too careful. But these'll thrive now." He seemed genuinely pleased with his output. "You don't mind if I continue, sir?"

"No. No, carry on." I busied myself with checking the duty log and incident reports. Of course, there were no incident reports. Now that we had some real cases on our hands, I'd banned the others from fabricating crime.

"So it wasn't him then," said Burley-Hogg, even as he lifted another seedling out of his nursery tray.

"What wasn't who?"

"The body. It wasn't our missing husband." The Sergeant always seemed to know things before I could tell him about them. It quite took the wind out of my sails. "The clerk at Headquarters phoned through."

"Ah. No, it wasn't him."

"A pity really. I could have bought four extra bags of compost with the winnings." Of course – the bet. The new turn of events would have thrown the odds into complete disarray. "Seems you had a lady visitor too, sir."

"Yes, Cake's sister. Victoria."

"I didn't know he had a sister."

"Nor did I. Nor did I." I was becoming mesmerized by the Sergeant's pricking and potting. The sight of that giant of a man bending his massive frame over those tiny green shootlets that quivered timidly, submissively in their little brown trays was actually quite moving. With such tender care did his stubby fingers, themselves completely dwarfing the seedlings, lovingly lift each one out in turn, teasing it with a dibber, silently communing with it in a language that only he and they understood. And with such boundless reassurance did he then implant them into their new homes, giving each a gentle caress and a little drink of water to welcome them in.

"Any thoughts on who it might be?" he asked one of them.

"Who what might be?" I replied on its behalf.

"The body, sir?"

"No. No thoughts at all."

"Back to square one, then."

"Yes. Back to square one." To be fair, we'd never even left square one.

"By the way, Sergeant. Is that autopsy report in yet?"

"No, sir. Not yet, sir."

"Right. So where's this courtesy car, then?"

"Oh! Yes," and at that the Sergeant looked up from his work for the first time. He even seemed mildly excited. "The courtesy car, sir. Well, in point of fact, the manager of the garage wondered if you'd like to go over there and choose one yourself. He has quite a selection to offer you."

"Go over where?"

"The garage. Curiosity Corner."

"Where is it?"

"By the old railway, sir. Turn left off the High Street opposite the Community Hall."

"Is it far to walk?"

"Not at all far. Five minutes at most."

"All right. Will you draw me a map?"

"Yes, I will draw you a map." He returned to his potting.

"And who exactly are *they*?" I asked.

"Beg pardon sir?"

"Who are the *they* who provided this courtesy car?"

"Oh. The courtesy car. Yes, sir, it was your insurance company, the Dribbleside and Mutual. They arranged it."

"I didn't know my car was insured with them."

"Oh yes. I arranged it for you. Before your arrival, sir."

"Did you? Well, thank you, Sergeant."

"Not at all, sir." He lifted another miniature seedling out with his tiny dibber. For another moment I watched in silence.

"So will you draw this map, then?"

"Oh, yes. Right, sir. I was completely lost. One moment." The Sergeant put his potting tools down, wiped his hands on his uniform, and took out pencil and paper. "By the way sir," he said after sketching a map. "Any news on the missing husband?"

"No, Sergeant. None at all."

"And what about the missing lizard?"

"Chameleon, you mean?"

"Chameleon, sir. Yes."

"It's still missing."

"Ah. Right. Fair enough."

Curiosity Corner resembled a kind of motorists' freak show. Parked on the gravel outside were bizarre vehicles of all kinds, known by some as 'classic cars'. I'd noticed it previously in passing, but had assumed it to be some sort of open-air museum.

"All lovingly restored, each comes with a five-year warranty sir!"

A man with a smile that seemed bigger than his face approached me on the forecourt. There were gaps between his teeth, but not because any of them were missing. There simply weren't enough teeth to fill the space.

"Actually—"

"The Wartburg 311 Cabriolet. A fascinating story attached to this one sir." The man patted waves of shiny golden hair back into place as he launched into his sales talk, an unending stream of rapid speech that defied the laws of nature. He even appeared willing to forego the luxury of breath, if it meant he could sell me a car. "The owner Gisela Krummschnauze drove straight through the Berlin Wall on the day after it came down sir – Didn't stop driving until she'd reached Calais – Looking for a J-Mart apparently – Ha ha ha – A beautiful car sir – Then there's the Trabant, also from the Democratic Republic – Driven by her partner Gerhard Geiselbock – Tragic story sir – Followed her through the rubble of the wall only to be caught in the cross-fire of an embassy siege in Düsseldorf – Truly tragic – Fine car all the same – Collector's item – Could have converted it to unleaded but decided it would lose its character without the smell of cheap fuel sir – Ha ha – Then there's the Robin Reliant sir – Much in demand with enthusiasts – A great little character – Excellent for city driving – Superb parking capability sir – Popular with the ladies – Or—"

That was quite enough. I had to interrupt.

"Actually, I'm here about a courtesy car. Inspector Gaskett? You know?"

He appeared stunned. For the first time since he'd started his performance, nothing of any substance would issue from his lips. Even the permanent smile started to crack. But the TV commercial look soon rallied and returned, like an engine springing back to life after momentarily stalling at a crossroads. "Ah – ah – ah – Yes! Yes. Inspector Gaskett. Of course I know. Yes indeed I do. Victor Sheen at your service and very glad to make your acquaintance. Well. Which of these fine cars would you like to use, sir? Take your pick."

"You are joking, aren't you."

"Joking? No, sir, I assure you most assuredly, I am not joking. One of these magnificent cars could now be yours! For a limited period only."

"Mine?"

"Until your insurance claim is paid sir!"

One of these magnificent cars was the last thing I wanted to be seen in.

"You mean... you have no other cars? No, how may I put it, more everyday models?"

"Certainly not sir. Unlike certain other insurers, Dribbleside and Mutual will not palm you off with anything but the best sir!"

"This is the best, then?!"

"Only the very best sir!"

"And what if I, er, damage the car while I'm using it?"

"I think you'll find they're indestructible sir! And besides, they're all fully insured. Peace of mind. This is what we offer sir."

Peace of mind. I could hear Mabey's mockery now, as I rolled up beside the police station in a Robin Reliant. It would do little to enhance my air of authority as a senior officer, I felt. The Wartburg was certainly very smart, a classic limousine. But quite apart from the inevitable connotation of warts, I wouldn't wish to be mistaken for a former KGB officer. The locals might begin to question whether liberty was inherently positive or negative, then conclude that it is not theirs to question anything.

"We do however have another vehicle sir," Victor Sheen continued, sensing my hesitation. He was human after all. "A BMW Isetta. A lovely car sir – Excellent for city driving – Superb parking capability sir – Popular with the ladies. Indeed."

BMW. BMW! Now that was better. A BMW would certainly keep the hounds of mockery at bay. Something more... yes, more commensurate with the dignity befitting my position. It, too, would no doubt be a 'classic', all rounded corners and chrome bumpers. But it would still have that unmistakable badge of authority sitting atop its radiator grille.

"Now I mention it," he continued breathlessly, "the Isetta is itself a former police car, Lower Saxony, radio telephone and optional blue flashing light, recommissioned by the Deutsche Bundespost and resprayed in yellow sir. Ideal for your situation I would say. Indeed." What was it with German cars and Victor Sheen? Perhaps it lifted his self-esteem to be associated with them. They certainly added extra 'Vorsprung' to his technique.

"Where is it?"

"It's being serviced at this very moment, sir. But I could have it sent round to the police station later this afternoon, if that should be your wish."

"All right. The BMW it is."

"It is on the small side, sir. But a lovely car, sir. I promise you won't regret it. An excellent decision, sir. An excellent choice."

Yes, yes, yes. A BMW was a BMW, whatever the size. The spring returned to my step as I strode back to the station.

BERLIN (Reuters): Detectives in Germany were dumbstruck after a man they'd just booked for burglary walked out of the police station and drove off in one of their cars, authorities said on Wednesday. "It's not just unusual, it's embarrassing," said a spokesman for police in the Berlin suburb of Babelsberg. Police said the 21-year-old must have pocketed the key of the car during his interrogation. After he was charged and released, officers were stunned to see the man easing out of the station in the unmarked vehicle, and immediately gave chase. Three cars, including the stolen vehicle, were damaged in the ensuing pursuit, which ended with the man's re-arrest on the Glienicker Bridge. "Good job it was a Trabant," said the spokesman. "We would never have caught him if it had been a BMW."

Bubble To Burst

"Piece off, Cake!" Mabey was yelling as I walked in through the double doors. *Moonlight Sonata*. I had my doubts about that one; a bit gloomy – not quite the desired tone, I felt.

"Cake, Mabey," I barked, suddenly feeling quite managerial in a BMW driver sort of way. Perhaps, like Victor Sheen, the very association with German cars had driven a new spirit of efficiency into me. We had pussyfooted around these cases for long enough; wheels now needed to be set in motion.

"Sir," they replied as one.

"In my office, please."

"What, now?" said Mabey.

"Yes, now."

They followed me in with varying levels of enthusiasm.

"Close the door and sit down."

They sat. I chose instead to walk around them like a predator circling its prey.

"All right. It's time the pair of you earned your pay. We've got a missing person and an unidentified body. Real cases to solve! Isn't that why you joined the force?!" They half-turned to each other with looks that said '*No!*' "So now it's time for some *action*. Dust off your truncheons, for we are about to get *real*. Is that understood?"

"Yes sir," they mumbled like schoolboys hauled up before the headmaster.

"Right. The Jollygoode case, Cake. I want you to discover all you can about this missing husband. And I mean all. I want to know his hat size, his waist measurement, his favourite tipple, everything."

"Sir."

"The business, neighbours, find anyone who knew him. Make yourself unpopular."

"Sir."

"And Mabey, you're on the body at the vicarage."

"On the body, sir?"

"Ask questions in the vicinity. Did anyone see this man go in? Any funny footprints anywhere? I want you to go over the area with a fine tooth comb."

"Sir."

"Get a photo of the victim. Show it around. Doesn't anyone know who the hell he is??"

"Sir."

"And of course the murder weapon. If it was murder."

"Sir?"

"Find it, Mabey, find it. It must be out there, somewhere. A blunt instrument, possibly a mallet. Could be something to do with fish."

"Sir."

"Any questions?"

"No, sir." Cake was happier now. Everything was as it should be, as he'd seen it on TV police dramas.

Mabey, on the other hand, was bound to raise a problem. "Well… There is one, sir."

"Go on."

"I've thought about this and reflected. What if the two are connected? The wife does the deed, out of some sort of greed, and before we know it she's—"

"Rejected. Rejected, Mabey, rejected!" It was Cake's turn to laugh. "I want to see written reports by tomorrow lunchtime. That's all for now."

"Sir."

"Oh, and do you mind?"

"Sir?"

"Stop calling me Sir, will you? It really is most irritating."

"… Right."

"Mr. Gaskett will do."

"Of course."

Strictly speaking, you see, I was no 'sir', nor even a 'guv'nor', but just an *ordinary man*. For I had yet to pass the paper test for promotion to Inspector. And I hadn't risen through the ranks either, but simply answered a newspaper ad. So I was, technically speaking, not the superior, but quite conversely the *gross inferior* of Burley-Hogg, Cake and Mabey. Still, Commissioner Painter didn't think they'd notice, and that was good enough for me. "They're even thicker than you are," he'd said. Jokingly, of course.

Mabey traipsed sullenly out of the office. It had evidently been some time since he'd actually been asked to do something. Cake, on the other hand, was delighted. As one of life's *completers-finishers*, he relished the thought of at last having something useful to do. He had never been happy with the boondoggle pretence anyway; it just didn't seem *right*. He vaulted out clumsily on his long gangly legs.

What sounded like an angry swarm of mosquitoes came droning along the High Street towards the station, increasing in volume as it approached. There must have been about 253,197 of the blighters. Worryingly, the droning stopped right outside the police station.

Burley-Hogg put his head around my door. He wore gardening gloves and still held a trowel in one hand. "The courtesy car, sir."

"Where?"

"Outside, sir."

Cake and Mabey were standing in the front doorway, sniggering. I brushed them aside and looked out across the road.

"Thank you very kindly sir!" a voice exclaimed brightly. I looked down, and there it was – what they used to call a 'bubble car'. Looking like a bald-headed egg-shaped four-wheeled dwarf, painted bright yellow with a picture of a posthorn on the side. And standing there next to the car, with one hand on the doorframe and another outstretched in display mode, was my shiny friend from the garage. The one and only, Victor Sheen of Curiosity Corner.

"...You said a BMW," I croaked.

"That is absolutely correct sir. BMW Isetta – Beautiful little car – Full of character – Excellent for parking – Popular with the ladies. Thank you very kindly sir!" He held the keys in his outstretched hand. I reluctantly accepted, not fancying the prospect of another encounter at Curiosity Corner. Behind me came another snigger.

"How does it, er… how does it work?" I asked wearily.

"The car sir? Yes, of course sir. The door opens like so." He opened the entire front of the vehicle. "The steering column operates on a universal joint, enabling it to come away with the door. Utterly ingenious sir." It was, indeed, utterly ingenious. "Originally designed for the continent sir. Ample room for passengers inside. Ignition here, gear change here. Indicators here. Radio telephone here, optional flashlight here. Fix it to the roof. Once used as a police car, later recommissioned by the Deutsche Bundespost. And so on and so forth. I guarantee this vehicle will give you hours of motoring pleasure. It has certainly given my wife a lot of pleasure sir."

"Your wife?"

"Yes, indeed sir. My wife usually drives this car sir."

"Won't she be needing it then?"

"Not at all sir. She will be glad to use the Wartburg."

"Oh. Well. Thank you very much."

"Thank you indeed sir. A pleasure to enjoy your custom sir. Thank you sir." And with that Victor Sheen strutted off like a peacock, leaving us with a cheery wave of his crinkly golden hair.

I turned to find Cake and Mabey recomposing themselves in the doorway. "All right you two," I said, vainly attempting to restore lost pride. "Haven't you anything to be getting on with?" They disappeared into the bowels of the station. "And Sergeant?"

"Yes, sir?"

"I'll be working at home for the remainder of the afternoon. If anyone should call."

"Very well, sir." I somehow didn't mind him calling me 'sir'; from him, it sounded like a genuine mark of respect. From the constables, it sounded like nothing but piss-taking.

"Oh, and Sergeant?"

"Sir?"

"Let's cut the Beethoven sonatas, shall we? We want to calm people, not drive them to suicide."

"As you say, sir." He saluted me with trowel and gardening-gloved hand. And with that ridiculous image still fixed in my mind, I stepped into my economic bubble car, swung the front door shut and turned the key in the ignition. The mosquitoes had evidently been busy in the interim, for there were now 506,014 of them. The din of their wing beats was sure to drown out all extraneous noise, rendering the owner immune from the taunts of children, builders and stray mongrels. It was accompanied by a vigorous vibration that shuddered through the lanky steering wheel into the palms of the driver. Hence the pleasure it afforded Victor Sheen's wife, no doubt, though whether that outweighed the downside would depend entirely on the individual's sensitivity.

The slightest pressure on the accelerator sent the vehicle hurtling down the road like a bumper car at a funfair. Nought to thirty in an astonishing twenty seconds.

Before I knew it I had returned, gratefully, to my signalman's hut by the railway. That had surely been the longest day and a half I would ever know. I collapsed into my armchair with a mug of Armagnac.

The late night express from London would pass through at 23.35. The points would have to be changed; I knew that very well. Otherwise the train would career straight down the disused track and hit the village headlong. There would be untold death and destruction.

But which of my levers operated the points at the junction? I tried them all, for luck. None of them would budge. They were all solidly locked in place, and probably had been for a hundred years or more.

There was nothing for it. I would have to go out there and prise the points apart myself. A crowbar leant against the wall. I took it in my hand and went down to the tracks, which glistened in moonlight moistened by pouring rain. With some considerable effort, I managed to move the points. But hold on. Which was the right way? This way, or that? I tried to move them back again. They were much stiffer now. I heaved, I strained, I pulled, but all to no avail. I knelt on the track, heaving and straining some more. Rain lashed down in relentless waves, sending miniature trails snaking along gleaming rails, forking into smaller trails, twisting and turning as the water sought the easiest route to the centre of the earth. Suddenly the train was upon me, screeching like ten thousand raging harpies. I was helpless. With a deafening noise and a blinding flood of light, the engine roared straight into me.

I woke with a headache that should have been legendary; it felt as if some kind of construction work was going on inside my skull. Men had put up temporary road signs and pitched a tent in there. A concrete mixer was churning. A pile driver smashed into the ground.

There was a familiar yelping sound. I looked around to see Four-Eyed Bob sitting in the other armchair. Miss Marple stood between us, enquiring after my well being.

"And how are we today?" echoed Bob. He'd let himself in with the spare key – I supposed.

"Awful, bloody awful," I replied, with far too little courtesy. "But of course, you know that already."

"Yes. It's only to be expected. You've been through a lot. But never mind. You'll be your normal self in a matter of days."

"Less than that, I hope. Er… Sorry, what time is it?"

"Just eight o'clock. Nearly time for a drink."

I looked down at the empty mug in my lap. "How long have you been here, Bob?"

"Since six. Couldn't wake you, so we let ourselves in. Hope you don't mind. Fact is, we've had a little snooze ourselves. Haven't we."

Miss Marple gave a muffled snort of agreement, then settled down to her preferred pose on the floor.

"Did you get your courtesy car then?" Bob asked.

"Yes, didn't you see it outside?" We did laugh.

"Let's just say I *felt* it." We laughed again. "Quite, how shall I say, low. And round. My guess is a BMW Isetta."

"Correct as ever," I replied. "Quite burst my bubble, I can tell you." Miss Marple was now fast asleep.

"No, don't get up," said Bob. I was just about to, before my brain smashed against the underside of my skull. "Let's make it another time. Saturday, say? Let me buy you one. I reckon you'll be ready by then."

"Fair enough. I think I'm through for today."

A brick came through the window. Miss Marple leapt up and made a dash for the door. It was closed. She howled as she'd never howled before. Through the gaping hole in the window, I could see a dark hooded figure running up Signal Box Lane towards the village. Running quite athletically, too.

"Oy! You! Stop! Desist!" I hollered. But my fleet-footed hurler of brick desisted not.

"Have you made enemies already?" asked Bob. He seemed unperturbed. Miss Marple stopped howling and looked over at him. As I led her away from the broken glass on the floor, she whined with a sense of unfulfilled retribution.

The brick was wrapped in a scruffy piece of paper bearing a crude inscription. 'KEAP AWAY FROM SUSAN JOLLYGOOD,' it warned in angry letters of uncloaked violence. It was the writing of a schoolchild.

"Lucky they didn't go for the bubble car," Bob quipped. We did laugh.

Who would want me to stay away from Susan Jollygoode? Not Susan Jollygoode, for sure, unless Henrietta Jekyll was her *alter ago*. Farmer Hector, perhaps? The violence of the act and the primitive nature of the message certainly suggested as much. But why? I could see no valid reason. And he would never run athletically. Cake would doubtless claim it was the missing husband, having changed his mind and returned from his journey of betrayal to ward off a potential rival. Luckily, I was not so easily fooled; there was more to this brick than met the eye.

I boarded up the window with a full-size advert for Skegness, mainly to keep the bracing wind outside. I couldn't honestly believe my physical safety had been threatened in this village of almost no crime at all. I would have the brothers Green replace the window in the morning, lest we should spark another boom of holidaymaking in that breezy east coast resort.

Dear Aunt Clarice,

Thanks for writing again. It cheers me up to hear from you, it really does! Nothing ever happens here, and as you can imagine, there isn't much for me to do. They've given me a job in the gardens, which I suppose gets me outside every now and then. But they'll only let me do menial tasks like wheeling barrows of weeds to the compost heap. It's very frustrating not being able to decide things by myself. Maybe if I do a good job they'll give me more responsibility in future. As for the book, I've been trying to write the story as you suggested, but I'm afraid I can't. It's supposed to be a detective thriller, but the story keeps straying into other things beyond my control. I can't concentrate properly. I find myself staring at the walls and drifting off blankly. I get quite depressed about it sometimes. Thanks for the clippings anyway. Yes, I would be glad to see some more, if you think the stories are funny. I might put them in the book, you never know! What happened to the vicar, by the way? Was he defrocked, or whatever?

love

John

Footnotes

Cake and Mabey duly delivered their case reports the following lunchtime.

"Sir," each said as he handed me a buff-coloured folder in the staff room. "Mr. Gaskett," each then corrected himself.

"Good. Thank you," I replied, inviting them to sit. *Intertribal Song to Stop the Rain* seemed quite an untimely choice, considering the devastating extent of the drought. But then again, it was never promised nor expected that the musical selection would reflect prevailing weather conditions. That would have been impossible.

Quite at odds with his poetic bent, Mabey's report was written in flowing prose. His questioning nature had clearly won the day. I read with some interest:

The Body in the Vicarage Garden— At approximately 15:05 on Sunday, June 20th, the Reverend Oscar Melon, vicar of Nether Hooey, discovered the body of a dead white adult male behind a rhododendron bush in his garden. How did the body get there, and how did the victim meet his end? I conducted a thorough search of the vicinity, and found no sign of forced entry into the garden at all. The wall around the garden, however, was low enough to be stepped over with ease by a white adult male. At a point approximately fifty feet from the house, I found damage to branches near the wall, and concluded that the victim had climbed over the wall at that point. I also found a very large footprint in the soil by the wall, which did not match the shoes of the victim. Radiocarbon dating has revealed that the print was not planted in the days subsequent to the murder. On interviewing the neighbours and several passers-by, I found none who had seen a man with very large shoes enter the garden.

I concluded that the victim was a prowler of some kind, and had been killed, whether deliberately or otherwise, by a very large-footed member of the vicar's family. I therefore interrogated the Melons. After an hour of intense grilling, the boy Peter broke down and admitted hurling his sister's croquet mallet into the bushes, near the spot where the body was found. The offending mallet has been bagged and is now with forensics. Neither the boy nor the girl Sarah has particularly large feet, but both are evidently hiding something. I therefore recommend they be brought in for further questioning at the station.

"Thank you, Mabey," I said on finishing the piece. "That was brilliant. Quite brilliant".

"Don't mention it." Mabey clearly felt he'd broken new ground. Which, in a way, he had.

"However," I persisted regardless, "I feel I must nitpick somewhat on your final point. Arresting children on suspicion of manslaughter, and with no tangible evidence whatsoever, is not something we should do lightly. And in the unlikely event that they *are* guilty, we wouldn't want to show our hand too soon, would we. No, I recommend a policy of covert surveillance for the while. See what you can pick up on the grapevine.

Listen to the locals. Are there any rumours of murderous minors? Of course, you're in the ideal position there, with you running a pub and all that."

"I don't like to mix the two", protested Mabey. "If I were to start making inquiries as landlord of a popular hostelry, I would lose all credibility."

"Jesus." I turned my face to the ceiling.

"What about this footprint?" asked Burley-Hogg. He was quite adroit at retrieving situations.

"Here." Mabey pulled a large, floppy rubber cast from his inside pocket and held it up twixt forefinger and thumb. As it unfurled in his grasp, it did indeed appear to resemble a footprint, but was at least twice as long as a full-sized man's shoe. To be more exact, the heel was more or less normal, but the rest of the sole was massively elongated. The significance of this was clear: we were looking for a murderer with feet of the most unusual proportions.

"Should make him easy to spot," offered Cake.

"Yes, but why just *one*?" I asked. "Have you thought of that?"

"Why *not* just one?" Mabey's tone suggested that he didn't think it relevant.

"Think about it. How would a person with feet that size ever manage to plant just a *single* footprint? It would be virtually impossible!"

"Perhaps he only had one leg."

"*ONLY HAD ONE LEG?* So we're looking for a one-legged murderer with a single, monstrously large foot?! A gigantic *monopod?*"

"It's a possibility. There are one-legged people," said Mabey.

"But the prosthetically challenged don't go around committing murder, do they!"

"Don't they? What about the one-armed strangler of Spalding, Lincs? She developed superhuman strength in her jaws to compensate, and killed both her husbands with her teeth and remaining hand."

"Yes, but we're talking about a one-legged man whacking someone over the head from behind," I argued. "He'd lose his balance and fall flat on his face."

"Perhaps he held onto a tree with the other hand," Mabey posited. I tried to imagine the scene. "And anyway, when did you ever see a one-legged person hop? He would obviously have some kind of prosthesis on his other leg."

"So where is it then?" I demanded.

"Where's what?" the wretched man asked.

"The *other leg*, man! Where is your trace of this famous *other leg?* He could hardly have planted only the good leg on the ground and kept the other leg dangling in the air."

"Ah well, it might have been a simple wooden or fibreglass appendage, something of the nature of a club or broom handle. I wasn't looking for that kind of shape. I was only looking for foot shapes."

"That wouldn't have worked anyway," added the Sergeant. "An appendix of the type you describe would have sunk into the soft ground behind the bush, which if I'm not mistaken consisted of an organic mulch to maintain acidity. He would have fallen over."

"Perhaps the print *is* the other leg," contended Mabey. "Perhaps there are no footprints from the *other* other leg because he was treading very carefully along the ground, almost gliding along the surface as it were, but conversely had no control over his replacement leg, the one with the enlarged foot, thus inadvertently planting the print."

"How do we know it was a man?" Cake asked somewhat uselessly.

Mabey turned on his colleague. "Ever seen a woman with feet this size?"

"On the other hand," intervened Burley-Hogg, "it is entirely plausible, is it not, that the footprint was planted there deliberately, by the murderer or someone else, in order to discriminate someone with very big feet? That would explain why there was only one print."

"So you're proposing someone planned the murder, then carried a gigantic boot into the vicarage garden just to pin the blame on someone else?" I enquired as calmly as was possible under the circumstances.

"Yes, that would be about it," answered the Sergeant, beginning to think back somewhat ruefully over his own logic. "Or it could have been one of those, you know, joke boot prints on the end of a wooden pole."

"All right. Let's go down that road. Put yourself in the murderer's shoes."

"Shoe sir," corrected Mabey with a smirk.

"Indeed. If you were trying to incriminate someone with very large feet, what would you do? Sergeant?"

"Me, sir? Well let me think," said Burley-Hogg as he raked his rough chin with the palm of his hand. "What I would do would be to make *a trail*. So you'd have a series of footprints going in a roughly forward direction. I'd then make a little cluster of scuffly footprints around the scene of the crime, suggesting a struggle. That's it in a chestnut."

"So the murderer would be carrying a rucksack," I added.

"Sir?"

"To carry the boots in."

"Ah."

"And since there were none of the signs you describe, I think we can safely consign your theory to oblivion."

"Yes, sir. I do see your point," said the Sergeant, a little deflated as he reached for his bottle of Baby Bio.

"The rain could have washed them away." Cake was keen to re-open the case, however. "Perhaps there were many more footprints, as the Sergeant suggests, but they've been disturbed in the intervening days. After all, the fact that there is only one footprint suggests we may be dealing with quite a devious mind here."

"So just being a murderer isn't devious enough?" was what Mabey slipped in with a smirk.

"What rain?" demanded the Sergeant, ruining the case for his own defence. "It hasn't rained for weeks. That's half the problem. It's sending us all bonkers."

"What?" I protested. "It rained the other day."

"No it didn't."

"Yes it did. It rained on the road to Upper Hooey."

"Ah," said the Sergeant with mystic cognisance, "that's different."

"All right," countered Cake. "Perhaps the abnormal *lack* of moisture due to the drought has caused some chemical reaction whereby footprints disappear? Perhaps the soil has, you know, risen up and messed itself about to cope with the abnormal conditions?"

"Yeah," said Mabey. "And perhaps you're a complete dickhead?"

"Er… May we continue with these reports?" I said in a vain bid to restore some semblance of normality.

"Sorry, Sir. Mr. Gaskett."

"Sorry."

I opened Cake's report. Inside the file was a single sheet of paper headed *The Case of the Missing Husband*. Beneath that, in the centre of the page, was a single word written in bold capitals:

NOTHING.

"Nothing?" I asked, aghast.

"Nothing," Cake confirmed, self-righteously unconcerned.

"Almost poetic!" Mabey exclaimed with vindictive animation.

"You discovered absolutely nothing about Duncan Jollygoode?"

"That's right. Absolutely nothing. Because there's absolutely nothing to discover. Anyway," Cake continued, turning to Mabey, "how can a single word be poetic? It doesn't even rhyme."

"Ah, but there you are," countered his colleague. "It doesn't have to rhyme to be poetry. There can be poetry in a single word. Like 'Silence'. That's one of mine. Then there's the *haiku*. Ah yes, the noble *haiku*. 'Stagnant pond. Frog jumps in. Sounds like water.' Poetry, sheer bloody poetry."

"Sorry, I can't be having that," argued Cake. "Where's the detail? You have to paint a picture, in my book."

"That's exactly the point, mate. The detail is there; you just have to imagine it. The words conjure up a mood, and you make of it what you will."

"No, no, no. The descriptive genre's for me. Look at this, for instance. It's a story I'm reading." Cake took out a book and actually began to read aloud. I looked on, powerless. "Hugo got up, put on a coral blue T-shirt, and went to partake of a shave. It was a gray, limp morning, rather like an old oatcake that had been left too long in a pool of yesterday's tea, but with a glimmering, a shimmering of silver light in the east that could barely be perceived. As Hugo dragged the cold metallic razor through the frothy swelling of bright white foam on his chin, he caught sight of a girl in a corner of his mirror, reflected in a roundish clearing on the steam-frosted glass. She was walking along the beech-lined street beyond the bathroom window, looking down at her custard-colored shoes as she went. She wore a lemon-yellow, billowing chiffon dress with olive-green polka dots, her highlighted hazel hair flowing behind her in the breeze like the trailing tail of a comet. Her legs were elegant and slight and shapely, the legs of a fawn, formed like newly pulled spring onions pinched tightly at the ankle. "Hmmm. Good enough to eat!" thought Hugo. Sensing his gaze as it burned into her reflection, the girl stopped and looked up into Hugo's steel-gray shaving mirror with an accusing glare, as if to reprimand him for intruding on her day. Her eyes were ultramarine, blue as the ocean, her face an enchanted landscape of gently rolling hills and babbling brooks. She lifted her head, a small, rounded head that looked as if it should belong to a child. Then she raised two long fingers, like sticks of asparagus manicured in sun-dried tomato, and spread them wide in a remarkably broad letter V. Her generous lips, imbued with the red of cherries, not cranberries, then parted, and through her brilliantly gleaming teeth, immaculately straight and upright like a newly erected henge of stone, Hugo was sure he could hear her say, "Piss off, you effing pervert!" The razor slipped and slashed his chin.'

There was a brief silence, before a crowd of passers-by who'd stopped to listen through the open door of the station burst into spontaneous and quite ecstatic applause.

"Move along now," called Burley-Hogg, having endured the whole thing with utmost stoicism.

"Now. How could you express all *that* in one word?" Cake continued.

"How about CRAP?!"

Mabey's laughter rang out like a cathedral bell as the last of the Dribblesiders reluctantly returned to her daily routine.

Dear John,

I'm so glad they've given you something to do. You need something to occupy yourself physically as well, you know. The devil makes work for idle hands, as it says in the Bible. After all, don't forget what you're there for in the first place. You're in no position to be laying down the law. As for your book, just make sure you stick to the story, that's what I say. I'm still not sure why you had to write about crime, after everything that happened, but I suppose it can't do any harm. The postman has been sacked for destroying mail. Apparently he opened every letter addressed to the vicar to see if there was any incriminating evidence against his wife. So now he's lost his wife and his job. The vicar has been sent to a new parish. So it's clear who the loser is there. Must close, or I'll miss the fish man.

> *love*
> *Aunt Clarice*

Bludgeoned by Fish

"Turnips."

Thud.

Burley-Hogg slapped his afternoon's baggings down on the counter in front of me.

"A good catch?" I asked, to jolly things along. *Ride of the Valkyries.*

"Not bad. Better than last year, and earlier too. It's this drought, you see. Seasons are all out of kilter. That and the chicken manure."

"Good. Good. By the way, Sergeant," I said, remembering my purpose.

"Yes, sir."

"Is that autopsy report in yet?"

"Oh, yes! I'd clean forgot. Yes, it came in this morning."

"And...?"

The Sergeant drew me closer to the counter by tapping the side of his nose. "Well," he said, casting a furtive look of reconnaissance about him, "it appears our mystery man was not killed by a blow to the head after all."

"No?"

"No. He was poisoned."

"*Poisoned?*"

"Yes. The pathologist found traces of a substance called Noxytoxypoxylene in his blood. Deadly. Murdered, for sure."

"Noxy...?"

"Noxy, toxy, poxylene."

"My God."

"The blow to the head must have been incremental."

"Perhaps the murderer – or *murderess* – hit him over the head, then injected him with poison to kill him?"

"Perhaps. Except the poison was swallowed."

"How do you know?"

"I don't. The pathologist said so."

"How did the pathologist know?" I persisted.

"Traces in the stomach, she said. But the funny thing is... "

"Yes?"

The Sergeant again looked around for listening ears before lowering his voice to a horse's whisper. "Noxytoxypoxylene is only available from the Pharmacy-General."

"The government??"

"That's right."

"My God."

"And anyway, he was hit on the head *after* he was poisoned. With a fish."

"...Poisoned with a fish?"

"Hit with a fish. Or by a fish."

116

"Hit with a fish?!"

"They found traces of herring scale in the wound, sir."

"Don't be ridiculous. A fish could never inflict such a wound."

"It was frozen, sir. The fish."

"Let me get this right. Our unknown victim was poisoned with… What was it?"

"Noxytoxypoxylene."

"Noxytoxypoxylene, then hit over the head with a frozen fish?"

"So it seems, sir. Frozen fish *is* remarkably hard, sir."

"Is it. Is it." I was doing my best to take it all in.

"But he was still in the pink when he was hit. Confusions and ruptured vessels around the wound proved as much. That means either he was deliberately struck on the back of the head to knock him unconscious, or that it was an accident – say, a crate load of frozen herring overturned and fell on him from a great height after he'd swallowed the poison. Out of the frying and into deep water, you might say. Unfortunately, it was next to impossible to determine the time of death, as the presence of the frozen herring had seriously impacted *algor mortis* and the readings from the rectal thermometer were all squew-whiff. It's possible, says the pathologist, that the body had even lain for some time in a frozen fish store, in which case we're right up the creek with that one, sir."

"What – you mean the body could have been *moved* to the vicarage garden?"

"Oh yes, sir, without a doubt, she said. The pools of lividity made that perfectly clear."

"Pools of lividity? Aren't we getting somewhat overly technical here, Sergeant? We are only supposed to be police officers, after all. Not scientists."

"I can't help that, sir. That's what it said in the report. The pools of lividity were all in the wrong place, meaning the body was moved after death, or *post mortem* to be more precise."

"All right, but how can you be sure the poison was swallowed first?"

"I can't. The pathologist said so."

"How can the *pathologist* be sure?"

"She said that haemorrhaging in the cranial cavity was consistent with subconsciousness. The blow would have been enough to kill him anyway. He wasn't going to drink anything after that, was he."

"Maybe the poison was forced into his stomach?"

"No."

"No?"

"Traces of oxygen in decontaminated blood cells suggest he was still breathing when he swallowed it."

This was hopeless. Like some imaginary game of word chess with a grand master, the Sergeant had me beaten at every move.

"Even so, that still doesn't prove it was murder. He could have accidentally swallowed the poison, then was passing a truck load of frozen herring when one of crates fell on him, then the owner of the poison or the herring – or both – moved him to vicarage garden to avoid a costly insurance claim and moreover to incriminate the vicar!"

"Yes, that's entirely possible, sir. Very plausible indeed. But there's a clue that shouldn't be overseen" – the Sergeant half-turned his head and pointed to the back of his head – "he had a small tattoo hidden behind his ear."

"Curious place for a tattoo. You'd usually want people to *see* a tattoo, wouldn't you."

"It said DEFF."

"Deaf?"

"DEFF."

"Was he deaf, then?"

"D-E-F-F."

"Ah. A code name?"

"Could well be. Perhaps he was some kind of secret agent. And this is my point, sir. A person carrying a hidden code name tattooed behind his ear is not going to mistakenly swallow poison or allow frozen herring to fall on him from a great height, is he. He's going to be vigilante, always on the lookout, waiting, watching. He's not going to be some kind of wally who lets casual accidents happen to him. He wouldn't last five minutes like that, would he now. Believe me, I know. I was in the commandos. No, sir. It's murder all right. Murder, deceit and subterfuge. In all my years, I never dreamed it could happen here on my own patch." He almost seemed pleased at the prospect. Perhaps he'd placed another bet.

"Well, in any case, we've got some checking out to do now. All known sources of that... What was it?"

"Noxytoxypoxylene?"

"Noxytoxypoxylene. All local handlers of frozen herring. Anyone with a grudge against the vicar. And the meaning of DEFF."

"Right you are sir."

DEFF. Where had I seen that before? I tried to think back. The clock on the Community Hall struck four. Footsteps, a man's and a woman's, passed the open door of the station, walking in opposite directions. A bus snarled noisily by. As it did, it sent a breeze swirling into the vestibule. The front page of the Daily Dribble lifted and danced in the air for a fleeting moment, only to furl silently back into place a moment later.

"Would you like one, sir?" asked the Sergeant.

"Pardon?"

"A turnip, or two?"

"Yes. Please. Yes, Sergeant, that would be good."

He split off a brace and handed them over with loving care.

Dear Aunt Clarice,

Things are getting out of hand. My missing husband is still missing, and it turns out the body they found in the vicarage garden wasn't his after all! Did I tell you about the body in the vicarage garden? No one has the foggiest idea who either of them is. To make matters worse, my Inspector is in love with the missing man's wife, but she seems to have a split personality and keeps giving him mixed signals. What's going on? I have no idea! I thought I would be in charge this time, but I can't even control the characters in my own story. They keep doing things out of the blue, quite unpredictably. I thought I'd created them, but now they're starting to have lives of their own! What should I do, Aunt Clarice? Keep sending those clippings anyway. Hopefully they'll give me some sense of perspective.

love

John

A Family of Sparrowhawks

"Excuse us," quaked the tremulous voice of a field mouse in the public vestibule. The Sergeant lumbered out to answer the call, shifting his weight from one tree trunk of a leg to the other in the manner of an ox pulling a plough.

We had been going over some potential DEFFs in my office. Cake's search had produced any number of them, mostly useless: Dartmouth and Exmouth Foot Fetishists. Deirdre Ermine's Furry Friends. Dario

119

Eniola Fancy Focaccias. Derek and Eric's Fish Farms. And many others. None or all of which might be connected to our mystery victim and his mystery tattoo.

"Inspector Gaskett." The Sergeant did at least knock before re-entering. "Some people to see you."

A terribly humble middle-aged couple crept in most apologetically, followed by a bespectacled girl in plaits. I'd seen her somewhere before. I was sure of it.

"Frank Sparrowhawk," said the man, leaning forward with head bowed obsequiously as he proffered a hand. Though not obliged to physically bond with the public, I reluctantly accepted the gesture. His handshake was limp and cold, like the skin flaps of a chicken taken straight from the fridge.

"Ivy Sparrowhawk," the wife echoed, and did the same. Her handshake merely belonged to a smaller chicken.

"And this is our daughter, Forget-Me-Not," continued the man. The girl twisted her fingers together and looked down at the floor in embarrassment. She was no more than about thirteen.

"*Adopted* daughter," corrected the woman.

"Take a seat," I offered baronially. There were only two seats besides my own. The girl stood nervously at the corner of my desk. "And how can I help you?"

"It's our adopted daughter," said Frank Sparrowhawk. No bird of prey, to be sure, he more closely resembled his quarry.

"Yes?"

"She... Well, she *sees* things, you see."

"My advice is that you take her to a doctor."

"No, you don't understand," protested the man. "She sees things of a criminal or otherwise suspicious sort of nature, if you follow."

Ah. Now he was talking. "What kind of things?" I asked with narrowing eyes.

"Tell him, love," said the mother, turning to her adopted daughter. With head still bowed, the girl looked across at her adoptive father, then at her adoptive mother, then back at the floor. Hands now clasped behind her back, she swung gently from side to side to cloak her unease.

"I... see... people. Men. Hiding. Watching. Taking photographs."

"Taking photographs is not against the law. It happens every day."

"I see *you*..." she continued, looking up sheepishly. Her line of vision now collided with the edge of my desk. Eye contact was imminent.

"Me?"

"She sees you," the mother confirmed.

"Going into a house," the girl continued, looking me squarely in the eye for the first time. "And I see men near the house. Hiding. Watching. Taking photographs." The words almost bounced as she spoke.

"What house is this?"

"The one next to ours," said the father.

"And where do you live, exactly?"

"None Pudding Lane," said the mother.

"Next to One Pudding Lane, if you follow," added the father.

"One Pudding Lane? Susan Jollygoode's house?" Of course. Forget-Me-Not was the basketball-bouncing girl in the property next to Susan's. This could well be the lead I'd been waiting for.

"That's right. The Jollygoodes' house," said the father. "Or rather, it *was* the Jollygoodes' house. But now another lady lives there."

I was taken aback. "You mean – Susan Jollygoode no longer lives there?"

"No. She's someone else, you see."

"No one told me about this! When did she move? Christ, I was only there three days ago."

"No, no. The Jollygoodes left some weeks ago. They just vanished. Gave no warning, left no forwarding address and haven't been heard of since. If you follow."

"So… the woman living there now is not Susan Jollygoode?"

"No," said the mother. "She is not Susan Jollygoode."

Hold on now. Was I hearing them right? That the case of the missing husband and the body in the vicarage garden had in fact been *preceded* by the double disappearance of the Jollygoodes, made doubly sinister by the impersonation of Susan Jollygoode by another woman? Perhaps there was a perfectly good explanation. Perhaps they'd gone on holiday. Perhaps she was looking after the house for them. Perhaps it was more convenient for her to assume their name, for whatever reasons. Perhaps she was on a tax dodge.

"And they haven't gone on holiday, either," the woman said telepathically. "They would have told us. They always did." Perhaps *they* were on a tax dodge?

"And they haven't moved house," added the husband. "There was no removal lorry. Forget-Me-Not would have seen it. Wouldn't you love?"

The girl swung her head in a gesture that clarified nothing but merely confirmed she was still alive. This was all getting too much. I needed time to think. I needed to rid my nest of these Sparrowhawks as quickly as possible.

I turned to the girl with a stratagem. "How do you see these things, these men?"

"From my bedroom window," she replied.

"And how do you know this activity is criminal? It could be a police operation."

"Ah yes, we thought about that," said the father. "But she saw them watching you too, you see."

"Me?"

"When you were there," the girl continued. "That night. They were watching you. Holding strange instruments. Hiding. Watching. Taking photographs."

"How many men do you see?"

"Sometimes one. Sometimes two. Sometimes three. Sometimes more." Bounce, bounce, bounce, bounce, bounce.

"Tell him about the lights dear," urged the mother.

"I... I see lights." The girl shifted her feet in acute embarrassment.

"Lights?"

"Lights. In the shed. At night."

"The shed in the next garden?"

"The Jollygoodes' garden."

"What used to be the Jollygoodes' garden," corrected the mother.

"Do you see anyone inside?"

"No. Just lights."

"And there is another thing," added the father. "That photograph outside."

"The Missing Persons photograph?"

"Yes. That's not Duncan Jollygoode, if you follow."

"What?"

"It's not Duncan Jollygoode."

"Who is it, then?"

"We have no idea," said the wife. "He was a lot older than that."

"Lights in sheds? People watching people? What makes you think any of this is criminal or otherwise suspicious?" I demanded, bringing my stratagem to its consummation. I was rapidly tiring of their excruciating humility and surfeit of community spirit. Nor did I feel entirely comfortable to think the girl had been watching me that night. Was nothing sacred?

"Well... It just is, you see" explained the man.

"Watching someone is criminal?"

"Suspicious, at least."

"So would you also call your daughter's activities suspicious?"

"Our *adopted* daughter?"

"Yes, your adopted daughter. She has also been watching people, has she not?"

"Yes, but—"

"I suggest you go away and think nothing more of it. Leave the criminal investigation to us. That's what we're paid for."

That was more like it! All those weeks of training hadn't been entirely lost on me. The girl's testimony was clearly of the very greatest importance, but I mustn't let them know it. The secret of true authority, you see, lies in controlling information.

As the family trudged away with an air of immense hurt, I did feel the slightest twinge of remorse.

BBC Health News: Many guide dogs for the blind have impaired vision themselves, scientists have shown. Seven out of ten labrador retriever guide dogs were found to be nearsighted in research at Harvard University. Despite their impaired vision, the dogs were still able to act as good guides for their owners. The dogs may rely on other senses to do their job, according to a spokesman at the International Dog Myopia Conference. "Dogs are also subject to absent-mindedness and lapses of memory," said the spokesman. "Past studies have shown that dogs selectively 'forget' unpleasant experiences in the same way as humans do."

Altered Ego

"Aren't you forgetting something?" said Four-Eyed Bob. We were having that drink at The Point of No Return. The double case of the missing husband and the body in the vicarage garden had been giving me a lot of grief; I seemed to have no control at all over either investigation, not to mention the missing chameleon and the missing Jollygoodes. Even my grasp of the barest facts was diminishing. Bob would put me on the right track, I felt, over a flagon or two of Highly Extraordinary.

"Forgetting?"

"*The victim is often the perpetrator.* Yes? Your so-called Susan Jollygoode, for instance. It's perfectly clear that every word she utters is a fabrication. Mere fiction." Miss Marple lay curled up at his feet as usual. "Think back to the Daz box case, my friend."

Ah, the Daz box case. The brothers O'Doyle had sued their local council for damages when the refuse collectors had mistakenly taken four black bags from the side of their property. The bags, they claimed, had contained irreplaceable documents pertaining to their roofing and guttering business. As it turned out, the bags had been full of detergent boxes stuffed with fifty pound notes, ill-gotten gains from numerous bank robberies and fraud scams, dirty money that they were planning to launder later that day. They'd left the bags outside as a disguise. They knew they were under surveillance and thought no one would ever open a bag of rubbish left outside – but had forgotten that it was collection day. The brothers only came clean when the cash was discovered flying out of the bags at a landfill site some days later. As one newspaper wittily mused, it was nearly the dirtiest yet most valuable load of old rubbish ever collected. *The victim is often the perpetrator.*

If the Sparrowhawks were to be believed, the woman who now called herself Susan Jollygoode had never been a 'victim' anyway, even if that term could somewhat tenuously be applied to the partner of a missing person. But 'perpetrator' she certainly was; she had fabricated a false identity and perverted the course of justice, at the very least.

"And there are some very obvious clues you've failed to notice," Bob continued. "Yes, the light in the shed. Yes, the burial in the garden. Yes, the missing photo on the wall. But who was in it? Who are those children? There is no record of any children. You should be asking these questions."

Bob paused for a very large gulp of Highly Extraordinary. I took a more modest drink of mine while Miss Marple licked her chops and yawned.

"What you need is surveillance. You need to watch the house, you need to watch the people watching the house, and you need to watch the girl watching the people watching the house. Something is going on over there, and you need to find out what it is, my boy."

"Yes, I'm aware of that."

"But the word is *covert*, yes? She must not know that you know. To all intents and purposes, she must remain hidden behind her alias, her alter ego. If you were to expose her now, you could lose a vital lead to the whereabouts of the missing couple and the identity of the murderer – even if it isn't her. For there must be no doubt in your mind that all these events are somehow connected."

"For sure. But recently, I've been wondering if she isn't suffering from some kind of mental problem as well."

"Mental problem…?"

"Schizophrenia. Dual personality, even. In that case, her alter ego wouldn't be something she could fake so easily, would it."

"Schizophrenia? What makes you think that?"

"The fact that she has two distinct personalities? Now she is warm and friendly, now a complete stranger. She has no apparent control."

"Well, I wouldn't admit to being a doctor, but you may be onto something there. Nevertheless, you would do well not to confuse schizophrenia with dual personality, my friend. Schizophrenics have an impaired perception of reality, usually in the form of hallucinations, paranoid or bizarre delusions, or disorganized speech and thinking in situations of social or occupational dysfunction. This is not the same as dissociative identity disorder, also known as multiple personality disorder or split personality, though the two are often confused in popular culture. And in any case, it is so very easy to put a label on such a condition, don't you think? Autism, dyslexia, bipolar thingy, what have you. It allows you to compartmentalize, file away and thereby forget all about the humanity of the sufferer. Perhaps I have said too much. After all, it is *your* case. But if I had to put a label on it, I think you may have a example of what's called *depersonalization* there. Then again, how do you know this woman has no control over her condition? It may just be a smokescreen."

"True."

"And what about the delivery through your window the other day? Are you any closer to identifying the culprit?"

"The message was that I should keep away from Susan Jollygoode, written in the hand of an illiterate. Deliberately so, to conceal the identity of the writer. Of course, the effect of the act was conversely to draw my attention to Susan Jollygoode as a potential source of trouble. Now who would possibly entertain such a motive? Surely not SJ herself, in light of recent revelations?"

"And certainly not the gentleman who is standing over there with imminent intent to harm," Bob added with a nod towards the crowded bar of the pub.

A beer glass was brought down on the counter with an almighty crash.

"You're the bugger that stole my wife's hat!" bellowed Farmer Hector Hodgkinson as he strode towards us with menace. Miss Marple lifted her head and pricked up her ears.

"What? Your wife's hat?" I replied, feigning ignorance.

"Don't try to be funny! You were seen wearing my wife's hat last Monday!"

"That hat?? You mean... Your wife is a *scarecrow*??"

"You slimey smart-arsed ponce! One more funny remark like that and I'll smash your bloody teeth in!"

"All right, all right! I'm sorry, all right? I tried to return the hat, but the scarecrow had disappeared." Only the second part was true; I had to stall for time.

"What's that?"

"The scarecrow had moved. Perhaps she preferred the next farmer's field?"

So he came to smash my teeth in. Instantly, Miss Marple leapt up from the floor and positioned herself between us, baring her teeth and snarling at the irate farmer with venom. She was utterly transformed.

Farmer Hector stared at the beast with a look of abject horror – as if he'd seen the hideous three-headed dog of Hades...

"That'll do now old girl," Four-Eyed Bob intervened calmly. Miss Marple withdrew to a less terrifying distance.

"All right, you'll get your hat," I said, with no clear certainty of that fact. "But first, you'll need to explain why your tractor has no number plate, why you failed to stop at the scene of an accident, why you threatened an officer of the law, and why you caused a disturbance in a public house."

Farmer Hector fell silent. Staggering under the weight of the charges against him, he backed off through the watching crowd, back through the back door, back onto his tractor, and back along the country road to his farm in Upper Hooey.

"There," said Bob through a nonchalant slurp of his pint. "*The victim is often the perpetrator.*"

Arise, surveillance. Noble though it sounded, the act was not of the noblest intentions. It meant to spy, snoop, peep on a person to collect information without their knowledge. In spite of her manifold personality defects, not to mention the identity fraud, I had always felt Susan to be inherently honest – yes, the *victim*… All right, I had feelings for her, feelings of a not altogether professional nature. It was hard to define, but I felt a certain affinity with her, as if we were somehow *connected*. It was more than mere lust, though heaven knows that alone should have been sufficient in my state of uninvited celibacy. Besides my old friend Bob, I felt Susan to be the only person in my current situation with whom I could have a meaningful relationship of any sort.

For this reason I agreed with Bob's analysis, but for a different motive. Ever since the Sparrowhawks had descended on my office to offer their myriad revelations, I'd made the conscious decision that I would not, for now, confront Susan with the questions they'd raised. To answer those and the many other shadowy uncertainties of this case, I first needed to develop a deeper bond of trust with the woman. For the time being, she would remain 'Susan Jollygoode', and her 'missing husband' would remain just that. Besides, I had no other name to call her by. Was I allowing my feelings for her to cloud my professional judgment? Most certainly.

'Depersonalization', Bob had suggested. Later that afternoon, I pulled out an old medical compendium from the sparsely populated bookshelf in my office. Its dusty companions included an encyclopaedia with black-and-white photographic illustrations, a world atlas that proudly proclaimed half the world pink and asserted the continuing existence of Nyasaland, and a Whittakers Almanac from 1935. I opened the compendium and read:

Depersonalization
In the field of psychiatry, *depersonalization* or *derealization* refers to a diminishing sense of reality. Sufferers feel that their personalities have changed and the world has become less real; it is vague, dreamlike or lacking in significance. This can sometimes be a highly disturbing experience, since many feel that they are indeed living in some sort of dream. Certain drugs can also cause the feeling as a side effect, especially hallucinogens.

Hmm. Really? Not a lot of that fitted my perception of Susan – or the woman I would continue to know by that name. Schizophrenia seemed far more fitting. Hallucinations, impaired perception of reality, disorganized speech and thinking… Or perhaps that was only one side of the story. Nevertheless, 'Susan' could aptly have been described as living in a dream world. That's how it always seemed to me. The vagueness, the contradictory statements, the lack of control, the inexplicable utterances, the frequent changes of atmosphere... Yes, she may even have been taking hallucinogenic drugs. Perhaps they were in the shed. That would explain her reluctance to let me in there. Or perhaps they were buried under the fig trees.

Whatever the case, I would need to tread with care. Susan's fragile senses might be a pressure cooker that could explode at any time. And so, rather than surrounding her house with more spies and bugging her furniture, I decided on a somewhat gentler approach.

I could hear the ringing tone. She must have had her phone fixed in the meantime.

"*Hello?*"

"Hello, Susan? It's John."

"*Yes?*" Both she and her voice were as cold as ice.

"I see your telephone's working now."

"*It is. What can I do for you?*"

"Well, a week has passed since your husband's disappearance..."

"*Yes?*"

"Well... What we usually do in such situations is send someone to counsel you."

"*Counsel? On what, exactly?*"

"To help you come to terms with your trauma."

"*What trauma?*"

"The disappearance of your husband, of course."

"*Oh. Yes, I see. But I don't need any counselling. I'm perfectly all right.*"

"Would you allow me to send a specialist? A female officer?"

"*A female officer?*"

"Yes, we usually find same gender counsellors most effective..."

"*How very patronizing!*"

"But Susan—"

"*Look, I'm all right. Just let me know when you find anything.*"

And with that, the line went dead. My attempt at gentle persuasion had failed miserably. My reading of our relationship also seemed to have fallen badly short. How could I have got it so wrong? Schizophrenic was the word. That was the only part I had got right. But perhaps there was another explanation; perhaps some despicable low-life had been holding a gun to her head even as we spoke. Perhaps she was in greater danger than I could ever have imagined... Whether from her own demons or someone else's...

There was only one thing for it: I would have to go to her house myself. I had to get to Susan that night. She was in danger, I was sure. People were watching her, but why? What were they hoping to find?

After my last ordeal there, the decision to go to Upper Hooey was not one I could take lightly. But go I decidedly must. The means of transport was a problem, however. I could hardly use the bubble car; I'd be spotted a mile off. The same went for Victoria's cake van. There was no bus service, naturally. And I surely wasn't going to walk again.

"Any ideas?" I asked the Sergeant, who was busily attaching a sprinkler hose to a tap at the back of the building.

"Can you ride a horse, sir?" he suggested as he tightened a clamp at the top of the hose.

"Of course not."

"Only there is the old police mare," he continued. "Old Nell. They put her out to pasture, but she still comes out for shows and the like."

"They'd hear us coming, wouldn't they?"

"Rubber shoes, sir."

"Ah."

"Yes, sir."

"Anyway, I can't ride a horse. I told you that."

"Right, sir." Burley-Hogg unreeled the hose and walked backwards as he pulled it out towards the bottom of the vegetable plot.

"And I wasn't planning on going alone," I said, stepping forward in time with him.

"No?"

"No. We need a full contingent on this one. It seems there's more than one suspect."

"More than one?"

"Yes. You're needed here, of course, but the other two can join me."

"The other two, sir?"

"Yes, the Constables."

"I'm sorry sir, you can't have both Cake *and* Mabey. That would be like having your cake and eating it. In fact, you can have *neither* Cake *nor* Mabey. Not today, sir. Not on a Friday." I'd clean forgotten – Friday evening was Cake's chess night. He was one of Dribbleside's grand masters, I'd been told. Clearly, some things were even more important to him than getting an early night's sleep.

"You're right. But this can't wait. There's something odd happening over there, and I need to get to the bottom of it." We had nearly reached the end of the plot.

"Yes, sir." His unreeling complete, the Sergeant now attached a rotating sprinkler head to the end of the hose. "But you will have to go alone." He marched back up to the tap at the wall, and I marched back up in time with him. "Perhaps someone can give you a lift?"

Flight of Fancy

The far horizon was tinged with the russet glow of dusk by the time the balloon was full. A veil of summer evening mist hung low over the riverside meadow, a magician's screen beneath which diurnal creatures clocked off and handed over to the night shift. A hot blast of gas from the balloon's propane burner sent a trio of mallards quacking off into the gathering gloom.

"*Et voilà, m'sieur. On y va,*" said the balloonist, the renowned Jean-Claude Monty of Wallonia. A novel form of investigative flight, the balloon had occasionally been used, in former times, for military reconnaissance when stealth and surprise were required. Its main failing, of course, was that it was completely at the mercy of the wind and utterly impossible to navigate. Monsieur Monty had assured me nonetheless, in almost impeccable English but with a maddening tendency to speak in rising arpeggios, that the prevailing wind this evening would carry us directly to Upper Hooey. And that was good enough for me.

I had hit upon the idea while leafing through the black-and-white encyclopaedia, that old shelfmate of my medical compendium. The aeronautics section on Page One proudly presented the latest biplanes as the pinnacle of human endeavour to date, adding the caveat that "the noise produced by the engine can regrettably be heard some miles away, effectively rendering the biplane useless as a means of reconnaissance in enemy territory, for which reason it will probably never replace the hot-air balloon". Of course! The 'enemy' would be looking on the ground, not in the air. Especially if there was no engine noise. If the balloon could hang low over the terrain and approach the village from behind, I could enter unseen and unheard.

"OK," I replied, summoning up every milligram of Dutch courage. "Let us go." It had to be safe, after all. Thousands of children had travelled in these things in the past year alone. The burner couldn't explode due to a loose fitting, the flames couldn't be driven onto the balloon's fabric by the wind, migrating geese would never be foolish enough to fly headlong into the thing in their arrowhead formation...

A cool evening breeze wafted gently past as we rose silently into the twilight. The first star of night twinkled in a Cytherean way, a beacon for others to follow. Laughing voices of happy children floated across from nearby playing fields. A burst of flame lit up the inside of the balloon, transforming it into a massive, roaring Chinese lantern. Sombre shapes of trees and sheep fell away below us as we lifted into the wind, while in the far distance, the sparkling lights of Dribblemouth offered a safe haven from the perils of the night. A cargo ship turned in a slow arc around the bay as it prepared to berth.

"...power lines?" ended the next arpeggio from my pilot.

"Pardon?" The roar of the burner was deafening.

"I said, it is not normal to go by night? One cannot see the power lines?"

"Ah. Yes. I do appreciate that."

"I am sorry?"

"I appreciate that," I said a little more loudly. "But surely we could go higher?"

"Higher? *Mais bien sûr*. We will. But when you go out, it will be no joke, no?"

"Yes, I'll have to be careful."

"My brother Pipi, he tried to fly once at night. He became wedged between two trees?"

"We'll have to avoid that then."

"Pardon?"

"I said..." A family of geese drifted by, honking ethereally. "Do you ever get hit by birds?"

"Birds? No. They have too much sense, I think?"

Jean-Claude Monty had already told me his life story, and how he'd established quite a name for himself in the field of balloonery. Together with his brother Jean-Pierre, he had invented a one-man hot air balloon aptly named the 'Monty', filled with patented 'Monty gas' and fitted with a device aptly named a 'levitator'.

The brothers had discovered the gas during a curious incident in their mother's kitchen. A saucepan full of potatoes had boiled dry while she was telling them in great detail about her latest chiropodical adventure. The brothers were then surprised to see the lid of the saucepan float clean off the stove and collide with the ceiling as she continued her tale. They deduced that the potatoes, a special variety grown only in the Ardennes region, produced a levitational gas when heated beyond a certain degree outside water, and started to experiment with balloons.

They tested their idea on animals of increasingly large proportions, starting with the humble field mouse, following through with an Oudenaarde duck and culminating in a Flemish goose. All were lifted effortlessly into the air by the brothers' gas-filled balloon, with no visibly adverse effects barring a modicum of surprise. The resulting invention was the 'Monty', a dirigible contraption lying somewhere between balloon and parachute, which would be harnessed to the owner's upper body and used for short-distance travel in urban environments. The balloon or '*ballon*' above the wearer's head was approximately the size of a small car, powered by gas from heated potatoes at its base, and steered by controls on the user's breastplate. The wearer could rise from ground level to ten metres in 4.5 seconds and could accelerate or decelerate at will.

Initially hailed as a breakthrough that could save the planet from carbon monoxide poisoning, the project suffered a setback when the first prototype was destroyed by 'the indiscretion of a passer-by'. A Paris fashion designer, enraged at the sight of the balloon rushing towards her, stubbed a cigarette on its underside causing it to explode. Confidence in the project then collapsed. The government withdrew funding and cancelled plans for traffic-regulated 'balloonways' in major cities. A number of potato farmers had their dreams of riches instantly dashed. The Montys would have been broken men, but for their life-saving counterfeit money printing business.

Jean-Claude eventually fell back on the traditional hot air balloon, the full-size variety, though similarly fuelled by Ardennes potato gas. He designed a sphere that resembled the Earth in appearance, its continents, oceans and even the Galapagos Islands clearly marked, then crossed the Channel to make his name and fortune with 'global warming events', as he wittily called them. It should be added that he used the Calais-Dover ferry to get across; he knew of the fate suffered by the Spanish Armada and didn't want to be at the mercy of any winds *there*, thank you very much.

Having succeeded where the Spaniards had failed, he found the people of England far more amenable to foreign ideas than King Philip II could ever have imagined. As long as it didn't involve work, responsibility or serious thought, they were open to any new ideas for extending their leisure time. Buoyed by the idea of getting high on potatoes, the English happily paid good money to be taken up in the air, led across a bit, then brought back down again.

It so happened that Monsieur Monty's busy summer schedule had brought him over to Dribbleside, where, the Daily Dribble proudly announced, a party of wealthy investors would be let down in Hedge Field that afternoon. All right, he overshot the field, and the next one, but still ended up within the parish boundaries. He was happy to accede to my request on condition that I bought him a meal and any beer except Stella Artois, in the nearest tavern, the poorly frequented and rarely mentioned *Golden Goose*. There he would tell me his life story, and how he'd established, etc., etc., etc. The fabric of the deflated balloon would hide the gear from prying eyes, and no one, he assured me, would have any idea how to steal it.

The one-man 'Monty' would certainly have been handier for my trip to the upper ward, but I felt somewhat relieved not to have it. After all, where would I have left the contraption on my arrival there? This was not some kind of spy movie, where the protagonist could simply dump unwanted hardware at the drop of a hat; this was the real world, full of real people and very real concerns.

"*Et maintenant*, we begin seeing the planets," enthused the ballooning Walloon. Our craft had risen to his preferred height of eighty metres, whereupon the frantic bursts of gas and flame had subsided to a more acceptable degree. "First, there is Venus, the brightest star? Then we shall see Mars, Mercury, Jupiter and Saturn. All of them named after days of the week. And if we are very lucky, we will also see Uranus and Neptune, but not Pluto. Pluto, it is too much?"

"Surely it is impossible to see all of those planets at the same time?" I quibbled needlessly.

"Ah, but yes! As we rise into the troposphere, the air becomes more clear? We can see for hundreds of millions of kilometres, even as far as the Trans-Neptunian objects!"

Poor chap was clearly off his rocker, but as long as he gave good balloon, that was fine by me. "Well," I said, "it certainly does clear the head, being this high up. One acquires – how should one put it? – an alternative view of the world."

"*Exactement*. And the universe! And beyond the universe!"

The Point of No Return loomed large in the semi-darkness ahead. It shone like a lighthouse in an otherwise darkening landscape as the main body of the village drifted away behind us. Outside the pub, standing with pint in one hand and fag in the other, tilting back on heels, arching backs and throwing laughter into the night air, semi-drunken revellers in short-sleeved shirts, cropped hairstyles and overpowering aftershave exchanged more hilarious anecdotes on issues as important as a centre forward slipping as he went to take a penalty. Others, seated at picnic tables in the illuminated back garden, held more meaningful conversation: Did you hear about the man who went missing? They say his wife did him in. Yeah. What about the body in the vicarage? What about it? Was it him, I mean? No. They say it wasn't. Who was it then? I dunno. Tell you what though. We never had all this going on before that Inspector arrived. You're right there. Maybe he brought it all with him! It didn't matter what they said. The mundane banalities of their lives seemed so infinitesimally small and insignificant, with them down there and me up in the air, communing with the cosmos. Yes, I felt a sense of release, liberation, to be in a world where no one mentioned Susan Jolly-goode.

"Is it really true that the planets are named after days of the week? I wasn't aware of that," I said to humour the balloonist yet.

"*Mais oui*. But only the Belgian ones. *Mardi, mercredi, jeudi, vendredi, oui? Les voilà*."

"What about Uranus? Saturn? Neptune?"

"We have no *uranedi*. What do you take us for – *imbeciles*?" He laughed madly. "They were discovered much later than the days of the week. The balloons could not go high enough then. And you English, you have stolen Saturn with your *Saturday*?"

I could but marvel at his absurdly illogical logic; the poor man's flights of fancy were growing increasingly insane with every centimetre that separated us from the ground. Perhaps gravity had a serious effect on his mind. Or perhaps we were approaching the upper ward...

"Greek gods!" I cried as we flew over another cuckoo's nest bereft of occupancy, its bird having flown. "The planets are named after Greek gods, are they not?"

"No, *mon ami*," countered my friend, "days of the week are named after the gods, and planets are named after days of the week. Mars was discovered on *mardi*, Mercury on *mercredi*, *et cetera*? Uranus and Saturn were discovered on Sunday and Monday, but it was thought too *disingenué* to name them the Sun and the Moon. So then, they were named after Greek gods, yes?" The pitch of his voice was reaching impossible heights as his excitement continued to grow. His accent was transformed to that of a Beano-type Frenchman spouting "*Zut alors!*" – to the point of using phoney words, even. This was clearly a subject about which he felt most passionate. "But, I would rather talk of Pluto! *I would rather talk of Pluto!!*" he shrieked insanely as he pulled on the gas burner for another roar of flame.

Pluto, the mad balloonist explained, was full of frozen methane. It was his life's goal to travel there and collect some of it for his experiments on weightlessness. The existence of methane proved beyond doubt that there had once been cows on Pluto, he claimed. I'd heard of moon cows, I said, but never Plutonian ones, and anyway, surely cows' stomachs weren't the only source of methane? Ah yes, he replied, but the planet was originally named by an eleven-year-old girl from Oxford, so anything was possible…

An almost full moon emerged from behind cloud cover to illuminate the scene. As we drifted over open fields, the rib cage of Copse Hill came starkly into view ahead. I had developed a dread of venturing anywhere near the upper ward, but now found myself positively willing our craft towards it.

We would have to climb further to negotiate the hill and reach our destination safely. In that case, there was no knowing what crazy flights of bizarre imagination my Walloonish pilot would reach next. Perhaps his body would fill with potato gas, his voice would rise to a supersonic squeak that only a dog could hear, and he would finally fizz up into the atmosphere like a released child's balloon, never to be seen or heard of again. Perhaps, like some latter-day Icarus, he would burn to a frazzle even as he met the sun-warmed surface of the moon.

But he did neither of those things. *Au contraire*, indeed, for he did quite the opposite; he grew increasingly normal as we approached the village. His voice returned to its lower register and his accent made him

Belgian Ambassador to the United Nations once more. But of course. We were gaining altitude, yes, but at the same time the hilly ground was rising to meet us. That was it! It was not so much his aerial elevation as the *distance relative to the ground* that sparked his madness.

"Ah, my friend," he now enthused in a wholly reasonable way, "we will soon arrive at your destination?" The rising arpeggios, however, were endemic.

"Yes, regrettably," I replied, trying my best to sound cool and unruffled. At that moment I could have done with a Gauloise to twiddle twixt forefinger and thumb, and possibly a long curly moustache to caress, but having neither of those, I made do with an insouciant waggle of the head. "And thank you."

"*Ça fait rien,*" he chortled most congenially. A moonlit expanse of hillside raced towards us with frightening speed. I'd chosen to land in fields at the back of the village, where I could arrive unobserved yet reach Susan's house with ease. Monsieur Monty released a rope from the side of the basket, and I used it to clamber out over the edge. "*Bon voyage!*" he called, though my voyage had ended, and then waved a cheery farewell as I dangled half way down.

I eased my way down the rest of the rope and jumped the final few feet to the ground, partially spraining my ankle. Oblivious to my discomfort, Monty blithely pulled up the rope and gave a hearty blast on the gas burner, taking his globe back up into the sky. I was sure I could hear his demented laugh once more as the balloon receded rapidly into the distance, now so small that I could almost take it in my hand. All that remained was an eerie silence, broken only by the faint whistling of the breeze through the grass.

I took a look around me. Down there, in the moonlight, I could see the old stone cross and the village green behind it. I limped out of the field and slipped unnoticed into Pudding Lane, concealing myself in the shade of trees opposite Susan Jollygoode's house. I saw her through the open curtain. She was performing Tai-Chi exercises in her living room, completely naked. Apparently motionless, a predator ready to pounce.

I panned across the trees that stood further along the road. I saw a glint of binocular, and yes, the figure of a man silhouetted against the moonlit lawn beyond. As my eyes roved across the scene, I could see three, perhaps four men, wearing hats and possibly also gloves, their binoculars trained on the house. One was perched in a tree. They appeared to be signalling to each other.

I turned and looked at the house next to Susan's – None Pudding Lane. There, in an upstairs window at the side of the property, stood the girl, watching from her darkened room. I watched her as she watched them watching Susan. Monty's balloon flitted across the moon, inducing a minor eclipse and sending its rotund shadow gliding across the village landscape. For the briefest of moments, nothing at all was visible.

"Are you spying on me?"

Susan was standing before me in her oriental gown.

"John!!" she gasped in genuine surprise as the balloon moved away from the moon. "What are you doing out here?"

"What? No, it's just that… Did you know you're being watched?"

"Watched? Well, yes, by *you*…"

"No… By those men… Over there…" But they were gone. "And that girl next door…" But she was gone.

"You'd better come back in. I don't know what's come over you, John."

A faint glow emanated from the shed at the bottom of the garden.

Shed Light On

Again, she was a different woman. Again, she was warm and accommodating now. Again, she served me mystical concoctions, again we played word games. Occasionally she would utter curious statements, ask curious questions: "Do you think they suspect?", "We'd better lie low," and the like. When quizzed most delicately about her true identity, she would only reply with a riddle: "No one is who they say they are… are they?" When asked about the spies outside her house, she would answer with no words but a simple hand movement and a tilt of the head to indicate that they were indeed agents of an unnamed organization who were not only watching her every movement but, yes, even listening to her telephone conversations using sophisticated sonar equipment. Ridiculous!

Of course I just laughed it all off. For I knew, by now, that these were merely symptoms of her illness. I'd come across personality disorders before, but never quite as complex as this. And since she and her missing husband – whoever they were and if he had ever existed – were probably tied up with the body in the vicarage garden, I somehow had to find a way through her conflicting disguises and get to the heart of the matter.

"Was that Tai-Chi you were doing earlier?" I asked with deliberate nonchalance as the night wore on.

"Oh. So you *were* spying on me?" was her retort.

"Er... I couldn't help seeing you. Your curtains were open."

"Anyway, it's *Taijiquan*, if you must know. Calms the mind."

"I'll take your word for it."

"You'd better."

"Susan, there's something you can perhaps shed light on," I said, shifting the discourse to more pressing matters.

"Shed light on?"

"Yes, shed light on. A brick came through my window yesterday. Attached to it was a warning – to keep away from you."

"You'd better keep away then, hadn't you!" she replied, laughing with abandon.

I could but share her laughter. "Who could it have been, though?"

"Who? What?"

"The brick. Who could have thrown the brick? Who would want to keep us apart?"

"Er... My husband?" Now she was giggling like a schoolgirl.

"Really?"

"Oh, come on. John. You know who it is."

"...Do I?"

She looked at me for what seemed like a very long moment.

"No," she said at length, the smile a distant memory. "On reflection, perhaps you don't. Perhaps *I* don't. Why should I? Ha ha!" She poured two more measures of *shochu* spirit, a variety made from potato and labelled 'One Hundred Years of Solitude'.

"What about the shed then?"

"What *about* the shed?"

"Why does it glow at night? Are you sure your husband isn't in there?"

She looked utterly stunned. "Of course I am! How could he be in there? What would he eat? Of course he's not in there!"

"You could always go and check."

"Now you're just being daft. Are you trying to wind me up?"

"How do you mean?"

"I told you, didn't I? I don't know where the key is. He must have taken it with him."

"He could have locked himself in there. Have you thought of that? Perhaps he's a nocturnal animal. Perhaps he creeps out at night and raids your larder while you're asleep."

Susan looked at me blankly for a few seconds, then burst into barely controlled laughter again. I took another gulp of *shochu*. "Very good, John, you nearly had me there!" she said, having regained a modicum of self-control. "Perhaps he lets himself out at night. Very good."

"Is it? Yes, I suppose it is. Very good."

"But you know, John, there is something that puzzles me. Where would he have left the key? If he wanted to hide it, for whatever reason, where would he have put it? John? If it was you, say. Where would you have put it? Where would you put the key to your own garden shed?"

"Well, let's see." I could but humour her, now well assured of another night on the couch – at the very least. "There would be a number of candidates. Under a plant pot is an obvious one. Another would be to bury it in shingle. Or tape it under the overhang of the shed roof. Or…"

"Yes, but where would *you* hide it, John?" she asked with greater urgency. And I thought I was supposed to be the interrogator here. "Where would you *actually* hide it?"

A sudden, irrational obsession with minor detail was clearly a symptom of her illness. Her subconscious was using the shed and its key to mask a deep trauma, protect her from further disintegration of her personality. But that was not my concern. I am not a doctor.

"Where would I actually hide it. Yes. That is a good question. Where would I *actually* hide it." I took another sip. Tonight's concoction also tasted strangely medicinal, though not as acrid as the *lao jiu* last time. "I *wouldn't* hide it. If it was me, I wouldn't hide it at all."

Susan appeared to jump. "What?! You wouldn't hide it?" Her eyes bore into mine with an incredible intensity. "What would you do with it then?"

"I would… I would leave it somewhere perfectly obvious. Yes. I would leave it somewhere so obvious that no one would think to look. Such as… On the key hook by the back door."

"Right…" Susan's eyes made an involuntary movement in the direction of the kitchen. She was obviously itching to go and check it out. Poor woman.

"Are you sure you're OK, Susan? Is the strain getting too much for you?"

"What strain?

"Well, the strain of wondering, waiting, not knowing if or when your husband will ever return? You seem a little disturbed..."

"You're not suggesting I'm off my head, are you? That's a laugh! I'm no madder than you are!"

There was a slight pause laden with uncertainty. Which way would she turn? Would she be for me, or against me this time? We both lifted our thimbeline glasses and sipped loudly at the same time. We laughed together innocuously, and the tension of the moment was gone.

There were one or two other questions I should have asked. I was almost certain of it. I surely hadn't risked my life and my sanity in Monsieur Monty's contraption to become mired in a discourse over keys. The problem was that I could no longer remember the barest detail of those questions. My mind was growing fuzzy, hazy, blurry. Sleepy, even.

"Night night," Susan eventually cooed as her satin nightwear swished out through the door.

There would be no dreams for me that night. For I had only one intention: to get to the bottom of the garden and shed light on that shed light.

Get to the bottom of the garden and.

Get to the bottom of.

The bottom of.

The.

Fig Trees of the Mind

It was Frank Sparrowhawk who opened the door. There was a distinct smell of cabbage cooking.

I'd failed miserably in my attempt to vanquish the demons of sleep and sneak out to the garden shed that night. Was it the irresistible lure of the couch? The strangely soothing reassurance of Susan's senseless statements? Or something she put in the drink...?

She'd woken me with a cheery "*Up you get!!*" followed by hot coffee and griddlecakes. "I have to be at the nursery this morning," she'd explained over a hard-boiled egg. "Can I take you anywhere?"

"No – thank you. I think I'll stay in the village. I need to make some enquiries."

"Oh. Enquiries!" she'd said with a wink and a giggle. "Yes, of course. You will need to be making some *enquiries!*" She was still laughing as she lopped off the top of her egg.

I had to get down to the shed somehow. But it would be risky in broad daylight. Someone might be looking... And then I remembered the girl. What was her name? She said she'd been watching the house. I'd seen her doing just that, the previous evening. From the vantagepoint of her side-on upstairs window, she was in a position to see all comings and goings in the Jollygoode household, and perhaps more. Of course. I would make her an ally in my strategy of covert surveillance; she would be my eyes, if not my ears.

Before that, I would have to order a double helping of humble pie with lashings of whipped penitence from her parents. Yes, I regretted not treating the Sparrowhawks with greater courtesy when they descended on the station that afternoon. Were they in the forgiving mood today? It was with some trepidation that I walked up their log-lined path and rang their antique ceramic doorbell.

The bell imitated the sound of a klaxon.

"Yes?"

Frank Sparrowhawk eyed me with a look of great hurt and immense suspicion, coupled with an obsequious self-effacement and an unthinking trust in authority. It couldn't have been easy.

"I think I owe you an apology, Mr. Sparrowhawk..."

"Oh yes?"

"Yes, it's just that, er, may I come in?"

"Oh. Certainly. Do come in, Inspector."

"Hedges may have ears," I added by way of explanation as I crossed the threshold. The Sparrowhawks' residence was modest in size, smaller than it appeared from the outside. The ceilings were exceedingly low; I could only imagine the thatched roof had been deliberately piled high to make the property look grander. It was in fact a bungalow with a converted attic.

"I—"

"Do sit down, Inspector."

I sat down. "Actually, I wanted to—"

"Will you have some tea, Inspector?" Ivy Sparrowhawk emerged from the kitchen, a little flushed, to be sure.

"Oh... Well... Yes. Thank you very much."

"I thought you were going to say *Not when I'm on duty*," Frank Sparrowhawk said with a chuckle. He'd forgiven me already.

I humoured him with a chuckle of my own. "It's just that I—"

"Milk? Sugar?" Ivy called from the kitchen.

"Oh... Both, please," I called back, then turned to face Frank again. "Anyway, as I said—"

"One lump or two?"

"Ah... Half a spoon, please. Mrs. Sparrowhawk."

"That wouldn't taste very nice," said Frank, overtly chortling now. The reassurance of being in their own home seemed to turn them into bubbly extroverts. "Half a spoon wouldn't be very nice at all. You'd have a job swallowing it, for a start! And how would you manage one half without accidentally swallowing the other? You see? Those are the problems you run into when you try to cut down on things. I'd just go for the whole spoon if I were you, and be done with it."

"No, I—"

"I know what he means, halfpennyworth," the wife chided as she brought the tea in.

"Yes, thank you. Very nice. Well, anyway, as I was saying—"

"Fairy cake?"

"Er... Pardon?"

"Would you like a fairy cake, Inspector? Freshly baked yesterday."

"Oh... No thank you. I've already had a sizeable breakfast."

"Next door?"

"Yes. How did you know?"

"We have our spies," inserted the husband.

"Your spies...? Ah. Yes. I see." I'd almost forgotten the girl again.

"She's not going to give you much, that woman, is she?" resumed the wife, referring of course to Susan. "She's all skin and bone, her. I don't know when she last saw a decent meal."

"Really? She seems very...er..."

"Would you like a fairy cake, Frank?"

"Yes, thank you dear."

"You should have come here for your breakfast, Inspector. Most important meal of the day, I say. Fill 'em up and send 'em packing, that's my motto. Frank never went out on an empty belly, did you Frank. Not before you retired. Well, I say retired. He didn't have much choice, did you Frank? It was that accident with the combine harvester that did it, that's what I always say. You were never the same after that, were you Frank. Of course, we couldn't afford to stay in the Lodge any more, not on his pension, so we had to be rehoused down here, but I ask you, None Pudding Lane, it hasn't even got the dignity of its own number, just because Number One was already there when they built it, but of course we'd only just adopted Forget-Me-Not then, she could only have been about three, poor little petal, not that we're not related, mind, well it was that devil from Essex, he messed my sister up good and proper, and I don't mind saying it, so what option did we have, I said I said, we'd be only too happy to have her, after all she's my own flesh and blood, I wouldn't think of doing anything else, only she did have the problem with the fits, and the psychic incidents, but we managed all right, didn't we Frank, are you sure you won't have a cake?" Not so much bubbly as garrulous.

"I don't think the Inspector's come all this way to eat cakes Ivy," Frank chipped in on my behalf.

The wife fell into a stunned silence and I awoke from my trance. "Ahem. Yes. Why have I come all this way? Well, there are two reasons. I wonder if you would first care to embellish your story about the Jollygoodes next door. The *missing* Jollygoodes."

"It's not a story," said Frank, once again wearing the expression of an unfairly scolded dog. "It's the truth."

"Yes, I'm sorry. I didn't mean to suggest you'd *made it all up*. What's the story, anyway?"

"Well, Inspector, it's more or less as we said, you see. They suddenly weren't there any more, and then she appeared in their place."

"Right away?"

"More or less."

"Did she introduce herself to you?"

"No."

"When was this?"

"About a month ago."

"And how long had you known the Jollygoodes at the time?"

"Oh, years. We'd known them for years, hadn't we Ivy. Ever since we moved here. Yes, we got on very well. Didn't we, Ivy."

Ivy took over, batteries recharged. "Oh yes, very well. You could say they were perfect neighbours, and you know, that's so hard to come by these days, don't you find? Everyone's too busy with other things, people don't even know each other's names these days do they, but then

I ask, what's it all for? Are their lives any better now, with their swimming pools and their conservatories and their second cars? It's just as I was saying to Clarice the other day, the world won't stop turning if people just had a bit of courtesy for one another, and she said well, what about the vicar and the postman's wife, now look at *them*, I mean what's the world coming to, this never happened in our day did it, and so I said no it didn't, you're quite right, these people never knew any hardship, that's the problem, they never knew hardship. That's what brought us all together in those days after all, wasn't it Frank. And so yes, well where was I, the Jollygoodes, yes, they were a wonderful couple, elderly mind, old enough to be your parents Inspector, but they knew how to look after a garden, oh yes they knew that all right, they were out there every hour God sends making it look beautiful, and look at it now. That woman has no idea, no idea at all, I mean what does she do all day? Could she not at least cut the grass?!"

"Well… She was planting some fig trees the other day," I said lamely on Susan's behalf.

Frank coughed. Ivy stared at me as she took a tea break.

"And the second thing?" Frank said to prevent a pause from turning into another silence.

"The second thing…"

"Your second reason for coming here?"

"Ah! Yes. Well, I was wondering if… Um… Is your daughter in at this moment in time, as it were?"

"Forget-Me-Not?" said Frank.

"That was it."

"Our *adopted* daughter? Our ward of court?"

"Yes."

"No. Well, of course, she'd be at school. It being a weekday."

"I see. And that is the school in…"

"That's right. The school in the village. Do you know it?"

"No. Well, I was wondering, anyway. Do you think we could station a man in her bedroom?"

"A *man*?" Ivy Sparrowhawk gasped in mid-cake.

"In her *bedroom*?" Crumbs flew from Frank Sparrowhawk's mouth.

"Yes, to conduct surveillance. There's something not quite right going on here."

"Too blooming right it's not right, a man in our adopted daughter's bedroom?!" There were certain lines Frank was not prepared to cross.

144

"A woman, then? A WPC."

"Surveillance of what, exactly?"

"Well… Acting on your adopted daughter's tip-off, I confirmed last night that there *are* people watching the house next door, and that there *is* a light shining in the shed at night. So now it would be useful to keep an official watch on the house to see what exactly is going on there."

"As long as it doesn't keep her awake at night," said Mrs Sparrowhawk. "She's a light sleeper as it is."

"The girl could sleep in the spare room, Ivy."

"Yes, I suppose she could. Of course she could," said the wife as she disappeared once more into the kitchen.

"You can't be too careful you see," explained Frank, leaning towards me conspiratorially. "Don't listen to the wife. She's off her head! Nothing like this ever happened in our day?! Pschoff! Take Christie, for a start. He murdered old women, and a boy. Well, I suppose you know all about that. And what was that about hardship? Pouff! We'd never had it so good. You used to find money down the back of the sofa in those days, but not any more. No, they were the good times all right. Do you follow the Spurs? Arthur Lowe, push-and-run. The coronation. Nobody minded the wind. The end of rationing – about time, too. Then the Swiss crisis. What was that all about?! Jazz. Never could stomach it. Rock About the Clock, that was the one for me. Alex Bedser, Denis Compden. Perfect gentlemen. Yes, those were the days all right. Do you ever feel you're actually in a mental institution, and all the things going on around you are just figments of your imagination? Or perhaps artificially created by doctors as part of your treatment? Do you think somebody who seems particularly close to you could actually be your nurse, or your doctor? I don't. No, I don't think that at all." I sat there pinned helplessly in my armchair, held back by an invisible straightjacket.

"What was that about figs?" asked Ivy as she skirted the wall and clambered up the stairs.

"To be honest," continued Frank, ignoring her, "I do sometimes wonder about Ivy. The girl and her, they're related after all. Perhaps it runs in the family."

It did seem, indeed, that everyone in this village had some terrible mental problem. Perhaps they'd been isolated from the outside world for too long. Inbreeding, perhaps. Or perhaps it was Frank's mental institution: open plan, minimal supervision. They were all harmless, after all. Weren't they?

"Would you like to see the upstairs? The room?" Ivy called from the top of the stairs. "I've made it look presentable."

"Ah yes," I said, gladly breaking out of the straightjacket and rising from my chair.

The Sparrowhawks had an open-style lounge with stairs ascending one wall. The ceilings were so low and the space so cramped that I had to duck my head on the way up; doffing the helmet would never have sufficed for Cake. At the top of the stairs stood Ivy, her spindly index finger pointing spookily towards an open door at the end of a low, narrow corridor that looked like a mine tunnel. The girl's room was unexceptional, its walls covered with childish posters of Snoopy, Scooby Doo and the Harlem Globetrotters. An orange basketball occupied the centre of her bed, like some pampered pet or favourite stuffed toy.

"She's loves her basketball," explained Ivy, who now clung to the frame of the door. "Not the game but the ball, you follow. She's never played you know, and so I said well, if you love it that much why don't you join a club? Then she said there weren't any clubs, except in America, and I said well couldn't you just start with netball" and as she droned on I surveyed the view from the window. It looked out over the side of the property, offering a perfect vista of the former Jollygoode residence. There were the fig saplings at the front, there the shed at the back, looking quite innocuous in the cheery light of day.

"Right. That'll do nicely," I said more to myself than anyone, taking care this time to add a "thank you."

"...the other children at school, she's always been what you might call a loner, but what's wrong with that, Frank says. Still waters run deep, it's often the dark horse that's first past the post, she'll be all right and we needn't worry about the trances too much..."

I was downstairs by now. Ivy had followed me down, keeping the volume of her delivery constant.

"So anyway," I announced in the hallway, "I'll be sending someone shortly. For the surveillance. A WPC."

"Right you are. A WPC it is." Frank seemed happy with that.

"Goodbye then."

"Nice to have met you again," chirped Ivy.

I turned to face the morning sun. I didn't have a WPC. I needed time to think.

Dear John,

I'm sorry to hear you're unhappy about your story. You must stay in control, that's what I always say. After all, if you're not in charge of yourself, then who is? That was the whole problem, unfortunately. You let things get the better of you, and look where that has got you. I suggest you take a firm stand, put your foot down and say, "No, Inspector, you must not get romantically involved with a potential suspect, it's unethical and you've a public duty to solve these cases." Go on, tell them who's in charge. After all, you could just get rid of them if you wanted, couldn't you? Of course you could. You need to get out more, that's what it is. You shouldn't be stuck in your room writing all day. You should always be sociable, always be willing to meet people whenever the chance arises, that's what I say. Well, I must get out to the shops now, as Frank and Ivy are coming for tea.

love
Aunt Clarice
PS. More clips enclosed

LONDON (Ananova): The Ministry of Hedges has defended its funding of secret tests into the use of psychic powers to "remotely view" hidden objects. In the study, conducted in 1972, subjects were blindfolded and asked to guess the contents of sealed brown envelopes containing pictures of random objects and public figures. Incredibly, 28% of the subjects managed a close guess at the contents of the envelopes, which included pictures of a basketball, Snoopy and an "Asian individual". But most of their guesses were hopelessly off the mark. One subject even fell asleep while he tried to focus on the envelope's content. A former MoH employee said: "It can only be speculation, but you don't employ that kind of time and effort to find money down the back of the sofa." The MoH refused to discuss the possible applications of such a technique, but said the study had concluded there was little value in using "remote surveillance" in the defence of the nation.

Who will be my WPC

Leaving the station in the less than capable hands of Mabey, I elected to join Sergeant Burley-Hogg on his monthly patrol of the village. Though it was nothing more than a chore to him, he was evidently something of a celebrity among the villagers – almost a deity, in fact. They regaled him with sweetmeats and feted him with hurrahs as his sturdy boots pounded the dusty streets of the parish.

"It certainly was lucky I had that brainwave," he said as we strolled between engagements. "Or else who knows how long you'd have been stuck up there."

"Yes, it was indeed fortuitous," I said with such gratitude. "But tell me, what made you think of attaching the bubble car to the back of your bicycle? Surely it would have made more sense just to drive it?"

"Ah well, I've never been fond of motor cars, if truth be told. They don't agree with me at all, sir. Anything comes out of the ground is fine by me, but machines I just can't abide with."

"It certainly was prescient of me to leave the keys at the station."

"A stroke of good fortune indeed, sir, thereby allowing me to release the handbrake."

"All the same, it couldn't have been easy. Especially going up that hill."

"I hardly knew it was there, sir." Yes – he was built like a draught ox, and now he had worked like one. "I've pulled heavier things in my time."

"...Such as?"

"Such as a QF Howitzer in North Africa during the war, after our tank had been demobilized, for example."

"Well, you certainly rescued me anyway. I'd just been bombarded by more lunacy from the Sparrowhawks. Is it true what they say? Is everyone really mad up there?"

The Sergeant laughed jovially. "They're no madder than you are, sir. It's six of one and a dozen of the other. Morning Ernest. Morning Brunhilda," he called cheerily as we entered *An Olive or Three*, the village delicatessen on the High Street.

"Morning Ivor," they called back in old-fashioned harmony. The place simply stank of continental cheese; 'twas a close thing between rotting cabbage and a broken sewage pipe. Bob's nose could easily have picked out *Plaisir des Campagnes*, *Le Coq de Bruyère* and *Le Vieux Pané*, though not necessarily in that order. Of course, the smell would have been a thing of the past once the offending item had been popped in the mouth, there to melt in paradisiac delight, giving an experience more akin to promenading through Elysian fields than the aforementioned unmentionables. Meanwhile, the more subtle aromas of pastrami, leberwurst, anchovies and double-roasted coffee put up some semblance of resistance to the pong.

"How those beetroots coming on?" asked Ernest in the meantime, casting an anxious glance at his half-empty organic vegetable racks.

148

"Not so good, I'm very sorry to say," the Sergeant said between short gasps, illustrating the hazards of breathing through the mouth and speaking at the same time. Even the old manure silos on his farm had nothing on this. "Blooming drought. Can hardly get anything to grow."

"An olive or three Ivor?" offered Brunhilda through the stench, temptingly introducing her wares with a flourish of the hand. All manner of marinaded green globules huddled together plumply in plastic containers under the glass counter. "Roasted artichoke? Baby peppers?"

"No thanks Brun," Ivor replied in a tone of apology. "Have you met the Inspector? He just joined us the other week."

"We've heard all about you Inspector, but never actually met," said Ernest, offering a hand over the counter. "Ernest Sellers."

"Isn't it exciting," gushed Brunhilda. "The Murder at the Vicarage. Like something out of Agatha Christie!"

"That is Agatha Christie," confirmed Ernest. "Ours was a murder in the vicarage garden."

"Oh yes. Silly me!" Brunhilda said with a silly giggle as she went to slice some more salami.

"Anyway Ivor," Ernest said to resume his discourse. "What about courgettes? Any sign of life?"

But before the Sergeant could answer: "Did you find that missing husband?" came the next query from the slicer of salami.

"Yes and no," my colleague replied, answering both but satisfying neither.

"Celeriac?"

"The chameleon?"

"Tomatoes?"

"The brick through the window?"

The Sergeant chuckled through it all with several shakes of the head. There were no answers.

"It certainly is strange," declared Ernest, yielding to his wife's will as usual, "that all these untoward incidents started happening the moment we got our new Inspector. Have you brought them with you or something, Inspector?" The three burst into unbridled laughter. It should have felt like mockery, but it was just their innocent way of passing the time of day.

The shop door opened with another tinkle of its bell. And without further embellishment, "Oy, can I put a poster up for a mediaeval joust?

Jesus Christ what's that stink?!" said a familiar voice behind me. I turned to see Penelope Slack standing in the doorway with a handful of bills.

"Is there any other type of joust?" Brunhilda quizzed knowingly.

"Watcha, Inspector me old mate," said the psychic. "Didn't know it was you from behind. Oh yeah, by the way! I found me Brains in the end. He was hiding in front of a picture of Leo."

"Hiding *behind*, don't you mean?" Ernest challenged with a puzzled look.

"No, hiding *in front of*. Camouflaged hisself, didn't he. Silly little bleeder." She took a drag from her cigarette and blew the smoke out through the door.

Ernest and Brunhilda exchanged looks of bewilderment in the *'Whatever will the woman say next'* vein. The Sergeant looked decidedly unimpressed. Whether it was the choice of vocabulary that disagreed with him, or the fact that the woman had failed to report her find, was hard to discern from the stony look on his face.

"Well, that's one thing less for the Dribbleside constabulary to bother themselves with," I muttered on his behalf, with the unspoken but necessary addendum *'And what a complete waste of police time'*.

"Sorry for wasting police time," said Penelope. She couldn't possibly have read my mind; it was surely nothing but a chance coincidence of ideas.

"What's this joust palaver all about, anyway?" asked Ernest.

"It's the Dribble & District Dangerous Pastimes Society, what I'm a member of. They're doing a mediaeval joust on Nilby Marsh in August. Can I put the poster up then?"

"Leave it over there, love," said Brunhilda, sympathetically indicating the broad shelf-like windowsill. She was understandably keen for the smoking cigarette to be gone in the shortest possible time. "We'll make room for it."

"Ta very much," gushed the medium as she placed a poster in the instructed location and turned to leave. "Expect I'll see you again, Inspector. Phworr!" Vigorously she waved the air in front of her face. The Sellers exchanged another look as she walked out, shaking heads in dismay at their near neighbour's nuttiness, not to mention her awful discourtesy.

"We'll be on our way too," said the Sergeant with a light tip to the unhelmeted head.

"See you next month, Ivor," sighed Ernest. "Let us know how the crops come on."

"Will do."

"Good luck with those cases, Inspector," added his wife. We bade them farewell and returned to the stifling heat of the High Street, the tinkling of the doorbell still ringing in our ears. The overpowering smell of soft cheese would soon be a distant memory.

"She could be your WPC," mused the Sergeant as we strolled past the Community Hall on our way to the next venue.

"Brunhilda?"

"No! The crazy woman. She would probably know what was going on before it happened," he said with a hearty chuckle.

"You *are* joking."

"Yes, sir. I am joking."

We were about to step into the post office when Penelope stepped out, having no doubt left a wad of posters with Nick Down.

"Oh! Sorry, Inspector. Didn't see you coming." And out came the smoke.

"That's OK," I said. "By the way, did you say you were a member of the Dangerous Pastimes Society?"

"Dribble & District Dangerous Pastimes Society, yeah. I did. What about it?"

"What do you do exactly?"

"Anything that's dangerous. Abseiling, paragliding, bunjee jumping, bronco riding, you name it. Wanna join?"

"No thanks. Life's dangerous enough as it is. But I wonder. Did you ever meet Duncan Jollygoode?"

"Jollygoode. Jollygoode. Where have I heard that name? No idea. Why do you ask?"

"He was – is – an Associate Member."

"No, sorry. Can't remember ever meeting anyone with that name."

"All right. Well, thank you," I said, inviting her to move on. She moved on. I turned to the Sergeant as I opened the post office door. "No, Sergeant. I think I know the very person."

The healthy, tanned smiles of Nick and Nicolette Down beamed at us from behind the security glass of the post office counter.

A Warm Reception

"How simply fab to see you, Inspector! And looking so smart!" Victoria Cake seemed quite surprised as I entered the marquee with the Constables. "I didn't spot you in church?"

"No. I'm agnostic."

"What does that mean?" Mabey whispered behind his hand.

"I don't know," Cake whispered back. Mabey sniggered with self-satisfied glee.

It was the little-awaited reception to celebrate the marriage of Angelica Green to one of the Fisher boys. Their union had been blessed earlier in the church of Saint Sebastian's, and it was evidently deemed appropriate to hold the reception in the vicarage garden. An odd choice, really, considering the discovery that had been made there less than ten days earlier. But then, I supposed, these things had to be booked months in advance, and the newly-weds weren't going to allow the loss of an insignificant life to spoil their carefully planned arrangements. I had no inclination whatsoever to witness the event, but had relented on learning that virtually the entire village would be in attendance. *"Everyone's more or less related to each other here"*, Cake had so helpfully remarked. Why so many people had nothing better to do on a Thursday afternoon was quite beyond my comprehension. Still, past research had suggested that the killer is known to his victim in the majority of murder cases, even if not actually related. And given half the chance, the killer will always, always return to the scene of the crime. If the vicarage garden murderer were local, he or she might also be at the reception, calmly sipping martinis or commenting on the bridesmaids' bouquets.

"Actually, I wasn't invited anyway," I continued. "I'm here on police business."

"At a wedding?!"

"Well, there's so little to go on. I'm clutching at straws here."

"Aren't we all, lovey. Aren't we all." Victoria took a sip of champagne as her eye started to roam. The marquee was nearly full already, but more guests kept spilling in from the sunlit lawns of the vicarage, quacking like families of geese as they came.

"To be honest, there's something I wanted to ask of you," I said, calling her back to attention.

"Ask? Of me? What?"

"I wondered if you'd care to help us out with some surveillance."

"Me? Why?" She began to look edgy.

"I need a woman." I heard suppressed snorts and guffaws from the pair beside me. "To do a job a man couldn't do." I heard overt gasps of mirth.

"I can do jobs a man can't do. That's for sure," Victoria said with a twinkle in her eye, winking at the two of them.

"I hoped you'd say that. It's just that I can't spend a night in a teenage girl's bedroom." I heard shrieks. I heard howls.

"Too right," said Victoria. "They'd have you struck off."

"So will you do it?"

"What?"

"Spend the night in the girl's bedroom?" Mabey was clutching his belly.

"What for?"

"To watch the house. The Jollygoode house. Where the dead man lives."

"Though he might not be dead," Mabey interjected through his tears.

"And he doesn't live there any more," Cake added more helpfully.

Victoria looked utterly bemused. "So it's a place where a dead man who's not dead doesn't live any more?"

"Yes. That's about the long and short of it. Anyway, there are some strange things going on out there, and I need someone to be on watch."

"Out where?"

"Upper Hooey."

"No way! Far too spooky. They're all nutters up there."

"Come on. I'll make it worth your while." I heard Ooohs from the constables.

"Now that sounds promising…"

"Fifty? A hundred?"

"Ah, she's quality, sir. You'll have to try harder than that," laughed Mabey.

"Shut up," said Cake, suddenly riled.

"No, no. I've a better idea," said Victoria. "Tell you what… Come on, you two. Shut your cake-holes, will you?" As she turned to reprimand the giggling duo, she seemed to catch sight of someone on the far side of the marquee. I sent my eye through the gathering throng to see who it could be. A sinister figure of a man was watching her from beyond the shrimp *vol-au-vents* as he calmly sipped a martini. Where had I seen him before? It was difficult to tell under his tuxedo. He gave her a small but meaningful nod.

"Er... Will you excuse me, Inspector? I have to be elsewhere."

"Of course."

"We'll catch up later," she said as she turned to go. Contrary to my surmise, she walked not towards the sinister figure but in quite the opposite direction, eventually disappearing from view.

The theme of the wedding reception was, naturally, fishery. The women wore fishnet tights and the men were encouraged to turn up with rods. The inside of the marquee was lined by a gigantic trawl net with begrudging openings left for doorways. The net was tangled with quivering slithers of kelp and other seaweeds, as well as lobsters, crayfish, starfish, shells and shreds of plastic rope. Tables were fashioned from upturned boats, tethered to fat mooring posts with frayed lengths of string. Converted rum barrels doubled up as seats. The screeching of seagulls sounded over the PA system.

Taking a look around, I could see that most of the village was indeed in attendance – the lower village, that is. The Melons were guests of honour, and yes, as I looked on, Peter was already kicking Sarah under the table. "I'm allergic to vegetables," he screamed. Sylvia Grainger and Karen Gutteridge were excitedly comparing hairstyles. Ralph Morpurgo argued the nature of reality with a Japanese guru of metafiction. Penelope Slack sat in a hypnotic trance, or perhaps she'd had one vodka too many, while the Downs were eagerly exchanging telephone numbers and underwear sizes with a newly divorced couple. Aunt Clarice was laughing happily with a friend. Victor Sheen from Curiosity Corner had arranged a display of classic cars on the drought-hardened ground outside the marquee, and was even now expounding the intricacies of double-declutching to a bemused couple as his obscenely fat wife scoffed sausage rolls. How she ever fitted into that bubble car was quite beyond me.

"Hullo there, Inspector." A voice called me from one side. Followed by another from the other side: "Hullo." It was the brothers Jeffrey and Jeremy Green.

"Sorry about the other day," Jeffrey continued, this time to Cake.

"Yes, sorry mate," Jeremy echoed, always half an octave higher.

"What about the other day?" I asked.

"The incident with the lunch box," Cake answered gravely.

"Ah yes. Well, never mind, eh?" That was a finished episode. We wouldn't want to open the lunchbox incident again, would we?

"When bearing a grudge, the boy just won't budge," Mabey interjected with a smirk.

"Oh, come on mate. We'll buy you a drink," offered Jeffrey.

"Yeah. Come on," Jeremy echoed again.

"Oh, all right. But only because it's your sister's wedding," Cake relented. Of course – they were all related as well.

"Angie lives with the parents in Dribblemouth," Jeffrey explained conveniently. "We call them the Town Greens."

"We're the Village Greens," added the brother, face as straight as a cricket bat.

"Actually, the family originally lived in the village," Jeffrey went on. "That's why we're having the wedding here. No decent facilities in Dribblemouth."

"No decent facilities," Jeremy.

"And how exactly are you related to the Cakes?" I inquired.

"Cousins," replied Jeffrey.

"We share a grandmother," said Cake.

"I see. Well, good," I said. "It's always useful to know who's related to who. Whom."

"Any luck with that missing husband, Inspector?" asked Jeffrey.

"Or the body in the garden?" added Jeremy.

"No luck at all," I replied.

"Where was the body actually found?" asked Jeffrey, recalling the coincidence of the location.

"Not a very nice thing to ask on Angie's wedding day," Cake said with a scowl.

Mabey saw a nice chance for some more sarcasm. "Yeah, let's not dwell on death, lads, we're only here to have a good time."

"OK, OK," said one brother, touchily.

"OK," said the other, equally so.

The brothers Green went off, exchanging notes of annoyance like a discordant two-part harmony. I released the Constables into the wild and took myself to the bar. Strangely, it had taken little persuasion to prise Mabey away from his day job; it must have been the prospect of drinking someone else's booze that swung it for him. Cake was related to the bride anyway, and Burley-Hogg was more than happy to remain on duty at the station. The whole village would be at the wedding, hence no trifling enquiries about lost cats and obviously no criminal activity. '*The perfect chance to dig that bean trench*', the big man had enthused.

"Wotcha Inspector," bayed Penelope Slack, evidently having awoken from her trance. Her timing was impeccable, almost prophetic; I was on the verge of ordering a drink. "I didn't expect to see you here!"

"Ah well," I replied, trying my very best to appear jovial, "nobody knows when an inspector may call. We move in mysterious ways."

"Fuck me that's funny," she said as she lit another cigarette. True to the theme of the afternoon, she wore what looked like a pink wetsuit, with pink diving goggles and snorkel around her head; only the flippers were lacking. Huge, spiky puffer-fish earrings dangled and danced at the back of her jaw, while her hair unintentionally resembled fronds of dead seaweed. I couldn't help thinking she'd taken the theme a little too literally.

"Would you, er, would you like a drink?" I offered, yielding under the unbearable weight of expectation.

"Vodka and lime please. Just the ticket, Inspector."

"Perhaps you could fill me in on some facts, meanwhile?" I asked as the white-jacketed barman made up our order without breaking into a smile.

"Yeah?"

"Yes. Why is a wedding reception held in the vicarage garden, for starters?"

"How the fuck should I know? Tell you what, though. I bet the vicar makes a bob or two out of it. Greedy git."

"I bet he does," I agreed. The po-faced barman sucked in his cheeks as he placed our drinks on the makeshift counter top in front of us.

"Your health, Inspector," said Penelope, raising her glass with fag-holding hand.

"Cheers." We drank.

"He uses this place for events," she resumed. "Rents it out by the hour. Not cheap either. All he thinks about is making money, the old turd. Their marriage is falling apart, it's just for show now. They haven't had it for years. So now she's having it off with a bellringer." How did she know all this? "How do I know? I just know. I hear the gossip. And then I think, they've just had a bleedin' body found in their garden, you'd think they'd cancel the reception. But no, that would be lost income for the 'oly man, and the Fishers couldn't give a fuck anyway. No matter that the whole village has to close down just for the occasion. So on it goes, Inspector."

The Fishers… Perhaps there could be a connection between them and the murder; the look the father had given me at the quayside was certainly nothing short of murderous. I could hardly take him in for questioning on that basis, however. I would need hard evidence for that…

"They're gypsies originally, did you know? Illiterate tossers."

"So why the boat? I thought gypsies lived in caravans."

"Their family used to live on common land in the upper village. But they had to leave when one of them knocked up a local girl and got her pregnant. Silly tart. There's a legend that says the village and everyone in it will one day be devoured by the illegitimate offspring of a virgin. The only way to save the village from its fate is to drive the girl into the sea. Being all stupid up there, they thought the folklore had come true and tried to drown her. So she escaped in a boat with the rest of the gang, gave birth to triplets and they've lived on houseboats ever since."

"So it's a kind of lore enforcement."

"Fuck me that's funny."

"What happened to the mother?"

"Disappeared soon after. Boys were brung up by their dad. There was a rumour the mother turned into a mermaid and swam off…"

There had been three shadowy figures, perhaps four, watching Susan's house that night. Could they have been the Fishers? If so, what were they doing there? Could Susan's house be connected to the story about the gypsies? Perhaps they were coming back to avenge their mother, or perhaps to reclaim their birthright, if they'd ever had one. The house might have been where the mother had lived. But I failed to see how any of this could possibly concern Susan; she was far too young to be the boys' mother, for a start. More likely the house itself was what interested them.

"Any luck with the missing husband, Inspector?" asked Penelope.

"No luck at all," I replied. It was becoming the standard answer.

"No progress on the body?"

"None."

"Want another session at my place, then?" A trail of smoke rose lazily from her cigarette as she held it at head height.

"I'm not sure it's the way forward, to be frank. I'll let you know."

"PENNY!!!" gushed a woman who, if it was at all possible, looked even more outlandish than the lizard-owning medium. She had what looked like a tasselled curtain draped over her shoulders, swirling around her body and almost down almost to her bare toes. Towels from a Turkish bath were piled high on her head and a long necklace of yellow beads swung freely around her torso. The fishery reference escaped me for the present. Penelope half-drunkenly took her leave and went off with the woman, the pair exploding like fireworks in paroxysms of excitement.

After some idle and not necessarily relevant chitchat at the bar, I went to sit at the Cake table, flanked by a PC on either side. The family had most graciously invited us to join them. Mabey's wife and boy were conspicuously absent, the wife looking after the Copper Inn, the boy playing cricket against Nilbymouth Juniors. Cake introduced me most dutifully to his kin: his mother Geraldine (she of the Greens), his father Phil, and his grandmother Granny Green. What did I think of the bridesmaids' bouquets, Granny Green asked. Weren't they lovely? The Cakes, meanwhile, wore permanent smiles and seemed utterly unaware that anything unpleasant might be happening anywhere in the world, at all.

Victoria's seat was empty.

Waiters dressed as lobsters circulated ceaselessly with a selection of drinks – champagne, cranberry juice or perhaps just both. The first course was crayfish bisque, followed by whitebait, followed by Cumberland stuffed herrings, followed by baked mackerel with gooseberry sauce, all served with greens and washed down with buckets of Chardonnay, finished off by lemon posset drizzled with lime puree in the shape of an island, served plain or with angelica.

Angelica was rather disappointingly plain. The pregnancy must have been taking its toll. Even then, I found it hard to see how she could have lured even one Fisher boy, let alone all three into her net. Perhaps their expectations of life were low.

The three brothers sat behind a long bridal table that broke all rules of wedding etiquette. Which was Declan, which Desmond and which Denholm was impossible to tell; they were virtually identical and virtually indistinguishable without their rugged woollens and sou'westers. I used my powers of detection to deduce that the one sitting next to the bride was in fact the groom. An older man, presumably her father, sat to Angelica's left, and a small, shrew-like woman, presumably the bride's mother, to the right of the groom. Each parent was flanked by a child bridesmaid, each bridesmaid by a Fisher brother.

As the guests settled into their after-dinner stupor, the brother on the far right – Desmond, shall we say – tapped on the side of his wineglass with a fruit spoon. He was obviously a master of ceremonies.

"May I, yes, all right, may I have yer attention everyone," he called, straining nervously to be heard above the hubbub. "May I have yer attention. Everyone."

"Sit down, you fool!" came a voice from the back of the marquee, followed by a round of raucous laughter.

"Get on with it!" called another voice. More laughter. The Fishers certainly seemed popular in these parts, despite their outsider status. Or perhaps they were just targets of fun.

"No, see, s'just that, may I have your attention, may I."

"You've got our attention, you twit, now just get on with it!" The original heckler, buoyed by his earlier success, was really getting stuck in now. Whole tables of revellers were clutching their stomachs in mirth.

"Right. Right. Well, I see I's got your attention, like, and—"

"Desmond, there's something in my soup!" came another call, from the side this time. "Could you come and fish it out?" The whole place was in uproar.

"All right. Very good, Arthur. Very good." The laughter subsided to a few coughs. Desmond composed himself once more. "We're here today to witness the union of our Declan—"

"Haven't they done it yet?!"

"…the union of our Declan with the lovely Angelica, whose virtues are renowned throughout the county."

"Is that what you call 'em?!"

"So, our father which art not here today, I'll now ask our Denholm, as best man, to make a toast. Raise a speech. You know."

"Speech!!!"

"Toast!!!"

"Is he the best man?!"

"Ask the missus! She should know!"

Desmond sat, completely crestfallen, and now Denholm stood to take the rudder.

"NOW WILL YOU ALL JUST SHUT YER GOBS!" he bellowed in the manner of a ship's foghorn.

The marquee fell into a shocked silence.

159

"Thank you. Now. As best man, I'd like to tell you a little story about our Declan here for the benefit of his beautiful bride…" – he paused – "Angelica." And he turned to give her a little smile. "Now, you may be thinking, what has this to do with the main story at all. Well, if you listen out, you might hear something you didn't know. When we was boys, not that long ago, one of us was given a very special toy. I won't tell you which of us it was, but the toy was a train that went chuff-chuff and made real smoke. Now that train was so precious that the other boys got jealous. They'd only been given racing cars and tractors, and none of them made real smoke. So the two boys made a pact together. When the other boy was asleep, they would sneak to his bedside and steal the train, then hide it in a place he'd never go. And secretly, they would then go and play with it when he wasn't looking. That was the plan. But each of the two boys thought he was more cunning than the other. After they'd stolen the train and hidden it, each of the boys planned secretly to go to the hiding place alone, take the train and hide it in another place that only he knew. Well, each went at his own time, planning to steal the train from the other. But when each arrived at the hiding place, he found that the train had gone. Immediately, each suspected the other of having had the same plan, which in fact was the case, and each spied on the other from that time on. And they've been spying on each other ever since. Thank you. What's that you say? What happened to the train? Simple. The first boy knew his brothers were jealous of his train. So he secretly listened to their plan. He pretended to be asleep, then followed them to the hiding place. He knew that each would plan to steal the train for himself, so he took the train from the hiding place and hid it in a box in the garden shed. And that's where it has remained to this day. What's the moral to the story? I don't know, but ever since that day, those three brothers have vowed that everything any one of them has shall always be shared with the others." Some of the guests laughed nervously, not knowing quite what he was suggesting – that all three brothers would share Angelika? Denholm raised his glass. "And so, I'd just like to say… Cheers, Declan!"

"Cheers, Declan!" echoed the throng.

"And Angelica!" they added. Declan glowered murderously at his brother on realizing the truth about the train.

Desmond stood up again. "Yes, thank you, and now—"

"Not him again!!"

"Boo!" More laughter.

160

"Ha ha, now I give you the father's bride. The bride's father."

"Farther than who?!"

"Come on, Gerald!" cried a more supportive voice.

Gerald Green stood up – a big, ruddy-faced man with a large nose. "Ladies and gentlemen," he started in a tone more befitting the occasion. "All the world's a stage, and all the people in it are just, you know, actors. That's the trouble with Shakespeare. He's full of bloody quotes!" A ripple of amusement did the rounds. "They have their exits and their entrances, but one man in his time plays many parts. You see, we're all actors in some kind of play. If you like, we're characters in a story. We must be! How else can you explain my lovely daughter Angelica's amazing journey to reach this day? It must sound like fiction. And you really have to ask yourself – is Declan the fisher, or the fished? For my Gelly trawled the seven seas searching for her little fishie. She may have caught some sprats along the way" – he glanced across at the other brothers with an ironic smile, which they returned – "but now she's got her Declan. She's got him hook, line and sinker. How shall we have him for supper tonight, Gelly? Well, ha ha, I think I'll leave that to you. Because, you see, I'm already in my lean and slippered pantaloons, with spectacles on my nose and pouch at my side. Got it? I'm now approaching second childhood, total oblivion, with no teeth, hardly any eyes, certainly no taste, and, above all, no daughter. So I hope you'll join me now in a toast, and let's do it properly this time: to Angelica and Declan – may they fish where none has fished before!"

"Angelica and Declan!!"

"... fished before!!"

The hearty cheers of inebriated guests echoed on into the afternoon.

Until the entertainment started.

On a prearranged stage to the side of the main seating area, a clown tumbled in and started to perform acrobatics. To anyone who bothered to watch, he communicated in mime. Occasionally, he would move to other parts of the marquee, where he would miraculously reveal handwritten signs that did the talking for him. "Hello!" "I'm Albert the Clown!" "What am I doing here?" "Help! I can't speak!" "We're being watched!" "It's a conspiracy!" And others, much to the amusement of the crowd. In fact, most of those present seemed to know him; they evidently knew, at each turn, what was coming next. The Cakes were in virtual ecstasies of laughter at the slightest provocation. Albert the Clown produced an apple from behind the ear of a young girl – the

Cakes guffawed as though their lives depended on it. Albert the Clown pretended to trip over his elongated boots – the Cakes almost fell off their chairs. Albert the Clown chased a fake chicken as it raced around his body – the Cakes were ready to join the Foreign Legion.

Elongated boots.

Elongated boots.

I turned to Mabey. "Notice anything about the clown's footwear?"

"The clown's footwear?" he said dozily. "Yes, it's stupid all right."

"Aha."

A moment or two passed. Then suddenly:

"Ah! Yes!! The clown's footwear!!!" And he pulled the rubber cast from his inside pocket. The footprint he'd found in the vicarage garden resembled in every discernible way the sole of the clown's gigantic boot. Why Mabey had transferred the print to his wedding suit was quite another matter. "That's it! A perfect fit! Cinderella, you shall not go to the ball! He's our man, Inspector! Let's go and arrest him right away!"

I made a hand gesture to contain his excitement. "All right, Constable. All in good time. It could be a different clown, after all. We'll let him have his fun, then speak to him afterwards."

Cake looked distinctly uncomfortable. And then I saw it all. The tuxedo'd gentleman behind the prawn *vol-au-vents* had been none other than Derrick Fisher, the missing father of the groom. He too was notably absent from proceedings now. He had nodded that knowing nod to Victoria Cake. Now she, too, was conspicuously absent. They were having an affair! Illicit relations between new in-laws! And with a difference of thirty years between them – cross-generational relations between in-laws! Not quite incest as such, but you get the picture!

Victoria's wedding cake now stood where Derrick had last been seen. She had passed it to him that day at the quayside; he was obviously Master of the Fish Cake. Had there been something in the cake, some message, some secret billet doux meant for his eyes only?

The clown had merely been a diversion, for no sooner had he ended his act by cartwheeling into the shadows than the cutting of the cake commenced. The initial pressure from Declan's knife sent his alter ego plunging into the sea, the passionfruit coulis parting as he fell flat on his face. Then, after bride and groom had ceremoniously eaten each other (to a round of applause), the cake was carted off to be divided up. Desmond clumsily announced the first dance, a brass band started playing, and pandemonium descended.

I instructed Mabey to seek out the clown and Cake to check out the cake, then made a beeline for the vicar's table. He would know if they'd had a clown on the premises before. The Reverend Melon sat alone, forlornly contemplating a large glass of brandy while his wife danced with a bellringer and the children chased each other round the bridal table.

"Ah, Inspector," he enthused, effortlessly switching from morose introspection to 'altar persona', and with such immaculate deception! "And how are we coming along in our investigations? Any sign of our missing husband? Or our murderer? Our chameleon? Our thrower of brick?"

Why did everyone keep banging on about the cases? Was it any of their business, strictly speaking? And how did they know about it all?

"One down, three to go," I replied as obliquely as possible. "We're working on the rest."

"Good, excellent," he said patronizingly, like a professor to a first year student, or a literary agent to a new client. "You know, nothing ever happened in this village before you arrived, Inspector. You've certainly brightened things up. Well done!"

"Though of course a man's death is no laughing matter, is it."

"No, indeed not," he said with a condescending smile. "Amen to that."

"I was wondering whether you recognized the clown, vicar. It's just that we found what could be his footprint in your garden the other day."

"Ah, the clown. Yes, we booked Albert for Peter's birthday party. Everyone knows who Albert is."

"Do they?"

"Why yes! Of course they do!"

"Who is it then?"

"My dear boy, it's—"

"BLOODY HELL! FIRE !! EVERYONE OUT!!!"

The shrieking, cavorting kids had knocked over a candle on the bridal table. The table was instantly engulfed in flames, which quickly leapt up to the massive net that enclosed us. As lines of flame shot along the fibres of the net, charred lobsters and flaming langoustines came crashing down on the startled wellwishers. The bride screamed in sheer terror and literally ran out of her burning wedding dress, blazing strips of which fell away from her as she went. For those already outside, it was evidently good sport to watch her racing across the lawn, haring half-naked through the lengthening shadows towards the vicarage. "You bloody bastard Declan! You did that deliberately!" she screamed as she ran through the open door wearing nothing but her saucy bridal underwear.

"Jesus Christ! That's five hundred quid up in smoke!" wailed Declan, stamping out flames on the smouldering strips as he picked them up after her.

Guests who chose not to flee in blind panic stayed on to douse the fire. Some patiently patted out flames with sheaves of napkins while others popped champagne corks to provide a liberal spray. Lingering everywhere was the now appetizing, now nauseating smell of half-chargrilled seafood.

Non Habeas Corpus

"Eventful day, sir?" asked Burley-Hogg as if it hadn't been. His huge farm hands were turning a very large aspidistra in a corner of the public vestibule. Didn't he ever do any farm work?

"No more than any other," I replied dryly.

Reinhardt grappled with Grappelli as the Hot Club Quintet kept the score. Hot was the word; despite the lateness of the hour, the heat of another rainless summer day had gathered in a stubborn, unmoving mass that sat on the High Street like a pregnant sow.

"It doesn't look right whichever way I turn it," the Sergeant sighed with a disconsolate shake of the head. "I've never been so flummoxed by a pot plant."

"Get rid of it then."

"Ah, but I can't, sir. It's been here since Victorian times. In those days the aspidistra was a sign of social standing, now it's a kind of joke, but the aspidistra has to stay at all times. It's a long-suffering member of the village community. Look here, sir." He pointed to an ageing photograph on the wall. It depicted a happy family of seven, well endowed with the Victorian virtues of charity and respectability, orderliness, obedience, thrift, temperance, fidelity, self-reliance, self-discipline, cleanliness, godliness, industry and self-improvement. "This picture was taken right where you're standing now. That's my grandfather, Constable Hogg, the village bobby back in 1893. Have you ever seen such a moustache! There's his wife, my grandmother Jemima Burley. A kind soul she was. She would never even hurt a fly. It did help that she was myopic, mind. And there are the five children. Three girls, two boys. The boy picking his nose is my father Jack. He was to become a Chief Superintendent in the city, sir. But he still kept a hankering for the country, and it was he who bought the farm with his retirement pension. Son, he said, which do you want to be, a policeman or a farmer, and I said 'Both'. The girl curled up on the floor is my Aunt Ada, the only surviving member. She lives in a town house near Nilbymouth. And there at the back is the aspidistra. You'll see it's hardly changed in all that time. Grown a few millilitres, that's all. Oh, and there's been another body, sir."

"—What??!"

"They've found another murder, sir."

"Why didn't you tell me?"

"I just did, sir."

"When? Where?"

"Just now. I just said it."

"No, the body, man! Where is it?"

"Oh, the body. Yes. Down by the old railway, sir. The call came in a few minutes ago."

"Our missing husband, perhaps?"

"Could be, sir." Ah – the elusive Mr. Jollygoode at last. A body come home to roost. Perhaps. "Except the caller did say it was a woman."

"A woman...? Do we know who?"

"No positive ID as yet, sir."

My mind was racing. It couldn't be Susan – *please*. But then everything would fall into place. Sinister figures had been watching her house. The Fishers, say. Perhaps I'd been right in my surmise: the house had belonged to their missing mother's family and they wanted to reclaim their inheritance. Except that, rather than go through the tedious process of a legal challenge, they'd decided simply to bump everyone off. They'd already done away with the Jollygoodes, and Susan's husband, if she'd ever had one. Now they'd done away with her, too. But that still didn't explain why she'd been hiding her identity, or that of her 'husband'. And in any case, how could the Fishers have committed murder this afternoon? They'd all been at the wedding reception. A pretty decent alibi, and with almost the entire local police force in attendance. Then again, the father had disappeared... So had Victoria... Could our charming patissière possibly have been an accessory to murder? If so, we had been well and truly duped, our minds cleverly diverted from our duty to the community.

"The railway, you say?"

"That's correct, sir."

"Right." I made a bolt for the door.

The Sergeant called to stopped me. "I think you'll find it's closer through the back, sir. Down past the vegetables, carry straight on and there's a path down to the tracks. You can't miss it, sir."

Guitar solo.

It was when the brambles and bracken had reached my knees that I began to regret taking the short cut. Was it too late to turn back? Yes it was. The towering slope behind me seemed just as forbidding as the path ahead. To go back would have meant a loss of crucial minutes, not to mention the loss of face with Sergeant Burley-Hogg. Besides, how else could I explain the loose threads and snag marks on my hired suit, without the excuse of having waded through the thorny thicket at the bottom of the police station vegetable plot?

I could buy the suit off the costumiers, I thought as I continued down the slope. It was starting to level out anyway. I lifted a vicious-looking bramble and stepped over another, my hand brushing against a gigantic stinging nettle in the process. Good job the blackberries weren't ripe yet. Those stains would never have come out.

Had the Sergeant ever actually used this short cut, I wondered, as a small rodent scurried across my path and back again. Yes, he must have done, when the railway was still in service. He would have slipped down to catch the afternoon train over to his Aunt Ada's town house in Nilbymouth. Of course, everything would have been neatly trimmed in those days, brambles kept firmly in check. Discipline, self-reliance, industry. The path would have been broad and green, the grass freshly cut. It would have led directly onto the platform, taking him 'station to station', as it were, and sparing him the inconvenience of having to pass the ticket office and pay for his journey. He would have enjoyed his tea and crumpet at Aunt Ada's, exchanged gardening tips with his erstwhile mentor of the green finger, and arrived back at the station before anyone had noticed the petunias needed watering.

A bee skimmed past my ear to wake me from my reverie. I was now at the foot of the slope, where the barely visible path led through a blanket of nettles to a crooked gate. Beyond the gate lay a flat expanse of weed-infested wasteland – the railway. As I reached the gate, I turned to look back. The police station, and the other buildings on the High Street alongside it, were now entirely hidden behind a mound of brambles and thorny undergrowth that instantly squeezed all hope from the soul.

I pressed down on the rusty latch and forced the creaking gate open, then stepped onto the discoloured gravel of the old railway line. Which way to turn? The Sergeant hadn't said. My signal hut stood to the right. Instinct told me to go that way.

The soles of my shoes crunched on the gravel of the track as I walked past the derelict station building. None but the ghostly shadows of bygone ticket collectors called out to stop me. The old station mistress sat knitting in the disused waiting room; the squeaking of her rocking chair could be heard clearly above the ghoulish silence. Huge sprawling thistles grew out of cracks on the platform above my head. Rooks nested in the chimney of the ticket office. The phantom of a slow freight train passed me on the opposite track, a ghastly line of oil wagons sliding gloomily past.

As I emerged from the shade of the station, I could see a small group of people huddled together near a bend some fifty yards down the track. Amid the huddle, an indeterminate lump lay on the ground, covered in a blanket.

"And you are?"

A youngish man in black leather coat and sunglasses arrogantly lifted his chin to challenge me as I approached the scene.

"Gaskett, Inspector Gaskett," I mumbled, vaguely brandishing my ID. "What's going on?"

"Ah, it's Gaskett, is it?"

"Yes, that's right. What's going on?"

"I'm afraid I'm not at liberty to divulge." The man lifted his eyebrows to suggest superiority.

"But there's been a murder!"

"Has there?"

"And who are you, anyway?" I demanded, disregarding his attitude. "What are you doing here?"

"Dribbleside County Constabulary," the man replied with infuriating calm. "This is our case now."

"You can't do that without consulting me! I'm in charge here!"

"In charge, are you? You sure of that?"

Another man, crouching over the indeterminate lump, called my inquisitor over and handed him what appeared to be a comedy nose. A freak gust of wind carried their conversation to my ear.

"It's her all right."

"Jollygoode?"

"Susan Jollygoode. No doubt about it."

"Right. Clear this lot up. And get rid of these ruddy onlookers."

Actually, there were no onlookers – just me and five or six men in black leather coats and sunglasses. Two of them, hefty fellows with thick elephantine necks, led me away from the scene with a degree of coercion I felt somewhat excessive.

"I'll be reporting this to Commissioner Painter," I protested yet.

"Don't worry. He's given the go-ahead," said one of the DCC henchmen.

"Yeah, he's given the go-ahead," said the other with a throaty chuckle that seemed almost threatening. I half-stopped and half-turned in a final attempt to reimpose my authority, only to find their steel-like arms propelling me away from the track bed. One of them grasped me a little too vigorously on the forearm. I felt a pain shoot up to my shoulder. The other bent my thumb back to force me along. The pain was excruciating.

Susan was dead. Of that I was certain. I walked the few remaining paces to my hut in a state of numb confusion.

Dear Aunt Clarice,

I'm afraid it's too late. They've taken over. They've started appearing in scenes on their own, when I'm not even there. I'm not in charge any more! I tried to get outside more, as you suggested, but it only makes things worse. The outside is full of demons. I think they've been drugging me. They must have been. Will you come and visit me? That's the only thing I can hope for now.

love

John

Afterlife

Susan was dead. Murdered. How? Why? When? Who by? What with? Was her death connected to the husband's disappearance, or the body in the vicarage garden, or both? So many questions rushed at once to

168

squeeze through the tiny portal of my mind. As now seemed almost customary, I'd fallen into a deep slumber almost upon entering my little hut. But a solid night's sleep had done nothing to offer satisfactory answers; it had merely raised more questions. Like, why was I no longer on the case? And why did it so interest the Dribbleside County Constabulary?

"There is no Dribbleside County Constabulary," Bob said calmly as a light spray of summer drizzle coated the windows of the hut.

"—What?!"

"In your confusion you have overlooked that fact. There is no Dribbleside County, so therefore there can be no Dribbleside County Constabulary."

"Of course! There is no Dribbleside County!"

"And if you go down to the tracks today, you'll find no body there either."

I passed through the jungle of cranks and levers to reach the window at the rear of the hut. It would once have afforded an unobstructed view of the railway line, that being its original purpose, but trees and undergrowth had grown to block the view. Even so, enough of the weedy gravel beyond could be seen to suggest that my visually challenged companion was right, as usual. There was no huddle of people, no indeterminate heap on the ground. Well, of course there wasn't – it was the following day. They wouldn't have left the body there overnight. More to the point, though, there was no crime scene tent surrounded by Police Keep Out ticker tape, no forensic specialists in white space-suits taking photographs. Nothing.

"So… Who were they? What did they want?" I asked dimly.

The telephone rang. Miss Marple pricked up her ears. I picked up the receiver.

"John, I'm frightened," said the voice.

"Susan??"

"I know I shouldn't call you here, but—"

"But you're dead!"

"Well, that's it John. I'm not!"

"Not what?"

"Not dead, John, I'm not dead!"

"You're not dead?"

"I'm not dead, John. What are we going to do?"

"We? What do you mean, 'we'?"

The voice hesitated. "Is there someone there with you, John?"

"No, just—"

"Can we meet tonight? We need to talk."

"Very well... Where?"

"Behind the old windmill. Six o'clock this evening."

"All right..." The phone went dead.

"Did you see the body?" asked Bob.

"Well, no... I saw something that looked... like it could have been a body..."

"But you couldn't be sure who or what it was? You couldn't even be sure a murder had been committed in the first place?"

"No... They said her name... And I just assumed..."

Nothing should ever be assumed. I should have known that. I'd assumed the indeterminate lump to be a body, on the Sergeant's say-so, based on a telephone call. I'd assumed the body to be Susan's – because I'd instinctively feared as much, because the men in the trenchcoats had said as much. Or so I'd thought. I'd assumed they were undercover agents, because they *hadn't* said as much. And now I was assuming Susan wasn't dead, after all... Because the voice on the telephone had said as much. But had it really been Susan's voice? It could have been someone impersonating her. It could have been a pre-recorded message. It could have been a ghost. But no. Ghosts don't make phone calls. Perhaps I'd imagined the whole scene. Perhaps it was some kind of practical joke. Perhaps this. Maybe that. Possibly the other. Where was the truth? My head was reeling.

With the six o'clock rendezvous weighing heavy on my mind, filling the rest of the day with meaningful events was not the easiest of tasks. Mabey had his feet on the table and was contemplating the point of a pencil when I arrived at the station. Both he and Cake had vanished amid the confusion of the marquee fire. I could have used their help in directing the public away from the scene, cordoning off the area and generally assisting in the firefighting effort. But at that precise moment they were engaged, at my behest, in fruitless searches for clowns and clues in wedding cakes, only to reappear empty-handed once the entire venue had been reduced to a smouldering pool of firehose water. As we stood by helplessly, watching the last damp scraps of someone's ruined afternoon being pulled away from the scene, I couldn't help wondering what on earth we were doing there in the first place.

The Boy with the Thorn in his Side was one of Mabey's suggestions.

170

"Dates us a bit, doesn't it," he said as he sucked on the blunt end of his pencil. "And brings the tone down. Greatest English poet of the last fifty years."

"Never mind that," I snapped. "Have we made any progress on the new murder case?"

"What new murder case?" he asked with unconcealed insolence, tapping the pencil on the tip of his nose.

"For Christ's sake, haven't you heard?"

"Heard what, sir?"

I looked to the heavens and back again. "Another body was found yesterday, down on the railway line. When I went to investigate, I found a group of men in sunglasses claiming to be from Dribbleside County Constabulary."

"There is no Dribbleside County Constabulary."

"*I KNOW THAT!!!*"

"All right sir. Keep your hair on." Mabey raked the point of his pencil through the bristles of his goatee beard.

I loosened my collar melodramatically. "So. The Sergeant told you nothing?"

"Nobody tells me anything, sir. A dickie bird is what I have not heard. And anyway, Sarge hasn't come in today."

"Oh? Why's that then?"

"Sheep had dysentery. Or something." He twiddled the blunt end of the pencil in his ear. The Sergeant's absence seemed merely to magnify Mabey's lack of respect. It was obvious that Burley-Hogg, and not I, was the figure of authority in these parts.

"Right. Well, as soon as Cake gets in, I want you down on that railway line. Scour the area."

"Right you are, sir. You'll have me down on the railway line, which of course doesn't exist any more. I presume you mean the old railway trackbed. Oh, and by the way. The Commissioner called."

"What did he want?"

"He wanted to know why we hadn't solved any of the cases yet. Didn't we realize it reflects badly on his thirty-year record of never failing to solve a crime? He's got a big regional conference coming up and he doesn't want the other Commissioners laughing at him behind his back. Specially as he's due for a national commendation and he's been invited to Buckingham Palace. He wouldn't be able to look the Queen in the eye, he said. And then I told him about the fire at the wedding reception."

"Was he mad?"

"Hopping. Why didn't we get it cleared with health and safety first. Why didn't we rescue the lobsters. Didn't we realize it reflects badly on his standing as Honorary Chairman of the Regional Association of Seafood Victuallers? I pointed out that we were just village bobbies, not a government enforcement agency. He said Shut up and get me the Inspector. I said you weren't in yet, probably having a lie-in with a naked photograph of Susan Jollygoode. Then for some reason he just went into a rage and slammed the phone down."

"Hmm. That didn't go too badly then."

How I would explain that there'd been another murder and that I'd allowed the body to be carted off by a shady bunch of confidence tricksters was another matter altogether.

I needed to buy some time before I could face the roaring torrent of Commissioner Painter's abuse. All these highly improbable events must be connected in some way. If I could only find the connection, then I would at least have something with which to offset his rabid glare from my bungling incompetence.

"*How to Appear in Control Whilst Others Are Losing Their Heads*" was a secret supplement to the standard issue MoH Policing Manual (1949). It had never been used and was sadly neglected. As I turned the cover, a small moth flew out from between the Contents Page and the Introduction.

The title didn't strictly match my situation, to be sure. If anything, everyone else (with the probable exception of Commissioner Painter) seemed perfectly calm, as if they all knew something I didn't. But inside my head swirled a maelstrom of angst. Events that were already quite beyond my control seemed merely to be mounting in scale. How could Cake still be at his bread oven, Burley-Hogg still watching over his flock and Mabey still chewing a pencil with his feet on the table when such terrible events were unfolding?

"The key is always to appear in control, even when you are not," the supplement started. "For this purpose, it is essential that you are accompanied at all times by junior staff who appear less capable than yourself." That was actually no problem. "Make yourself appear busy and never give the impression you have time to spare." So what was I doing reading a book? "Always be on the move. Be curt to others to the point of rudeness. Ignore notes and messages. Never do yourself what you can delegate to others. Always appear to have an undisclosed plan that is beyond the comprehension of those around you. When the truth of a case is revealed, nod knowingly, even when it is as much a surprise to you as it is to everyone else. Be on familiar terms with journalists, tradesmen, artisans and labourers, whom you must appear to consider well-meaning rogues. On the odd occasion, mysteriously and quite unexpectedly work through the night on piles of papers or old case files. This need consist of nothing more than transferring the papers from one pile to another, but do be sure the piles are never neat. Rough corners must protrude at random angles and the occasional newspaper clipping is *de rigueur*. It will help if you can smoke while fulfilling this task. Do your best to create the effect of billows filling the room, indicating that you have been sitting in the same position for a considerable length of time. If you are a non-smoker, what are you doing in the police force. Alternatively, you may prefer to make do with a bottle of whiskey – *less than half full, never more* – and a glass beside it – *ditto*. Of course, the brand of whiskey must always be a cheap one, blended, not a single malt from some remote Hebridean island. Finally, make sure you are never seen in a bubble car."

That last note seemed prophetic indeed. Given that bubble cars didn't even exist in 1949, I took it to be some kind of metaphor. In any case, times had changed since the Manual was first printed. Congestion on roads and public concern over atmospheric pollution had rendered the point somewhat moot, whatever was meant by it; you *had* to think small these days.

"Oh and by the way, they've got something for you at the post office," Mabey called rudely from the staff room.

What could the Downs possibly have for me? I was sure I'd already made my feelings clear. "It's a parcel of some sort," Mabey said to answer my unspoken question.

"Why couldn't they have brought it here?"

"Personal mail. Has to be signed for in person, the postwoman said."

"Couldn't you have signed for it?"

"Official mail only, I told her. All personal mail to be dealt by the person it's addressed to. Otherwise I would become liable for your property, and I'm not insured for that. What if it went missing whilst it was in my possession? It doesn't bear thinking about. This is a police station, not a personal courier service, I said. We have serious work to be getting on with, stamping out crime, apprehending villains, protecting the public. What would happen if a bank was robbed while I was signing it? And anyway, I didn't have anything to write with," the idiot concluded even as he flicked his pencil up and caught it in mid-air.

It was my chance to get out, after all. And this I now did, disregarding the supplement and leaving Mabey in charge. I had to get away from the station, away from the village – as far away as possible. I needed time to think before I could face the Commissioner. I would collect my parcel from the post office, then drive off to some secluded spot. There I would ponder matters further.

SKYNEWS (PA): Three laptop computers containing payroll details for the Metropolitan Police Service have been stolen. The computers were stolen from the London offices of Angelica CMG, responsible for the Metropolitan Police's pay and pension services. The Metropolitan Police said in a statement: "We are here to protect the public, not to keep a twenty-four hour watch on computers. What do you think we are?! Anyway, we believe the risk of staff members falling victim to either fraudulent activity or identity theft is minimal if not non-existent."

Time is Ticking

On climbing the timeworn steps to the post office and opening the door, I was surprised to see a different pair of faces sitting there behind the counter. In the usual places of Nick and Nicolette Down were two complete strangers of distinctly Asiatic origin. They clearly didn't have a single clue what to do; both of them were busily consulting manuals, or their customers, to decide whether a letter was standard or large, a parcel small or bulky, a stamp first class or second. Luckily, there were few who would tax their resourcefulness at this late morning hour, but come five o'clock, the queues would surely be stretching down the High Street.

"Road tax? Now what must you give me for that?" asked the subcontinental gentleman.

"I've got everything here," replied the young woman in front of me, passing a sheaf of documents under the bulletproof glass.

"Ah good," said the stand-in postmaster with a carefree smile, "I'm glad you have your wits about you today," and the deal was concluded in no time at all.

A senior officer of my standing should never need to stand in a queue. I should have had lackeys doing this kind of thing; I should have

174

been able to click my fingers and the job would have been done for me. Where had everything gone so horribly wrong?

"Gaskett's the name," I said as I advanced to the front. "I believe you have a parcel for me?"

"Ah yes," said the man, whose name, according to the badge on his jacket, was Nick Down. "Where would that be, I wonder?"

"Barcels are over there," interrupted his partner, whose name, curiously, appeared to be Nicolette Down. She pointed to a disorderly pile of bulky mail items at the back.

"Ah yes," said the man, swivelling to reach the pile without leaving his seat. "And what did you say your name was?"

"Gaskett."

"Does that begin with a C or a G?"

"Pardon?"

"I am most apologetic, but was it Casket with a C or Gaskett with a G?" In his vernacular, they sounded the same.

"Gaskett with a G."

"Ah yes, thank you most kindly sir." And he rummaged. "Casket. Casket. Casket. Let me see…"

"I wouldn't want to be called Inspector Casket. Makes me sound like a funeral director," I quipped.

"Ah yes," the man said with the same carefree smile, ignoring my well-constructed jibe. "Here it is. A parcel for Mr. Casket. Addressed to the police station. Were you in custody there? Well, that's none of my business."

He lifted the bulletproof partition and passed a box-shaped parcel through the gaping hole. That would have been the window of opportunity for anyone with a gun.

"Don't I have to sign for it?" I asked, knowing instantly that the man wouldn't have the faintest idea.

"Ah yes, do you? Does he?" he asked his partner.

"Barcels must be signed for," she replied without turning.

"Not always," weighed in her customer, a man wearing knee-length shorts, who appeared to be a dry stone walling specialist.

"Well, mine had to be signed for," I protested, wasting more time. "Otherwise what have I come all this way for?" The ersatz postmaster ran his finger down a clipboard in the meantime.

"Ah yes, it does have to be signed for. Would you pass the parcel," he said, opening the hatch again. "Pass the parcel back."

175

"What for?" I asked feebly as I passed it through.

"I can't give you the parcel until you have signed for it, you see, strictly speaking," he explained as he took the parcel and handed me the clipboard instead. "Please sign and print your name."

"By the way," I said as I did his bidding, "where are the Downs?"

"The Downs? I don't know. Aren't they near Brighton?"

"Silly," chided the fake postmistress. "He means Nick and Nicolette."

"Oh, the Downs! Yes. Golly me. Well, we met them at a party for swinging couples and they suggested a threesome with the delicatessen. We're calling it a 'shop swap'. If all goes well, we will become sleeping partners in each other's businesses. So they're looking after the deli, the deli people are minding our grocery and we're working here, you see. Dilip and Javindra Patel. We're from Bombay originally, did I tell you? We have to call it Mumbai now, but it's still home!" He laughed, then gave a little bow of the head to underline the belated self-introduction.

"Pleased to meet you," I said to return the compliment. "John Gaskett. Inspector John Gaskett."

"Oh!!! *Inspector* Casket!" yelled Dilip Patel, now suddenly reaching enlightenment. "You are *the* Inspector Casket? The *police* Inspector Casket?"

"That's right."

"Well, that is a very great pleasure to meet you, sir. We have been hearing about your successes, oh yes we have. And what about the disappearing husband? Is there any sign of him yet?"

"No, I'm afraid not."

"What about the body in the vicar's garden?" asked Javindra. "Do you know who it is yet?"

"And the brick through the window, sir?" continued her partner. "Who could have thrown it?" Curious. Even people I'd never met were asking the same questions.

"Have no fear," I answered with false reassurance. "We are making our enquiries."

"Oh yes, you must be making your enquiries," said Dilip with several vigorous nods of the head. "But it is highly odd, isn't it. There were never any incidents in this village before your esteemed arrival. You must have carried them here with you!"

"Road dax? What must you give me for that?" the woman was asking her next customer as I gladly slipped away, clutching the box-like parcel under my arm.

I started back up the High Street towards the station, passing the tanned smiles of Nick and Nicolette in the deli as I went. Nick pointed at the parcel and gave me the big thumbs up. Nicolette mouthed "An olive or three?" A wave of the hand sufficed to answer both.

It was then that I first heard a ticking. The parcel I now held in my other hand – a perfect cube, yes, perhaps eight inches by eight – was ticking. There was definitely a ticking.

It was a bomb. Someone had sent me a bomb. A time bomb. I was carrying a time bomb. Think! What to do? Drop it and run of course! But then several desirable Georgian properties in the High Street would have been destroyed by the blast, their occupants reduced to atoms. It was my duty to protect the public from harm, not blow them up. I could have hurled it over the rooftops, aiming at the meadows beyond; but it could have fallen short and landed in a child's back-garden paddling pool, causing a much bigger splash. There was only one thing for it: I would have to carry it to safety. The bomb would obviously not be triggered by being moved; it had, after all, survived transportation by the Royal Mail, whose employees take great pride in their ability to hurl things. I took off my jacket – gladly so, as the heat was once again stifling – and wrapped it around the deadly missive for good measure. And I started to run. Run. Run. Run. I raced past Bill the Butcher's, legged it past the police station and hared past the Copper Inn. I was heading for the open fields, where I would deposit the parcel safely before calling for reinforcements. Run. Run. Run, run, run.

But as I ran, I started to think again. If the bomb was not triggered by movement, then it must surely have been timed to explode at a specific moment. When? Soon after I picked it up at the post office? Perhaps not. How could they have known I wouldn't be at the police station when it arrived – whoever 'they' were? How did they know what time I would pick it up? Why hadn't it gone off during its morning sojourn at the post office? There was only one answer: it must have been set on a twenty-four hour timer, primed to blast me to smithereens as I lay in bed that night. Perhaps my haste was not so wise after all. Besides, by agitating it as I ran, I could have set it off prematurely after all.

But then again, surely I would have opened the parcel before going to bed? That settled it. The bomb was set to explode when the parcel was opened.

Who had sent me this murderous pandora's box? I stopped to examine the parcel. The sender's address was illegible, the postmark smudged. That was only to be expected; only a fool would leave a return address on a parcel bomb. But since it was 'signed for', the post office would surely have some record of the sender, even if only the place of origin. The problem would be how to prise that information out of the Patels. No, it could wait. The first priority was to get the thing dismantled, or else exploded in a controlled environment.

Sergeant Burley-Hogg had finally appeared and was brushing earth off a hand hoe as I walked back towards the station. He'd made good use of his idle hours to brighten the station's appearance with window boxes, flower borders and hanging baskets. The front of the building was awash with flowering plants of all colours, a tribute to the Sergeant's profess-ional dedication.

"Weeds'll grow in any weather," he grumbled grimly as I approached. "Specially if you keep watering them like I do."

"And how are the sheep?"

"Sheep? What sheep?"

"I hear you had ovine problems," I said, wishing I'd come straight to the point.

"Oh, it was nothing really, sir. Nothing a good flushing out wouldn't fix."

"Good. Good. It's just that I've got a bomb here." I weighed the cuboid package up and down in my hand.

"Oh yes? And how do you know it's a bomb sir, if you don't mind my asking?"

"It's ticking, that's how."

"Couldn't it be a clock?"

"Who would send me a clock?"

"Who would send you a bomb?" As usual, the Sergeant had his mind planted firmly on the ground.

"All right, let's say it's either a clock or a bomb," I posited. "How do we find out which? One: we open it. If it's a clock, all well and good. If it's a bomb, we're history. Two: we explode it. If it's a bomb, all well and good. Our lives are saved for later use. If it's a clock, all well and good. All we've lost is a clock. And I don't know who sent it anyway."

The Sergeant silently placed his hoe against the wall and went inside to call the Regional Bomb Disposal Unit. As if to test his conviction, he then took the bomb to the foot of his vegetable plot, where a whole season's hard labour would have been ruined if his surmise were proved wrong. "I know a bomb when I see one," he said, "and that is not a bomb." He probably knew what he was talking about, having served in North Africa. But I was taking no chances.

We sat eating sandwiches as we waited for the Unit to arrive. Home-cured ham from the Sergeant's farm, cucumber from the vegetable plot and yesterday's bread from Cake, who had yet to make his appearance. Mabey was nowhere to be seen – still scouring the railway track, no doubt.

"Oh, and by the way sir," Burley-Hogg somehow managed to utter, with moistened clumps of wholemeal bread wedged into all the gaps between his teeth. "The Commissioner called."

My heart sank. In all my concern over the bomb, I'd clean forgotten about the Commissioner. An irascible man at the best of times, he would now be bouncing off the walls.

"Oh?" I said disingenuously. "And what did he want?"

"He wanted to know where you were, for a start."

"What did you say?"

"I said I didn't know, sir. Because I didn't know."

"And what did he say to that?"

"Oh, I couldn't repeat what he said, sir. And then I told him about the body on the railway line. Or the lack of it."

I made immediate preparations for the journey to Dribblemouth. I would think of my excuses on the way.

My little bubble car sprang into action with a familiar phut-phut-phut. I'd grown somewhat accustomed to her quirks, her failings, and had come to see her more as a friend now. Together we drove, away from the station, past Signal Box Lane, along the High Street towards the Dribblemouth turn. Man and machine in perfect harmony.

It was another searing hot summer afternoon. Mirages appeared on the road ahead, strange alien craft hovering on a sea of molten asphalt. I found it somewhat regrettable that the mighty Bayerische Motorwerke hadn't thought to install a cooler in this car, a suntrap already as it was. But still we chuntered merrily along.

Isetta spoke to me in Morse code, a language only she and I under-stood. A nifty transmitter had been attached to the radio telephone on her dashboard, probably put there by the Bundespost. It was the epitome of German efficiency; the postman could have delivered cable messages on the go.

The knob of the transmitter jumped up and down in excitement as we trundled along the bumpy road; its piercing 'dits' and 'dahs' were even audible above the racket of the engine. "*Straight ahead for half a mile,*" they said. "*Turn left here.*" "*Sharp bend approaching.*" This was a calm, authoritative, female voice, with a reassuringly light accent that spoke more of technical prowess than towels on beaches.

The Commissioner was not at all the raging fury I'd expected; on the contrary, he was a picture of *bonhomie* itself. I had nothing to reproach myself for, he said. Events were already beyond our control. But they would resolve themselves in time, he was sure. There was no point in trying to force things; restraint was needed. In any case, we would pull through together. We would beat this thing, knock it on the head. Every day, and in every way, it would get better and better.

I came out feeling that, well, at least someone was on my side. It even appeared that *time* was on my side. Word came through that the Bomb Disposal Unit had safely dismantled my mystery parcel – and found inside it *a clock*. And nothing else. Who would have sent me a clock and nothing else was, frankly, of less concern to me than who would have sent me a bomb. "Well, that must be a weight off your mind," the Commissioner remarked.

Dear John,

I'm very sorry to hear about your situation. But remember, you brought it all on yourself and you've only yourself to blame. Of course no one is drugging you! They wouldn't be allowed to, would they? These are just the kind of times when you have to put your trust in the Lord and hope that, somehow, he will find forgiveness for you. I know you're not a bad person, you were just acting on impulse. Now we need to get you back on the right track. As for your story, you should just finish what you started, that's what I always say. I wish I could visit, but I'm getting less and less mobile now. I'll come if I can.

love

Aunt Clarice

PS More clippings enclosed

Vicar in a Twist

Buoyed by the Commissioner's compassionate understanding, I went back to the village for an audience with the vicar. Not that I needed his spiritual guidance in any way. He'd been on the point of divulging some important information when the fire broke out in the wedding marquee; there was still plenty of time before six to continue the interrogation.

The vicarage was conveniently stuck at the far end of the village, on the road that led out to the old windmill. I left Isetta at the station and set off on foot, passing the Copper Inn on my way. That was a curious edifice, to be sure; unlike the surrounding structures, it had three storeys, each of which seemed unduly high. What made it more conspicuous was that each storey seemed to consist of just one room, making it look something like a castle tower. The gable windows in the roof merely reinforced the image.

As I passed the open door of the hostelry I could just see Mabey pouring illicit liquor into a bottle marked Remy Martin. The usual Friday night crowd was beginning to gather, the din not yet loud enough to drown out an Irish fiddler on his opening number. I found it hard but walked on by.

"Are you one of us, Inspector?" enquired the Reverend Melon as he fingered another macaroon. He appeared remarkably calm under the circumstances. For not only had a body been found in his garden, but a conflagration that could have halved the village's population had taken place there just the previous day.

"You mean…?"

"Faith, Inspector, are we in the same boat?" he enlarged.

"You're asking if I'm a churchgoer?"

"No. I'm asking if you have faith."

"God…"

"Yes, God, perhaps. That would be most welcome. But we all have our gods, do we not? It's the soul that matters in the end."

"Are you saying, as a member of the clergy, that you don't mind what people believe as long as they believe *something*?"

"Well, yes. That is more or less it, in a nutshell."

"But shouldn't you be promoting your own God, actually?"

"Well," and he laughed, "I think the days of such luxury are long gone. We have to move with the times, after all. If Mohammed won't come to the mountain, and so on. But faith is important, don't you agree. So once more I say unto you, do you have a faith? Do you believe?"

"I'm not sure. So many people believe a god to be something more or less human, yet superhuman at the same time. Not only the Christian god – with respect. It's so difficult to get away from. 'He' this, 'His' that. But there's obviously no gigantic superhumanoid out there in space, watching our every move with loving care. He's watching over us, they say in Swansea. He's watching over us, they say in Swaziland. How can he be watching over all those people? I mean, how many pairs of eyes is he supposed to have? What is he, Father Christmas?! Then you get people saying, Ah, it's not really a person as such. It's an idea, an atmosphere, a mystique. So, what? An idea is watching over us? And how is an *idea* supposed to have fathered Jesus Christ? I mean, come on."

"Sugar?" The vicar's wife eyed me sternly.

"Ah. Just half a spoon, please."

"God is not an idea. God can be real, God can be a He, if you really want Him to be," the Reverend Melon expounded with a hint of reprimand. "Inspector, I was once like you. Did you know I used to work in the entertainment industry? Yes. I enjoyed a modicum of success in the West End, Broadway, Hollywood and the Shanghai'd Theatre. I was an agnostic, just like you. I thought I had everything I needed in life. I wasn't poor, or depressed, or lonely, or ill. I wanted for nothing; every day was like a party! But one day, with no warning whatsoever, God spoke to me. You may not believe this, and there's no reason why you should. I could hardly believe it myself. I was standing backstage one day, waiting for my cue – it was *A Streetcar Named Desire*, if I recall correctly – when the creator of the universe came sidling up to me through the lighting cables and said, 'Hi, Oscar. I'm real.' And I knew He was. One moment there was no God, the next moment I couldn't have denied the fact if you'd been burning me at the stake. Now, if you're not a believer this may all seem unbelievable, and there is no way I will convince you otherwise – but God can. Take it from me, He is real and you were created to have a relationship with Him. If you're not having that relationship, your life is not complete. You may not like me telling you that, but somewhere deep down inside yourself, at some time in the future if not now, you'll know it. The Bible tells us that God never changes, that He is the same now as He was when Moses or Abraham were alive. If they met God and talked to him, so can you. But I stress, that is only my view. My inner view to which I adhere most deeply. Others will have other views. What is important is that we *believe* in something; all these individual gods are merely pegs upon which to hang that belief. If we had no belief, we would have no society. We would have nothing but chaos. Would that be preferable to an orderly society blindly following a god who is in fact six thousand million different gods? No, I don't think so. Now let me ask you something. What do you think will happen to you when you die?"

"Die? I'm not going to die."

"Yes you are. You are going to die."

"Ah, in the sense that we all have to go some time, yes."

"Amen to that. So what will happen then?"

"Happen?"

"Your soul, Inspector. Where will it go?"

"My soul will go nowhere. It will simply cease to exist."

"Cease to exist? A *soul*?" The vicar seemed to find that immensely funny. "But how do you know? You don't. It's something no one can possibly know. The afterlife, as people imagine it, could be nothing but a fantasy based on faith. But it could equally be true, something that really exists. To put it another way, the belief that there is *no* afterlife could itself be nothing but a fantasy based on our limited observation of physical phenomena. We *see* no life in a dead body, and therefore we assume there to *be* no life. But how can we really know what happens when someone dies? We can't. Because no one has ever died and lived to tell the tale. It is quite possible, for example, that after we die, we start to live in a virtual world where marvellous magical things are happening all the time. We may find ourselves doing things we always wanted to do when alive, but were never able to. Like writing a book. Flying a hot air balloon. Acting in a play. We may find ourselves in joyful, blissful union with those marvellous magical things, or governed, confused and destroyed by them. I don't mean to be judgmental – that's the Lord's job – but our reaction to these marvellous magical things, the effect they have upon us, may be the result of deeds we have done or not done in our previous, material life. If you have done good deeds, you might enjoy yourself in the virtual world of souls. If you have done bad deeds, you could find the virtual world closing you down in a most unpleasant way.

183

Death may not be the end, but the beginning of the real life, the real journey of the soul. What we're doing here is hedging our bets."

My, how the vicar liked the sound of his own voice. Was I here to take an eternity discussing eternity? No. I had cases to solve, in the real world, in the here and now. I took a sip of tea, then launched into what I felt would conclude this fruitless discussion.

"I believe the 'soul', as you call it, to be a complex and admittedly wonderful combination of electrochemical impulses governed by the brain. The brain cannot function without oxygen. When breathing ceases, the supply of oxygen is cut off, the electrochemical impulses fade to nothing, and the 'soul' can no longer exist."

"Aha! *The man of science*! But you are wrong, so wrong! So narrow in your view! The soul lives on after death, is liberated, flourishes even, goes to join the celestial Maker in the grand scheme of the heavens! We have to believe that, otherwise there is no hope. Electrochemical impulses? Pah! Next you will say the universe created itself!"

"The universe created itself. Yes, I believe it did."

Oscar Melon stirred his tea once more. A perfect right-turning spiral formed at the top of the brew. "Good. Good. Well, at least you believe something. Perhaps we can take some comfort from that."

"Actually, I'll tell you what I believe. When I was a boy, everyone told me there was a god; it wasn't even questioned. School, family, church, they all tried to drum it in. Thing is, they all believed it too. Why? Because someone like you had told them it was true. It was too much trouble for people to think for themselves, challenge the accepted scenario. Not that I was unhappy with that. On the contrary, it was very easy to go along with it all. Then one day, as I sat in church waiting for the Te Deum, it suddenly hit me. There is no God. A certain nothingness came up to me through the choir stalls and said, 'I'm nothingness.' In myself, I knew it was true. You mentioned Moses and Abraham – and that's what it's all about, to me. God is a figment that was invented in their time, for their convenience, and has no place in the modern world. That is what I believe."

"*You little bastard! I'll bloody kill you for that!*" Peter came crashing into the room, hotly pursued by Sarah.

"Sarah!" the vicar's wife gasped in shocked alarm as Peter dodged behind the sofa. "WALK, DON'T RUN!"

"But he—"

"I don't care what he did. Can't you see we have a guest?"

"Oh. Yes mum. Sorry mum."

"And, er, mind your language," added Dad. "Just you mind your language."

"Yes dad. Sorry dad."

"Now please leave the room."

The children edged their way silently past the sitting room furniture and out through the door. No sooner had they left the room than they careered off up the stairs, squealing and shouting and cursing and blinding murderously, just as they had done before.

The Melons shifted uncomfortably in their seats and exchanged mutually reproachful glances. *It's your fault, woman. Those children are spoilt! Allergic to vegetables? Whatever next?! – Huh! If you'd got off your backside once in a blue moon they'd never have turned out like that in the first place! – What do you mean?! I've been a perfect father to them! – Perfect father? You have got to be joking! Some days they never see you from dawn to dusk! – Of course they don't! I have my church work, you know! – Church?! Ha! I'm in there more than you are! – Only because you're having it off with the bellringers! – And if you'd done something in that department in the last five years that would never have happened either!*

"So," I interjected with a little cough. "What happened at the theatre?"

"What theatre?" asked the vicar, visibly flustered.

"The theatre. You were waiting for your line."

"Ah. Yes. God accidentally tripped on the main spotlight cable and I never worked again."

There was the briefest of pauses before I asked the main question.

"And who is Albert the Clown?"

"Albert the Clown is Victoria Cake. But surely you knew that."

A fragment of Shrewsbury biscuit fell helplessly onto my plate. The sound reverberated until it filled the room.

Windmills of the Mind

The clown was a woman!! I thought in wonderment as I made my way to the old windmill. And the clown was our killer? But of course! It all added up! The suspicious looks, the unexplained disappearances. The clownish footprint and the comedy nose at the respective crime scenes. It all made perfect sense now.

And yet – Victoria Cake a murderer? Sweet, bubbly Victoria Cake? Surely not! No, it made no sense at all. She was a policeman's sister, and what's more, she made cakes. No, no, no, no. No.

The old windmill stood on a grassy knoll overlooking the river. Why they couldn't have built a watermill would surely become clear. A stroll from the vicarage took me through the older part of the village, where the road narrowed and started to meander lazily. Fine Georgian residences facing directly onto the street soon gave way to modest country cottages that hid demurely behind tall hedges and colourful displays of hollyhocks. The odd Dribblesider would give me the time of day with an "*Arrr*" or an "*Aye*" or a "*Eeeee*" as I passed. As another quaint bend, another roof of thatch came into view, the whole scene started to resemble a series of picture postcards from a bygone age.

The road dipped and turned then rose again, whereupon the old windmill appeared among the open fields beyond. I'd read about it in the *Village Almanac*. It had apparently fallen out of use in early Victorian times, when the sail frames were pulled down for firewood during a particularly cold but windless winter. A village association was now trying to raise money for its restoration, which struck me as a kind of reverse Quixoticism. For the windmill no longer represented the threat of technology, but a lost innocence that some so wanted to preserve. Perhaps that was why it would never be fully restored; if complete and working, it would be too modern, too efficient. And that is why, despite the association's gallant tilting, their windmill continued to resemble a giant upturned thimble. Grasses and wild plants grew from its exposed crevices; nesting birds darted in and out of gaping holes with wisps of straw quivering in their beaks.

"What kept you?" Susan was waiting in the shadow behind the mill. She had her hair tied high, and wore what looked like army fatigues; she was obviously prepared for some kind of action.

"A plate of Peak Frean's family assortment."

"What?"

"I've been at the vicarage. Why do we have to meet here, Susan?"

"It's about the only place that doesn't have ears. No one will find us here."

"Oh. And why would anyone want to find us, actually?"

Susan eyed me sadly. "You really don't know, do you. You poor thing." She turned away and looked out over the river behind the hill. As a shaft of summer evening sunlight fell obliquely on her face, I was sure

I could see the glint of a tear in her eye. "You really don't remember, do you."

"Don't remember what?"

She turned back to face me. "You've lost your memory, John. I thought it would all come back to you. But it hasn't. You don't even know who I am, do you."

This was getting ridiculous. Each time we met, Susan was acting a scene from an entirely different movie. Her personality was split in more ways than one, it seemed – far more severely than I'd initially feared.

The woman was obviously deranged, at the very least. I had to humour her, buy some time. Her mental health was not altogether my concern anyway. Above all, I had to discover her true identity, and how she was connected with the murders in the village. That she *was* connected, in some way, was now beyond doubt.

"Are you not Susan then, Susan?" I asked, testing the water.

She sighed. "Don't you remember me asking if your memory had returned? Saying what we should do until it did? Why it was so important to do that?"

I feigned hesitation. "No… I don't remember any of that."

"You don't remember losing your memory?"

"No. I'm sure I would have remembered that."

She sighed again, this time with an air of fresh resolution. "All right. I'm going to tell you again. But you must promise to remember this time."

"All right, I'll try. I promise I'll try."

"This will take time. Let's sit down." She beckoned me onto the grass.

There was humouring, and there was humouring. My earlier desire for Susan had nosedived somewhat; it was no easy task to carry a flame for a madwoman.

"No. I've a better idea." My eye caught sight of a rowing boat tethered to the riverbank down beneath the grassy knoll. The Dribble really was little more than a dribble; perhaps that explained the name? It certainly explained the absence of a watermill. Aha! For despite the relative proximity to the estuary at Dribblemouth, the river was barely wide enough for a pleasure steamer and barely swift enough to wake a sleeping cat, but meandered inoffensively through rustic fields of scorched brown as it trickled down to the sea. "Let's go to the river. There's no one listening there. No one but pike and sturgeons. You'll be all right. And anyway, we must have been on the river before? Before I lost my memory? It'll be like old times…"

"Why, yes… We must have…" She seemed momentarily stunned. Never let the other party take the initiative. Another ploy I'd learnt in police training – and it worked. Now the dissembling Mrs. Jollygoode was like putty in my hands.

A broad gravel path led us down from the windmill towards the Dribble. On the far side of the river were meadows filled with cattle a-lowing; beyond them stood a line of trees at the edge of Nilby Great Wood. Amid the bulrushes at the riverside was a small landing stage, and there our barque awaited us, complete with oars. I felt only the briefest moment's compunction at requisitioning the property of another; but then, if stopped, I could always pull rank. *This is an emergency, man! Stand aside!* And who was there to stop us anyway? All I could see were aquatic fowl, coots circling on the river's surface, webbed feet thrashing madly in the greenish water beneath them.

"Are you sure this is OK?" asked Susan.

"You are forgetting. I am a senior police officer."

"Oh yes," she laughed heartily as she stepped in. "So you are."

I loosened the rope knot that tied the boat to its mooring, and we slipped away noiselessly into the slow-moving water. The surface swung and lilted to welcome the new arrival, little arc-shaped pockets of brightness glistening in the soft light of the early evening sun. I sat, took up the oars and began to row away from the village, accompanied by no sound but the plunging of oars into the river's deep and the plip-plop of water falling thickly from their tips as I raised them.

Susan sat facing me on the boat's honest wooden bench, propping herself on arms that gripped the hindmost edge of it. For a few minutes she gazed vacantly into the mesmerizing flow of languidly moving water. She seemed preoccupied. She tossed her head and leant backwards to watch swallows gliding and dipping over the water. She stretched an arm over the side of the boat, allowing her fingers to dangle lazily into the oncoming stream. Streaks of sunlight, reflected from the water's surface, danced and jiggled on her face. At length, she turned to look at me.

"John—"

"Not yet!"

I continued to row downstream in silence. Munching cows drifted by at head height. Mosquitoes hovered over the water, displaced only momentarily by the motion of air around our craft. Midges and gnats became mired in beads of perspiration on my forehead. Birds darted in from the river's edge and back. Plovers, wagtails, all those other ones. Curlews and kittiwakes. Over the tops of the bulrushes, the windmill and the tall tower of the Copper Inn receded into the distance behind my silent passenger. Here and there willows bent, rinsing their supple bows in the gentle flow.

A crumpled piece of paper came floating past, dancing on the water's surface amongst the duckweed and algae. It was some kind of public notice. The river's current and our own movement were so slow that I could read every word: *"Calling all Dribblesiders"* it announced. *"Say NO to the Nilbymouth Bypass! There will be a Public Meeting at"* and the rest was torn off.

Hastily pencilled over the notice was a message, almost but not quite washed off by the river's flow. *"SHE'S LYING"*, it said. Had I known then that it was written in Victoria's hand, I may have saved myself a lot of wasted time and effort. But I didn't know that then.

Even so, I still knew something Susan didn't know. The drought had become so severe that, to conserve water in the valley, the sluices downstream had been closed. Now the suction of groundwater recharge was drawing so much water that it pulled the current backwards. Miraculously, the river was actually travelling upstream.

I decided I would stop the boat at exactly twenty minutes talking time from the windmill, then let it drift back upstream while Susan tried to convince me of her story. That would give her time to empty her bag of air, but not so much that I would start to dislike her in any serious way. Meanwhile I could ascertain her true intentions, or her true mental disorder. And finally, we would be back in the village in time for a good old fashioned pint at the Copper Inn. Yes. It was good.

"Fire away then," I said as I rested the oars along the inside of the boat. "Off you go."

Susan seemed confused, as if she thought I were the one with the problem. But of course she did. She looked at me for a moment, took a deep breath, and finally spoke. "What's the first thing you remember, John?"

"The first thing I remember. What, ever?"

"Yes. What's the first thing you remember."

I gave it some thought. "Now that's a hard one," I said coyly. "Well, I suppose it would have to be... Sitting in the back of a council careworker's car... Yes, that's it. When I was two."

"So you remember your childhood?"

"Yes. Don't we all?"

"And yet you don't remember me? Anything at all?"

"The first time I saw you was when you walked into the police station."

"Oh, come on. That is ridiculous!"

"Is it?"

"All right. Let me ask you something. What do you know about the Nanosecond Protocol? An organization called DEFF? The quantum mechanics of time?"

"Nothing. None of those mean anything to me," which was not altogether true.

Now Susan appeared genuinely shocked. Her mouth was open, her eyes wide in disbelief.

"John. You are an *expert* in the quantum mechanics of time. You *control* the quantum mechanics of time! What else do you think that shed is for?"

"...Shed?"

She looked away across the river, biting her lip in apparent exasperation. For a moment, she seemed to be saying something to herself, muttering as if cursing, mouthing as if remembering...

She turned back to look me in the eye. "John, I'm your wife. You're my husband, for God's sake! It's driving me round the bend! Why can't you remember *that*?!" She put her hands to her eyes and sobbed uncontrollably. I swatted at a midge that had landed on my cheek.

This woman was sorely testing my patience now. But I had to stay calm. I had to buy more time, find out what was really going on.

"I'm sorry, Susan. I don't remember any of that."

"And for Christ's sake, STOP CALLING ME SUSAN!" she screamed. A startled pair of mating pheasants flew up from a nearby wood.

That seemed to bring her back to her senses. She looked around nervously for hidden spies, then wiped her cheeks and recomposed herself. "I'm sorry, John. I'm sorry. It's not your fault, I know it isn't. Let me explain it all again. Will you promise to listen?"

"I'll listen."

"Well," she continued, as if talking to a child who had already stretched her parental cool to its limit. "Before you lost your memory, you discovered the secret of controlling time, using quantum mechanics and the nanosecond protocol." I looked on aghast. "You were working for the government. It was all top secret, hush hush. No one was to know. The scientific community realized it was only a matter of time before someone controlled time, and the Chinese were onto it. If they'd discovered it before we did, the consequences would have been dire. They could have sent us back into the dark ages at the flick of a switch. Our own intentions were wholly honourable, of course. We needed to control time so that nobody else could control it – a kind of temporal deterrent." That seemed to amuse her. She shifted herself into a more relaxing position.

The boat drifted into the riverbank. I pushed it away with an oar.

"You cracked it late one night. Called me from the lab to tell me about it. I'd never known you so happy, you were delirious. But you had to hide it, you said. You had to hide the apparatus, the papers. Why? Because word had leaked out to DEFF. They might even have a mole in the lab. Could you put it in the shed, you said. What shed, I said. Your parents' shed in the country, you said. Is it safe? I asked. Yes of course, you said, no one would think of looking for a quantum time converter in a garden shed. So that's where you put it."

She seemed to be making it up as she went along. Still, I listened. Perhaps some good might come of it. "So then DEFF started looking for it. They ransacked your lab but found nothing. You had to disappear, of course. So you went to Holland for the plastic surgery, then came back pretending to be a police officer. The local force fell for it and gave you a job in your home town. It helped that there was hardly any crime around here in the first place. All the other officers had far better things to do with their time, so no one would ever notice you didn't know the first thing about law. Then I had to come up with a reason for your disappearance, which is why I reported you missing."

It seemed a natural place for a pause. A chub rose to the surface near our boat, seemed to gasp in surprise as it mouthed the top of the water, then turned abruptly and vanished into the depths with a swish and a plop.

"All right," I said, feeling the need to add some light relief. "If that's all true, why did you make me sleep on the sofa?"

"John. For goodness sake! We're being watched, you know that! They'd know it was you!"

"All right. What's my real name then?"

"Your real name?"

"Yes. I'm obviously not John Gaskett, am I. We made that up, didn't we."

"Well… Your first name *is* John."

"My name is John? So why didn't you guess it that night?"

"John, I didn't believe for one second you would use your real name. Otherwise I would have got the joke straight off."

Enough of this. The time had come to bring the subject round to my own interests. "What about the body in the vicarage garden?" I asked. "The body on the old railway line?"

"Tragic. Really tragic. It shows the lengths these people will go to."

"What people?"

"DEFF, of course. The two bodies were undercover agents on our side. They were tailing DEFF, but they must have blown their cover."

"So you're telling me those men on the railway track were DEFF agents?"

"What men?"

"They claimed to be from a non-existent constabulary. Said they were in charge."

"Quite probably then."

"But why did they say the dead man was Susan Jollygoode?"

"Did they? Are you sure?"

"Well… One of them said it was you."

"How could they mistake a dead man for a dead woman?"

"And how do you know it was a man?"

Susan looked away. We drifted towards the opposite bank. "Both of the agents were men. And now they're both dead. That's why I'm scared."

"All right, if you say these DEFF characters are the killers, where are they? How do I get hold of them? I'll go over there with my men and take them in for questioning."

"They'll kill you first."

"We'll see about that."

"And anyway, you're forgetting something, aren't you? You're a scientist, not a police officer. The law is not your responsibility. Your responsibility is to make sure you stay alive."

"Ah yes. I'm not who I think I am."

"That's right."

"So how did I lose my memory?"

"…What?"

"How did I lose my memory? How did it happen?"

The thimble of the windmill started to rise behind Susan's head as we drifted back towards it. Time was running out. For one who was supposed to have cracked the secret of controlling time, I wasn't doing very well. A coot made a raucous squawking noise as it skated madly over the river's surface to the other side.

Susan, or whatever her name was now, let out another deep sigh as she started to explain once more. "It all happened when you were having the plastic surgery. They made a mistake with the anaesthetic control, and there was a risk of brain damage. They gave you too much lidocaine. When you came round, you didn't know who or where you were…" She quickly lifted a hand to her mouth, evidently to control the tears that now welled up. "I explained it all to you at the clinic. I told you who you were and why you were there. Just like I did just now. You not only seem to have lost your memory, but also your capacity to remember anything at all. You'll probably forget this conversation, too. You poor, poor thing." And she started to sob again.

"It can't be easy," I said at some length, "being married to someone with a different face and no memory of you. That must be hard."

"It's hard, John," she agreed, her convulsions subsiding conveniently. "It's really hard. But as long as we're together. As long as you know I'm on your side…"

"What should we do, then?"

"We must leave the country, John. It's imperative that we act immediately. But first, we must get the quantum controller and papers out of the shed. I'll pass them to others on our side. They can send a helicopter at a moment's notice. We just need to get them out of the shed."

"OK. So why haven't you done that already?"

"The key, John! The key!"

"What key?"

"The key to the shed, of course! The shed is protected by a gamma ray device, don't you remember? No, of course you don't. First the gamma ray device has to be disabled, and you're the only one who can do that. You're the only one who knows where the key is, the key to disable the gamma ray device. You've hidden it somewhere, and no one but you knows where it is."

"God. Well, I'm afraid I have no knowledge of that." Susan put a hand over her eyes in growing impatience.

"So we'll have to try," she said. "We'll have to try and think, together, where it could be."

"All right. We'll do that." The windmill loomed high on the hill up ahead; the landing stage would soon appear round the next bend. "But that's it for now, I'm afraid. Journey's over." I used the oar to steer us around the bend. "By the way…"

"Yes?"

"What's your name? Your real name?"

"My name…?"

"OY!"

Farmer Hector Hodgkinson was waiting impassively by the landing stage as our boat approached it. He looked mad enough already, but when he saw me he was practically jumping up and down.

"*You* again! I'll bloody kill you!!" he roared. The boat was undoubtedly his.

"What's all that about?" asked Susan.

"Ah, nothing much. I've just developed a habit of purloining his property."

"Let's disembark as normal," she said with surprising reassurance. "Leave him to me."

I agreed; perhaps she somehow possessed the charm to disarm him. It seemed unlikely, though, since he stood there with legs akimbo, fists flexing impatiently with head tilted slightly to one side in that certain manner suggesting imminent violence. And so it proved. For no sooner had I stepped out of the boat – after Susan, of course – than he came rushing at me with right arm raised behind his head in the style of an Olympic javelin thrower combined with an Olympic discus hurler and an Olympic shotput chucker, and swung one almighty punch at my face.

I ducked and feinted to my right. The agriculturalist's fist swiped thin air. He lurched forward and staggered towards the water's edge, but, to his immense credit, regained his footing and prepared to launch another attack.

Then something really quite peculiar happened. Susan's right foot, arched and pointed at the tip of her rigidly extended leg in the manner of a cobra poised to pounce on an armadillo, suddenly appeared from nowhere, hung momentarily in mid-air, then delivered a powerful blow to Hector's midriff before returning obediently to its owner's side. The farmer, winded by the blow and stunned at the turn of events, recoiled and turned aghast to face his assailant. "Whaaa—" he moaned in slow motion *and* in a very deep voice. Susan now circled around him, knees bent, legs wide open and hands wheeling devilishly in the air. "*Heee-YAH!*" she screamed like some demented banshee as she dealt a lightning-quick rabbit chop to the side of his neck, then kneed him in the cobblers for good measure. The unfortunate muck-spreader keeled over forwards, groaning in shock and agony. He was completely spent, his manly challenge at an end. I couldn't help feeling sorry for Farmer Hector Hodgkinson; for not only had he had his property stolen, again, but he'd had to suffer the humiliation of a beating-up for his pains, and by a woman at that.

And I'd witnessed yet another side to the many-sided personality of Susan Jollygoode.

"Where did you learn to do that?" I enquired casually.

"I have to protect myself somehow," she replied as she dusted herself down, barely perturbed by her rigours. "We'd better split up. DEFF are everywhere now."

"Is he one of them?" I asked, proffering a chin over my shoulder towards the pathetic emasculated heap that now scrabbled about on the gravel.

"Him? No. He's just a pain in the backside, and irrelevant to boot." Her 'boot' had certainly given him a pain somewhere. "Can you get over to the house?" she asked, recovering some of her coquettish charm.

Getting over to her house was actually the last thing on my mind. "Sure," I replied with false certainty. "Just wait for me there."

"Then we'll get to work finding this key."

"Ah yes… the key."

Susan cast me a look of fond farewell, then turned and walked briskly back up the gravel path.

I would now arrest Farmer Hector for almost assaulting a police officer, and probably owning a boat without a licence. He had simply gone too far this time. I stretched myself to my full five-foot-eleven and turned to perform the duty entrusted to me as a custodian of the peace.

And he was gone. There was no sign of any farmer, no trace of any boat.

The river was still there though.

Too Many Notes

"Evening, sir." Mabey greeted me with a casual lack of concern as I entered the Copper Inn. "And what can I get you."

"A pint of Highly Extraordinary. And don't call me sir."

Mabey diligently turned his attention to the tap. "Ah, but we call *everyone* sir here, sir. Except the ladies. In that case it's madam. You could see it as a kind of etiquette, sir. One fine word all tension will defuse, then off you go and drink your booze. That'll be one pound eight and six in the old money, sir."

Quite apart from his ridiculously low and moreover impossible prices, Mabey displayed a professionalism and gentle charm that were utterly at odds with his cynical uselessness at the station; this was, after all, his *proper* job. At the same time, he was deliberately treating me with courtesy as a way of keeping his distance; he obviously wouldn't want to alienate his crowd of regulars. I was having none of it, of course.

"What's the progress on the new murder case?" I asked loudly enough. The pub was heaving with its regular Friday night clientèle; there was no point in lowering my voice anyway. Even the Irish fiddler could no longer be heard above the clamour.

"New murder case, sir? What new murder case?"

"Come on, man. We spoke about it this morning."

"Ah. Yes. *That* new murder case. I thought you meant a *new* new murder case." He plucked up a tea towel and started to wipe glasses that were already dry. "Apparently it's a bit of a mystery, sir."

"Murders usually are mysteries."

"Yes, but this one's particularly mysterious. There is as yet no evidence to suggest anything happened in the first place."

"No evidence?"

"I proceeded – I mean, *went* – to the scene of the so-called crime, whereupon there was nothing to be seen at all. Nothing to be seen at the scene. I scoured the gravel, as you suggested, though not with a fine tooth comb but with a miniature plastic rake Sarge keeps under the counter. The crime scene was of clues bereft, the body must have upped and left. So we've got no murder, no perpetrator, no motive, no clues and no victim. Not much to build a case on, is it."

A great roar of laughter came from the table at the window, where sat six or seven well-watered locals. "You should all be ashamed of yourselves," tutted the barmaid as she came away with the empties. "Keep the change love!" called back one of the inebriated pack, setting off another loud explosion of mirth.

"Did you find the clown then?" I continued regardless.

"What clown, sir?" Mabey asked back with an expression of surly disinterest.

"Must you always feign ignorance, man?! The clown! The clown at the wedding!"

"Ah. *That* clown." He lifted a shot glass from above head height and helped himself to a single malt from an optic. "Vanished, sir. Never to be seen or heard of again."

"And did you perchance discover that the clown was in fact Cake's sister?"

"Sister? I didn't know he had a sister."

"That's just what the Sergeant said."

"Are you sure you've got that right, sir?" He popped an ice cube into his whiskey after checking the coast for disapproving Scots. The coast was clear.

"Of course," I answered indignantly. "She told me herself."

"What, that she was a clown?"

"No, that she was his sister."

"So how do you know she's the clown?"

"The vicar told me," I said with diminishing confidence.

"Ah," nodded Mabey, "I understand completely. The vicar wouldn't lie, would he." He leaned over the bar towards me, lifting his chin in a manner suggesting sudden secrecy. "Cake wanted you to have this, sir." He passed his hand across the counter like a croupier's rake, then lifted it to reveal an untidily folded piece of paper.

With a quick glance over my shoulder to check for prying eyes, I unfolded the paper under the lip of the bar and read: *You might like to visit the theatre tomorrow. Victoria is in the second cast and would be glad of your support.*

Another explosion of drunken laughter erupted from the table by the window. Looking more closely, I spied the erudite features of Dr Ralph Morpurgo, Professor of Philosophy, no longer questioning the nature of reality but quite palpably drunk. His companions this time were very much of the flesh: postmaster Nick Down without postmistress Nicolette, two of the Fisher boys – the third presumably 'indisposed' with his new bride – Jeremy and Jeffrey Green, Peter Mowforth and another with his back to me, faceless. But yes – I recognized the monklike bald spot at the back of that greying head. It was the Reverend Melon, now waving his arms wildly in drunken imitation of a man falling off the edge of a cliff. Or a stage. The others all guffawed and rocked in their chairs, slopping beer onto the table top and wiping merry eyes with their sleeves.

"Our thespian crowd," offered Mabey as he rang up another pint's worth of cash. "In here every night these days."

"Actors?"

"Not all of them. Morpurgo's the fartistic director. A couple of them are stagehands. Lighting technicians. Set designers. Sound effects. Props. Front of house. Box office. Takes more than actors to put on a play, you know. Oh yes. Far more than actors."

"What about our good Reverend, then?"

"Director and leading man, of course. Always has to be in charge. It goes without saying."

Oscar Melon was evidently recounting some hilarious anecdote from his West End days, making the most of a tame audience made captive by drink. "Now Sir Michael, well, he had a habit of reading over his script just before he came on," he declared in his loudest Shakespearean boom. "Then when his cue came, he would roll the script up and wodge it in his back pocket. Every time he showed his arse, the audience would burst out laughing. And this was Ibsen's *Brand*, mind." Roars of merriment. Mowforth fell off his chair. Morpurgo entered a solipsistic coma. Jeremy Green laughed half an octave higher than his brother.

I turned back to my host. "Are they doing a play, then?"

"Something about a dog and a thief. They had the dress rehearsal tonight. Total bunch of wallies, if you ask me." I could see it wasn't quite his thing. Too many words, for sure.

"Where?"

"The Shelled Onion. Starts tomorrow. Who's next? Yes sir," he continued, turning to a fresh prospect with a little tug of his goatee.

The Shelled Onion – of course. A converted Methodist chapel in Florence Nightingale Street, annexed by the Community Hall. Often used for political meetings to gather support for anti-Nilbymouth campaigns, according to the *Village Almanac*. A curious name, to be sure; onions aren't there to be 'shelled', strictly speaking. It had reportedly been the scene of the odd kerfuffle, but since Nilbymouthers rarely ever set foot in Dribbleside, grievous bodily harm had never been known to ensue.

As I contemplated the half-fullness of my glass, I thought back over the facts as I understood them so far. Cake's sister was to appear in a play – the same play, surely, as the one being cooked up by the vicar and his cronies. She must therefore be a member of their troupe. In that case, our Victoria was not only cakemaker, clown and suspected killer but also histrionic castmember. But if she *were* the killer, why would she draw attention to herself in that way? Or was it all a smokescreen, reverse psychology? I would have quizzed the thespians there and then, if only I could reach their table. No. A more opportune moment would surely present itself.

The bar was now crammed with locals touting notes in growing desperation. I decided to sup up and head for a quieter venue. Soon my glass was no longer half-full but, in fact, completely empty. I made a peremptory '*Be seeing you*' gesture to the otherwise occupied Mabey and turned towards the door.

As I squeezed my way through the throng, a hand clutched mine and thrust something paperine into it. I grasped the paper as an instinctive reaction, then turned to identify the mystery donor. But he, or she, had already melted into the simmering crowd, leaving nothing but the back of a hooded jacket in my muddied line of vision.

I would perhaps have waded back in to resolve the matter, had I not been physically swept out into the street by a sudden surge from the madding crowd. It all had something to do with making room for the weekly indoor skittles competition, as I gathered from the cries.

Out in the relative cool of the street and the softening glow of sunset, I dusted myself down and restored my dignity as best I could. As whoops of gay merriment and the occasional sound of smashing glass emanated yet from the brightened windows of the hostelry, I fished the crumpled paper from my pocket and uncrumpled it there. "*Be at the theatre, ten o'clock tomorrow.*" The theatre – again?! Two notes directing me to the same place? Something distinctly odd was afoot, but of course, there was nothing new about that. I strode off down the street towards the station, the manly clip-clopping of my heels ringing out on deserted flagstones as the sounds of partying receded into the distance behind me.

Quantum Mechanic

"Know anything about quantum mechanics, Sarge?" I asked on my return to the police station. Burley-Hogg was closing up for the day – and that, of course, meant watering all the potted plants inside the building, not to mention the hanging baskets outside, taking careful note of all new shootlets and deformed leaves, and removing pots from east-facing windows.

"I know of *a* mechanic, sir. Cousin of mine. Good lad, reasonable rates," he replied as he continued his tasks.

"Quantum mechanics, Sergeant. Physics. Science."

"Ah. I thought you meant the other type. You know, the type that mend motors."

"Or someone who does know?"

The Sergeant fetched an aluminium stepladder from the back room. "Well now. You could ask Professor Morpurgo about that. He has a lot of recondite friends."

"Yes. I've met some of them."

"He'd be your best bet."

"Where's Cake, by the way?"

"Gone home," the Sergeant replied curtly as he mounted his ladder in the glimmering afterglow of dusk. Water cascaded from the spout of his green plastic pourer, permeated a basketful of fuschias interlaced with pink begonias that hung by the doorway, and coursed through the amply moistened soil before spattering down onto the pavement below. There it gathered up the dust of a dry summer day and formed little viscous pools, which soon linked together to form little puddles, which in turn rolled over the kerb into the street. "He has to get up early, that one."

"Yes, of course." Cake's dough, well kneaded and patted, would have to be introduced to the oven in the small hours of the morning. "Did he say anything about a play?"

"A play?" The Sergeant stepped down and shifted the stepladder to the other side of the doorway, its harsh metallic scrape disturbing the still of twilight. "A play. What sort of play?"

"At the theatre? The Shelled Onion?"

Water tumbled joyously to the waiting ground once more.

"Ah yes, sir. Hysterical, or some such name they call themselves. Yes. Something about a detective and a dog, if I remember correctly." He plucked a few withered flowers from a hanging basket. "There's a leaflet inside. Would you mind, sir?" Nipped deadheads fell from his outstretched hand into my waiting palm.

The deadheads duly found their way to the bin, and sure enough, there on the wall was a flier for the play. *Dribbleside Hysterics present a Double Bill of Spoofs on Spoofs: "A Burglary is Announced" by Chris Taggart followed by "The Genuine Sergeant Pooch" by Pam Doorstopper at the Shelled Onion Theatre, Sat-Sun 7:30pm, Sat matinee 2:30 pm.* The text was accompanied by an unhysterical cartoon of a bloodhound wearing a Sherlock Holmesian hat and cape, and, at the bottom, *With the generous support of the Church of Saint Sebastian's.*

I stepped outside again. Burley-Hogg was folding up his stepladder as watery afterthoughts still dripped from his hanging baskets onto the ground.

"What about the second murder? Any developments?"

"Well, it's funny you should ask that, sir," the Sergeant replied, suddenly growing conspiratorial. "I am of the opinion it was a hoax. A hoax call, yes."

"A hoax? But I saw the body, for God's sake! I saw those men…"

"No, well, it must have been some kind of miscomprehension, sir. No body has been found."

"No body?"

"No body at all."

"So who made the call?"

"Of that I cannot be certain, sir. I received the call shortly before your return yesterday afternoon. Sadly, the caller hung up before I could get identification."

"Did you trace the call?"

"Yes, sir. It came from a public call box in the upper village. It was a woman's voice, sir. That would narrow it down, I should think."

"But that's bizarre!" I protested. "Why would someone go all the way up there to tell us about a fictitious crime down here?"

"My point exactly, sir," said he, attaching cycle clips to his legs. "A hoax call." The Sergeant strode over to an old iron bicycle that stood by the wall. "Well, that all appears to be in order now. Will you lock up, sir?"

"Er… Yes. Yes, of course."

"Very well, sir. Good evening, then." And off he clanked down the dusty road on that old iron bicycle, leaving me with nothing but the gentle pitter-patter of water from his hanging baskets.

LONDON (Reuters): Two police officers have been arrested on suspicion of stealing sweets from their own police station. The two officers, who are free on bail, have been suspended and a number of other staff and officers have been removed from front line duty while an investigation into the "significant stock loss" is carried out, police said on Friday. The confectionery at Burley Police Station in Hampshire operates on an honour system whereby officers help themselves to food and drinks before leaving money in a tin. "The integrity of our staff is very important to us, and when we identify problems such as this, we act swiftly and positively to resolve the issues," said Chief Inspector Pat Baker.

Distance Relative

"Tell me about your sister, Cake," I said as the Constable stepped into the station the following lunchtime.

Cake looked decidedly edgy as he started to unstrap his helmet; John Coltrane did his best to calm the mood.

"Well... What do you want to know?"

"Shall we start with why you didn't mention her before? Why you didn't say she was the clown? Why she has left traces at the scene of one crime and another place that apparently wasn't the scene of a crime at all?"

"Sorry, but I don't know anything about that stuff. We don't talk much."

"You don't have much in common?"

"You could say that." He turned to the mirror on the wall and started dabbing down his sideburns.

"What if I were to tell you she's a suspect in the vicarage murder case?"

"On what basis, sir?"

"On the basis of her footprint being found near the body?"

"Highly circumstantial as evidence goes," Cake said in mid-dab, eyeing my reflection in the mirror.

"Well, who else goes round the village in clown's boots?"

"Yes, but how can we be sure the boot print has anything at all to do with the murder?"

"True, of course. But in that case, why has she disappeared?"

"Has she disappeared, sir?" Dabs done, he turned and started to adjust his uniform.

"Well, I haven't seen her, and to the best of my knowledge, no one else has either."

"Pardon me, sir, but not being seen by someone doesn't mean a person has disappeared. Or is a murderer."

"You want hard evidence? Proof that someone has disappeared?"

"Well…" Cake shifted his feet uneasily. I began to wonder if he wasn't telling me everything.

"All right then," I continued undaunted. "Tell me where I can find her. Where does she live?"

"I don't know sir."

"*You don't know?* You don't know where *your own sister lives?*"

"It's complicated, sir. We're not a close family, not particularly."

"Not a close family? But you work in the same business!"

"Yes, but that's different. That's business."

Cake was at his very best: stubbornly punctilious to the point of absurdity. If there was anything Cake and Mabey had in common, it was that they were both singularly useless at supplying information in an intelligible way.

"Very well, we shall have to track her down at the theatre," I said as I turned to enter my office.

"The theatre, sir?"

"Yes, the play. The play will be the thing."

"What play, sir?"

"*For Christ's sake, Cake!* The play, the play! The one you wrote about in your note! The Proper PC Plod or whatever!"

"What note, sir?"

The silence was life-threatening. A tumult of swifts mocked me as they wheeled high in the sky outside the open window. Cake really knew nothing about it at all. He knew nothing about Victoria, nor the play, nor the note he had allegedly written. Either he too had lost his memory, or *someone else had written the note.*

(Press Association) Speed camera administrators have apologised to a farmer after they tried to fine him for doing 85mph in a tractor. Hector Hodgkin, who runs a farm in the Ribble Valley, was surprised to receive a ticket claiming his tractor had been snapped by a camera in North Wales. With a top speed of 25mph, it would have taken Mr Hodgkin's tractor more than four hours to cover the distance from his farm in Hebden Bridge to Caernarfon, where the alleged offence took place. The farmer pointed out that not only was the tractor incapable of racking up such a speed, but he had been mending his boat at the time. Mr Hodgkin told BBC Wales: "It's a good tractor, but not that good. It can just about get up to 25mph, but that's downhill, with a following wind and no rain on the road. And anyway, I can't be in two places at the same time, can I."

Another Time, Another Place

"Here's a good one." Mabey held the Dribbleside Echo up to the light. A gamelan orchestra played as Rama did battle with the demon-king Ravana. "Irish police have told a man dubbed Ireland's dumbest crook to give up his disastrous criminal career before it gets the better of him. The unnamed man in his thirties has been arrested three times and each heist has brought him closer to the hereafter. Police took the man to a hospital at the weekend after he was hit by a lorry while making a getaway from a betting shop robbery, the Irish Sun reported. He has also been plucked from a chimney where he got stuck while trying to burgle a house, and from the ceiling of a bank where he was pinned by a security device. When they arrived at the bank he was dangling by one leg and stuffing cash into his pants. 'Go straight before you kill yourself,' the Dublin police reportedly told him."

The Sergeant gave a hearty chuckle as he wiped the leaves of an ornamental palm.

"Yeah – and?" Cake was rather less impressed.

"What do you mean, *Yeah – and?*"

"I mean, what's that got to do with anything? It's not relevant to this situation."

"Did I say it was relevant? Did I?"

"What d'you read it out for, then?"

"Because it's funny, that's why."

"I didn't think it was funny."

"Sarge did. Didn't you, Sarge?"

The Sergeant barely grunted.

"We've got two or possibly four unsolved cases, and you're just sitting there reading funny newspaper articles?" Cake continued. "Don't make me laugh."

"I'll try not to," Mabey said with a sarcastic snigger.

"All right. Imagine this was a book. Right? You're reading a book, and we're all characters in it. You've read about the missing man, and the murder in the vicarage garden, and the missing couple, and the missing body, and you're just itching to know what happens next. Does our intrepid copper find the husband? Does he track down the murderer? Is the missing man the murderer? Who'll be next? Could blackmail perhaps be involved in some way? You'd want to know, wouldn't you? You wouldn't want to listen to some lightly bearded twat spouting crap about bungling Irish burglars!"

"OY! Watch it mate!" Mabey was riled, possibly for the first time.

"No, no, that was just a metaphor," Cake said hurriedly. Though a full truncheon taller than his colleague, he was still scared witless of him. "I'm just saying, if this was a book…"

"If this was a book, a policeman wouldn't be given this bloody hairy chin! A poet in his own right wouldn't be holed up in the middle of nowhere talking to a sanctimonious prat like you! And yeah, that was just a *metaphor*, so you can shove it up your arse with the rest of it!"

"Now, now boys," Burley-Hogg refereed. "Just you watch your language."

"Come on Sarge, who's listening?" said Mabey.

"Not listening, but *reading*. What about the readers?" Cake thought he was being clever. With some self-satisfaction he took an apple out of his lunchbox.

"The readers, as you call them," said the Sergeant, "would ask me to point out that you should eat that apple elsewhere, Constable. Don't you know they let off small quantities of ethylene gas that shortens the life of flowers? Those freesias were fresh in today. I don't want them spoilt already, thank you very much."

The Constables exchanged dumbfounded glances. "Blimey Sarge," said Mabey. "That was well off plot."

"Now there you go again," moaned Cake. "If we're going to be in this book, hadn't we better to find one story and stick to it? I mean, is it supposed to be a comedy, a thriller, a slice of life or what? People need to know. I can't be having all this genre-hopping."

"Ha! What, and you think you're not *funny* and *sad* at the same time? Look at the real world, mate. You won't find people living their lives by genres."

There was a brief pause.

"Talk about off plot," Cake then muttered.

"Look," the leaf-wiper said. "If this was a book, you boys wouldn't be loafing around arguing over what would happen if it was a book, would you. You'd be getting on with something useful. You'd be hot on the heels of distortionists or embezzlers, or something. The devil finds work for idle hands, as they say."

"I've heard it said," Mabey agreed. "But seeing as this is reality, we can more or less do as we please, can't we? I mean, beyond protecting this rural community, which isn't hard, let's face it, we don't owe anyone anything, do we. This is real life mate, people loaf around reading funny things out of newspapers, get over it."

"Let's face it, you're just a lazy git," Cake hurled at him.

"Ah. You may say I'm a lazy git, but what I am is a poet," responded Mabey with woeful meter but smugly nonetheless.

"Daaah."

"Anyway Sarge," Mabey continued through his colleague's despair. Winding up Cake was daily sport for the bearded one. "What did you call us here for at this ungodly hour? I've got customers to serve."

"I thought you'd never ask," scoffed the Sergeant.

"I've got ovens to prepare," said Cake, a little slow as usual.

"If this was a book," the Sergeant continued, "the readers would certainly be wondering that. What did I call you here for? It is a good question."

"What did you call us here for?" Mabey repeated.

"Boys. We have an undissolved problem here, don't we. I think you know what I mean."

Mabey raked the goatee beard. Cake twiddled fingertips on the tabletop. No, they didn't know what he meant.

Burley-Hogg resumed his thrust. "All right. Cast your minds backwards, if you will."

"Our minds backwards? How far?" said Cake.

"Before he arrived."

"Who?"

"Our Inspector, of course. He's somewhere else now. Gives us the perfect chance to thrash things out. So I ask you. What was it like before he arrived?"

"What was it like? Normal. Nothing happened. We made up the crimes."

"And after he arrived?"

"A husband went missing… A man's body was found… Various other things… Ah."

"Yes," the Sergeant said with a look of triumph. "Before he came, everything was normal. Nothing ever happened. We just got on with our daily lives. Falsicating incidents, planting, baking, pulling pints. Then after he came, everything changed. People started disappearing. People started getting murdered. Don't you think that's odd? And the worst of it is, we're getting detracted from our main tasks in life. My livestock have been neglected and there's weeds all over the vegetable garden."

"True," agreed Mabey. "My ale has been going stale."

"My buns have been going hard," echoed Cake.

"My haiku have gone yahoo."

"Plants need repotting, sow's got a cyst."

"OK Sarge, I think we get your gist."

"All right then lads. Something has to be done."

"What, though?"

"Well, there's only one thing for it, as I see it. We'll have to tell him."

"Tell him….?"

"Tell him….?!"

"Tell him… About the boondoggle. The real boondoggle."

"No need to, Sarge," concluded Mabey, pointing up at the closed circuit TV camera. "He'll see it on the video."

"Yes, of course," agreed the Sergeant, "he'll see it all in the video clippage."

Cake swivelled in his seat to look in the direction indicated by Mabey's finger. "Jesus!" he exclaimed, looking straight into the camera. Being tall, he'd never felt the need to look up before. "How did that get there?!"

I switched the monitor off.

LONDON (Reuters): A trainee landscape gardener who killed his parents last June has been found not guilty of murder due to insanity. John Goode, of Yellow Brick Road, Swansea, was arrested at the scene covered in blood and wearing only his boxer shorts. He told police he thought his father was the devil and that he had been sent by god to kill him. Summing up, Judge Oscar Melon said: "When you committed this appalling act of violence, you were suffering from a severe schizophrenic illness." Forensic psychiatrist Ralph Morpurgo called Goode "one of the illest people he had met in his entire professional career". David Mabey QC, prosecuting, told the jury Mr Goode had stood outside his parents' house with his hands outstretched, saying "I am Vincent Van Gogh and I work for MI5". Sentencing Goode to spend the rest of his life in

Broadmoor Hospital, Judge Melon described the murder as "the beginning of a nightmare that will never end".

Cryptic Cue

"*Custard Cream, madam?*" squawked Penelope Slack in the guise of Mrs. Sludge the drudge, fag hanging most convincingly from the side of her mouth.

An audience of well-meaning burghers, their critical faculties further stymied by interval drinks and hula hoops, erupted with laughter. All the usual suspects were there: the Greens, brimming with admiration for the brothers' set-building skills, though lacking the honeymoon-bound Angelica; the Melon siblings, eyes only for papa, accompanied by Nanny as Mama was presumably inspecting the bell tower at St Sebastian's again; Victor Sheen and his fat wife Molly, still shuddering from their journey hither in the Wartburg; even Patricia the postperson, keen to see how Nick and Nicolette would deliver their lines. All more than willing to sense entertainment in any small scrap, eager to feel pride in knowing that their fellow villagers could produce anything at all of worth. As a result, even utterances of little or no consequence earned snickers and snuffles of amusement somewhere in the half-packed auditorium.

The need to complete vital paperwork – among others, my report to Commissioner Painter on the latest developments in the missing husband case, the mystery murder case, the missing murder case, and the missing couple case – had forced me to miss the first part of the evening's entertainment, 'A Burglary is Announced'. In any case, I'd been informed that Victoria Cake would be in '*the second cast*'. I took that to mean the cast of the second play, 'The Genuine Sergeant Pooch'. Of pooch there was no sign, but a feline presence was assured: Aubergine the post office cat had obviously been given a complimentary stage pass. She could be found wandering across the set at will, hunting behind drape curtains for mice or curling up on armchairs at various points in the piece.

The Shelled Onion Theatre, converted from a Methodist chapel, was a modest venue accommodating some two hundred souls. The origin of the name was anyone's guess, but it certainly had nothing to do with Methodism. Quaintly enough, the moniker was perpetuated in the form of a large onion-shaped lamp that hung over the front entrance, illuminated at night.

The theatre was surprisingly spacious inside; it was a virtual cathedral to the arts. There had clearly been some method to the Methodists' madness. The seats came in rows of pews, as they would have done in more spiritual times, with an aisle running down the middle. An arcade of huge pillars restricted the view for anyone foolish enough to sit at the sides, and most of the sound was lost high in the vaulted ceiling anyway.

The stage was where the chancel and altar would once have been, only a step or two raised from the nave. The vestry on the left provided a dressing room, the pulpit on the right an ideal spot for the 'Wherefore art thou Romeo' scene, if ever that were needed. Choir stalls to the left of the chancel provided seats for a fictional 'jury' of cardboard cutouts, jostling for space with two judges played by Nick Down and the Reverend Melon. Visible through an ornate wooden fretwork behind them was a magnificent Edwardian organ. It was a gift from an anonymous donor, according to the *Almanac*. "The organ is the heart of any church," Oscar Melon had told me, but this one was no longer beating. The Pre-Raphaelite stain-glassed windows at the rear proved more useful, bearing in mind the play was set in a remote country hotel with Pre-Raphaelite stain-glassed windows, cut off from the outside world by bogs…

"*We interrupt this programme for an emergency newsflash. The police search for psychopathic killer John Goode has narrowed to the bogs around Goodefellows Country House Hotel…*"

Mrs. Sludge nervously switched off the television and resumed her collection of empty cocoa cups.

Each member of the cast had made an appearance by now, but none of them was Victoria Cake. Of that I was certain. Though she was capable of disguising herself as a clown, there was surely no hiding place behind the characters in this play. So where was she? Why did Cake's note – which Cake claimed not to have written – tell me quite distinctly that she would be in the cast?

A telephone rang on the empty stage. The hotel guests and staff had all retired for the night, leaving Mrs. Sludge to tidy up and reveal the body, inadvertently, before herself leaving the stage. The 'judges', Nick Down and the vicar, were discussing the story so far – the story within a story – trying their best to ignore the cardboard cutouts and the continuously ringing telephone.

The rings came at amusingly irregular intervals. They were clearly being operated by a member of the backstage crew, whose task was to press some doorbell-like contraption behind the set. Whoever it was had no sense of timing; it could only the stammering Peter Mowforth. Finally, Oscar Melon, as Judge Moor, lost patience and strode over to the phone on the opposite side of the stage, skilfully stepping over the cat in the process. No matter that the final ring came after he'd lifted the receiver; the audience had already downed too much drink to be overly concerned with technicalities.

"*Hello!*" Judge Moor barked in obvious irritation. There was a pause. He seemed genuinely taken aback. Then: "It's for *you*," he called, shading his eyes from the lights as he sought me out in the audience. A cold sweat instantly engulfed me as the entire audience, and cast, turned to stare. Even Peter Mowforth, the sound technician, peered around the flimsy set to share the moment.

I rose to my feet uncertainly, not sure whether it was some kind of practical joke, a dream, or possibly both. Faces still stared at me in silence. They all had the same look: genderless, expressionless, character-less faces apparently devoid of soul, unnervingly vacant, like some ghastly gathering of the half-dead. In the deathly hush of the desanctified auditorium, the sound of my beating heart grew to deafening pitch. I passed along my pew towards the aisle and made my way to the stage. The sea of faceless heads turned to follow my every move.

And then I realized the awful truth: they all thought it was part of the play! Their credulity already stretched by the 'story within a story', these fine citizens of Dribbleside were willing to see anything that happened in this unhallowed venue tonight as a piece of fiction designed solely for their entertainment.

I moved over to stage left, where the vicar, rooted to the spot and apparently turned to a pillar of salt since his last utterance, still held the receiver towards me in his outstretched hand. I took it from him with some apprehension and put it to my ear.

"*Inspector?*" said a woman's voice.

"…I told you never to phone me at work!" I answered in mock indignation, half-winking towards the pews. The audience burst into desperately contrived laughter, the tension of the moment gone.

"*What? Never mind that. Meet me in the crypt at ten o'clock,*" said the voice.

"No thanks, I've already got one," I countered with a knowing grin, sparking another ripple of glee. I was fast learning how to work this audience.

The line went dead. I replaced the receiver and looked up to see the faces of more than a hundred souls eagerly awaiting a punchline. "Wrong number," I declared, and the place exploded.

The phone rang once more, with impeccable timing. 'Judge Moor', still standing there expectantly, snatched it up without a moment's thought. Poor Peter Mowforth had no chance. The phone was still ringing merrily as the vicar barked his "*Hello!*" into the mouthpiece for a second time.

Oscar Melon turned back towards Nick Down as 'Judge Broad' on the bench of cardboard cutouts, stage right. "*It's for you,*" he said with a look of practised astonishment, tinged with a look of unpractised relief. It was then that the rolled-up script wodged in Melon's back pocket came into full view for the first time. Cat miaowed loudly; audience dissolved into helpless laughter. Attention thus diverted, I slipped away into the shadows, stage left, in search of the crypt.

Methodist chapels don't generally have crypts. After the 10th century the need for crypts diminished when Church officials permitted relics to be kept in the main level of the church, and by the Gothic period crypts were rarely built. But I wasn't to know that, was I, not being omniscient. So I searched on.

The audience remained transfixed in convulsions of merriment as I continued my search, watched only by a small boy sitting on the end of a row. Ignoring his curious gaze, I reached the side of the stage and passed below the high pulpit with suitable stealth. And there, hidden in gloomy shadow behind the pulpit, was a door marked 'CRYPT'.

"*I'll kill you for this, Sergeant Pooch!*" cried a voice on stage.

"*Over my dead body, madam!*" Generous laughter echoed through the auditorium.

I opened the door quietly and crept into the crypt. Disappointingly, there was no flight of stone steps spiralling down to a cavernous space where grisly stone skeletons lay covered in cobwebs on dusty stone tombs. Instead, two fairly shallow steps led down to what appeared to be a refreshment room, the ideal spot for interval drinks. Lushly carpeted, the room was dotted randomly with armchairs upholstered in red leather, nestling around randomly positioned coffee tables. One side of the room was lined with automatic vending machines selling drinks, opal fruits and other confectionery; a large transparent dispenser marked 'Holy Water' could be seen at the far end. The walls were of barest stone, occasionally hidden behind luxurious drapes of crimson and purple velvet.

The blood red carpet was cut away in places to reveal ancient headstones lain flat in the surface of the floor. Some bore images of skulls and crossbones accompanied by barely legible inscriptions in Gothic script. Whoever was buried there had it cushy all right. I imagined the scene as the spirits of the dead partied the night away while the rest of the village slept. Perhaps it would be better to join them.

Two shots rang out on the stage above.

"*Bang Bang!* You're dead," intoned a sonorous voice at the back of the crypt. Near the far end of the room was a large high-backed chair, facing away from me to conceal its occupant, the owner of the voice. Who could it be? My secret informant on the telephone? But no, this was a man's voice… A voice I recognized well…

Miss Marple gave the game away with an involuntary sneeze. The high-backed chair swivelled to face me. "*Welcome to the Land of the Unliving*," said Four-Eyed Bob in his best Vincent Price voice, and I was almost inclined to believe him. Hound looked up to master with unseeing eyes of apology. Bob patted her on the head as if to say "There there, he would have found us anyway."

"Bob! What are you doing here?!"

"Waiting for the end."

"The end of what?"

"The end of the Double Bill of Spoofs on Spoofs, of course. Been here since the interval, my friend. Seen the second play before. A largely visual piece, don't you find?" He raised a paper cup of Holy Water to his lips.

"So you're not—"

"Well, no. I'm not the person who contacted you on the phone. Despite my manifold talents, projecting a woman's voice into a telephone is not one of them."

A peal of thunder rang out above. Church bells rang. The clock on the Community Hall struck ten.

"What's happened to you, Bob? You've changed…"

"No, my friend. It is you who have changed. But you don't yet know how."

The play was over. Charitable applause was followed by the sound of millions of army boots treading solidly over a hollow wooden floor. I had changed but I didn't yet know how? I needed a drink. I walked over to the Holy Water dispenser. Bob swivelled his chair to face me there. The door to the crypt creaked open, and a shadowy figure slipped in. Bob put a finger to his lips. I moved back across the carpeted floor to be confronted by Victoria Cake in the doorway.

"I'm sorry it had to be like this," she said in a restrained yet urgent tone as she reached into a pouch slung over her shoulder. She would then pull out a gun and shoot me. Why she would shoot me, I had not the slightest idea. These things were well beyond my comprehension already. But shoot me she would. She'd left traces at the scenes of both crimes, and I was next on the list. Perhaps Susan had been right after all. I was being hunted by DEFF agents, and the clown was one of them. Victoria had killed the two agents who were trying to protect me. After all, she'd disappeared from the wedding reception at around the time of the second murder.

But then why would she be about to kill me? If DEFF had to find the whereabouts of the key, they would need me alive… wouldn't they? Perhaps the whole story was a fabrication after all. Perhaps Victoria was nothing more than a homicidal maniac who would kill anyone, given half the chance. Fragments of my life started to flash before my eyes. I particularly liked the scene where I was receiving a gold medal at the Chelsea Flower Show. I'd worked hard for that one, to be sure, and I think I deserved it. The Californian woman on the next patch had produced a very innovative display of timeless aesthetics based on the principles of postmodern spiritualism, but the judges had obviously preferred the down-to-earth practicality of my country garden with its long grasses and sunflowers.

Victoria pulled out not a gun but a floral handkerchief from her pouch and started vigorously mopping her brow. "It was the only thing I could think of," she continued. "My cover's completely blown! They recognized me yesterday… You are alone, aren't you?"

I turned towards the high-backed chair, meaning to introduce my lifelong companion. "Well…"

"Good. Let's sit over there, shall we?" she said, hurrying towards the Holy Water dispenser.

"But…"

Victoria swivelled the high-backed chair and planted herself where Four-Eyed Bob had been sitting only moments earlier. There was no sign of my visually impaired friend, nor of his visually impaired best friend. They must have slipped out through a side door.

That was a funny thing about Bob. He was always appearing and disappearing in the most inexplicable ways. I usually put it down to his uncanny speed and guile, but how a blind man could make so many hidden entrances and exits was a marvel as yet unexplained by any philosophy.

Victoria corroborated Susan's story in nearly every aspect. Except for one vital difference: Susan was not my wife, nor my ally, but my foe. She had been the mole in the laboratory, and it was she who worked for DEFF. That would explain everything, of course; why she was so keen for me to find the key, the apparent personality changes, even her proficiency in martial arts...?

Very clever. Very clever indeed. Why the pair of them would collude to fabricate such a story was something I would consider later.

"The problem is, John, with your memory loss and everything, we can never really be sure whether you're faking it or not. We can't keep blurting out 'We're undercover agents, we're here to protect you', our cover would be blown immediately. But when you started looking for me in the marquee, I realized you didn't have a single idea what was going on. You must have forgotten what you'd remembered after you lost your memory. So then I had to do something to alert you, didn't I. It wouldn't have looked too clever if you'd arrested me and locked me up for murder, or something. Trouble was, they found my nose by the old railway, when they eliminated Y. So then I had to go into hiding. I couldn't contact you openly. They'd have realized immediately if I had. Because you see, they don't know you're you, seeing as you've had the plastic surgery. So I've been in hiding ever since then. I wrote that note and pretended it was from Vince, just to get you here. Of course I'm not in the cast! I was hoping you'd get to the end of the play, when the sergeant turns out not to be a sergeant, as I thought that might jog your memory. I left the note in the station when no one was looking, hoping that twat Mabey would pick it up and give it to you, if you'll forgive my French. Then I started thinking he might not find it, or even if he did he might not give it to you, so I went to the pub to give you another one. I knew you were there, I'd been watching you all day. How else could I have put that first note in the river?! But when it came to the play, I

214

couldn't think how to get your attention, to tell you where I'd be. Then I hit on the idea of the telephone. I knew the line was live, I'd seen them rehearsing with it. It was all done by intercom. The vicar kept forgetting his lines and they used the phone to remind him."

A cleaner slipped in noiselessly and started dusting headstones at the far end of the room.

I was happy to go along with the charade, for now. Victoria was in cahoots with Susan, of that I was certain; but for now I could see no point to their deceit, save that of driving me out of my mind. I would persevere.

"All right, but why did you have to draw attention to me like that? For that matter, doesn't dressing as a clown make you pretty easy to spot, too?"

"Yes, but it's reverse psychology, don't you see? DEFF are looking for someone who's trying to be as anonymous as possible, someone who blends into the surroundings. Albert the Clown is the opposite of that. They'll look straight at me and not see anything at all. To them, I don't exist. Well, until they spotted me on the old railway line, that is. The same goes for you being a detective, especially such an incompetent one. Nobody would suspect you of attempting to be incognito. And as for the trick with the telephone… well, they all thought it was part of the play, didn't they?"

"Not the actors. Not the director. I think they would know the play, don't you?"

"But they're not DEFF, so what does it matter?"

"Next you'll be telling me Cake isn't your brother."

"That's right, John. He's not my brother. What's more, I'm not his sister. It's just my cover, you see. I'm sorry. I'm really sorry to have involved him, he's such an innocent boy. He kept coming to me and saying he couldn't keep it up much longer. He was nearly wetting himself at the wedding. His parents don't know anything about it, of course. It all has to be kept strictly hush-hush."

"So why did you leave clues at the murder scenes?"

"It wasn't deliberate! What kind of a fool do you think I am?! It so happened that I was Albert the Clown when they eliminated X in the vicarage garden and I was Albert the Clown when they eliminated Y on the railway track. I was trying to warn them, X and Y I mean, but I was too late."

"And who's Z?"

"Z? That's me."

"So you'd be next?"

"Well, yes, if they were bumping us off in strictly alphabetical order. But it doesn't always work that way, does it."

The cleaner started hoovering the carpet in the middle of the room.

"What about the Fishers then?"

"Er… P, Q, R and S. The boys are sub-agents. That means they don't really know what's going on, they just do as they're told. And very good boys they are too. But P, that's Derrick Fisher, he's the Regional Controller."

"And talking of controlling, I suppose you know all about quantum mechanics?"

"Ah. Good old quantum mechanics. I had to read up about that before I took the job. But you know more about it than I do."

"Sorry. I know nothing."

"Of course. Wiped from the memory. Well, it goes something like this. In the real world, things can only be in one place at one time; that cleaning lady, for example, is either *here* or *there*. But in quantum mechanics, things can be both here *and* there. Or *neither* here *nor* there. The cleaner could be in two places at the same time – or in neither! Isn't that weird? Strictly, the theory only affects tiny things that can't be seen with the naked eye, like electrons or microparticles. You know. Basically, they can be in two places at the same time, but only if we don't look at them. As soon as we look at them, they seem to be only in one place. We destroy their quantum nature; they become 'less quantum'. So quantum objects don't like being looked at. That makes it very hard to do anything with them, and that's one of the reasons why building a quantum time controller was so difficult. But you did it by applying the principles of quantum teleportation and negative information. Apparently."

"How, exactly?" I was doing my best to stay awake.

"Well, if I knew *that*…"

The cleaner was right behind the high-backed chair now. The sound of the hoover was deafening; its thunderous din went on for more than a minute.

"…in two places at the same time!"

"Have you finished, love?" asked the cleaner at the far side of the room. "Only I need to lock up, see."

Quantum Leap

How I transported myself from the crypt of the Methodist chapel to Susan's shed in Upper Hooey is not something I can easily explain. But there I was, standing by the shed door on that late summer evening with a wispy breeze passing over my face.

Victoria – or perhaps I should call her Z – had said something about quantum teleportation. Microscopic matter acts in a 'quantum' way, which means it can be in two places at the same time, but only when we're not looking at it. In other words, it's a science that only makes sense if you don't think about it too much. How very convenient. But since all visible matter is composed of masses and masses of microscopic matter, everything, including sentient beings, could then logically be in two places at the same time. When someone claims to have seen you in the street even though you were miles away at the time, they could have been seeing your other self – not your *alter ego* but your *alibi ego*. The key lies in mentally overcoming the faith barrier and just believing the theory. All matter, including ourselves, can be in two places at the same time, but because we cannot *believe* it we also cannot comprehend it; we are convinced of our monotopicality and all other propositions are targets of scorn.

In that case, we need only believe we can be in two places at the same time, and we will be. This is a far cry from controlling time, of course; it would be nothing more than controlling awareness of diatopical existence. What I had somehow managed to do, according to Victoria's fiction, was to develop this awareness into a device for time travel. My invention was based on the principle that, if a mass can be in two places at the same time as long as we don't look at it, then that mass can also be *in the same place at two different times* as long as we don't look at it, since time and space are merely variants of the same plane of existence. Much as merely being in the right position – centre forward for England, say – can win you notoriety in modern times whereas simply remaining alive longer than other members of your clan could yield the same effect in ancient societies – *tempus qua locus*, and vice versa.

All well and good, albeit with questionable science. But what was the real purpose behind the web of deceit spun by 'Susan' and 'Victoria'? It could have been one of at least three things. First, to drive me insane, as I'd previously suspected. Why would they do that? No motive presented itself. Second, just to take the mickey. Well, I wasn't laughing. Third, to throw up a smokescreen, thus diverting attention from their homicidal tendencies. That was much more likely. For that they were both involved in both murders was now quite clear. *'It's Susan Jollygoode, all right'*, the bogus officer had declared. Quite right – not the victim, but the perpetrator. Those shady agents from 'Dribbleside County Constabulary' might be on my side after all. Secret service, perhaps. Now the two women were deliberating blurring what was essentially a simple case of felony by giving me too much information. *But what information it was!*

The brick through my window, the unexploding clock, the secret hooded informant in the Copper Inn, even the piece of paper floating by on the river… They were all Victoria's work, she'd claimed. She'd been trying to warn me that time was running out, alert me to the danger I was in, subliminally even, without blowing her cover. If that was her intention, it palpably hadn't worked. Her wanton acts had merely served to add confusion to an already perplexing narrative, and placed an added burden on already stretched public finances. If I couldn't get her for murder, I'd give her the rap for wasting public time and money.

"Come with me," she'd said, leading me towards a dark alcove in the crypt. The alcove concealed a low side door, through which we stepped. Maybe that was where Bob had gone. On the other side of the door was a rectangular room with high windows. They were all sitting there on bench seats, looking distinctly gloomy: the Downs, Ralph Morpurgo, Penelope Slack and the rest, all present to a woman. Victoria led me past them to the front. I turned to greet them as I passed, but they either looked straight through me or ignored me altogether. It was as if I didn't exist. Victoria spoke in respectfully hushed tones to some as she went by. A solemn classical piece played over a hidden loudspeaker.

We passed along the room and through another door at the far end. The door opened onto a dark alley – Florence Nightingale Street. Parked outside the building was Isetta, my little bubble car, engine turning over noisily. The optional flashlight had been installed above the driver's door, where it now protruded at an angle. It was rotating somewhat irregularly and looked as if it could fall off at any moment.

Cake, Mabey and Burley-Hogg were wedged into Isetta's passenger compartment, which now resembled a live re-enactment of Picasso's Guernica. The Sergeant's bulk was squeezed into the only passenger seat, the more diminutive Mabey sitting on the Sergeant's lap with his head bent to fit the contours of the roof. Cake was squashed into the rear compartment, a leg hooked over the driver's seat and an arm on Burley-Hogg's shoulder. Strictly speaking, it was illegal, and moreover quite impossible. But the situation clearly demanded haste and a blind eye to violations of law, both natural and juridical.

"Quickly sir," squeaked Cake, full of boyish enthusiasm and apparently not at all perturbed by his discomfort. "We must leave now. He's in the tractor!"

I walked round to the driver's door, still wondering who '*he*' could be and why he would be in a tractor. I got in, yanked on the universal joint steering wheel to pull the door shut, then stepped on the gas. A billion angry mosquitoes sent the bumper car hurtling along the darkened street, rolling along like a big yellow egg. Top speed fifty, but now, with all this undesigned weight in tow, her best effort was a law-abiding twenty-six. Had my colleagues taken this into account?

"................!" shouted Mabey, pointing vigorously ahead, but of course I couldn't hear him above the din. I merely guided our craft like a homing missile towards the tractor that now appeared at the far end of the street, spewing filthy clouds of diesel smoke. It looked a lot like Farmer Hector's vehicle, but then again I was no expert on tractors. Why were we following it?

"................!" shouted the Sergeant.

"................?!" I shouted back, unable even to hear my own voice. I used my finely honed powers of deduction to answer the question. I had to drive the vehicle, as I was the only one with a clean licence. How had they taken it to the theatre? Mabey must have broken his driving ban. But since the only people who could charge him for his misdemeanour were his two colleagues in the bubble car, he'd been able to do so with impunity and much turning of blind eyes. Far from having to fabricate offences, now they just couldn't help committing them.

More importantly, all four members of the local police force, including myself, had been mobilized to apprehend the driver of a tractor. This was therefore no ordinary felon. They must have found some irrefutable evidence linking him to the murders, the only crimes of note to have occurred in Dribbleside for some years. Whoever he was, the driver was the root of all our ills.

The tractor turned clumsily, carelessly into the High Street and headed off in the direction of the upper village. Determined to show an example of civic duty, I stopped at the junction to ensure no pedestrians would be needlessly crushed or maimed. That there were no pedestrians at all was largely incidental.

"................!" shouted Mabey, and we chuntered off down the High Street after the agricultural machine. Past the side of the Shelled Onion we flew, past the delicatessen, past the post office. It was a game of wax and wane. The tractor was thundering along at a top speed of, say, twenty-five. We would gradually gain ground on it, only for a dog or a cat or a fox to suddenly wander into the street, forcing us to slow down. The tractor, ignoring such minor inconveniences, would merely send the creatures flying to the side of the street and roar on regardless. Then the gap between us would narrow once more, only for the same thing to happen again.

So along we trundled, each on either end of a gigantic, invisible rubber band that was now stretching, now contracting in constant forward motion. It was when the tractor passed the Point of No Return that I realized it was taking us home to Upper Hooey.

"................!" shouted Mabey, pointing across me at the pub. He should have been saying 'How about a swift half?', but it felt more like 'We've passed the point of no return!' or even 'Have you seen the prices in there?!'

We were now travelling through open country on our way towards the white marker post. The tractor seemed about to drive straight past it – straight to the joke village, Neither Hooey – but just as it reached the junction, it performed a screeching ninety-degree turn to the right, its body tilting to the left with offside wheels dangling in the air. The Isetta being more stable, and with the benefit of hindsight, we slipped smoothly onto the Upper Hooey Road, crossing diagonally over the oncoming lane and nearly colliding with a girl on a bicycle in the process. The girl wore thick-lensed glasses and had her hair in plaits. I could just see her now in the rear-view mirror, through a tiny peephole exquisitely formed between Cake's bent elbow and the gap beneath Mabey's right ear. The girl wiped her specs with a crooked finger, looked back in anger, then started pedalling desperately after us, occasionally raising an arm and calling out, but in vain. There was something she wanted to tell us, yet stop we could not. We just had to catch that tractor.

A dog raced through a farm gate by the road and started chasing the bike as it chased the car that chased the tractor, barking madly as it went.

A farmer's wife ran through the farm gate by the road and started chasing the dog as it chased the bike that chased the car that chased the tractor, waving her arms wildly as she went.

A farmer rushed through the farm gate by the road and started chasing his wife as she chased the dog that chased the bike that chased the car that chased the tractor, putting a hand to his mouth and calling loudly as he went.

Thus we continued in a bizarre procession up the gentle slope towards the village, a farmer chasing his wife chasing a dog chasing a bike chasing a car chasing a tractor to the back of beyond.

And then the rain started to fall. In torrents it fell, in buckets.

"................!" shouted the Sergeant, thrusting a carrot-like finger back towards the road behind us. Whatever. We had to carry on. The gradient of the road caused surface rainwater to flow back towards the lower village, turning the road into a river. Isetta's tiny wheels could hardly cope with the onrushing force; the car slowed perceptibly. To the tractor, on the other hand, this was bread and butter. Its towering wheels ploughed proudly through the stream, leaving us literally in its wake.

Even the girl on the bicycle was making ground on us now. She came so close that she could almost have slapped a hand on Isetta's rear window. But as the road started to climb Copse Hill, the surface water eased and we pulled away again. The increased strain of the gradient slowed the tractor's engine, allowing us to gain ground on it once more. For all her frantic pedalling, the girl would soon be caught by the dog, though not by the farmer's wife and certainly not by the farmer, who was however gaining on his wife.

By the time we reached the crest of Copse Hill, we were no more than twenty feet behind the runaway tractor. The rain had abated somewhat, and as the road levelled out, I could palpably sense victory.

Soon we were approaching the turning onto the chalky farm track that led round to the back of Upper Hooey. The tractor skimmed breezily past the turning and headed towards the open field.

"................!" shouted all four occupants of the bubble car. Yes, we all knew instinctively that we could never compete with the tractor's massive tyre tracks on the softened earth of the field ahead. Yet we had no other option; we would have to go in after it. I made a calculated decision. We would take the long route around the field, avoiding the ruts made by the tractor's wheels, in the sure knowledge that our quarry would gain an almost unassailable lead, but that parity would be restored on the gentle slope leading down into the village at the other end.

Our flimsy craft hopped and bobbled over divots in the field, sending sundry body parts hurtling into the roof of the car. The bespectacled girl guided her bike along the tractor's wheel ruts, followed by the dog, then by the farmer's wife and the farmer, who had both presciently donned galoshes.

The gate at the far end of the field had been replaced since my last encounter. Now, a sturdy diamond-braced field gate stood where the heap of rotten timber had then lain. Even from a distance and in a moving vehicle, I could see it was a good gate, a strong gate, a bright yellow gate, almost a work of art, full of old-fashioned craftsmanship and dedication. The tractor smashed straight through it and swerved violently onto the chalky lane by the orchard.

In spite of our lengthy detour round the field, we still arrived at the sad remains of the gate before the girl on the bicycle, not to mention the dog, the farmer's wife or indeed the farmer himself. I carefully eased the vehicle over the shattered lengths of timber, soon to reach the freedom of the chalky lane and gain ground on the tractor once more. Down the lane we careered like a teardrop in the wind, our little egg freewheeling gaily past the Old Post Office, the Old School and the New School (a yellow house), neither of which looked remotely like a school, the Old Bakery, the Olde Pubbe, well that was a pub, the Old Stables, the Old Barn, the Old Lockup, the Old Forge and the Old Policeman's House, had there once been a police presence here or was it where an old policeman lived, before eventually arriving at the old village green.

As I'd already anticipated with doom-laden trepidation, the tractor veered left into Pudding Lane, then promptly stalled just past the turning. I took my eye off the road for the tiniest fraction of a second and collided frontally with the stone cross on the village green. The girl hit a rut in the road and fell off her bike.

"..................!" we all shouted or barked in unison. This broke down roughly into:

"Who's the actor in the tractor?"

"It's not our Hector, of that I'm sure!"

"We'll have him for speeding then!"

"Design fault in a German car?!"

"Don't go to the house tonight!"

"Rough!"

"Heel, boy!"

"Silly cow, you left the frying pan on!"

What the driver of the tractor said was, regrettably, unprintable.

Isetta's front door was jammed shut against the cross, forcing us to escape through the canvass sunroof. Design fault indeed. It was like climbing out of a collective straitjacket.

First, Mabey had to reach up and release the sunroof handle with his one available hand. Then Cake raised the canvass roof straight up with his left knee while Mabey pushed the central crossbeam to the back edge of the roof opening. He next insinuated himself under Cake's left leg and pushed his upper torso through the half-open roof as he folded the rest of the roof towards the back. Strictly speaking, he should have ended with the sunroof neatly folded into three layers, but since there were rather more pressing things on his mind and he couldn't be arsed anyway, he simply let it flap inertly down the back of the vehicle. Next he gripped both edges of the open roof cavity, lifted his paltry body weight in the style of an acrobat on parallel bars, and then, in a single motion, swung his legs up, over and out through the rear, narrowly missing Cake's gaping groin in the process. He finally slithered down the back of the car and landed in a large puddle on the chalky road behind.

The Sergeant, now free to move and desperately snatching for air, quickly followed but with considerably less agility, opting rather to lever himself out to the left using his stomach on the edge of the roof opening as a fulcrum. I stood on the driver's seat and heaved my left leg up into the void and out onto the windscreen, momentarily sitting astride the rim of the roof opening before hauling the other leg out and sliding down onto the grass next to the cross. How Cake got out was his own affair, for I immediately rushed to the aid of Mabey and the Sergeant, both of whom appeared to have sprained their ankles.

And all the while, the tractor driver had been frantically trying to restart his engine, the girl to adjust her handlebars. Now the dog, the farmer's wife and the farmer were almost upon her. I checked my men for serious injuries, found none, and so the four of us made a dash for the tractor on six good legs. We must have resembled the pistons of an engine, the two with sprained ankles bobbing up and down in regular alternation to mitigate the pain. But they neither minded nor noticed their discomfort; the adrenaline was flowing now.

The tractor driver turned to see us bobbing and hobbling towards him *en masse*, like a cast of hellish ghouls from some horror movie. The shadow of the cabin made it impossible to identify the man, though it certainly wasn't Hector Hodgkinson; his insolent blondish coif would surely have glowed in the dark. The man now abandoned his frantic turning of the ignition key, climbed out of the cabin and raced up Pudding Lane towards the house.

"Don't go to the house tonight!" shrieked the girl behind us, now also running. The mystery man made a beeline for One Pudding Lane and disappeared from view into the driveway. The girl, the dog, the farmer's wife and the farmer had all turned into Pudding Lane by the time we reached the front of the house and stood, panting breathlessly, wondering where the driver could have gone.

But I knew, instinctively, where he had gone. Everything pointed to the shed. I could think of no known reason, no visible motive for this man to go to that shed. Yet I had no doubt he would do just that. Both Susan and Victoria had spoken at length about the shed. It could have been part of their smokescreen of disinformation, but I recalled how anxious Susan had suddenly seemed when we went to the shed on my first visit – when life had been less fraught…

That the shed was linked to the murders was now quite certain. *How* it was linked would soon, surely, be revealed. I started up the drive towards the side of the house. As before, a faint glow emanated from the shed, just visible in the back garden. All else was shrouded in pitch darkness. There was no light nor sign of life in Susan's house, nor in the Sparrowhawk residence next door. All was perfectly silent, but for the sound of my footsteps crunching on gravel. The rain had eased to a fine spray. A micro-droplet would occasionally settle on my eyelash, creating a soft focus effect through which the shed light shimmered.

Shed Load

And that is how I arrived in front of the garden shed at One Pudding Lane that late summer evening. An icy unseasonal chill danced across my face as I contemplated the door. Susan had promised "a gamma ray device" – sufficiently vague to be disregarded. Part of the smokescreen, for sure. If the door were really protected by a gamma ray device, I would be history the moment I opened it.

I took hold of the cast-iron doorknob and hesitated. I wondered, for the briefest of moments, what had happened to the rest of my entourage. The deathly silence told me there was no one behind me at all, and I turned to confirm that fact. Where they'd all gone was anyone's guess;

224

mine was that the officers had been diverted to the front of the house and the others had followed them there. Somehow, it didn't seem too relevant anyway. I felt very strongly that this shed was my personal business. Mine to deal with in my own special way.

I tugged at the cast-iron knob. The door opened easily. It was not locked; there was no gamma ray device. My surmise, so far, had proved correct. Of course, the tractor driver could have already activated the device and been instantly vaporized by it, leaving me free to enter with impunity. The greater likelihood, though, was that it had never been locked at all, even on that first day here with Mabey. Susan's motive for claiming the contrary, and adding the baloney about the gamma ray device, would then be obvious: to prevent me from entering and seeing what was inside.

I opened the door wide.

The inside of the shed was deceptively spacious – the opposite, in fact, of the Sparrowhawk residence next door. A token collection of garden implements rested against walls or hung on hooks; a lawnmower and other heavier equipment had been stowed efficiently to the sides. Yet there was still room to open out a couple of collapsible garden chairs and enjoy a hearty lunch on the chequered lino flooring in the middle of the shed. *Pâté de fois gras*, buttered slices of wholemeal bread and a bottle of Bollinger. There could perhaps be a game of cricket going on in the background; the score would of course be immaterial. Cotton wool clouds would drift harmlessly across a deep blue sky, challenging artists to capture them on canvass. Four-Eyed Bob was sitting on a director's chair at the back of the shed, half hidden in the shadows. That I could see him at all was thanks to an ephemeral glow that seemed to emanate from the walls and ceiling of the place. There was no visible light source; just a glow.

"Perhaps it *is* a time machine," suggested Bob, pointing his chin at the contraption beside him. "Perhaps you could turn the story around and have him travelling through time after all. What do you think?"

I paused before replying with a question of my own. "Were you driving that tractor, Bob?"

He paused in turn. "I can do many things, my friend. I can ride a bicycle guided only by a blind dog. I can appear and disappear in the most unlikely of places. But a blind man cannot drive a tractor. There would be untold mayhem and carnage. No one would ever believe it."

225

Judging by the driver's apparent lack of concern for anything else on the road, it wouldn't have been so hard to believe.

"So do you know who it was?"

Bob took a breath of middling length. Miss Marple aroused herself and sat on her old haunches in anticipation. Bob exhaled, then revealed the ghastly truth.

"It was you, my friend. It was you."

"What?! No, no no no. I was following behind with the others. I was in the bubble car."

"I'm very much afraid you imagined all of that. *You* were driving the tractor. It was your *conscience* that made you wish you were driving the chase car."

"…My conscience?"

"Ah. There is so much to explain, yet so little time left to explain it. First, let us locate the whereabouts of our elusive Mr Jollygoode."

Were they all in on this deception? Including my old friend Bob, whom I trusted implicitly, on whom I depended for words of good sense?

"That won't be easy," I warned. "He's already eluded four highly-trained officers for more than a week, after all."

"Of course he has. But now we have access to his potting shed, do we not. We now have new material at our disposal, don't we."

"True…"

"Take, for example, these gardening gloves." He reached across to take a pair of gloves from the worktop beside him. "These will have been worn by our vanishing friend. They will carry his scent. Won't they, old girl?"

He invited Miss Marple to sniff the gloves, then gave her an affectionate stroke of the head followed by a barely audible whistle. At that, she lifted herself off her haunches with an air of new resolve – at last, some work to do! – and started sniffing around the shed. Her tour took her past earthy pots, past rusty forks, past rolled mesh netting and finally to my feet, where she sat once more and looked up at me as if to say, "I'm really sorry, but it's you."

"No no no…" I protested. Dog looked back at master to double-check the findings. He nodded. They saw each other with unseeing eyes.

"Would you like to sit down?" offered Bob, waving vaguely in the direction of a collapsible chair. I thought I'd better, and opened it out. In a way, I found it most satisfying that a dog, and a blind one at that, appeared to have solved a missing persons case. I'd certainly never heard of such a feat, but I was sure there would be more. What was somewhat more troubling was that she'd identified me as the missing person. How could I not have known I was missing? I mean, you'd know, wouldn't you? On the other hand, there was no doubting Miss Marple's integrity. She was always right.

If I really was the missing Duncan Jollygoode, then the two fatal women would have been right all along. I had lost my memory. Their story, though smoothly coordinated and effortlessly corroborated, had been so utterly bizarre as to be dismissed instantly. But when Four-Eyed Bob and Miss Marple pointed to the same conclusion, I felt somewhat more inclined to suspend my disbelief – for now.

"So it's true then? I've lost my memory?"

"No, no," chortled Bob. "That was all made up. It's much more complex than that. Rather a case of *selective* memory loss, if anything." He opened a little cabinet below the worktop and produced a small phial. "Noxytoxypoxylene," he declared nonchalantly with another swishing whistle to the dog. Miss Marple once again went to sniff the phial, once again toured the shed in search of a match, and once again terminated at my feet with the same apologetic look. The implication was that I'd poisoned the man in the vicarage garden, and incredible though it may sound, a myopic labrador had now solved two baffling cases in the space of less than a minute. I just had to pat her on the head for that.

"You see, this story's all about you in the end. But of course, you haven't actually 'killed' *anyone*, have you." I didn't think I had. "Not in this story, at least. Let's take the first case, the body in the vicarage garden, as you call it. This faceless man, this unidentifiable victim, represents your subconscious wish to do away with your father, do you see? Your father was a religious man, a good Christian, wasn't he. You resented him for denying you freedom, but more so for monopolizing your mother, whom you wished to possess for yourself, in a classic Oedipal sense. You saw him as an adversary, a competitor, a rival for the exclusive love of your mother. There's nothing unusual about that. But once you'd done away with him, aptly enough in the vicarage garden, you could then go about claiming your mother as your own. This you attempted, more or less unsuccessfully, in the form of Susan Jollygoode, but first there was a problem to overcome. How would you explain the loss of her partner without incurring her displeasure and thereby losing her affection? Simple. You would invent another partner who had disappeared, and in so doing relegate your sense of guilt to the depths of your subconscious. Your visits to your mother were retreats to your childhood, and herein lay the second problem: namely, the paradox that you could never truly possess your mother in the here and now. Your sexual frustration then transformed her into an enemy, and you symbolically killed her too, on the railway line. Once you'd severed the bond of trust with your mother, her image was free to haunt you as a wrathful spirit, punishing you again and again for your guilt. And when your sister turned on you and joined your mother in her mission to destroy you, you knew the game was up."

Bob paused. Was there more? It was sometimes difficult to know. I didn't want to burst his bubble too soon.

"And where do the others fit in?" I enquired nonetheless.

"Others?"

"Yes, my colleagues at the station, for example? Are you going to tell me they're not real?"

"Of course they're not real! Whoever heard of two policemen called Cake and Mabey? *Cake*, yes, maybe even *Mabey*, but never Cake *and* Mabey! They are your genital substitutes, don't you realize? Your subconscious self has invented them, and your role as custodian of the peace, as a way of legitimizing your existence and your true objective. Once you've determined yourself as an officer of the law, corruption and incompetence notwithstanding, you can place yourself in a position of authority, a position from which you can judge *others* instead of judging *yourself*. This then releases you from your heavy burden of guilt. That you have done so with some good humour is to your credit. It may have saved you from more serious self-harm."

"And the others? The people in the village, the village itself?"

"Figments of your imagination. Fiction. Not always very original, I have to say. The amnesia thing has been done to death in popular culture, and the idea of government agents with the name of their organization tattooed behind their ears is just plain daft."

"But you're real of course? Or am I imagining this conversation as well?"

"No, no, my friend," Bob said with a good-natured chuckle, "I'm very real. I'm here to help you, after all."

I hated to admit it, but I was beginning to tire of the pretence. I knew very well that I'd imagined nothing – except, perhaps, that Bob was my ally. His motive in spinning this tale remained opaque. What I found particularly grievous, though, was that my old friend Bob had apparently betrayed me. 'Helping' me he certainly was not. He had joined the others – Susan, Victoria – in attempting to divert my attention from the cases at hand. To be more precise, they were trying to make me imagine I was the problem. Why they would all share such a goal was a mystery; I could think of no plausible connection between them.

They were obviously protecting someone. It was now my task to discover the object of their protection, and the reason for it.

"There are a couple of holes in your theory, Bob," I sighed with a degree of sadness.

"Holes?"

I looked down at Miss Marple, who sat uneasily in the middle of the capacious shed floor. She was still waiting for the good-natured laughter that would put her at ease. She was just a dog, after all, but her unquestioning loyalty embodied the sadness I felt at questioning the integrity of my lifelong friend.

"Holes, Bob. You said I'd been driving the tractor but at the same time imagined myself in the chasing police car to deny my guilt. Then you said *everything* was in my imagination. In that case, I couldn't have been driving any tractor. Miss Marple identified me as the missing husband, but you said I'd invented him to hide my guilt from Susan. You said the body in the vicarage garden represented my subconscious desire to do away with my father, but then presented me with a phial of some substance with which I'd apparently done the deed. If the murder really had been 'imaginary' or the product of some subliminal wish, it would have been utterly illogical for there to be anything tangible to connect me to it. Those are the main ones."

"Ah. You've got me there," Bob conceded. "I hadn't thought of that. Of course, I was talking figuratively, but you can obviously see far better than I can."

There was a pause before we concurred in convivial laughter. Miss Marple at last curled up on the floor.

KOBE (AFP): Asian piracy syndicates are trying to assassinate two black labradors after the dogs helped find millions of dollars of fake CDs, officials said Thursday. Hercule and Jane sniffed out the discs during a raid by Japanese officials at an office block in Kobe. "Sources informed the Ministry of Hedges that syndicate members were looking for the dogs," said the Ministry's spokesman, Yasha Tsuchini. The two dogs are said to be the only ones in the world trained to detect the chemicals used in optical discs. They sit when they sniff a nearby haul, and are rewarded with a game of chase the basketball when their job is done. "Dogs make good detectives," said Mr Tsuchini. "It's only a matter of time before an absent-minded half-blind canine will solve a major criminal case."

Endgame

And so it went on. I returned to the station and resumed my search for Duncan Jollygoode, the vicarage garden murderer, the disappearing railway line corpse and the missing couple, aided and abetted by my Sergeant and my two Constables. As yet we've had no luck in any of these quests, but time is still very much on our side.

Susan and Victoria have disappeared altogether. Cake has denied any knowledge of his sister's whereabouts; all too convenient, I'm inclined to feel, but I'm willing to let it drop for the greater good.

Bob continues to puzzle me. He'll muck along as usual for a while, then quite unexpectedly come out with a load of Freudian guff again. His 'special moments' usually occur in Duncan Jollygoode's shed, where I frequently find myself rummaging for clues. I have long since accepted that it's some kind of practical joke on Bob's part. Perhaps his blindness takes him onto a different plane of practical jokery; perhaps it's his way of cocking a snoot at the seeing world. It has now become a kind of game between us; he will throw some more psychoanalytic mumbo-jumbo at me, I will find the flaws in his argument, then we'll have a hearty laugh together as Miss Marple at last finds her moment of comfort. I've never managed to fathom why we do that.

And I've yet to understand the meaning of the Paris Metro anecdote he told me all those years ago, the mysterious case of the human pyramid. Perhaps he merely meant to say that nothing is ever quite what it seems.

My latest visit was a case in point. Bob kindly informed me that the whole fantastic story, including Susan, the Constables and the Hooeys, had been concocted by my mind as a side effect of treatment using noxy-toxypoxylene. An experimental drug developed to treat severe cases of personality disorder, it had the effect of sending the patient into an illusory world of hallucination and make-believe. Bob and his medical research team had invented a device that allowed them to tap into that illusory world using brainwave patterns and quantum theory, thereby gaining a glimpse into the patient's mind and the hope of a cure.

The device they'd developed was the 'time machine' in the shed, which of course wasn't a shed but a psychiatric unit. The machine was otherwise known as DEFF, and I'd been unwittingly attached to it by means of sundry cables and electrodes implanted in my skull. DEFF stood for 'Decidedly Environmentally Friendly Facility', Bob told me, but that didn't seem to make sense either; the words, in the end, threw up more questions than answers.

Everything had happened while I lay there in a semi-comatose state, he claimed, and then proceeded to show how the patient's 'bed' swung down from the front of the device. I'd also undergone exploratory brain surgery in another unit, and there had initially been some concern over potential damage. But I'd soon reverted to my crazy hallucinations, which, as Bob explained, were helping to reveal certain truths about my childhood. Why are you telling me all this now, I asked, to which he replied that, well, I was coming to the end of the treatment and there were good signs of a recovery. The very fact that I was realizing the importance of the 'shed' and his role in it was a sure sign I was emerging from my world of self-delusion and entering the realm of reason. What's more, as my body was now acclimatized to the drug, its extreme effects were beginning to wear off. A crazy hallucinatory world that I'd previously accepted without question as reality was beginning to strike my reasoning mind as just that – a crazy, hallucinatory world. So Bob now felt it appropriate to answer my questions as openly and frankly as he could; it could no longer do me any harm to know the truth…

Had the whole world gone barking mad? Or was it something they put in the water? Me, a 'patient'? Bob, a 'doctor'? I had one last question to ask. Why did I need this 'treatment'? What had I done in some past life to earn such special attention? Normally, a person with a personality disorder would be treated in the normal way, gently, knowingly. Not drugged to the eyeballs and hitched up to a machine.

"Ah. I wondered when you'd ask that," said Bob. "I'm afraid this is, as they say, the last of the great boondoggles. We acquired significant public funding to conduct this research; it would make a valuable contribution to the advancement of science and would moreover help restore this country's faltering image as a leader of nations. But while the facility was being built, the government suffered that landslide defeat in the general election, and the market economists took over. Public spending was halted if it could no longer be justified by a quantifiable economic outcome. We could continue our research and be paid for it, but no new investment of any sort would be made.

"So then I thought, what a shame. All this equipment designed and developed, and nothing to do with it. Gallons of hallucinogen and no one to treat with it. Well, nearly no one. There *was* the curious case of John Goode. No conventional analysis would ever explain what he had done, no existing therapy could cure him. So then I thought, we would put this facility to good use after all. The injections of public money would continue for a while; a thundering train takes time to stop, after all. With the remaining cash, we would graphically reveal the inner workings of a psychopathic personality disorder, thereby entering contention for the Nobel Prize and ultimately acquiring international investment for the furtherance of our research. But why *you*, you rightly ask? Well, take a look at your feet."

I looked down. The chequered lino floor of the shed was now, in fact, a gigantic chessboard.

"Shall we start the game?" Bob said, and people started appearing on the squares in their rightful positions. I was a bishop's pawn. Bob was already the opposing king. A woman who markedly resembled Susan Jollygoode took her place next to him as queen. Oscar Melons hovered beside Bob as a bishop. Ralph Morpurgo waltzed in and became the queen's bishop. Next to the bishops stood Nick and Nicolette Down as knights, flanked severally by Dilip and Javindra Patel as rooks. A line of white-coated lab technicians filed in and squatted in front of the back line as pawns. I turned to see Burley-Hogg enter the fray. He gave me a nod that was simultaneously deferential and condescending, then took his place as my king. The queen was a slip of a girl wearing thick spectacles and her hair in plaits. Cake and Mabey were my rooks, Victoria and Penelope my knights. I craned my neck to see Jean-Claude Monty ready for flight as queen's bishop. Behind me stood Victor Sheen as the king's bishop, already trying to sell a car to the knight next to him. Now that was a surprise, and quite unsettling. But why was I only a pawn? Surely I was more important than that? Not to worry – it was only Bob's little game.

Alongside me in a line stood the hapless Fisher boys, the Green brothers and the Melon children, all pawns too. One of the lab coats, given a hefty push by the vicar, stumbled two spaces forward. Jeffrey Green, queen's bishop's pawn, mirrored the move by advancing two spaces, and his brother of course followed with a single step of his own.

As I protested yet about the proper rules of chess, the other lab technicians advanced in alternating patterns of one and two spaces. Penelope Slack, never one to hold back, vaulted over our pawns to threaten one of the lab coats. The vicar slipped forward obliquely then slid diagonally to take out the naïvely exposed Cake. Ironic, as the Constable was supposed to be an expert in the game. Cake shattered into thousands of soft fragments that sparkled for a brief moment before vanishing into the ether.

"*Crumbs!*" quipped Mabey with a hint of Schadenfreude.

"*Offside!*" shouted one of the Fisher boys inappropriately, moving forward a brace as the clergyman slithered back. I figured that if I could just sneak along unnoticed while they were all arguing, I might get to the other end and convert myself into a knight. That would be good.

Mayhem ensued. Pieces were moving simultaneously and at random, it seemed, with massive casualties on both sides. "*Advantage us!*" called Nick Down as his wife trampled Peter Melons under her hooves. Now that wasn't supposed to happen to a child. "*En garde!*" was Monsieur Monty's riposte as he took the prematurely triumphant postmaster off his guard. Professor Morpurgo snaffled the balloonist with a well-reasoned "*Quid pro quo!*", only to be rendered *nihil* by Penelope's rampant steed. The man of reason overcome by occult powers – whatever would happen next?! The innocuously advancing Greens took out a couple of lab coats in a 'pawn sandwich' before Jeremy was nabbed by the vicar and Jeffrey by the waiting Javindra. "*Caught at silly mid-on!*" she sang as she went on to destroy the last unprotected Fisher Boy.

I had advanced in the meantime, almost unnoticed it seemed, and now stood within sight of the back line. I was on the threshold of a transformation. Rebirth, even. At every step of the way Victoria had hovered around me, staving off attacks from the more potent pieces. They all had far more important foes to contend with anyway. Now, as I reached the end of my journey, I was faced with a choice. Move one step forward and I would be promoted. But if I eliminated Oscar Melons by moving diagonally to my left, I would then have the king in checkmate, trapped, his escape prevented by the positions of other pieces. Should I aggrandize myself for personal gain, or stand aside for the common good?

The vicar evaporated as I stepped straight through him. The game was over, the king defeated. Bob took off his sunglasses and looked me firmly in the eye. He was my father. The icy glint of his evil stare pierced straight to the core of my soul. I stepped into his space, drew a large knife and thrust it repeatedly into his abdomen. He collapsed in a pool of blood in front of the bathroom door. Mother rushed out of the bedroom. "What have you done? What have you done?!" she screamed. And so I did the same to her.

"There now," said Bob. "Doesn't that feel a lot better?"

Dear John,

    You haven't written in a while – are you all right? And how's that book coming along? I suppose you're still busy writing it. Don't forget to stick to the story. I always find it very confusing when they go off on a tangent. I'm off to the Royal Albert Hall with the Women's Institute on Thursday. We went last year and had a thoroughly good day out. They'll be playing "Music from the Musicals", which sounds much more my kind of thing. They say it's going to snow, but it shouldn't be too bad down here. Are you keeping warm enough? Would you like me to send you some woollens? I wouldn't want you catching a cold. Well, that's all for now. Do write as soon as you can.

    love
    Aunt Clarice

Dear Mrs. Sharpe,

    It is my painful duty to inform you that John Goode passed away at this facility on the night of Sunday January 5th. He fell from a third floor window, but we cannot be certain that he took his own life. It may simply have been a tragic incident. However, he had been showing signs of depressiveness recently. Please let me assure you that we will be holding a full and exhausting inquiry to ascertain how this tragedy could have taken place, and I will be sure to let you know the outcome. John possessed very few possessions, but among them was the enclosed manuscript, along with some letters from yourself. I understand you are not a blood relative, but since you were the only person he communicated with, and we have been unable to trace anyone more closely related, you are the nearest we have to his next of kin. So I am sending you the manuscript in case you should like to see it. I will be in touch again with details of the investigative enquiry and other arrangements. For now, may I close by offering my sincerest consolences.

    Yours faithfully,

    Ivor Burley, Facility Administrator

www.ingramcontent.com/pod-product-compliance
Lightning Source LLC
Chambersburg PA
CBHW020834260626
47169CB00003B/983